THE HOLLOW GODS

Moon's End

Also by Rebecca Levene

The Hollow Gods series
Smiler's Fair
The Hunter's Kind
The Sun's Devices

REBECCA LEVENE

Moon's End

THE HOLLOW GODS
BOOK 4

HODDERSCAPE

First published in Great Britain in 2026 by Hodderscape
An imprint of Hodder & Stoughton Limited
An Hachette UK company

The authorised representative in the EEA is Hachette Ireland,
8 Castlecourt Centre, Dublin 15, D15 XTP3, Ireland (email: info@hbgi.ie)

1

Copyright © Rebecca Levene 2026
Map by Clifford Webb and Dewi Hargreaves

The right of Rebecca Levene to be identified as the Author
of the Work has been asserted by her in accordance with the
Copyright, Designs and Patents Act 1988.

All rights reserved. No part of this publication may be
reproduced, stored in a retrieval system, or transmitted, in any form
or by any means without the prior written permission of the publisher,
nor be otherwise circulated in any form of binding or cover other
than that in which it is published and without a similar condition
being imposed on the subsequent purchaser.

All characters in this publication are fictitious and any resemblance
to real persons, living or dead, is purely coincidental.

A CIP catalogue record for this title is available from the British Library

Paperback ISBN 978 1 444 75385 1
ebook ISBN 978 1 444 75382 0

Typeset in Plantin MT Pro by Palimpsest Book Production Limited,
Falkirk, Stirlingshire

Printed and bound in Great Britain by Clays Ltd, Elcograf S.p.A.

Hodder & Stoughton policy is to use papers that are natural,
renewable and recyclable products and made from wood grown
in sustainable forests. The logging and manufacturing processes
are expected to conform to the environmental regulations
of the country of origin.

Hodder & Stoughton Limited
Carmelite House
50 Victoria Embankment
London EC4Y 0DZ

www.hodderscape.co.uk

For my mum, Muriel Levene.
I wish you could have stayed to see the end,
but I would never have reached it without you

Prologue

It was not, she knew, unheard of for a monarch to kill her brother. And even as the thought came to her, she knew that her brother would be having precisely the same one. They should never have ordered the Crimson House to begin a study of the mind of trees. But they had, and now the harvest they had reaped must be milled, or else left to rot in the granary.

Her eyes opened, as they did every morning, to a vision of gold. Each wall of her chamber was inlaid with it, embossed images of tigers roaring with golden teeth. The tribute of a dozen conquered peoples had been melted down to fashion it. Its message pleased her, if not its gaudiness.

Her servants glided silently to her side when she descended the sleeping platform, her robes already in their arms. Encrusted jewels made the cloth as heavy as armour, but the servants never faltered as they slipped the robes around her. They were pale-skinned and golden-haired, captives from the barbarous and nameless lands to the north. Their eyes remained downcast, faces inscrutable, but she wondered if the rumours had trickled low enough through the soil of the court to reach them. At least they, she could be confident, would never speak of what they knew. Their tongues had been severed before they had been given to her.

Not so Illac. She found him waiting outside her door when she opened it, rough-featured face set in an ingratiating smile she knew to be entirely false. He fell to his knees at her approach, forehead bent to the floor.

'Rise,' she said impatiently, 'and walk with me.'

She led him to the western face of the Gem of the Delta, onto the balcony that was hers alone. The wall of the palace sloped to the ground far below, glittering white and gold in the sunshine, the marble inlaid with geometric patterns that foxed the eye, leading it through cunning spirals. A gem indeed. And beyond, the city. The last census had counted 926,571 inhabitants: 427,971 people, and the rest slaves.

'Eminence,' Illac said. 'Unworthy as I am to offer advice to the lynchpin of the nation—'

'You have something to say,' she told him coldly. 'Say it.'

'Your brother is preparing to move against you. He has recalled the Honoured Band from the glorious war in the east, and the Leaf Army from its patrol of the ice frontier. They have always favoured the left-hand aspect of the Indivisible Throne. If you were to summon the militias—'

'Then we would have war here at the heart of the world. Would you wish to see the City Without Limits burn?'

He swallowed at the sharpness of her tone and bowed so low his hair brushed the floor.

She looked away from him across the realm she'd been born to govern. The city lay on the tip of a vast promontory, sharp mountains to its north and east, and sea to guard its other borders. The water was filled with ships: small fishing craft, war galleons and a dozen new quinqueremes bought with the spoils from the eastern front. It was said that a woman could leave the deck of a ship in the Golden Bay, walk a thousand miles with a full purse, and at the end of the journey she would still have both her coin and her virtue. Five generations of their dynasty had ruled a land of peace before she and her brother had ascended. Why must it be in her time that this problem came?

She sighed and turned back to Illac, who could be trusted in nothing but his own self-love. 'The Crimson House must be razed to the ground, every brick ground into dust and every paper turned to ash. A knife across the throat for every Priest of Blood.' She considered for a moment. 'And for their children too. No, more – every family member to the third degree. Every scroll that names the Crimson House must be written anew without mention of it. And for every person who speaks its name, evisceration. The Crimson House has never been and never will be again.'

He let his shock show only for one beat of a heart, then he nodded. 'Eminence, it will be done. But there is much which the Crimson— which the house that never was provides for the populace. Who will disburse grain to the destitute or teach the children of the rich their history and letters?'

'The House of Stars will grow to take on this responsibility. You will, of course, continue to lead your fraternity through this troubled time.'

She saw the effort it cost him not to smile. 'It will be done as you command.'

'Good,' she said. 'And now we must speak of my brother.'

*

He liked to walk the streets of the city without servants or guards. He went bare-faced, in the green robes of a farmer-merchant, and not a single person knew him. To the great mass of his people, he was a stranger. When he looked upon his subjects from the towering peak of the Gem of the Delta, they were an indistinguishable horde to him and he no more than a distant, glittering speck to them. Here, he could look in their eyes. He could smell the unwashed bodies of runners labouring in the traces of curricles, the cheap floral perfumes of women of the fourth rank. He knew them in a way his sister never would, secluded as she had always remained in the world of the court.

He knew, but she could not understand, that they needed a god. Not the idols that his people had worshipped when they lived in caves, or the star spirits that his ancestors had installed in their place. Stories for the ignorant, void of true power. Nor could kings alone answer their needs. He saw it in their tight expressions, the worry creasing their brows. It was in the failed harvest of the last two years, starvation in three of their five provinces and rebellion in a fourth. The two-fold crown had always been a mistake. The people needed absolute rule, absolute trust. And for this, he must have absolute power.

He felt a tickling against his foot and kicked out, flinging the rat to the roadside. The city was crawling with rodents. The grain stores in every district were a feast for the rats and the rats themselves a feast for the very poorest in this city. He was approaching one such neighbourhood now, where the only meat they ate was the rodents that plagued them.

The sun was hidden by high brick walls and the washing strung between them. He'd never been here before, and for the first time he felt a little unease. This was a place in the shadow of the law. Untrusting eyes followed him as he walked. But the directions had been clear and soon enough he came to a small, dusty square around a well and the red house at one end that was his destination.

The door opened before he could knock, admitting him to a low, dark room in which his co-conspirators were already gathered. The court was his sister's, but the army was his. He'd fought beside them in two long and bloody campaigns and they loved him for it.

He waved the conspirators back to their seats when they would have risen to make obeisance. Sellian alone made no move to rise. The First Brother of the Crimson House stared frowning at a scroll, tapping a pen absent-mindedly against the table. Any other man in his position would have been a dangerous rival, but Sellian had no ambitions; he cared only for knowledge.

'It isn't ready,' Sellian said, the moment their eyes met. 'If we could set every scribe to work on the problem . . . but your sister is consumed by the trivial. She's ordered us to find a way to make wheat grow without water. A waste of time better spent on deeper matters.'

Only Sellian would call the famine that had already taken half a million lives 'trivial'. But then the man had probably never stepped foot beyond the bounds of the city.

'The question isn't whether it *has* been done,' he said. 'It's whether it can be. If time is all that's needed, that can be arranged.'

'Can it?' Sea Lord Felmis's square face flushed red with shame at his own temerity.

'You're concerned my sister will stop us?'

Felmis nodded gratefully. 'Eminence, the rumours multiply by the day. They say she plans to send spies to poison the wells that the Honoured Band drink from. It's feared they'll never reach the city.'

'I've heard she hired assassins from a land beyond the lands we know,' Enioc added.

'Too soon, too soon,' Sellian muttered. 'This is knowledge unlike any we've found before. Knowledge not of what lies outside us, but of what is within us – within everything. The potential is there to . . . domesticate it. But it was a hundred generations of careful breeding before the wild mountain ibex became our placid cattle. And to tame ourselves must surely be an even harder endeavour.'

'A hundred generations?' Felmis asked, face paling.

Sellian's absent look sharpened at the horror in his voice. 'Oh, an example merely. I hope to see a result in my own lifetime. Yes, I should certainly hope so. But in the next year? No.'

A brief silence fell at the absoluteness of that 'no'.

But he had been prepared for it. 'It's not unheard of,' he said, 'for a king to rule without his sister, if she should by some tragic accident be stolen by death too young. My sister is a hunter of some renown. There is little she loves more than the coursing of tigers. The beasts are dangerous, of course, but my sister's skill has always been a match for their ferocity. So far, at least. My sister grows no younger or faster with the years. And there is to be another hunt at sun-high on the morrow.'

His eyes pinned each of them in turn, but he saw no doubt. They had always known it would end with this. He'd always known the same, and he found it gave him little pain. When he was a god, he would make a place in his heaven for his sister to spend an eternity hunting at her leisure. And before that, he would need to have words with the tiger-masters.

★

The day of the hunt, the sky was a blue so light it was almost white. The moon was a pale disc near the horizon. It was considered an ill omen, and to compensate she'd ordered that three of the strongest beasts be released into the royal preserve at the north of the city. When she killed all three, her people would be reassured.

Her fine, proud black stallion whickered as she approached. She stopped to rub his nose, then stepped into the chariot at his back. Custom dictated that she wear her robes of state for the occasion. They weighed heavy in the oppressive heat of the day. Her hand was clammy as it clasped her spear-thrower, the first spear already positioned within it. Two more stood ready in front of her. Custom also dictated that there be only as many spears as there were beasts. To miss would be more ill-omened than not to hunt at all.

Crowds thronged the high wooden stands that looked out over the parkland. Hunts were free and always well attended. She often wondered if they came to see her kill, or in the hope that just this once the tiger would triumph. Her brother and his cabal were absent from the stands, but then he was known to despise the hunt.

A hush fell as her carriage entered the ground. Then, swelling, the sound of drums. The beat of them was maddeningly irregular. A thousand years ago, a king of some other line had designed it to drive the beasts into a rage. Starved as they'd been for five days, their skin tormented with goads, she hardly thought they needed more reason to be angry.

They were impossible to see at this distance in the long, wheat-coloured grass. And, a secret the crowd would never know, the creatures were equally incapable of seeing her. Bright lights were shone into their eyes moments before their release. The tigers would be blind for the duration of the hunt, though still able to smell and hear, and still fiercely hungry.

She spotted the first of them. A female, if she was any judge. The beast seemed to sense her at the same moment, and its lip curled in a snarl. It shook its head, as if to clear its eyes, then reared on its hind legs to scream defiance. The soft flesh of its belly was exposed for no more than a moment, but it was enough.

Her arm jerked forwards and the spear flew. There was a thrill of tension in the crowd, an instant to wonder if her aim had been true.

She turned away before it struck. She knew that her throw had been good, even before the desperate, dying roar of the tiger. The metal stink of blood flooded the air, a lure to snare the tiger's brethren. She saw the second of them, slinking through the grass, elegant and lethal still despite its blindness. But she was more lethal yet.

The hunt was proceeding exactly as intended.

*

He woke to a sharp pain behind his eyes and the musty smell of soaked timbers. The world rocked. He thought at first that it was the after-effects of whatever had happened to him. But when he opened his eyes and saw wood beneath him, wood above, and still the rocking, then he knew. He was on a ship.

His sister. Had she struck just before the fruit of his own plans was ready to pluck? But then why did he yet live?

Whatever had gone amiss, it was still salvageable. He lived, that was enough. He had confidence in his ability to turn disaster into victory. With this ability he'd won more battles than any living general and stretched the empire's borders to the boundary of the known world. It wouldn't fail him now.

He could hear nothing but the slap of waves against hull and the creak of the rigging. He tried the handle of the door, expecting a lock, but it opened easily. He passed through three sections of hold stuffed with sacks of grain and sides of cured meat before he saw his first sailor. The man's eyes widened in shock.

He brushed past. At the foot of the stairs that led up on deck he paused, allowing his eyes to become accustomed to the light. It was midday above, he judged. He must have been unconscious for a full day.

As he climbed to the deck, he heard the shouts of sailors labouring at oars and others in the rigging. Further off, there was a more muted hubbub. As he climbed higher, he saw that it came from shore, a huge crowd gathered at the Antelope Point dock, only a few hundred yards distant. Something that had been clenched inside him unclenched. He had feared that they were in the open sea already. It would be a trivial matter to turn the ship around and head back to dish out to his sister the meal she'd tried to serve him. He need only show himself and the crowd on shore would force his return, or else have his sister exposed for a kin-killer and a regicide.

And then he noticed the man standing at the prow of the ship as it swept a broad turn through the harbour on its way towards the teeth-like rocks that guarded it. He'd taken the man for a figurehead, but now he saw that his arm moved, waving at the crowd on shore. And the robes he wore glittered in the sunlight, gems winking like eyes.

'Your sister announced that you're leading an expedition to root out the pirates who plague the Western Roads. The people love you, Eminence. See how many have come to cheer you.' It was Felmis, who'd come to stand beside him.

'And the pirates will kill me, I suppose. A glorious death in battle. I could hardly have asked for more.' He couldn't keep the bitterness from his voice.

Felmis shook his head, eyes downcast. 'That isn't her plan.'

'And how is it that you know her schemes?'

'I had no choice, you must understand. She had my son and my twin girls. She promised them the rotting death if I didn't do as she commanded.'

He saw now that others of his followers were on the boat. They watched him in silence, their faces tense.

'She knew that we were meeting?' he asked Felmis.

'She knew everything. She'd been following us for weeks.'

He peered around those gathered on the deck, looking for Sellian. He wasn't there. Not a single Priest of Blood was.

Felmis seemed to realise what he was searching for. 'She killed them all. The Crimson House is no more. She burned it to the ground. She burned every book. And, Eminence, we can never return. She said we must sail for the horizon and never alter course.'

He nodded. In a way, it was a kindness. There were far crueller methods she might have used to dispose of him. But he supposed this would leave her conscience free. She hadn't, after all, ordered his death. To either side, other ships had taken to sea, sleek galleys of the Seventh Guard, whose loyalty had always lain with her. They would be forced to keep to the course she'd set, and the food in the hold wouldn't last long.

And yet.

'Books can be burned,' he said, 'but knowledge can't be killed so easily. I read every word that Sellian wrote. I studied every stroke of his pen, every avenue and narrow alley of his research. I know it all. We can recreate and continue his work. If we can't go back, then we'll go on. And when the work is complete, we'll return, and teach my sister regret.'

The hopelessness hadn't lifted from Felmis's face. 'Go on to where, Eminence?'

He peered ahead at the endless blue. 'Whatever lies beyond the water.'

PART I
The New Gods

I

The emptiness inside Dae Hyo was gone. That was how he knew the rune had worked. Well, that and the way the whole cursed place was collapsing all around them. The dome high above shuddered as a long, jagged rent like a lightning strike tore through it, and tiles shattered on the floor. The Hunter was forced to dodge aside to spare her head.

'We need to get out of here!' he shouted.

His voice drowned in the sounds of destruction, and she didn't seem to hear. She was staring at the far wall. Moments ago, it had been covered in black marks, fragments of the rune that had occupied the whole room. All those marks were gone.

A marble block fell from the ceiling no more than a foot in front of her. A splinter of rock scored a bloody line across her cheek and finally seemed to startle her awake.

'We need to go!' he shouted again, and this time she nodded and followed as he sprinted for the door.

They made it with bare moments to spare. The deep booming crash as they fled could only be the entire dome falling in on itself.

*

Dae Hyo was surprised to find the ancient city outside still standing. Only here and there a few buildings had tumbled into ruin. Magic must have been used only sparingly in the construction of this place. But then, what man would want to live under a roof held up by nothing but the will of the gods?

He slowed to a walk as they neared the battlefield, and his stomach churned with dread. But he'd done what he'd done. A man must face the consequences of his actions.

And here at last was the square where the battle had been. It was nearly silent, except for the occasional groan of pain. The living had departed and only the dead remained, and a few who were taking their time about dying.

The Hunter made a terrible, choked sound. She seemed diminished since the power had been taken from the runes. Skin that had once shone golden now looked merely sallow, and there were deep shadows beneath her eyes. The scars that had scored her face were gone entirely. He followed her gaze to the battlefield and understood why she'd cried out.

The servants of Mizhara were dead. Their corpses lay scattered among those of the Sisterband. Dae Hyo could hardly bear to look at them, all these women he'd killed without meaning to.

He looked at the others instead, the thousands who'd thrown away their lives in this useless, meaningless war. Birds had already descended to feed on them, gimlet-eyed crows and green-feathered hawks. The stench of blood and the first hints of decay lay over everything. There would have been more battles like this, a war across the whole land, if he hadn't stopped it.

'She is gone,' the Hunter said. 'They have both gone.'

Dae Hyo's mind was sluggish with shock. He ought to have noticed far sooner who *wasn't* there. They were the two whose bodies he should most have expected to see. But neither Krish nor Mizhara was among the dead.

'Is Krish alive?' The possibility gladdened him, although the gladness was muted by guilt. Another thought occurred to him. 'You survived. You were a servant too, weren't you? Why them and not you?'

She ran her fingers down her face, along the tracks of the absent scars. 'I was a servant once, but I no longer served. I suppose that is why the end of the runes did not end me too. I thought it would. I thought I was nothing except what she made me.'

There was almost disappointment in her voice. It angered him. 'I tell you what, if you meant to die and leave me to bear this alone, you could have told me. Belbog's balls, you could have told me what taking the magic would do!' His eyes were drawn helplessly back to the bodies of the servants and the Sisterband.

'Indeed I could,' she said wearily, 'but then you might not have done that which was needed. It was the work of my life to rid the world of gods. I will not regret it.' But her expression, tight with grief and pain, made her a liar.

People weren't the only broken things here. The statues of the city had come to life to join the battle. Now they lay among the corpses, the white marble of their casings cracked and all their fantastical workings stilled. A stone eagle had crushed someone as it fell to earth. There was a pool of congealed blood all around it and only an outflung arm visible beneath the marble. Stone children had frozen into statues once again, their innocent faces lifted to the sky, but their arms in gore up to their elbows.

Perhaps Krish and Mizhara lay beneath the stone creatures. They must be somewhere on the battlefield. Or perhaps they'd fled in the aftermath of Dae Hyo's great and final working of the runes. If they had, they couldn't have travelled far. If Dae Hyo set out now, he could catch them up.

But what could he say to his brother? How could he explain what he'd done and why? And what would they do next, now Krish was no longer a god and Dae Hyo no longer a mage? No longer a man with any purpose in the world at all.

In the centre of the square was the raised platform on which Krish had stood and flung his magic at his enemies. A long scorch mark stretched from its foot towards the setting sun. In its path, a string of bodies had been reduced to charcoal. But at its far end a golden-haired figure was standing.

For a moment of hope, Dae Hyo thought that one of the servants had survived what he'd done. Maybe more than one. But no, it wasn't a woman. It was a youth – it was the boy, Eric. A different sort of hope stirred. Eric had been right beside Krish when Dae Hyo left the battle. There were more people beside him, and at least two seemed to be on their feet.

Dae Hyo sped into a run, the Hunter close behind. When he was within fifty paces, he saw that there were four figures upright and two on the ground. Twenty paces, and he knew the two lying down were Krish and Mizhara, with Dinesh and Eric standing over them. The other pair were strangers to him.

Dinesh's expression was dazed, like a man just woken from a deep sleep, but Eric's head snapped round as Dae Hyo and the Hunter approached. His shoulders relaxed when he saw who it was, but the expression on his delicate features was sombre.

'Are they dead?' Dae Hyo asked.

'They ain't dead, but they ain't in the rudest of health neither. When . . . whatever happened happened, they just fell down like puppets when the showman drops the strings.' Eric must have spotted something in Dae Hyo's face, because he squinted at him, suddenly suspicious. 'What exactly did happen?'

'It was I who was responsible, Eric,' the Hunter said. 'I took the power from the gods, and with it, their magic from the world.'

This was the time for Dae Hyo to do the noble thing and tell the others that he'd been just as much to blame as the Hunter. He didn't. He dropped to his knees beside Krish, who was lying by Mizhara like a married couple asleep in their tent. There wasn't a wound on Krish that he could see, and his breathing was even and clear. But when Dae Hyo shook his shoulder, he got no response. His too-thin, over-serious face looked unusually peaceful. If this was sleep, it wasn't one he could be woken from.

He looked at the last pair in the group, the ones who looked almost, but not quite like servants of the sun and moon. Whatever had happened to the Hunter when the magic left hadn't happened to them. She was still golden and his skin was still a sickly grey. The cheekbones beneath it were far too sharp, but his moon-silver eyes and her sunburst yellow ones didn't have the feverish look they'd had before.

'Is it truly over?' the woman asked. 'Is our land truly free of gods?'

The Hunter nodded gravely. 'For now and forever.'

The man reached a cautious hand towards the woman, as if unsure how it would be taken, but she grasped it tightly. 'La,' he said. 'We are free then, if not . . . unchanged.' He looked down, frowning at his grey-skinned hand.

'Will Drut wake up?' Eric asked the Hunter. 'Will either of them?'

'I do not know. The working that we – that I – performed has of its nature never been done before. But they yet live. You may take hope in that.'

Dae Hyo didn't trust her further than he could spit, but if she offered hope he'd take it. A starving dog would eat old bones. He scooped his arms beneath Krish, flung him over his shoulder and rose. 'We should get out of here. A battlefield's no place to chatter like knife women. The best people fight and the worst come to harvest after. If luck's with us, no one knows who caused the war or led the armies. But I'm not a man fortune's ever favoured and my brother has ill luck follow him around like a fart.'

'Bachur,' Eric said abruptly, addressing the Hunter. 'When the runes died, what would have happened to Rii?'

Dae Hyo saw in her face as she weighed how much of the truth to dole out.

'I don't want no lies,' Eric said.

She sighed. 'Eric . . .'

'She was carrying my son. My son and all her sprogs. And she was flying, this great fat thing that ought never be able to fly.'

'I think . . . that which magic has built was not *unbuilt* in that moment.' She gestured to the man and woman, the almost-servants with their changed faces. 'Things that the runes once made still have an existence outside of them. But the runes sustained too. And that, Eric, I fear must be gone.'

Eric's milk-white face whitened even further but he set his mouth in a stubborn line. 'She set off east, towards the sea. That's where we need to go. Where *I* need to go. Don't suppose I've got the right to command the rest of you.'

The two almost-servants looked at each other, then shrugged as one. 'We can hardly remain here,' he said. 'The River Natadik runs east, if we can find a boat.'

'I have . . . crumbled a bridge or two with my former employer,' she added. 'Undermined them to their very foundations, if I'm to be entirely honest. The sea is as good a destination as any.'

*

Eric lay on his back in the riverboat, staring at the featureless sky, his mind endlessly replaying the last moments he'd seen Rii, as she bore Arwel away from him. She'd been no more than a dot on the horizon, black against blue, and then . . . he couldn't remember. Had she dropped, plummeting a hundred, hundred strides to the ground? Or had he just imagined it so much it had begun to seem real?

The sails creaked as the boat shifted course with the wind. The shore was distant now they were so near the river mouth. Muddy, gently rippled water made up most of the scenery. It was a dull landscape, only the occasional island to break up the sameness and none of them with much to boast of beyond the odd scraggly tree. It was too familiar a sight to distract him from the pictures that kept forming in his mind of what they'd find when they reached the end of the sluggish river. He'd give all the gold of the Worshippers to stop the images. He saw Rii's vast body, crumpled and lifeless on the ground. He saw her children's bodies scattered around her, their delicate infant bones broken and their brief lives snuffed out.

He saw his son beside them.

He felt pushed and pulled in opposite directions, desperate to learn Arwel's fate and terrified to know it. Perhaps it would be best to stay forever in this moment, travelling and never arriving.

Sandals rasped on the deck beside him and then the blank sky was filled with the oval of Renar's face. 'Rouse yourself,' she said. 'We have need of your aid.' At first she and her brother had spoken to him gently. He'd found that easy to ignore. Now she snapped instructions.

It took almost more energy than he had to pull himself to his feet. It was so hard to do anything, to care about anything, when the thing he cared about most in the world lay— But no, he wouldn't let himself believe it. Not until he had to.

Dinesh knelt on the deck, Krishanjit propped up against him. Krish hadn't woken in the whole day they'd been travelling, him nor Drut neither. Dae Hyo often sat beside Krish and talked. He seemed animated by his one-sided conversation. Sometimes he laughed at his own jokes. Sometimes he spoke to Drut too, but there was never any response. She looked so small now the power of the god Mizhara had left her. She seemed much more like the servant Eric had known, the woman he'd tricked into loving him and had come to care for too, in his own way.

Eric raised her with a gentle arm around her shoulders. She was as limp as a wet mop and he had to use his other arm to raise her chin so Renar could tip the water bottle into her mouth. Her throat bobbed as she swallowed, though her eyes didn't open. Dae Hyo was clumsier with Krish, spilling half the water on his naked chest.

'Be careful,' Renar said sharply, 'unless your aim is to choke him.' She was the one who'd suggested watering them. She'd said the blazing Ofiklanod sun would dry them like cured goat meat.

Eric felt heat-shrivelled himself. His clothes were clogged with sweat, the warm, moist air too full of its own water to suck up any of his. It seemed to him the heat had increased in the last day, and the greenery to either side of the river grew less green and more withered with every mile.

By the next dawn, they'd reached the river delta. The hundred weaving channels of the river were filled with boats, fellow refugees from the destruction of Täm. The stink of suppurating wounds floated across the water along with the pitiful cries of the injured. Lanalan took one look at their faces, taut with grief or shock or anger, and lowered his own to hide his moon-grey skin and eyes. Eric quickly flung a sheet over the still-unconscious Krishanjit and Drut.

They were close, he could feel it. His gut was in a knot of fear and he paced restlessly from one end of the boat to the other, his eyes always on the silver and brown expanse of the delta. In this flat land, Rii's form would surely be visible – it must be, great lump that she was – and he searched desperately for a sight he dreaded to see.

It wasn't there. In all the miles of land there was nothing bigger than a boat or a low, mean riverside shack. Hope began to swell painfully inside him. Who's to say it was only magic that had kept her in the air all those years and not those ugly, leathery wings of hers?

They stopped at the last town before the sea. It was a lonely outpost whose houses stood above the marshy ground on stilts. Rah Bonwah, a one-legged acrobat with the Queen's Men, had once told Eric that his tribe built their homes in the same way. And here some cullies were on the other side of the world, with the exact same thought in their heads. It just went to show, people were only different on the outside.

Other refugee boats crowded the dock, and the town was thronged with strangers. Lanalan eyed them warily. Perhaps unconsciously, his hand rose to touch his face, tracing the outline of cheekbones warped by the moon's magic.

'You don't look half as awful as you did,' Dae Hyo said, clapping him on the back hard enough to rock him.

It was true. The grey skin on Lanalan's face was flaking and underneath there was a far healthier dark brown. It was the same with Renar, slowly changing from gold back to oak. It made sense, Eric supposed. Skin grew all a person's life. How else would wounds heal? And their new skin was growing in a world without magic. But eyes were eyes, and he couldn't see theirs changing back. They'd never be people who could pass unnoticed in the world. Was it the same with Arwel? He'd been born a servant, not made one like these two, but he was still flesh-and-blood and changing and growing every day. Maybe Eric would hardly recognise him when he saw him next.

'Perhaps 'tis wise to move on all the same,' Lanalan said.

'Move on where?' Renar asked. 'We're at the very edge of the land.'

Eric scanned the cullies the way he would have in Smiler's Fair, weighing them up. The anger he'd sensed earlier seemed drained. These people only looked exhausted. But anger was the easiest emotion to wake back up. That was another thing people shared in common from one shore to the other. 'I'll go into the town,' he said. 'Get us some grub. Find us a better boat, one that ain't gonna sink in waters deeper than a fathom.'

'You think to sail our way to safety?' Lanalan asked. 'Why, it's not such a terrible plan. We can put to shore away from these others, and then . . . Renar, what then?'

'Ofiklanod can't be a home to us now. We'll go to Ashanesland. The King must welcome us there if we bring him his son.' Her voice was firm but her face frowning.

Eric shook his head. 'We can't sail to Ashanesland, not right off. We need to find Rii first and then she can fly us. None of us are good enough seamen to make it there without her.'

He didn't like Lanalan's expression. It seemed pitying. 'You think to find her then, in all the wide waters?'

'She'll have landed on an island, won't she?' Eric said. 'I just need to get a map and find the nearest. Rii's a mum now. She'll want to feed her babes. An island with water, that's what she'll want, and maybe a place where there's delicious fat sea beasts for her to hunt.'

Lanalan looked like he meant to speak again, but Renar held up her hand to silence him. 'Buy your maps, then, and we'll see what's nearby.'

Eric left the boat in good spirits, despite the stares and murmurs his fair hair and fairer skin drew. He'd be back in Ashfall before you knew it, where he didn't look any more a local than here, but at least he had a place. Krish would wake up and Drut too. And when she'd had a chance to spend a bit of time with Arwel, Eric knew she'd come to love her son. She'd be the mum to him she was meant to be, and Eric could let go of the guilt he'd been carrying all this time.

The sand sucked damply at his sandals as he walked from the docks to the heart of the settlement. There were no smooth amber roads here and no graceful arches carrying water high above the ground. Only the dark skin and tight-curled hair of the people marked this as a part of Ofiklanod. It was as ramshackle and charmless as any place he'd seen in Ashanesland.

The refugees milled around the simple houses, as directionless as Eric. They were as much strangers here as he was. More, maybe. He'd lived poor and slept rough. The nobs of Täm lived in luxury and hadn't done an honest day's work between them. They'd probably never travelled beyond the city or the gentle countryside around it.

There might be no market and no traders to buy the map he wanted, but Eric wasn't as green as a bud. These were fisherfolk. Their boats bobbed in the water, dwarfed by the pleasure craft and skiffs of the strangers. They'd know these waters and any land that was in them.

He followed the line of the shore into mud-clogged grass, until he reached a group of fishermen, hiding from the throng. They sat on thick coils of rope beside barrels of salt-stinking fish. Some of them had gutting knives and were hard at work, but most were gossiping. The glances they cast askance at the refugees told Eric the topic. Their conversation sank into silence as he approached.

'No Tämish man, you,' a stoop-shouldered old codger said, his eyes fixed on Eric as his fingers worked mindlessly to mend the net in his lap.

'No,' Eric said. 'I'm new, from the godlands.'

All eyes were fixed on him now. The youngest of them said excitedly, 'No rumour then? Truth that the borders opened?'

'Ain't I the proof of it?' Eric said, but they looked at him blank-faced until he added, 'Yes, it's truth.'

'And Täm is gone, truth too?'

'That as well,' Eric said. 'Look, I'll tell you all you want about it, but I got a question first.'

The young man shrugged. 'Ask your question, stranger.'

'It's about a creature, a . . .' but he didn't know the Ofiklanod word for 'bat'. 'A flying creature, very big, as big as a house – did she come this way?'

'The monster?' the old man asked. 'Black against the sky, flying out to sea.'

Eric's heart sped painfully in his chest. 'Yeah, that's the one.'

'It fell,' he told Eric. 'This morning, at sunrise.'

His gut was fizzing, but he'd guessed that, hadn't he? Didn't have to mean anything bad. 'Where did she fall, though? Which island?'

The old man shook his head. 'No island. A water grave for her.' He was looking at Eric oddly, at this boy who cared too much about a monster.

'Not necessarily,' Eric said, 'not if there was land near. Somewhere she could swim to.'

'Are your eyes not made for looking?' the old man asked impatiently. 'This is seashore, not landshore. And the sea brings back what it takes.'

He pointed towards the water, behind the other men. They parted at his gesture, letting Eric see at last what had brought them here.

It was one of Rii's children, her new-born babes, washed up to shore. The body rose and fell as each wave took it. Its eyes were already gummy with death and flies had begun to settle on the corpse.

2

They were three, and they were one. There were three bodies, that much was certain, but the bodies weren't quite right. They had imagined themselves otherwise.

There were memories too, deep layers of them. They were a boy and the boy was afraid. His brother had his arm twisted behind his back, and a hand in the front of his britches. Shame burned in him, for the way his body responded to what his brother was doing.

They were a woman, hot from the forge. There were fragments of pain in her cheek where sparks had landed. The metal was cherry pink, and she raised the hammer—

They were inter. No thought, only sensation, warmth and wet and protection all around *omas*. But there was a pressure beginning, a squeezing of the wet red walls that was meant to force *omas* out, into the world—

They were three but they were also—

She felt herself falling apart, or maybe falling into place. *One*, she thought. *I'm one, not three. I'm Alfreda.*

She fell to her knees at the strength of this nameless new thing inside her. She kept her eyes fixed on her hands, focusing on each fine hair. She stared at her ragged nails and the long thin scar on her thumb. She knew that it – this new power – wanted her to be something else. There was a shape it wanted to fit her into, but she wouldn't let it. The shape would have to fit inside her instead.

When she'd regained some sense of herself, she stood. Marvan was already on his feet, leaning against the wall with one long leg crossed across the other, his head tipped back as if he was sunbathing in this dark corridor. Nabofik remained sitting cross-legged on the floor. *Omas* eyes were closed and *oms* was humming a tune that seemed to pull at the shape inside Alfreda and draw it out.

'Stop it!' she said sharply and Nabofik's eyes opened, startled.

'Well,' Marvan said, scratching his long nose. 'That was certainly interesting. What in the world did they put in that stew?'

'Maybe it was a drug. Like the purple sorghum that the traders bring from the god-ridden lands?' But Nabofik didn't sound convinced.

Alfreda wasn't either. Algar had tricked her once into taking some mushroom that the Eom cultivated and that was said to offer visions of the future. She'd lain on the blanket in the meadow he'd chosen and watched an ant crawl up a flower. The ant had been as big as a horse, the flower the height of a tree. She'd looked at Algar to tell him what she'd seen, and suddenly been uncertain if she was him, or he was her.

That had been a little like what she'd just experienced. But even in the depths of the mushroom delusions, she'd known on some level that everything she was feeling came from inside herself. This was different. She knew with absolute conviction that the fragments of Marvan's memory and of Nabofik's had been real. And that beyond even the three of them, something else was present, something of which she was somehow both creator and creation.

'Where do you think we are?' Marvan asked.

She found that she could remember everything up until the last few hours. 'The Mortals were heading to the Cinderlands, weren't they? That's what they were saying on the docks. And we got trapped on one of their ships, so I suppose this is where we landed.'

'The Cinderlands. Doesn't sound promising,' Marvan said.

She shrugged. 'Probably named for a fire mountain, just like Ashfall, and that's green and pleasant enough.'

'The Cinderlands aren't green,' Nabofik said. 'It's so far south they say it's nothing but sand and rock. The Mortals made the centre of their power here as a penance for summoning the old gods.'

Marvan peered out of a window. 'I see at least a dozen houses, all quite big. Definitely not a desert, more like a jungle, although . . . there's something not quite right about some of those plants. The Mortals have been lying.'

'But we knew that already, didn't we?' Alfreda said slowly, reckoning it out. 'When we met you, Nabofik, at your parents' house. The Mortal there was doing some sort of, I don't know, some sort of ritual. And it was him who told us to come here. I remember now! He said we'd find what we wanted here.'

Marvan rubbed his hands together briskly. 'Well, we won't find any answers in here, will we? I suggested we try to find our hosts.'

★

The sensation passed through Olufemi like oil. She knew it immediately, having felt it once before. This was how it felt when the world changed.

She and Yemisi had been left in the clearing where the children had died. The midday heat filled the air with the stink of spoiled blood, though the bodies had been removed. The only evidence of the slaughter was the stains left on the grass and the silver metal balls that the children would never again play with.

'It worked, didn't it?' Yemisi said.

Olufemi nodded. She'd given a monster the secret of god-creation. And now the new gods had emerged from their womb, slithering into life on a stream of blood.

'Should we go and see?' Yemisi asked.

They'd seen the younger almost-gods as they wandered unsupervised through this place. The children had been indoors in a nursery. Olufemi's family were map makers and she seldom forgot a route. It took her only minutes to lead Yemisi back to the place, through the dusty, tree-lined streets of the settlement. But when they got there, the crowd of Mortals she'd expected to find was absent.

The door was open. The children had been watched over when

Olufemi saw them previously, but they'd been deserted now. A chair in the corner of the room, adult-sized, had been kicked over as if its occupant had leapt up in alarm and fled in fear.

The children were dead. If Olufemi hadn't seen them living, she might not have recognised them now. They were mere husks, their dry skin sucked hollow like a spider's leavings. One of the husks still held a rattle in its hand, with bells which gently rang in the breeze. Another had a book open in its lap. It was impossible now to tell the inter from the girl or the girl from the boy. Death had robbed them of their individuality.

Olufemi's first thought was that the god-meal Bruyar had meant to use to empower them had destroyed them instead. But there was no sign of the terrible feast made of the flesh of the older children, the gods who'd already failed to be. Olufemi knelt beside the nearest husk and reached out a cautious hand to touch the desiccated flesh.

She jerked it away as the door was flung open. Bruyar stood beneath the lintel. A mass of Mortals and guards milled behind *omas*, held back from the room by *omas* bulk.

'What did you do?' *oms* asked. *Omas* eyes took in the husks of the children, then swivelled to bore into Olufemi, dark and bright and furious. *Omas* fleshy, jovial face looked anything but. 'Where is the food you stole?'

'I didn't steal or do anything. We walked from the clearing to this place and found the children as you see them.'

'But it worked,' Bruyar said. 'I felt it. Why, we all did.'

Olufemi rose on creaky knees. 'It worked, but not here. Did you say the food was stolen, the god-meal?'

Bruyar's face hardened into its usual cunning mask. 'Every scrap of it gone. The cooks claimed no knowledge. Is it possible, do you think, that the meal could serve to spark godhood in anyone, not just those we've primed for it?'

'I can tell you nothing,' Olufemi said. 'I know no more than you.'

But that wasn't true, she realised. There was a wordless knowledge inside her, a magnetic pull in a direction that wasn't north.

The others must have felt it too. As a group, they turned their backs on the hollow children and walked from the nursery.

The Three were waiting for them. The shock as Olufemi saw their faces emptied her lungs. The woman and the inter were strangers to her, but she *knew* the man, his long nose and that mouth twisted with ironic amusement. It was Marvan of Smiler's Fair. Marvan of the Drovers, whose appetite for blood the whole fair had known and feared. This man had followed Krishanjit to the lands of the Rah to kill him. He'd been their prisoner in Mirror Town.

The woman opened her mouth to speak, and for one moment a musical note emerged, deep and resonant and irresistible. It left room for nothing in Olufemi's head except itself. And then the music was gone and it was just a voice.

'What's going on here? What's happening to us?' the woman asked. She was very tall, with a broad, innocent face and the pale skin and loosely curled hair of the Moon Forest folk.

As she spoke, Marvan stared at Olufemi. She was quite sure he was trying to remember where he'd seen her before. She looked away, easing herself into the shadow of the man in front.

Bruyar smiled, all steel and no humour, although perhaps someone who'd only just met *omas* might not recognise that. 'Why,' *oms* said, 'for us to answer that question, you'll need to answer ours. The first being what precisely it is that you believe is occurring to you.'

The woman stared at *omas*, expressionless. Olufemi thought that perhaps she *had* recognised the inter for the serpent *oms* was.

It was the young inter who replied. *Oms* surely couldn't be past *omas* sixteenth year. 'We feel like we've been smoking blind-man's reed for three days straight, or at least it feels like what cousin Sinistium said blind-man's reed is like, and he's smoked so much that my father said he's certain never to amount to anything.'

'But we haven't smoked reed,' Marvan said. 'Or purple sorghum or bliss or the Lady's Favour. Unless something was slipped into our food.'

'Your food!' Bruyar pounced on the word. 'Did you by any chance – and there'll be no judgement here, my darlings, I promise you that – but did you by chance purloin some stew from our kitchens? Flour cakes too, perhaps.'

'We did.' The woman's voice shook and she ducked her head, like a shy child. But when she raised it again, her expression was fierce. 'What exactly was in that food?'

'Power, my dear, that's what. We set out to perform perhaps the greatest feat imaginable: the creation of new gods, three new and perfect gods to replace the two who let us down so badly. And' – *oms* swept as low a bow as *omas* belly allowed – 'when I look at you, I can be in no doubt whatsoever that we succeeded.'

★

Olufemi didn't have anything resembling a plan. She only knew that she needed to get away before Marvan remembered where he'd seen her before and just why he might want to hurt her. Yemisi followed in her wake, throwing questions that Olufemi didn't have time to answer.

The settlement was surrounded by jungle, with shaded earth paths leading out of it in three directions. One must lead to the fire mountain and the harbour beyond, but there was no way to know which. Olufemi chose the leftmost on a whim and had taken her first step on it when Yemisi caught her arm.

'Where are you going?' she asked.

'Away. You know who that man is – but no, of course, you've forgotten. Yemisi, that man, that new god, is a killer. I know him of old: he murders for sport. And he knows me, and has no reason to love me. It was at my bidding that he was held captive in Mirror Town when we came there with Krishanjit. We have to get out of here.'

'*You* need to get away. He doesn't know me.' Yemisi chewed her cheek. 'And there's the woman and the inter too. This is a threefold god they've created. No one knows what that means. The transformation from human to god might have transformed their natures too.'

'Perhaps it has, but I've never been a gambler. And if we

remain, my life hangs on the spin of a coin. Besides, you know what gods are, and these aren't even ones of my own making. I shan't make the mistake of trusting in them again.'

'If you didn't make them,' Yemisi said, 'perhaps they're better made. Your gods took everything from me, Olufemi. They stole my memories, my past. They stole me. Maybe these new gods can reverse the old magic and give me myself back.'

Only four paces separated them, but Olufemi didn't know how to cross that distance. Before Olufemi had brought Krishanjit to Mirror Town, Yemisi had been a wise old woman and Olufemi's mentor. But the moon's magic exacted a price and Yemisi had paid it with her years and experience, turning in an instant from an elder to a callow youth. She couldn't be blamed for that, but Olufemi had found this version of her almost incessantly irritating over the months of their travel. Yet the thought of being separated from her left Olufemi adrift.

'Why,' Bruyar said, 'just the women I was looking for.' The inter stood with folded arms, blocking the path back to the settlement. 'Oh, no need to look so alarmed. Our interests may be more aligned than you believe.'

Olufemi balled her hands into fists and kept her voice calm. 'You may choose to believe me or not, but one of these new gods of yours is a monster. A ruthless killer and a man without conscience.'

'Is he now? So he's known to you. How small the world is.'

'I shan't interfere with you,' Olufemi told *omas*. 'I shan't try to prevent . . . whatever it is you plan for these things you've worked so hard to create. Though I will say, you're a fool if you believe you can control them. But I need to be away. Please, just let me go. You've had all you require from me.'

Bruyar smiled. 'I don't mean to stop you. I and certain of my people will also be leaving here with some haste.'

'You are?' Olufemi stared at *omas*, trying to see the lie, the trick behind the pleasant mask.

'I am,' Bruyar said. 'I'm sure you have many thoughts about me, some perhaps less charitable than others. But I doubt you think me a fool. And as you so rightly say, only a fool would stay to see what those three wreak. Even more so, if what you say of the man is true. The gods I meant to make were my creatures, raised by my hand since their birth. Unlike your ungovernable moon, they would have done my bidding. But la! 'Twas not to be. And these three, grown to adulthood and beyond, full of their own plans and desires? These I will not stay to watch overturn me. There are ships in the dock waiting – we sail by sunset, if you care to join us.'

3

Sang Ki wanted some time alone to think, but had the misfortune to be among a people who disapproved of solitude. *Be calm*, he told himself. The tea was still in his system; he wasn't thinking straight. He stared away from the circle of the obec and tried to ignore Jalena squatting on the ground to his left. The people of the obec stopped to stare at him whenever they passed by. He tried to ignore them too.

The grass stretched in every direction, featureless except for the lone trees and the broad, flattened track of the obec's passage two days previously. The trees were elegant things, flat-topped and many-trunked. There was a sort of beauty here, very different from the icy drama of the mountains in which he'd grown to adulthood. He had, he realised now, grown to love this place in the short time he'd made it his home.

Had he thought he might live out his life here, a respected man among a generally joyful people? Well, he'd been a fool. The vision that the tea had given him told him so. But why now, curse it? For months the tea had given him nothing but a headache. And when he'd imagined what he was meant to be seeing, he'd pictured hallucinations of greenery and light. The world he'd seen in his trance hadn't been like that at all. It had been a purple-tinted, sharply angled maze, like a honeycomb made of triangles. It had been a place of fear.

He tried to call to mind exactly what it was he'd seen, but all he could remember was the terror and the knowledge that something new and evil had entered the world above. That, and the absolute certainty that wherever he hid, it would find him.

A horn sounded behind him, summoning the food-beasts back

from their pasture. They lumbered past Sang Ki, great walls of scaly flesh. He always expected some smell to accompany them, but like the lizards they resembled, they were entirely odourless. It made him uneasy, as if they were some figment of his imagination and not truly there.

As one of the beasts veered into his path, Jalena hurried forwards to slap its flank and shout, 'Careful, you hollow-head, the plant-speaker's here!' She looked anxiously at him. 'It didn't tread on your foot, did it? My mother's sister's daughter in Cervene Obec was trodden on by a house-beast, and first the foot turned green and then they had to cut it off. But I suppose house-beasts are much bigger.'

'It didn't tread on me,' he reassured her.

She grinned. 'There, you see! Aren't I good eyes for you? Better than Mircia or Radu. I think you should tell them so, that I'm the best eyes you have. Then they'll give me the job more often, and I won't have to be crushing up the grass-grain for the midturn feast. Mother says I'm very slow, but who can be fast when the work's so boring?'

'Who indeed,' he said. Jalena's chatter was sometimes irksome, but he found it restful today. He liked her complete ignorance of any world outside the small circle of the obec. She never asked him about his life before he and Mahvesh had made their way across the Silent Sands to this place and these people. None of her folk asked. To them it was as if he had sprung into existence on the day he stepped foot on the savannah.

Unfortunately, the world outside did exist, and these people might soon have no choice but to care about it. 'Go and speak to the horn-holders,' he told her. 'Tell them to sound the call for a conclave.'

*

It was night by the time the conclave met with the plant-speaker. The house-beasts were giant shadows in the darkness. Jalena usually liked this time, when the work of the day was finished and she could slip from kin-fire to kin-fire. She was always welcomed to sit and share braised meat and dumplings. Everyone knew that she was a good friend to the Lucky Woman, and they thought that maybe some of that luck would pass from Jalena to them. And while Jalena ate, she could hear what every family of the obec talked about, all the private things they didn't share outside their own fire.

But the conclave was only three people: the chief gatherer, the chief harvester and the chief crafter. Not even old Agata was invited, who was very wise, so they would never have let Jalena come to listen. That was why she was slinking through the darkness like a snake, only maybe not quite so silent. It didn't matter. By the time she'd slithered up to them, they were already in the middle of their talk and their voices were very loud. If they kept shouting so much, the whole obec would know what they talked about and not just Jalena.

'You're not listening to me!' That was the plant-speaker. His pale face was flushed red with anger. Jalena had never seen him angry before, or really anything except happy.

'We *are* listening, plant-speaker,' the chief gatherer said patiently. 'We're very glad the plants spoke to you so loudly. This is a good thing.'

'Then you have to do what they told me. We have to go.'

'Go where?' the chief harvester asked reasonably. He always spoke very reasonably and calmly.

'I don't know!' the plant-speaker said, and then again more quietly, 'I don't know. Not . . . not east. It's coming from the east. I don't know how I know that, but I do.'

'North, then?' That was the chief harvester again. 'Into the lands of Statecny Obec? You know there's been much raiding between us. If we go north, there will be blood.'

The plant-speaker shook his head from side to side, which Jalena had learned meant no among the Ostatni Ludia. 'We can't go north. There are . . . I have enemies there.'

Jalena gasped. A plant-speaker didn't have enemies. Who would hurt a man who touched the world-beneath-the-world? It would be the illest of all ill luck.

'What lies to the south of the grasses?' the plant-speaker asked.

'Or . . . or over the ocean, I suppose. If we could build boats. But it can be done – history says we all came to these lands over the water, your own people included.'

The three conclave members flinched and clapped their hands over their ears. For anyone to speak of the long-ago past was a bad thing, but for the plant-speaker to do it was even worse.

He looked startled at their reaction, and then seemed to realise what he'd done. 'I'm sorry,' he said. 'I only meant a sea voyage is possible. But maybe south is the best way.'

The conclave exchanged looks. 'Tell us again what it was you saw,' the chief crafter said softly. She was a very old woman, her face as wrinkled as a house-beast's ball-sack. Soon she would not be, and so everything she said was listened to very carefully, before it all had to be forgotten.

'I told you, I don't remember very clearly,' the plant-speaker said. But when they all stared at him silently, he added grudgingly, 'There was a maze, and I was running through it, but I could also see myself running through it. The maze had a centre but I couldn't reach it, even though reaching it was the only way to get out. And in the maze I felt—' He stopped abruptly.

'You have remembered something,' the chief crafter said.

'I saw the moon and the sun,' the plant-speaker said slowly. 'I knew, somehow, that they were asleep. I think I shouted to wake them up, but they didn't hear me. And then suddenly I couldn't see them any more, because . . . because something else had come to be. It was both inside and outside the maze, and it was somehow three people and one person at the same time. The centre of the maze – whatever was in the centre of the maze – these three were using its power. It's the greatest power in the world, and I knew that they'd use it very, very badly.'

There was a silence when he'd finished speaking and the conclave cut their eyes at each other again, as if they were speaking without moving their mouths.

Finally, the chief gatherer said, 'Well then, this is a very clear vision, and a very lucky one. A seeing of very great luck.'

'Luck? Did you not hear what I said?'

'Yes. You were not always a person, plant-speaker. You were a not-person before, one of the Ostatni Ludia. This isn't to ill-speak you. You're the best plant-speaker on the grasslands, everyone knows it. But you didn't grow up with our ways. A plant-speaker sees, yes. But understands? No. The plant-speaker sees, and others understand. This is the way of it.'

The plant-speaker smiled, but Jalena saw that there was no laughter in his heart. 'So you're readers of tea-leaves and I'm merely the cup. I had my fortune told me once, you know. A man of Smiler's Fair read my palm. I thought it would be amusing. He described in great detail the meaning of each line of my hand. The broken upper line had some connection to monetary wealth, as I recall, and to secret noble blood. It was almost as if my provenance and history were common knowledge at the fair. And the fact that the true meaning of my visions here is precisely what serves *you* best? I'm sure that's mere coincidence too.'

Jalena nearly laughed at the expressions on the faces of the conclave. The plant-speaker always talked in knots and tangles, but she had become skilled at unpicking them. It took the conclave longer to understand they'd been insulted. At first their expressions were stupid, and then angry, and finally they made trying-not-to-be-angry faces, because a plant-speaker must always be honoured, even when he called you a liar.

'Plant-speaker,' the chief harvester began carefully. 'I see that—'

'Enough!' The plant-speaker heaved himself to his feet and held out a palm. 'We understand each other. I've given you my vision, and you've told me what it means. What else is there to say?'

He strode away into the night, but Jalena stayed behind. She wanted to hear what the conclave said when the plant-speaker wasn't there. Because she knew his vision was true. She'd seen his fear when he woke from it. He'd seen disaster in their future, and the stupid conclave would walk the obec into the jaws of it, if they couldn't be stopped.

*

It was his own fault, Sang Ki reminded himself. When he and Mahvesh had first come here, and the people had welcomed them so unexpectedly, he'd been more than happy to play the role they handed him. When he'd drunk the tea and it had given him little more than a headache, he'd used his imagination to furnish them with the visions they wanted. And he'd been delighted to let them understand them as they pleased. The obec prospered and everyone was happy.

The dinner fires were mere embers as he walked through them, the kin groups having already retreated to their house-beasts. In the dim light of the stars, it was hard to make out his own beast. He approached the nearest vast shadow, only for it to grumble unhappily. The house-beasts were bonded to their families, as good as guard dogs. They seemed placid, but he had no desire to find out the damage something ten times the weight of a mammoth could do to him if it chose.

He was greeted by two more deep, resonant rumbles before he heard the familiar cooing of his own home. It always amused him how much like a bird it sounded, a giant bird welcoming an equally outsized chick back to its nest.

A stepladder hung from the creature's back. Sang Ki had balked the first time he'd used one, but he barely noticed the climb now. These days, some of his bulk was muscle, and not fat. The people here weren't pleased. They saw his size as a symbol of plenty and they encouraged him to sit still and plied him with food. But Sang Ki enjoyed the unfamiliar sense of his body as a tool rather than an encumbrance.

At the top, the fibrous stepladder turned into wooden stairs, running up the curve of the beast's back and to the door of the low wooden hut that sat on top. His first night here, Sang Ki had barely slept, afraid that the hut would tumble from the beast's back and fall the very long distance to the ground.

In the morning he'd seen the hardwood nails hammered through the hut's floor into the creature's flesh. The flesh had grown over the wounds long ago, making the hut and the beast one.

The interior of the house was dim, lit only by a single candle burning on the low table. Mahvesh sat beside it, weaving a rush skirt for one of the dozen babies in the obec. Her burn-scarred face was abstracted, but she looked up the moment he entered.

She studied him carefully before saying, 'They didn't listen?'

'As indeed you told me they wouldn't.'

'You had no plan to offer them. "A danger's coming, I don't know what it is, and I don't know how to get away from it." What did you expect them to say?'

'Precisely what they did, I suppose. But I do have a plan.'

'Oh?' She didn't look thrilled at the prospect.

'Well, perhaps plan is too grand a word for it. But I've certain ideas about how to get away.'

'You're really going to leave?' While she talked, her hands never stopped working on the rush skirt. Her work was highly valued in the obec, though he suspected more for its connection to the 'Lucky Woman' than for its quality. Mahvesh had once been – well, according to her, she'd been the proprietress of the Laughing Rabbit in Smiler's Fair, and he'd chosen not to gainsay the story. The murder of his father, for which he'd once blamed her, seemed so very long ago. But whether she truly had been the woman who was his father's unwilling bride, unrecognisable now beneath her burn scars, she certainly hadn't been one who was accustomed to manual labour. The skirt was decidedly lopsided.

She's happy here, he realised. Why wouldn't she be? She had respect, company when she chose, solitude when she didn't. The people of the obec believed her scars showed her to be the possessor of tremendous luck. How else could someone have survived so terrible a fire? He supposed it made a sort of sense. He was fairly certain that Jalena's second cousin had begun to woo her, though he wasn't sure if she returned the feelings. Life here was simple, but sweet.

He couldn't be content with it, though, not now. What *was* Krishanjit up to these days? Sang Ki had last seen him during the battle of Mirror Town, leading the freed slaves against his own father's men. He and Sang Ki had been, ostensibly, allies then. But Sang Ki had never much cared to be his vassal. Could he be the danger that Sang Ki had sensed in the world-beneath-the-world? But no, the moon was sleeping and wouldn't wake, whatever that meant.

'Well?' she said. 'What *is* the plan?'

She was happy here, he reminded himself. She had a place. 'Nothing,' he told her. 'No more than idle dreams.'

★

The next morning, the obec moved to new pastures. It was a lengthy and sweaty operation in which Sang Ki was expected to take no part. He sat on a lizard-leather tuffet and plotted. He'd head south, he decided, into unexplored lands. It was a strangely exhilarating prospect. When he'd sat in his father's library in Winter's Hammer, devouring book after book about the world and never seeing an inch of it, he hadn't dreamed he'd become an adventurer. But sometimes the world served a dish to meet your needs and not your appetite.

He wondered what his father would have made of life in the obec. He'd have considered it barbaric, but perhaps he would have enjoyed its efficiency. It seemed the most terrible, chaotic mess now, as the lumbering house-beasts were prodded into motion, children still scampering up and down their legs. The friskier food-beasts were saddled and mounted, and all the cook-pots and spindles and woodwork tools were gathered and stored. But despite the chaos, Sang Ki knew that they'd be in motion by the time the sun had moved a handspan.

Tasks completed, a laughing group of youths approached from his left. 'Ho, plant-speaker,' Drogan said. 'Want to have some fun?'

The whole group was smiling and jostling each other as if acting on a dare.

'I suppose it depends what form the fun takes,' Sang Ki replied.

'Zayna found a grass-cat nest by a watering hole,' Drogan said. 'We're going to catch them for pets.'

'That certainly does sound fun,' Sang Ki allowed.

'Come with us then, and you can have a pet of your own.'

But there was something about Zayna's smile that Sang Ki didn't trust.

He rose to his feet, suddenly not liking the feeling of the youths towering over him. 'It's a kind offer, but I think I must decline. My world is the world of plants, not animals.'

Drogan and Zayna exchanged a look, and now he was quite sure they were up to something.

Drogan leaned in closer and spoke softly. 'The truth is, plant-speaker, we have a bet. Wendolin and that jackal Piotr said that you thought us very low. They said you think we're the joke of the obec. And we said we were your favourites of all the almost-grown. And he said, prove it then. And so we said, just you watch tomorrow, the plant-speaker has promised he'll take us to a nest of grass-cats he's found. And Piotr laughed, and so Zayna bet her favourite bead necklace on it. And so now you have to come with us. Unless you really think we *are* very low, and no more than a joke.'

Well, that was a very neat bit of blackmail. And after all, he *would* quite like one of the creatures as a pet. A memento of his time here he could take away on his travels.

'Well . . .' he said, and the youths whooped and cheered, already knowing that they'd won.

No one troubled them as they left the camp, except for an adult or two who shouted at them to be back before the move began. Sang Ki had worried that the conclave might think to put a guard on him, but no one followed when they left. There was a charming naivety to these people. Or perhaps it was just an inability to imagine that anyone would want to leave the obec which was their whole world.

The savannah looked flat from the back of one of the house-beasts, but it wasn't truly. The obec and all its beasts and people were soon lost to sight behind the brow of a hill. The grass grew greener and taller as they walked, and here and there he saw a dusty pink flower. Despite the peacefulness of their surroundings, Sang Ki felt a tension growing in his shoulders, the knowledge in his spine of some hidden danger.

He could see that the youths felt it too. They held themselves stiffly, and there was no laughter now.

'How much further?' he asked.

'Don't worry, we're nearly there.' Zayna's voice cracked halfway through the sentence.

Just when he'd decided to turn back anyway, the grass parted to reveal the watering hole, and a surprised antelope dipping its head for a drink. As the antelope bounded away in high leaps, Sang Ki gasped in relief. The after-effects of the tea must still be with him if he was sensing danger in so innocent an outing.

'Well then,' he said, 'where are these grass-cats?'

'I'm sorry, plant-speaker,' Drogan said, 'it seems there are no grass-kittens after all. We were mistaken. But look, a pig-beast in the water.'

Sang Ki saw quite clearly that the watering hole was unattended now the antelope had fled. He looked at Drogan, then at the dozen or so other young men and women. They were all wearing the same intent expression.

'What's going on here, Drogan?' he asked. 'Is this some game or joke, or a part of the bet? I'll happily lie for you and say there was a pig-beast if it will help Zayna to keep her bead necklace.'

'But there *is* a pig-beast,' Zayna said.

Drogan nodded. 'We were very surprised and frightened. We tried to run away, but you were too slow. By the time we came back for you, the pig-beast had already hurt you.'

Sang Ki tried to take a step away, but the young people were all around him. 'Is that the story you want me to tell?' he asked shakily. There was a knife in Drogan's hand now.

'No story,' Zayna said. 'Everyone knows pig-beasts have a certain way of hunting. They go for the legs first, for the cord that holds the foot. They use their horn to cut it. That way the prey can't run from them.'

Two of the youths grabbed Sang Ki's arms.

'This is the conclave's doing, isn't it?' he said. There was no reply, but he knew that he was right. 'The conclave asked you to do this, but they won't do it themselves. And you know why. Hurting a plant-speaker is terrible bad luck. They want misfortune to fall on you and not on them.'

He'd managed to unsettle them. A few of the youths backed away, and the one holding his left arm dropped it. But Drogan and Zayna seemed unaffected. They both wore serene expressions that terrified him, as if completely happy with what they planned to do.

'The obec is safety,' Drogan said. 'Plant-speaker, there's danger out in the grass. When the pig-beast gores you, it will only hurt a little while, and then the wounds will heal.'

'And I won't be able to walk!' Sang Ki said. He knew his voice sounded high and desperate.

'There are beasts that can carry you,' Zayna said. 'And everyone in the obec will be your legs for you. For a gatherer or a hunter, the pig-beast's goring would be a harm. But for a crafter or a plant-speaker, it's nothing. You can sit and put many plants inside you. You will be safe and you'll tell the obec all we need to know, so everyone will be happy.'

The others seemed to take heart at their words. Two of the burliest young men reached for him and panic took him. He surged forwards, running three paces before a youth leapt onto his back and others grabbed his arms, some flinging themselves down to hold his legs. He flailed and roared until he heard Drogan shout, 'Tie him up! Don't hurt him!' and twine was bound around his arms and legs.

He was gasping, sweating like a pig-beast himself as Drogan knelt at his feet, knife in hand. Carefully, he lifted Sang Ki's ankle to position it for the blade just-so.

'If you do this,' Sang Ki told him, 'when I next visit the world-beneath-the-world, I'll tell all the growing things to shun the obec. I'll tell the wild wheat to produce no grain for you, and the fruit to rot on the bough before you pick it. Your people will be the poorest in the grasslands, and everyone will know that the luck is gone from Juh Obec. The daughters of the other obecs will spit on your sons, and their sons will turn their backs on your daughters. No babies will be born and no futures made. All this will happen if you use that knife.'

For the first time, Drogan's face showed doubt. The other youths muttered and stepped away from him. He was left in a clear circle with Drogan at his feet and Zayna standing at his head. But in her eyes, the certainty still shone bright.

'He's angry now,' she told Drogan. 'We all say not-true things when we're angry. When the anger goes, the not-true things never come to be.'

Drogan's face cleared. He touched the knife's cold flint blade against Sang Ki's ankle – and jerked away again as a roar shattered the tense silence.

There was a babble of fear and confusion among the youths. Zayna stared at Sang Ki, as if he'd somehow been responsible, and Drogan at his knife, where a single bead of Sang Ki's blood hung.

One of the young men pointed to the far side of the watering hole and shrieked, 'Tiger!' in a voice thin with terror.

None of the youths were holding Sang Ki now. He struggled onto his elbows, helpless in his bonds. His neck twisted at a painful angle as he tried desperately to see where the youth was pointing.

All he saw was grass, dyed yellow by the relentless heat. Was that a fang? But no, it was only one of the strange white crickets of these lands. And the stripes were just stalks. Surely they were. Except, that ring of deep golden-orange could almost be an eye. And then all at once it resolved into a clear shape. A tiger, unquestionably a tiger, its teeth bared in a snarl.

Two or three of the youths screamed. Then they were all running – past Sang Ki and away.

'Don't leave me here!' he yelled. 'Drogan! Zayna!'

Drogan spun to look at him. For a moment he hesitated – and then he too fled.

The tiger's roar came again. Sang Ki whimpered and his bladder released a spurt of warm urine. With the absolute clarity of the doomed, he thought how much he wished he could have died a more dignified death.

The grasses shook as the tiger's head pushed forwards. It was moving in silence now. Stalking its prey. Until finally the beast broke through the underbrush and he saw it whole: the furred head of a tiger on a slender human body.

Fear had slowed his mind and for a moment he wondered if this was some terrible new hybrid. And then his wits returned to him and he saw it for what it was: a human wearing a mask made from tiger skin, with glass beads for eyes. The figure raised its hands – thin and long-fingered, surely a woman's hands – and pulled off the mask.

'It worked!' Jalena crowed. 'I knew it would. I threw some luck stones this morning and they all came up on the star-side, every single one of them. I was afraid they'd catch me sneaking into the festival hut where all the masks are held, only they didn't. And I thought maybe Drogan would recognise the mask, because it's his father who usually wears it at the summer dance. But that didn't happen either. And then I was worried because – oh, but I haven't untied you yet, have I? And they'll probably come back, when they realise how much trouble they'll be in for leaving the plant-speaker to be eaten by a tiger.'

She sliced through the ropes at his wrists and ankles and offered her hand to help him to his feet. He felt almost too shaky to stand. He was weak with the emptiness that's left behind when fear is gone.

He looked at Jalena. Her cheeks were flushed with triumph and her straight hair fell at an angle over her sharp face.

'You saved me,' he said. 'You knew what they were going to do.'

'No, not really. I listened to the conclave last night and so I knew they wanted to stop you leaving. Then I saw them whispering with Drogan and Zayna and I knew they were planning a not-good thing. Only there were more of them than me and I couldn't stop so many of them with my strength even if I was very strong, and I'm not very strong. But the week before you came to us, in the bad year, two babies were eaten by a tiger and three obecs had to work together to hunt him down. So I knew that I could frighten them and maybe make them stop the not-good thing.'

On such a slender thread his future had hung. 'I can't go back,' he said. 'The conclave tried to do this. They'll try again.'

'Yes, we must leave,' she said.

'*We?*' He studied her. Her youthful face was mulish, almost comically determined. 'Jalena, I don't know where I'm going, but it will be a very long way from here. A very long way from your home. You've never seen the rest of the world. I don't think it's a place that would please you.'

She shrugged, the rolling one-shouldered shrug that was distinctively hers. 'But the plants spoke to you. *They* know where you're going. I saw your face after the vision. You saw a very-true thing, whatever the stupid chief harvester and chief gatherer and chief crafter think. The plants have a purpose for you, and I want to be part of it.'

4

Dae Hyo followed a careful twenty paces behind Eric. Any closer and the boy scowled at him. Any further away, and Eric would be lost to sight in the growing crowd of refugees washing up in this nowhere town on an ugly brown coast.

It was strange to see Eric so angry. Dae Hyo wouldn't have thought he had it in him. Eric had been a boy whore of Smiler's Fair, which was close enough to being a knife woman, and knife women were gentle-natured. But Eric's son had been taken from him and it had wakened a rage in him. In Dae Hyo's opinion, it should have been grief instead. Eric's son was lost in the sea, never to be found. But Eric refused to believe it. So here he was, hunting for a boat to follow his boy's trail and snarling every time he was thwarted.

Eric approached another group of fishermen clustered protectively around their small dinghy. Like all the rest, they sent him on his way with barely a word. There were too many people here wanting too few boats. Men who made their living on the water knew better than to give up their livelihood for a few coins that would be gone in days, and then how would they catch their fish?

Eric was on a fool's errand, but Dae Hyo meant to see that he didn't get hurt while he pursued it. Tempers were high here. Those with sea-worthy boats had already taken to sea, and those who remained grew more desperate by the day. Dae Hyo had a nose for a fight, and he could sense one brewing here. A part of him looked forward to it. A bit of bloodshed concentrated the mind, and his thoughts had grown unpleasantly noisy since he'd taken the gods from the world.

The rune tattoo that Krish had put on him was itching and flaking, as no tattoo should. The rune had been made to save him from bliss and keep him from drink. It made it impossible for him to take any pleasure from them, or it had. He was trying very hard not to wonder if the gods' departure had taken the rune's power with it.

But they couldn't stay in this dirt-poor town forever. Food was already running short. They'd have to start walking soon, north towards the border with Ashanesland that was five hundred miles or more distant. Someone needed to make Eric face the truth, and maybe it should be Dae Hyo.

He'd been so lost in his thoughts that he almost tripped over Eric. The boy was small, but he'd puffed himself up with anger. Dae Hyo nearly bounced off his crossed arms.

'Stop following me, will you? Eric snarled.

'I'm not following you, boy. It's a fine day when a man can't walk down a street without being accused of following someone.'

Eric glared at him.

'All right,' Dae Hyo said. 'I may have been keeping an eye on you. But only to keep you out of trouble. My brother seemed to like you, and he'd want me to take care of you.'

'I don't care what Krish likes! He ain't said a word for near a week now, has he? And none of you ain't lifted a finger to help me. Except you skulking around and making the cullies think I'm up to no good. Go away.'

Dae Hyo opened his mouth to tell Eric that he'd never find what he wanted. All he was doing was riling people up, and he ought to be grateful if Dae Hyo made sure his face didn't get broken while he did it. But he saw the boy's expression, the tight lines around his mouth and the red of his eyes, and shut his mouth.

He'd let Eric keep trying for a little longer. There was no harm in having hope. It had kept Dae Hyo on his feet after his people were slaughtered, and probably hadn't been the reason the drink had taken such a hold on him.

It was a short walk for Dae Hyo back to their makeshift

campsite in the ruins of a fisherman's shack. It was a cold home and a cold welcome he got when he came back to it. Dinesh sat cross-legged beside Krish and Drut, staring at his own hands. Lanalan lounged on a broken bench, his gaze equally distant. Renar was probably off looking for more food.

Only the Hunter looked up as Dae Hyo approached. 'How is Eric?' she asked. It was the most interest she'd shown in anyone. She seemed to have a soft spot for the boy.

Dae Hyo shrugged. 'About to get himself in trouble.'

That drew Lanalan's attention. 'Then why have you left him? Had you not set yourself as his guard?'

Lanalan had a soft spot for Eric too, Dae Hyo was certain of it.

'It is past the time for us to depart,' the Hunter said. 'This was always a desolate region, where few crops would grow. Mizhara had plans to bring the canals here, and with them life, but war broke out before she could.' Her golden eyes scanned the rough shacks of the town and the flat dry landscape around it. 'It seems that in a thousand years, nothing has changed.'

'If we go by land, how, how, how will we carry them?' Dinesh asked. He was looking at Krish and Drut. Dae Hyo couldn't read his expression, and nothing in his voice told whether he thought leaving Krish and Drut behind would be a good or bad thing. The rune he wore had forced his loyalty to Krish, but his tattoo, like Dae Hyo's, was fading away.

'There is one boat big enough to take us,' Lanalan said. 'It arrived yesterday morn on the early tide.'

Dae Hyo smiled. 'Well, there's half the problem solved, then.'

'And the other half?' the Hunter asked.

'Getting whoever owns the boat to give it up.'

Lanalan nodded. 'Precisely why my sib has gone to speak with them. They are acquaintances of hers. Although, 'twould be more accurate to say rivals. Renar promoted the other candidate in the last Triumvir election. Her tactics were much admired in the news-sheets for their cunning and ruthlessness.'

'Did she win?' Dae Hyo asked.

'Why, of course!'

Dinesh smiled, more twisted and less sunny than any expression he'd made before the magic left the world. 'Then, then, then let's hope they don't bear grudges.'

*

Renar approached the centre of the village with little delight. Though it was barely past mid-morning, the sky had darkened to an ominous grey and thunder rumbled in the distance. No rain fell to quell the heat, though. It seldom did in these parts. The province of Ofzib had contributed little to the economy of Ofiklanod over the years and even less to its culture.

As she rounded the corner into the village's muddy central square, she saw Verik herself, the woman whose boat she needed to somehow procure. Renar had almost forgotten what she looked like. Once she'd eliminated her from the race to become Triumvir of the Land, she'd barely spared the woman a thought. She wasn't looking forward to playing the supplicant with her now, but need dictated, and so she gathered herself, stepped forwards – and was nearly knocked from her feet as a man pushed past her.

'The boat!' he shouted. 'Verik, someone's stealing the boat!'

Renar stared, dumbfounded, as Verik leapt to her feet, and the crowd around her turned seawards, where a proud, two-masted vessel was indeed heading out from shore towards the bank of storm clouds that blotted the horizon.

*

Smiler's Fair winked its eye at all sorts of wrongdoing, but Eric had never held with thievery. He didn't care now. No one would sell him a boat? Then a boy wasn't left with any other choice. He couldn't sail her, of course. When would a sellcock have learned how to put to sea? But that didn't matter. Dinesh had grown up in a land that was half water, and Eric would lay a wager that the Hunter knew a thing or two on the subject.

The wind was blowing away from shore. He'd checked that before he nicked the boat. But he hadn't accounted for how strong it would be when it grabbed hold of the sail. The rope pulled halfway out of his hand, taking his skin with it, and he struggled to tie it off with the sail still at half-mast. Even so, the boat was fair racing through the water. Eric took hold of the helm and tried to curve her round to shore, but even a land-hugger like him knew you couldn't point a boat dead against the wind.

He'd counted on his companions to follow him, once the deed was done. Or at least the Hunter, and probably Dae Hyo too. They would have been enough to manage the boat between them. But they'd have to reach it first, and the shore was growing more distant by the moment.

Well, Eric would manage on his own if he had to, and every inch away from land took him nearer to Rii and to Arwel. He didn't like the look of the sky, though. The sea was gentle, at least. The tiller was easy enough for Eric to hold, and the boat answered when he pulled it. She was a pretty thing, near forty-foot long with a cabin down below. He could stay dry in there when the storm hit – and he admitted to himself now that it *would* hit, sooner than he'd like. The sky ahead was almost as dark as night, rent by brilliant flashes of lightning.

The boat heaved and the rigging sang unhappily. Eric looked back to shore for the twelfth time and . . . those little dots? Were they dinghies coming towards him? And if they were, how could he tell if they were friend or enemy? His boat lurched as a bigger wave caught it and Eric's stomach lurched too.

The smaller vessels were gaining on him. There were two of them, both under oar. A sudden gust struck the boat and the tiller wrenched out of his hand. It flung him to the deck as the boat twisted sideways, dropping the wind from its sail. The waves over which it had raced now buffeted and rocked it. An inch of water sloshed along the deck, growing deeper by the second.

There was a reverberating bang, and Eric thought the hull had been holed. Then he heard the yells, feeble against the roar of the wind, and he realised that he'd been boarded. He pulled himself to his knees, staggered, and fell on his back instead, staring up at the angry black sky.

Hands grabbed and pulled him upright. He struggled against them, until the salt water blinding his eyes cleared. It was Renar.

Behind her, Dinesh and Bachur pulled Krish's limp body over the railing.

'You idiot!' Renar yelled. 'Do you have any idea what you've done!'

And then the storm struck.

5

Sang Ki had learned much about the savannah in his short time among its people. He knew its dusty plants and elegant trees. He'd learned to love its multi-coloured sunsets, its gentle weather and even the alarming, shrieking laughter of the chichochat birds that lived off the obec's leavings. But he hadn't been alone in it since he and Mahvesh first stepped over its borders and into the waiting arms of Juh Obec.

Now with only Jalena beside him and no supplies, no spears or nets, no more than the long bone knife at Jalena's belt, he felt the savannah's vastness and its hostility. In the first few hours of their flight, Jalena led him to a river. It flowed westwards, broad, shallow and sluggish, towards the distant sea. Thirst hadn't been a problem since, but the same couldn't be said of food.

Though zebra and pink stilt-birds and horn-beasts flocked to the riverbank, they knew far faster and stronger predators than Sang Ki and Jalena. Their second morning, he watched a lion savage a water-mouse twice its size. Jackals devoured its leavings before he could get near them. And Jalena only managed to down one hare, which proved to be so riddled with disease that they left its meat untouched.

That day, they walked until sunset and found a crooked tree to sleep beneath. The water drew insects in profusion, and the next morning Sang Ki woke scratching at their many bites and with a gnawing in his stomach.

As the second day drew on, he began to yearn for the obec. If they turned back now, they could retrace their path – or find the hunters who must surely have been sent after them. Sang Ki had feared pursuit in the first hours of their flight. Now he found himself hoping they'd left a trail broad enough to follow. The hunters would have food, even a mount to carry them back to the obec. And perhaps the conclave would stop at one attempt to cripple him.

But when he turned to Jalena to tell her as much, she gave a glad cry and pounced on a thorny bush wedged between two boulders. 'Flour-root,' she said. 'Help me, we need to pull it up.'

He knelt to scrabble beside her in the dirt. Jalena seemed oblivious to the thorns scoring her face and hands. When she'd dug a little deeper, he saw why. The unpromising plant had hairy, tuberous roots, similar to the potatoes that Sang Ki's father had imported from the lowlands of Ashanesland at exorbitant cost.

'See, the plants are giving to us. They want us to continue,' Jalena said.

'And will the plants instruct us how to cook it with neither flint nor coal to hand?' he asked.

He regretted his sharp words when her face fell. 'No. And you can't eat it raw. My cousin Ladislao tried and he was sick for a week.'

'Well,' Sang Ki said, 'we'll just have to find a way to make a flame, won't we?'

Her face brightened. 'We can use sticks!'

'I had indeed heard that wood may be used to make a fire.'

She smiled, apparently oblivious to his sarcasm. 'Yes. It was many rainfalls ago, I think, before I was grown. My uncle Jaroslav showed me – oh, but I shouldn't say that name. He's been forgotten.'

By this, Sang Ki knew, she meant that he was dead. He'd found this fake forgetfulness a fascinating quirk when he'd first arrived among the people of Juh Obec. 'I think there is a distinction to be made,' he said carefully, 'between memories of a person and knowledge that was acquired from them. Else how would anyone know anything?'

She frowned. 'Do you think so? I've never heard it said, but perhaps the plants gave you knowledge of this.'

'Yes, indeed, the plants have spoken. You may relate what your uncle told you.'

She chewed her lip in indecision, looking very young. He felt a little guilty, but not enough to outweigh the gnawing of his stomach. 'Jalena, I swear to you, if you tell me this, no harm will come.'

It didn't seem much good would come of it either. Jalena broke two slender branches from a nearby tree and diligently stripped them of their leaves. But when she rubbed one against the other, all it produced was an unpleasant grating sound.

It was easy enough to guess what the intention was. Heat came from friction, as anyone who'd rubbed their own hands together to warm them knew. But any fool also knew not to throw green timber on a fire. The sap quenched the flames.

He returned to the tree from which Jalena had chosen her branches and searched for ground-fall instead, the dryer the better.

Jalena looked up when his shadow fell over her. 'I need your knife,' he said.

He drew the blade down the centre of one of his branches, up and down until he'd worn a groove nearly its whole length, then trimmed the end of the other until it fitted inside the groove.

'We need to build up the heat in just one area,' he told Jalena, who'd abandoned her own attempt to watch him work.

Her face cleared. 'Oh yes, I see. Give it to me, plant-speaker. I can do it. I'm stronger.'

But he found himself reluctant to let go of his work. It took a while to master the sawing motion, until he found his rhythm. His shoulder began to ache and then to throb, and then, finally—

'Smoke!' Jalena yelled. 'Plant-speaker, it's smoking!'

'Quickly, find me some dry leaves!'

It took her too long. By the time she brought him the kindling, the smoke had dissipated. It was three attempts later when he thought to use the matted coating of butter nuts to hold and grow the flame, and another hour until the embers were hot enough to roast the tubers.

The meal that followed was the blandest he'd ever eaten, and also the best. In his entire life, this was the first time he'd eaten a meal he prepared himself. Even on their journey from Mirror Town to the savannah, Mahvesh had done what cooking there was. They had mostly lived on supplies looted from the ransacked city. And before that, when he'd lived in Winter's Hammer with his father and mother, he'd eaten as befitted a lord's heir, though as a bastard he'd hardly been one. He tried to call to mind that soft, confident young man who thought he knew the path that lay ahead of him, but he felt so changed by the events of the last years that his younger self was a stranger to him.

The next day dawned without a sun. The sky was striated orange and red and lowering black. A wind had risen, rare in these grasslands, but seemed uncertain which way to blow. It bent the grass first one way, then another, and shook twigs and overripe fruit and one startled monkey from the tree under which they'd camped.

Jalena stared warily at the horizon. Her shoulder-length brown hair whipped around her face, softening its sharp angles.

'Should we find better shelter from the storm?' Sang Ki asked.

She shrugged. 'The storm is nothing. Where to go next is the question. This is nowhere land, between the grazing of Krasivaya Obec and Umnny Obec. Here we must decide: Krasivaya or Umnny.'

'We've avoided any encounters so far. Can't we continue to slip by unnoticed? It's not as if an obec is hard to see coming. The dust cloud alone is visible for miles. Not to mention the odour.'

'If these were any other obecs, yes. But there's been much raiding between these two. More than normal, a not-good amount. Gatherers have died. Now they send patrols all over the grazing lands to watch for trouble.'

'But we're not trouble. They can hardly see us as a threat. And I'm a plant-speaker, which isn't a title your people take lightly. Or is it different in other obecs?'

'No. It's the same.' But she still looked worried.

A hazy memory surfaced. 'I seem to recall having heard of Umnny Obec before. Something about them keeping the ears of their enemies for trophies? Can that really be true?'

'Yes,' Jalena said. 'That's why Mirko has only one ear and is very ugly.'

'Then I suggest we make our route through Krasivaya lands.'

She nodded, though she didn't seem entirely convinced, and angled their path north-west. He'd lived here long enough that the sounds of the savannah were like silence to him, soothing in their way. But Jalena's twitchiness had him on edge, and he couldn't stop his eyes darting around like hers, looking for threats. It was only because of this watchfulness that he spotted the small, shrivelled plant.

'Purple sorghum!' he said. 'I had no idea it grew here, so far from the Hundred Islands.'

Jalena frowned. 'Of course the dream-flower grows here. Very rare and very precious. What else do you think they put in your tea? It's the best of all the plants for clearing the path to the world-beneath-the-world.'

He stared at her in shock. He supposed it was his own fault for never asking what precisely went into the concoction they gave him to facilitate his visions. Still, he wasn't delighted to learn that he'd been taking a substance that was a key ingredient in the making of the drug bliss.

The clouds cleared as noon approached, the promised storm scudding eastwards to drop its rain elsewhere. But just before the sun reached its zenith, he noticed a different cloud on the horizon, dusty and brown.

'Yes,' Jalena said. 'Krasivaya Obec is there.'

Though they walked for another hour, the obec's cloud didn't seem to draw any nearer. Sang Ki's shoulders, which had been hunched with tension, gradually relaxed. He began to wonder when Jalena might think it was time for lunch. He opened his mouth to ask her – and a branch snapped beneath his foot, leaving nothing at all beneath it.

He cried out, flailing his arms for purchase. They caught only twigs as he fell into darkness.

★

He opened his eyes on that same darkness. He was on his back, staring upwards. Above him, the night sky was freckled with stars. He floated above himself, drawn to their lights – and then his body shifted, very slightly, and he crashed back into the searing agony in his leg.

'Oh,' Jalena said, 'you're not dead.'

The stars disappeared as she bent above him. A tentative finger brushed against his cheek. He flinched away from it. He felt skinned alive, every part of him agonisingly sensitive.

'I think . . . I think my ankle is . . . broken,' he gasped.

'Yes. I can see the bone.' Her voice was very small, and there was a thickness to it, as if she'd been crying.

His gorge rose. He forced himself to swallow it down. He was afraid he might choke on his own vomit. 'Can you help me sit up?' he asked.

She slipped an arm behind him, a warm comfort against his back. He could feel her straining upwards, but it was no use. He was too heavy for her. He pushed her gently away, and then pressed his palms to the ground, bracing himself before pushing upwards.

When he next knew anything, his back was propped against a dirt wall and both his legs were stretched out in front of him. It was lighter now. He could see the first hint of the sky's shift from black to blue. Unfortunately, more light allowed him to see his own ankle. He'd seen a horse with a similarly mangled joint. His father had slit its throat to put it out of its agony. Sang Ki should have been in pain too, but there was only numbness. He wasn't fool enough to think that was a good sign.

'Do you think you can stand?' Jalena asked. His expression must have spoken for itself because she added, 'I know your leg is hurt, but Mirko's dog only has two legs and he can run faster than me. Not that I want you to run. But . . . I think we should get out of here.'

'Here' was a space little more than ten paces square and tall enough that Jalena would have needed to be twice her height to reach the top. Above, he saw the ragged edges of broken branches and a scattering of leaves to hide the trap.

'You should go,' he said. 'Return to your people.'

'I won't leave you.'

'You must. I can't climb out of here. You can. There's no point us both . . . there's no point us both being trapped here.'

She turned to the wall of the pit and began to dig at it with her knife, one groove at knee height and then another a pace above it. When she made the third groove, he realised that she was making footholds for herself. He tried not to feel hurt at how quickly she'd accepted his suggestion.

There was something in the wall at his back, a rock or a tree root, pressing into his kidneys. He shifted to ease the discomfort and a lance of agony slammed up from his leg. It knocked his thoughts into blackness.

When he next woke, Jalena's face was framed by the sky above him. She was frowning. 'Oh good. I thought you were going to sleep forever.'

'You're . . . you're still here,' he croaked.

'I'm not going without you, so you can stop arguing. And anyway, I've found a way to get you out.'

The only thing that seemed to have changed about his situation was that a vine now hung beside the crude footholds Jalena had dug in the pit's wall.

He smiled crookedly. 'If you're planning to pull me up, I hope you've found a dozen burly men to help you.'

'I'm not going to pull you up – you are.'

'I most certainly am not. Jalena, my leg . . . I can't stand. I can barely move.'

'I know. That's why I fixed it.'

Fixed was perhaps too strong a word. She'd strapped his leg from knee to ankle, using strips of cloth to bind two sticks to it. Her shirt was shorter by inches, baring the pale flesh of her stomach and the indentation of her belly button.

'I put the bone back inside while you were sleeping,' she said. 'I thought if you were asleep you wouldn't feel it, but you screamed when I did and I felt very not-good. But then you went to sleep again, so I carried on. I used water to clean it, only the water was muddy. That's bad, but it takes time for flesh to start rotting from dirt. My cousin Ivan lived for four days before the sickness in his arm spread to his heart and killed him. We can worry about your leg tomorrow.'

He started laughing and couldn't stop. He'd seen hysterics in others. It was very strange to feel it in himself. And then he caught sight of Jalena's frightened face and all the laughter left him.

'You've done a good thing,' he told her, 'but I won't be able to walk on it.'

'You will. Look, I made a stick for you to lean on.'

It was quite cleverly done, a branch with a cloth-wrapped fork on top to rest beneath his armpit. He could see that she'd torn another strip from her own clothing to make it. He began to feel the first stirrings of real hope. 'That still won't help me climb,' he said.

'No. You'll have to pull yourself up with your arms. I'll be behind you and help to push.'

'I'm not strong enough.'

She shook her head stubbornly. 'You've eaten a thousand, thousand plants. You have their strength inside you. Plants are more powerful than anything. Their roots can break rocks and they live in the deepest water and on the highest, driest land. You are a plant-speaker. You live half in this world and half in theirs. Be in the other world.'

Three days ago, he would have considered this complete nonsense. But he *had* visited the world-beneath-the-world. He'd walked through its terrible strangeness. Perhaps there truly was more strength inside him than he knew.

He used the stick she'd made for him to lever himself to his feet. It cost him pain, so he found that place again, outside his body, and placed the agony there.

The hardest was the first step. He had to lift his good leg to the foothold in the wall and leave the bad to bear his weight. But then it was done, and the vine was in his hands. He pulled himself to the next foothold, and the next. Jalena's shoulder was wedged beneath him, giving him support when his own strength failed.

At barely fifteen paces upwards, it was the longest journey of his life. His body was soaked with sweat and wracked with shivers by the time he reached up mindlessly for the next handhold and found empty air instead.

When he could feel the sun on his face and smell the grass he'd crushed beneath his elbows, he fell onto his back, closed his eyes and simply breathed.

He heard the huff of effort as Jalena heaved herself over the edge too. There was a brief pause before she said, 'Plant-speaker, I think you should open your eyes.'

He opened them to the mottled blue-white of the sky. And then a corner of it was blotted out by a face. It was a young man with a fierce scar running from forehead to lip through an empty eye socket. A moment later another face joined it: a middle-aged woman.

'It's him, isn't it?' the man said.

The woman squinted at Sang Ki. 'Maybe.'

'What do you mean, maybe? Look at his face. And his belly! This is Juh Obec's plant-speaker.'

Sang Ki levered himself painfully into a sitting position. The man and woman weren't alone. Around them was a ring of warriors, their weapons drawn. They all had a hungry, angry look about them. One young man shifted restlessly from foot to foot. His hand clenched and unclenched around his spear as if he was itching to use it.

Should Sang Ki lie about who he was? These people seemed to have been looking for him. But his position as plant-speaker was the only shield he had, flimsy as it might be.

'I am the plant-speaker of Juh Obec,' he said. 'I mean no disrespect if I – if myself and my apprentice – have wandered into your territory. I was speaking with the world below, and my visions led me to this place.'

The man who'd first spoken smiled at the woman. 'There, you see. I told you it was him.'

Her gaze swept over Sang Ki, like a farmer inspecting a goat at market. 'He's broken, though. Look at his foot. I've seen men die from a wound like that.'

The man shrugged. 'Then we'll have to get him there quickly.'

★

Janela and Sang Ki were kept bound together. It was hot and uncomfortable, but he was glad to know she was safe. That first day, it had taken some fast talking to persuade their captors not to take her from the camp and slit her throat.

No amount of talking, though, would make their captors tell them why they'd been imprisoned or where they were being taken. Jalena's mouth was bruised from the number of times she'd been slapped to silence for asking those questions.

'They can't do this,' Jalena said, more loudly than she should. Conversation between them was discouraged too. This evening time, when the sun was red on the horizon and their captors were busy making camp, was one of the few opportunities they had to talk.

Sang Ki was glad of the distraction. During the day, when he was carried on a litter by dour, silent men, he had nothing to divert him from his pain. His whole leg felt like it was on fire. He'd begun to smell something putrid, something that he feared was his own flesh.

'They very clearly *are* doing it,' he said to Jalena. 'Is it possible that other obecs don't respect plant-speakers as much as we'd imagined?'

'No. Impossible.' She stared murderously at their captors.

'Then why have they taken us? Have we transgressed in some way?' It alarmed him to notice that his speech was slurred, as if he was drunk. Did he have a fever? His thoughts were too clouded to reach a conclusion.

Jalena turned back to him. Her expression softened. 'The

blame sits at their fire, not ours. These aren't obec people. I've heard of them, but I didn't believe. In Juh Obec it would never happen. But in other obecs, sometimes people who are gatherers don't want to be gatherers any more, even though it's a job that needs doing. These people want to be hunters instead, and so they leave the obec and become almost like not-people, like the Ostatni Ludia. They hunt and travel and they have no house-beasts to live in. They sleep on the earth like beasts themselves.'

The description did seem to fit this group who'd taken them. There was a feral look about them.

That night, his dinner of dried antelope meat and wild thyme sat untouched on his plate. The thought of food nauseated him. He stared at his fingers instead, the way they seemed to grow and shrink. He was dripping with sweat. Jalena insisted that he had a fever, but he didn't feel warm. He was freezing.

The scarred man, the one-eyed warrior who'd first captured them, knelt in front of Sang Ki. He offered a clay cup. When Sang Ki didn't take it, he lifted Sang Ki's hand and wrapped the fingers one by one around the cup. 'Drink, plant-eater. You're dying. They say plant-eaters take great strength from the world-beneath-the-world. Drink, then. Take strength.'

Sang Ki fell into the world-beneath-the-world like a rock. It had been a far more gradual sinking the first time. There was a blur of colour around him, and then a bodiless landing that jarred his mind like a blow. It seemed to knock all the confusion out of his head. He felt absolutely himself again, and horribly aware of how quickly his body, the real one in the real world, was succumbing to infection.

He was, as he'd been before, in an angular maze, strange triangular rooms stacked together like a honeycomb, but entirely the wrong shape. The walls shimmered a translucent purple, like coloured glass. But when he touched one, he realised that it was something quite other. It was soft and velvety, like a petal, and his fingers were left flecked with pollen.

There were no doorways on any surface. He felt, for an instant, horrifyingly trapped. But then the knowledge came to him that he could pass through the walls if he chose. And he knew, without knowing how, that he could walk up them too. Did up and down have any meaning here?

He could see no one else in the maze, but he knew he wasn't alone. There was a presence, emanating something that wasn't light. It felt a little like madness. But it wasn't the evil that he'd sensed when he first came here. This thing, whatever it was, was far older and colder and stronger. And he realised, suddenly, that this was what up and down meant in the world-beneath-the-world. Wherever you were in the maze, this thing lay *downwards*, at the very bottom, or the very centre. It was at the root of everything.

He noticed for the first time that there was a window in the wall. When he looked through it, he saw his own room on his house-beast in Juh Obec. The view through the window shifted downwards and he saw hands, brown-skinned and scarred, sewing. Those were Mahvesh's hands, he was sure of it.

He passed through the wall, with a sensation like sinking into water, and in the next chamber of the maze found another window. He saw nothing but darkness through this one. The next gave a view of a moonlit landscape. The view shifted, as if the window was slowly moving forwards, and then lowered, as if whoever was holding this strange window had crouched. He looked through the next window in the next triangular chamber to see a babe suckling at a breast.

'They're eyes,' a voice said at his shoulder.

It was Krishanjit. He looked, impossibly, younger and thinner and frailer than when Sang Ki had last seen him. Perhaps it was the form he'd imagined, the way he still pictured himself, made real in this strange place. Just as Sang Ki's own body, it occurred to him now, was whole and uninjured here, while his true flesh rotted in the world above.

'Where are we?' Krishanjit asked.

'The world-beneath-the-world.'

Krish frowned. 'And where is that?'

'I don't truly know,' Sang Ki admitted. 'Somewhere that the mind goes when certain plants are consumed.'

'I didn't eat any plants.'

'Didn't you?' Sang Ki studied him. Krish was dressed in the simple clothes of a landborn Ashane. Was this the boy he'd once been, before his fate had found him? 'What were you doing, then, before you came here?' Sang Ki asked.

'I . . . was in a battle.' Krish seemed to be struggling to remember. Then his eyes cleared. 'I was fighting my sister. She's here too.'

And in that strange way that this placeless place seemed to operate, as soon as he said those words, Sang Ki knew that they were true. There was another here, distant. The sense Sang Ki had of her was hostile; she didn't wish to be known by him. Or perhaps it was Krish she wanted to avoid.

'I let it go,' Krish said. He smiled suddenly. It looked like an expression that seldom visited his face. 'I let the power go, the power of the runes, and then I came here. I think I might be dead.'

Sang Ki felt an unpleasant sensation that would have been his stomach lurching, if he'd still been in possession of a real one. Was he dead too? But he'd come here before, when he'd most certainly been alive. 'This isn't a place for the dead. It's . . . somewhere else.'

'A gaol,' Krish said, with sudden knowledge.

Sang Ki looked at the translucent, doorless walls, stretching infinitely into the distance in every direction. 'It certainly has the appearance of one.'

'No. Not here. This is freedom.' Krish's gaze turned to the nearest window. It showed a scene Sang Ki recognised, the vertiginous view from the treetop mansion of a Moon Forest thegn. 'They're the ones imprisoned. We—'

With nauseating suddenness, Sang Ki was falling away, falling back into his body. All the pain and confusion returned. The night sky of the real world hung above him. In front of him was a woman, someone he knew he should recognise.

'Well, well, well,' she said, but not to Sang Ki. 'This is the man. My friend, you found him, and you shall have everything that was promised.'

'Who are you?' Sang Ki asked. His voice was weak, little more than a whisper.

She seemed to understand. She crouched in front of him. 'I am Bone Dancer, betrayer.' Her face was as smooth as a young woman's, but her eyebrows were steel-grey and her hair stringy and white. She wasn't a woman of the savannah. She was a tribeswoman, a very long way from home.

'Have we met before?' he asked.

She didn't answer. She looked down instead at his foot. 'That might need to come off, if I mean to keep you alive. And no, we've never met.'

He couldn't make sense of it, her presence here or what she was saying. 'Then who did I betray?'

'My brother, Little Cousin. You led him to his death. And now, betrayer, you're mine.'

6

Marvan had found a garden to sit in, on a bench carved with trefoil leaves. There were toys strewn around but no children to play with them. He tapped his foot absently against a wooden play-wagon as he considered whether they would really allow him to do it. He didn't see any way that they could deny him, but that slight doubt made the anticipation all the sweeter.

At first, he'd been very interested in what precisely had happened to him. But after an hour at table with Alfreda talking to the Mortal leaders about histories and theories he didn't understand and didn't particularly care to, he'd stood and walked away. The Mortals had glanced at him out of the corners of their eyes, never meeting his. No person had, since he'd woken to this strange new reality. No one but Nabofik and Alfreda.

He knew the skeleton of it anyway, the part on which all the rest hung. He'd been made a god, the master of some strange and powerful new magic, or at least its co-owner. Nabofik and Alfreda shared his godhood. For a while they'd shared more than that; he'd been lost inside a mind of which his was only a part. He'd always felt a peculiar kinship with Alfreda, the anger in him calling to the anger in her. But this had been far more than that. Now she'd seen every ugly part of him from the inside, and rather than pushing her away, it had drawn her closer.

He wondered what it meant to be a god. Krishanjit of Ashanesland had been one, and yet he'd looked no more than a boy when Marvan had captured him as a plaything in Smiler's Fair. He'd certainly bled as red as any man when Marvan had his fun with him. And in Mirror Town, when Marvan had been his prisoner in turn, Krish had the air of a fox with its foot in a trap. His godhood had seemed to burden, not bolster him.

It appeared to Marvan that Krish had been the kind of god whose power served his worshippers and not himself. Well, that sort of godhood wasn't for Marvan.

He'd noticed one particular man at the meeting with the Mortals. It was hard to say what about him had drawn Marvan's eye. Maybe the arrogant twist to his lips, or the contemptuous drawl he couldn't quite keep from his voice, despite the sweaty, fearful clenching of his hands.

Yes, that man would be the one. The test.

The meeting had broken up by the time Marvan returned. Most of the Mortals had headed to a long, low building, shaded by trees with dark green leaves an armspan wide. Every head turned as Marvan entered. He smiled but didn't speak. He savoured their fear, their reluctance even to question him. But his quarry wasn't among them.

He wasn't in one of the two dozen or so near-identical houses either. Marvan enjoyed himself, even so, searching through strangers' rooms. He enjoyed it most when the strangers were there to watch him. He held one man's eye as he rifled through his wardrobe, pulling out expensive silks and throwing them to the ground. The Mortals were priests, meant to be humble. The fools even cut off their own hands. But here, away from the eyes of the people they supposedly served, they dropped the mask. They were hypocrites, all of them.

He considered amusing himself with one of these people, but he'd chosen his quarry. Now only that prey would satisfy him. Besides, he could always return to them later. How long did a god live? An eternity, he'd heard.

He found the man at last in what looked like a workshop. There were glass bottles everywhere, some empty, others filled with a murky liquid holding deformed things. Marvan thought they might be embryos, but not human.

The man himself crouched over a bench. He appeared to be working on the corpse of a black-feathered bird. There was a device attached to the stump of his arm that ended in a narrow scalpel. He used it to gently tease apart the wrinkles and folds of the bird's guts. There was a book open on the bench beside him, and every now and again he peered between its pages and the dead bird, frowning.

Marvan watched him in silence for a while before saying, 'I don't believe I know your name.'

The man's shoulders twitched violently. But when he turned round, his face was composed. 'I am Hilautan . . .' There was an empty space at the end of his sentence that Marvan saw Hilautan struggling to fill with an honorific. But if he understood correctly, the language of Ofiklanod had none for gods.

'And what are you doing here?' Marvan asked.

'Searching for changes.' Hilautan's tongue flicked out to lick his lips.

Marvan glanced down at the eviscerated bird. 'Changes from what?'

'From what it was. Many animals have been changed, you see, by the magic here. It had been theorised that the gorse crow is an ancestor of the carrion birds of Ashanesland, which are undoubtedly creatures of the moon. And so I thought perhaps that the birth – I mean to say, *your* birth – your rebirth . . .' His lips thinned as he collected himself. 'I wondered what effect this recent change might have had on the creatures of the moon.'

'Fascinating,' Marvan said, as if he meant the opposite.

Hilautan smiled patronisingly. 'I understand that you are outlanders. There will be much of this you don't understand. La, 'tis fortunate we Mortals are here to guide you.'

'Is it?' Marvan stepped forwards.

Hilautan tried to back away, but the bench stopped him. 'I only meant to say that we Mortals are here to serve you, as we've served the people of Ofiklanod so long and so selflessly.'

And there it was again, the supercilious tone that Hilautan couldn't seem to keep from his voice. It flooded Marvan's mouth with saliva.

'There is one way you could serve me,' Marvan told him. He

looked at the scalpel attached to Hilautan's arm and a wonderful idea occurred to him. 'You Mortals sacrifice your hands for your people, don't you?'

Hilautan's eyes were wide with fear. It was everything Marvan had wanted.

'Very well then,' Marvan said. 'Now I'd like you to sacrifice your foot for your god.'

'My . . . my foot?'

Marvan grasped Hilautan's wrist and twisted it until the scalpel-bladed prosthesis was inches from his eyes. 'This looks sharp enough for the job.'

'I can't,' Hilautan gasped. 'Please, my master, I can't!'

Marvan turned his wrist to press the blade of the scalpel against Hilautan's throat. 'Then I have no use for you.'

He saw the precise moment when Hilautan's will broke. Something died in his eyes. The human light extinguished to leave only the terrified beast behind. Marvan smiled as Hilautan lifted up his robe and set the scalpel's blade against his own skin.

*

Nabofik couldn't believe they'd left *omas* free to explore. *Oms* had heard stories of the Mortals' island home *omas* entire life. *Oms* had never thought to be granted the honour of visiting it. But it was the Mortals who seemed to be the ones feeling honoured by the visit.

Marvan and Alfreda were still there, nestled snugly in a corner of *omas* mind. There was a flavour to their thoughts. Alfreda's were crisp and dry with a hidden heat underneath, like rice wine. Marvan's were stronger and richer and just a little wrong, like a stew made with spoiled meat.

Their presence didn't fade as *oms* got further away from them. It was as if they were connected in some other place, where space meant something other than distance. But Nabofik didn't waste too much time thinking about it. There was so much else that was interesting here.

Oms liked Rorön, the Mortal they'd given *omas* as a guide. He was tall and thin with a long, thin face. He reminded *omas* of *omas* father. His head bent towards Nabofik whenever *oms* spoke, keen to catch every word. And he left a little pause after everything Nabofik said, truly considering it rather than just pretending to as *omas* parents did. But then, they still saw Nabofik as a child. Nabofik definitely wasn't a child any more.

'Was there anything in particular you wished to see?' Rorön asked. 'We're only a small settlement here, and recent. When I was a child this was nothing but rock and sand. The Mortal Council met elsewhere on the island.'

'But you're not any older than my father! The trees can't have grown that fast!' The nearest brushed their lowest leaves over the roofs of several huts.

'They've grown at an unnatural rate,' Rorön said. 'We hoped it indicated our efforts to summon the gods were bearing fruit. And so they were, if not entirely in the way we anticipated.'

'We may not be the gods you wanted,' Nabofik said, 'but we'll be good all the same. I swear to you. My father always told me: treat others as you mean to be treated and the world will give you kindness back. Of course, my maker always said that was nonsense and that I shouldn't listen to him. *Oms* thought people weren't to be trusted – they always got into a row about it. But mother would calm them down, and – but you don't want to hear about that, do you? I'm sorry. I ramble on too much; that's something Father always said, too.'

Rorön studied *omas* face. His own tilted to the side with a light frown. 'How old are you, exactly?'

'Oh, I'm nearly eighteen. I'm not a child.'

'No indeed,' Rorön said gravely. 'An inter grown. Still, I imagine you'll be wanting some advice from those who've seen a little more of the world than you. Advice, merely, of course. The final word would be yours. But there are battles ahead. The sun goddess and her followers must be dealt with. And there'll be others in the world who resist your coming.'

Oms studied him in turn, not so innocent that *oms* didn't understand what he was really saying. 'How much power do I have?' Nabofik asked. 'What can I actually do?'

'We have little idea, quite honestly. But certainly a very great deal. You have enough power to reshape the world, if the elder gods are any guide. And we made you to be stronger and better than them.'

'I *will* be better,' Nabofik said. 'The . . . the other two gods. Can I say their names? I suppose there's no reason not to now. Yron and Mizhara made a mess of everything. They were meant to bring peace and prosperity, that's what my tutor told me, and instead they brought war and destruction. I won't let that happen again. I've only been thinking about it for an hour and I've already got all sorts of ideas about how we can fix things. I – all three of us – we want to do right. You won't be sorry you made us into your gods.'

★

Alfreda made the Mortals bring her to the place where the experiments were done.

The room was lit by narrow shafts of sunlight through its high windows. They fell in broad lines across a floor tiled in volcanic grey rock, and over the many piles of books. The light warped into rainbows through the glass of bottles and tubes twined in complicated set-ups that she thought were stills. She couldn't guess what they were meant to distil. But by far the largest area of the room was taken up with musical instruments.

'The nature of your godhood is tied to music.'

Alfreda spun to confront the speaker. She didn't recognise the young woman's face.

'I'm Yemisi,' the woman said. She held up her hands. 'A stranger here, not a Mortal. They think they can help you, but they've never dealt with gods before. I have.'

'You're not from Ofiklanod. You're from Mirror Town,' Alfreda said.

The corners of Yemisi's full lips shifted downwards. 'You were at the battle of Mirror Town?'

'I was there.' Alfreda took a step towards Yemisi, looming over her with her greater height and bulk.

Yemisi held her ground. That sensitive mouth drew into a

tighter, stronger line. 'You would have been among the Hunter's forces, and I was on the moon's side.'

'Yes.' Alfreda's shadow engulfed Yemisi.

Yemisi's throat moved as she swallowed. 'Did you lose friends there? Or family? A lot of people did. I lost something too. I was ninety-five years old during the Battle of Mirror Town. Then the magic hit me.'

Alfreda looked at her seamless face and sturdy body. 'That doesn't seem like much of a loss. Being given back your youth and health – who wouldn't want that?'

'Anyone who's had it. The magic took my memories along with my years. The person who fought that battle – who used the magic – she died that day. And I was born, into a world seventy years after the one I knew. They say that those who lose a limb in battle feel a phantom of it still, that it sometimes pains them even in its absence. I feel it too: a phantom past, constantly with me, constantly unreachable. There isn't a moment waking that I don't feel the loss of what I once had.'

Alfreda could see in Yemisi's face that she was telling the truth. It was the emotion she saw there that confirmed it, a bitter anger that Alfreda knew well. 'Then why did you come here?' she asked.

'I didn't. I was brought here. Kidnapped. But I'm glad I was. I want back what I lost. All those years of experience, of memories, stolen from me. The moon's magic didn't reinvigorate me; it diminished me. Maybe yours can make me whole again.'

Alfreda picked up a round-bellied instrument with three strings. She ran her hand across them and a discordant jangle sounded. 'You said that my . . . my magic is connected to music.'

'The power lies in chords,' Yemisi said. 'Three notes in one, that must be how it works. A whole that's greater and more beautiful than its parts.'

There was a sheaf of parchments on one shelf, marked with a notation that Alfreda couldn't read. 'My father played the flute, while he was alive. But I never learned. Maybe I need to now.'

Yemisi chewed her lip. 'No, I don't think so. *I* do, just as the mages once had to learn the runes. But Yron never did. You *are* the magic. The music. And the music is a language and the language describes the world. That's how it works. Maybe . . . maybe you just have to listen.'

It seemed absurd, in the silence of that underground room, but there was something. Alfreda wouldn't have called it music. It was a deep, subliminal resonance. She touched the parchment gently with her fingertips, but the soundless sound of it was too complex. She thought she knew why. Paper was made of wood and wood was made of a hundred things. That was why a smith couldn't work it. She needed the simplicity of metal.

There was an iron cauldron beside one of the benches. She felt foolish at first, staring at it, trying to stare inside it somehow. But after a moment, she heard the music of it. This note was far simpler. It was a thousand, a million voices singing in harmony, and the voices were the tiny, identical fragments of which this larger thing was made.

The song was what bound them. It told them how to be. But Alfreda could change it. *That* was the power she had, which had never been in the world before. She could make things other than they were.

She held the cauldron between her hands and changed its song. The metal softened in her fingers, toffee-like. She pulled it apart until there was a sheet of iron between her hands as thin as silk. She knew she could pull it thinner still if she chose. She could make it become anything, as long as she worked with its fundamental nature, the unchanging chord at the heart of it.

Today she could melt metal with her hands. But she already knew that wasn't the limit of it. Perhaps there was no limit, and nothing in the world she couldn't utterly transform.

7

Olufemi gasped in a breath that was more water than air. She rolled to her stomach, retching, and swallowed another mouthful of seawater when the next wave came in.

There was barely any strength in her. She dragged herself over rock and sand on her forearms, inch by painful inch. The waves continued to wash over her as she moved.

She kept her mouth closed and waited for them to draw back, then crawled on.

She remembered a ship. Yes, she'd taken sail with Bruyar. And then . . . But no, after she'd boarded there was only darkness. Still, looking at the beach, it seemed clear what had happened. Along with the pebbles, and the strands of seaweed, and the skeletal driftwood branches, there were far larger pieces of debris. She couldn't tell what the board to her left might once have been, but she recognised the torn white fabric trapped beneath a rock as part of a sail. Further down the beach, a carved wooden chair that had once sat in the captain's cabin rested in the sand.

There was no sign of other people. Olufemi stumbled up the first of the dunes that rolled inland from the shoreline, but there was nothing much to see from the brow of it. Beyond the beach, a pine forest covered the land to the horizon. No smoke rose above the trees and there was no other sign of human habitation.

There was no sign of fresh water, either. Olufemi's lips were cracked and her throat felt coated with salt. The beach stretched straight and featureless into the distance on her left. To her right, it ended at a rocky headland. There might be a stream beyond it. There would at least be a different view.

Her robes were sodden. They tore on the sharp edges of rocks as she clambered over them. The sea spray made the rocks slippery, and the sun emerged from behind the clouds to scorch any remaining moisture out of her.

It was all worth it when she finally crested the rise. There was a rocky bay beyond, more fragments of a ship shattered beyond repair – and at last some other survivors.

She heard a shout, muffled by distance, and one figure began to mount the rocks towards her. There seemed to be at least two dozen on the beach: not all the ship's complement by any means, but a substantial portion of it.

As the figure drew closer, she recognised Bruyar. *Oms* had lost *omas* robes. A white undergarment stretched over *omas* ample stomach and breasts, stained here and there with blood.

'I'm glad to see you survived, my darling,' Bruyar said. 'Are there any others where you came from?'

'Just me. But I don't remember what happened. How did we end up here?'

'A storm – one such as I had never seen before. I sensed forces moving within it. Or perhaps colliding would be a better word. If I had to guess, I'd say the newly birthed magic met the old, and the commingling of unlike with unlike raised the storm.'

'Just as your experiments caused deformities in nearby people, I suppose,' Olufemi said.

Bruyar smiled at the barb. 'Indeed. This is why I'm glad to see you, dearest. Alas, too many Mortals were lost in the shipwreck.' *Oms* held up the stumps of *omas* hands. 'We're not well suited to swimming. Most of those who survive are the servants, useful people but not on the whole great thinkers.'

'What is there to think about?' Olufemi asked.

'Why, a great deal. Apparently you don't recall, but the storm winds blew west to east. Before they drove us onto these rocks, they drove us a very long way from land.'

'How long a way?'

'All I know is that we've made landfall on what I presume to be an island somewhere in the centre of the ocean. Our vessel is in fragments and there isn't a shipwright among us. We're stranded far from home with no means of escape. And if that's not enough for you to ponder, Olufemi, think on this. We've left behind us new gods of unknown power and suspect motive. A long path lies ahead of us, and we've yet to find its start.'

*

It seemed improbable that they'd made it to shore. Renar took one last look at the small boat they'd left on the beach, still unaccountably intact. There were gleams of silver all around it: fish thrown ashore by the storm.

Memories flashed into her mind unbidden even two days after they'd reached land. She saw sea foam scudding above them like clouds as the deck tipped almost vertical between the crest of one wave and the next. Lanalan lost his grip on the boat's side and was flung towards the water. He'd been saved only by a sudden tipping of the boat that spilled him back into it.

And yet they'd survived. Them, and perhaps no one else. They'd made a crude camp on the beach and waited a day, but no other boat had appeared. When the storm struck, she and Lanalan had been on one side of the vessel, and Eric and the rest on the other. She hadn't hesitated before climbing into the only lifeboat and dragging Lanalan into it beside her.

'He might still be alive,' Lanalan said as they walked the narrow track that led from the beach inland. Renar knew he meant Eric.

'He might,' Renar agreed. 'They all might. But they could be anywhere on five hundred miles of coast. We're more likely to find them in Ashfall than by waiting here. That's surely where they'll head once they're ashore.'

Lanalan studied the scenery. There were fenced fields, freshly ploughed, with clumps of woodland between them. 'And you're sure we're in Ashanesland?

She wasn't sure of anything until they came to their first village. It wasn't much to look at – a scattering of wagons surrounding a well – but it confirmed their location. No Ofiklanders lived their life in wagons.

She ran a hand through her hair. The roots had grown back mercifully its old dark brown and she'd cut off the rest. Her eyes, though, remained luminous yellow. Her sib's were moon-grey crescents above unnaturally sharp cheekbones.

It was midday when they arrived and the village was mostly empty. She was reminded suddenly of the first time they'd arrived in Ashanesland and their less than warm welcome. But now she had the winning card. She spotted a group of four elderly women hunched over spindles, nudged Lanalan towards them and took a step back.

As ever, he played his part well, but to excess. 'Good morning to you, friends!' he proclaimed, flinging his arms outwards in a gesture he'd learned in the theatre. 'We are in need of your aid.'

Two of the women jumped up in alarm and a third fell backwards off her stool. The fourth, a sour-faced old matron as sturdy as a cow, said, 'Who by the Lady's tit are you?'

Lanalan approached them until he was close enough for the women to see his eyes.

The woman who'd fallen from her stool scuttled backwards in a half-crouch. One of the others shrieked, but the one who'd spoken merely frowned. 'You're an odd-looking fellow, and that's the truth. What do you want here?'

Lanalan smiled disarmingly. 'La, merely some assistance. We're servants of your Wheelheir, as you can see.'

'Then why aren't you with him?' the woman asked.

'Alas,' he said, 'we were at sea and shipwrecked by a storm. In short, we're lost.'

'You've got the Smiler's own luck then. The Oak Wheel and his army, may the Five protect them, are marching for the border. They passed by here only yesterday.'

The women provided them with bread and cheese and withered apples along with a waterskin and directions towards King Nayan.

"Tis a pleasing country, is it not?' Lanalan said as they walked a path between two white-flowered hedges.

'It's not so different from Makat,' she agreed. 'The fields are smaller.'

'And no sof-bug nests. Or stib bugs or lac bugs, I suppose.'

'They've never learned to husband them. That's something we can teach them – some value we have, beyond the ability to tell them that their prince is missing.'

'We shall need that, shan't we? Renar, do you truly think we can never return home?'

'How can we, looking like this, and with the memory of war so fresh? And Lanalan, Bruyar is out for my blood. Where in Ofiklanod could we be safe?'

'Maybe not now. Maybe not yet. Maybe not even for a year. But Bruyar will need you, Renar, to mend what's been broken. *Oms* doesn't bear grudges if there's a cost to them, you told me that years ago. You're the cleverest person I know. Of course *oms* will want your help.'

'Maybe,' she said. 'Yes, you might be right.'

An hour later, they crested a low hill crowned with trees, and stopped short. It was amazing the havoc simply walking could wreak, if there were enough people doing it. The army itself wasn't in sight, but its trail cut a scar a hundred paces wide across the land. Wheat fields had been trampled into mud and hedgerows broken into splinters.

'I suppose King Nayan's worried about Krish,' Lanalan said.

'I imagine he is.'

'Does he plan to invade Ofiklanod to find him? Doesn't he know what happened the last time Ashanesland fought us? They don't call it the Fool's War for nothing.'

'We can all be made foolish by love.' Although Renar hadn't sensed any great affection between Krishanjit and his father. 'We should catch him up before he commits to a needless war. Although with all that's happened, I'm not sure which side would seem foolish by the end of it. Ofiklanod is in no position to repel an invasion.'

After not more than an hour they began to hear the noise of the army itself beyond a small patch of trees. Renar recognised the land around them from their first visit here. They were very close to the border with Ofiklanod and a futile battle. She didn't think she could endure another. And then they were through the trees and both the army and the Great Rift lay before them.

'Oh,' Lanalan said. His mouth was gaping like a figure from a comedy. 'Oh. I don't suppose we'll be going home soon after all.'

'No. I don't suppose we will.'

Not ten paces in front of them lay two corpses: a huge, vulture-like bird that Renar recognised as an Ashane carrion mount, with its rider crushed beneath it.

There were hundreds more, strewn across the barren land in front of the chasm. In places the army's ranks had been broken by their fall, with a dozen men left dead or wounded beside the giant birds. It was clear that the entire force of carrion riders was gone. Like Rii, it seemed the birds had lost their powers of flight with the going of the magic. And that aerial force, Renar knew, had been the foundation of every Ashane king's power.

Beyond them, something else was broken. The single bridge spanning the Great Rift was gone. Only its jagged ends remained, splintered like wood: one on the Ashane side, and one far distant where Ofiklanod began. Just as the carrion mounts had been products of the moon's magic, this bridge had been the work of the sun's, and just like the carrion mounts, it had been unable to survive the magic's passing. It had been the only path home for her and Lanalan, and it was broken beyond repair.

*

Eric had once watched a very bad play about a man stranded on a lonely island at sea. There'd been some line in it about being surrounded by water while dying of thirst. He hadn't paid it any mind at the time. Now he understood what the cully who wrote it had been getting at.

It was probably his own fault. No, it was definitely his fault, but he couldn't bring himself to care very much. As he'd lain drifting on this chunk of a broken ship, slowly slipping closer to death, he'd finally let himself accept that Arwel was gone. It made the end easier to bear. It made him long for it.

If he'd been alone, he might have just tipped himself over the edge of the oak board and held his breath until he'd sunk into the depths. He could have shared a watery grave with his son and his . . . Had Rii been his friend? He supposed she had, after all that. They could all have slept on the seabed together.

Only he wasn't alone, and Dinesh and Dae Hyo and the Hunter wouldn't let him have any peace.

'Your turn,' Dae Hyo said, pressing one of their crudely made oars into Eric's hands. They were already red and blistered from his last stint. Eric had tried to explain that with fewer fingers than the normal complement he ought to be exempted, but Dae Hyo was having none of it.

'What's the point?' Eric asked again. 'We ain't gonna get nowhere and it's just making us hungrier and thirstier. We don't even know where we are.'

Dae Hyo used his own hand to close Eric's remaining fingers around the oar. 'It doesn't matter where we are. We know where the land is. Svarog's cock, there's a whole bloody lot of it. If we row west, we can't miss it.'

Even if he'd been able to row like a Rah, it wouldn't have moved them much faster. The part of the ship they'd clung to as the rest fell into the depths wasn't much more than ten paces square. Krish and Drut lay in the middle, still unwaking. Their faces were turned up to the relentless sun. It hadn't stopped shining since the storm cleared. Dinesh had soaked two strips of his own shirt in seawater and put them over the sleepers' faces to cool them down. Eric didn't like it. It made them look dead. It felt like they were travelling the sea with two corpses for company.

The hours drifted into each other. An ache set up shop in Eric's shoulders and arms, his blisters burst and his blood slicked the oar. His mind began to drift too, slipping its mooring in time and heading into the past. He remembered another journey over these waters. They'd been distant then, flat and empty and blue, seen from Rii's back. Who had the boy been who made that journey? Eric wasn't sure he knew him any more, though it was his choices that had led Eric to this place.

He remembered the island Rii had landed them on, where she'd hunted the wrinkly grey sea cows for food. It had been little more than a black line on the horizon at first – or, wait, was that what he was seeing now? Eric shook his head until he'd snapped back into himself and looked again. It was there. He wasn't imagining it.

He leapt to his feet, thinking to see more of it, but even upright it looked just the same: a black line stretching a long way to left and right.

Dae Hyo's eyes followed Eric's gaze. 'You see! I told you we'd find land.'

Dinesh moved to stand at Eric's shoulder. 'It's land, but it isn't home.'

'Of course it is,' Dae Hyo said. 'Where else would it be?'

'I don't know, but it's an island, it's got to be. Unless home's shrunk since we left it.' Eric pointed to the part where the black line ended in blue.

Dae Hyo folded his arms stubbornly. 'Then it's a headland. I tell you what, wherever it is, it's better than here.'

Eric didn't resist when Dae Hyo took the oar from him and set them moving with long, steady strokes. He couldn't figure out his own feelings. He was ready to die, but there was a stubborn bit of hope too. He didn't know the point of living in a world without his son, and yet a part of him clearly wanted to.

They made good distance over the water. But the closer they came, the less it seemed like an island. Or if it was, it was the lowest, flattest island Eric had ever seen. Nearer still and he saw what looked like buildings on it, also very low, but no sign of grass or rock or sand. And then, as the wind brought them the first murmur of voices, Eric realised what he was looking at.

'It's a raft!' he said.

Dae Hyo stopped rowing briefly to squint ahead. 'That's no raft. It's the size of Mirror Town.'

'Eric is correct,' the Hunter murmured. 'What we see ahead has no roots in the earth.'

It wasn't so much one raft as a whole bunch of them roped together, bobbing up and down on the waves out of time with each other. And those *were* houses Eric had seen.

There were people too, scattered over the vast fleet of rafts. A crowd stood at the edge of the nearest, watching them approach. Eric thought they were children at first: short, thin and dark-skinned. But when he looked at their faces, he knew they were grown adults. They weren't of any people he'd ever met, and he'd met all sorts during his days at Smiler's Fair.

The strangers chattered to each other excitedly – or maybe fearfully – in a sing-song tongue. They shouted questions to the newcomers too, but Eric shook his head and then shrugged, not able to understand a word of it.

That didn't seem to please the raft people. There was a movement in the crowd and three or four men came forwards with poles in their hands. They used them to push the hunk of wreckage away. When Dae Hyo took a step towards them, arms held away from his sides and the various knives and axes there, they pushed harder on the poles until there was a broad stretch of empty water separating them again.

'They believe we have come to do them harm,' the Hunter said, not looking up. Eric realised that she was trying to hide her strange eyes.

'Belbog's balls, why would I row over half the ocean on a piece of driftwood just to stick a knife in someone?' Dae Hyo growled. 'If it's blood I'm after, there's enough of that at home.'

Eric heard several of the people on the raft gasp, suggesting that they weren't as ignorant of normal language as Eric was of theirs. 'That sort of talk definitely ain't helping,' he said.

'They want to know if you bring sickness with you,' a new voice announced.

Eric saw that the crowd had parted to let a single man through. He was a head taller than the rest and sallow-skinned like a tribesman. He *was* a tribesman, unless Eric missed his guess.

'We ain't got no sickness,' Eric said. 'We was shipwrecked.'

'Then what ails those two?' the man asked.

Eric realised he was looking at Krish and Drut's motionless bodies.

'Oh, them two?' Eric said breezily. 'They was knocked out. It weren't no sickness, just something broken inside their heads.'

The man's gaze swung between the six of them, while his companions on the raft all stared at him, as if awaiting his judgement.

'You're a strange group to be travelling together. Ashane, Moon Forest, Mirror Town and plains. Since when did groups like that set sail together?'

'What does it matter?' Dae Hyo asked. 'We want water and directions. And maybe the loan of a boat, if you have one. And if you'll take a man's word on repayment. We're a little short on coin.'

There was a long tense moment as the man stood firm. Then at last he nodded and the poles were pulled back, freeing them to approach. 'You can come aboard then,' he said. 'But there's no boat and there'll be no directions. You're a thousand miles from land with no way to reach it. You've found the Drifters of the Warm Seas, and you'll make your home here, or you'll make it in the ocean.'

PART 2
The Old Lands

8

It was the cold that Renar found hardest to bear. Even after three years stranded in this land, she found it as strange as on the day she and Lanalan had been shipwrecked on its coast.

In this bleak, flat delta landscape, not a tree stood to block the wind. It blew with an icy chill over the silvery network of waterways and the mud between them. Even the birds seemed to dislike the climate. The endless grey sky was home to only a single formation of geese, wisely heading south. Her first winter in Ashfall, King Nayan had seen her shivering in council meetings and ordered hunters to supply her with wolfskin. She wore the greatcoat they'd made her every frosty day and the guards called her 'the Bear'.

Among her own people she'd been known as the Fox. It was hard not to feel that the bear was a step downwards. But then, the cunning that had earned her the name in Ofiklanod had landed her here, in the freezing north, among a strange and uncivilised people. Perhaps a bear, sour-tempered and slow-witted, was all that she remained.

Nevertheless, it was for her wits that King Nayan had employed her as counsellor and envoy three years ago, when she and Lanalan had found themselves exiled and friendless in this land. The old man was wily, and while his vassals had grumbled at a foreigner being raised so high, he'd understood that the political skills she'd honed under Bruyar were of value to him. Or so she'd been able to persuade him.

'It was a success, was it not?' Lanalan said.

And her sib, of course, whom Nayan had also engaged in his service. Not for his wits, certainly, but for his pleasantness. Renar had come to value that quality more than she once did, especially during the current negotiations.

'A successful hunt, certainly,' she replied. 'I hear you were the master of it. You brought down a fine stag of sixteen tines. Since when did you become so adept a bowman?'

'My arrow grazed its haunch. It was Lord Harjas who killed the beast and gave me the credit to curry favour. I don't believe I'll ever understand the way these godlanders bow and scrape to mere men. 'Tis a wonder they have any worship left over for their gods.'

'They say the words, but do they mean them? Perhaps their respect is as empty as their prayers. Lord Harjas calls himself a loyal vassal of King Nayan, yet there's treachery in his smile.'

'At first maybe,' Lanalan said. 'You made him King Nayan's offer, didn't you? To adopt Harjas's firstborn as heir to the Oak Wheel?'

'I hinted at it. I've hinted at it in every shipfort across this wretched land. A tease is only potent so long as people believe its promise will be fulfilled. I fear King Nayan's shiplords have begun to doubt. Besides, who's to say Lord Harjas will ever have a son? They say he'd rather lie with his hounds than that weasel-faced wife of his.'

The pace of their horses slowed as they spoke. There'd been a flagstone road for the first half of their journey. Now there was only ever-thickening mud. They'd be able to go no further without assistance.

Renar's horse whickered irritably as she pulled the reins. As ever, she found herself longing for the ease of travel along the canals of her home. But even they must now be stagnant. The magic wind that swept boats along them for a millennium had been forever stilled.

Besides, if Ashanesland held such waterways, Delta's Strength wouldn't be the place or the power it was. It was the hub through which all river-borne trade passed. The shipfort was tiny in the distance, surrounded on all sides by water and sand and mud. There was a path through, but it shifted with the tide. Only the lords of Delta's Strength knew it.

'Are those our guides?' Lanalan asked, peering over the waters at an approaching cart.

Renar recognised its riders. The rulers of Delta's Strength themselves had come to greet them, the twin sisters Nimrit and Amila. King Nayan had sent them word of the visit by messenger bird.

'You will be Renar, then,' Nimrit said, when the cart stopped in front of them. The twins weren't difficult to distinguish. In truth, they were different enough to look unrelated. Nimrit was the taller, thin and austere, while Amila was all smiles, wavy-haired and round. Renar didn't trust either of them.

'I am Renar,' she confirmed, 'and this is my sib – my brother, Lanalan.'

Nimrit flicked her eyes up and down them. 'Well,' she said. 'I suppose you'd better follow us.'

'Please do,' Amila said. 'I'm dying to hear what dear Nayan has to say to us.'

Renar exchanged a glance with Lanalan. Her sib looked calm, but her sib had a regrettable tendency to see people in the brightest light. Renar had spent too long in the shadows to do the same. She knew they weren't among friends.

There was no conversation as they travelled, only the dull thud of the horses' hooves, and the occasional croak of a frog. The air smelled faintly of decay, as if the mud had swallowed unhealthy things. Renar ran her fingers along the golden torc that Nayan had given her to mark her rank. It was a nervous habit she abhorred but couldn't seem to shake. The gold was icy cold.

The landscape around remained flat and drear. Only the proportion of water changed. As the shipfort approached, rivulets grew to streams and then to great shallow rivers, with the sand between them not much wider than the cart.

When the shipfort was close enough to see its great red sails, the cart stopped. Renar realised that what she'd taken for land still ahead was a collection of broad reed rafts. They were covered in soil that was prickled with the first green shoots of spring.

'We learned the trick from the Rah,' Amila said. 'They're an interesting people, very enterprising. Our trade with them has been extremely profitable. The rafts allow us to grow our own grain and vegetables, so we're no longer dependent on the inland forts for food. Ah, but here's our barge. The horses can take us no further.'

The boat was wide enough to take them all along with their mounts. The rafts shifted as it rowed through them, until they were past the last of them, and the fort lay before them.

'La, 'tis hardly possible!' Lanalan exclaimed.

Nimrit smiled thinly. 'King Ashane said the same, many hundreds of years past. Yet here we still are.'

There were no mammoths to pull this fort on its circuit of the lake and no ropes connecting it to the shore. Even its great sails were slack. The force that moved it was in the water itself, a whirlpool of extraordinary size around whose outer edge the fort travelled. A churning white vortex led from its centre to uncharted depth. The rough, roaring sound of it was more like wind than water.

The lake was so shallow on its outer edge that only a barge such as theirs could traverse it. If Renar chose to trail her hand in the water, she could brush the leaves of plants rooted in the sandy bottom. But only a dozen paces ahead that sand fell away into blackness. There was a cliff edge in the lake so sheer and fathomless that Renar flinched as their barge crossed its boundary. She felt an irrational, animal fear that their boat would tip and plummet down that underwater cliff.

She realised that Nimrit was observing her closely, a small smug smile on her lips.

'Your home sits on the edge of destruction,' Renar said with studied calm. 'One moment of inattention from its steersmen and it would be lost.'

'Fortunate for us, then, that we never waver,' Nimrit replied.

Lanalan had stood to stare at the whirlpool with guileless curiosity. 'What could possibly cause it?'

Amila shrugged. 'No one knows, or ever has. The landborn

blamed the gods, of course. They said the Smiler and the Lady once fought over a golden comb that they both coveted. The Lady, who is mistress of the weather, flung a storm at the Smiler. He laughed and turned it upside down. Their legend doesn't record who ended up with the comb.'

'But you don't believe this tale?' Renar asked. She'd never quite deciphered the way the Ashane felt about their gods. Perhaps an Ofiklander never would.

'I thought it was the moon's work,' Nimrit said quietly. 'Even we Ashane, who weren't in these lands for the moon's first birth, remembered that he was an ill-luck bringer. But the moon is gone and the maelstrom is still here. Some things are more mysterious and more powerful than gods.'

Their barge raced towards the shipfort that dwarfed it, carried by the whirlpool's currents. Perhaps their strength accounted for the sturdiness of the fort's construction. Long, shiplapped planks covered a framework of oak. There wasn't a crack or a warp in any of it. Renar suspected, though, that the shipfort had been made to withstand a different foe.

A hundred paces short of the fort's broad dock, their barge veered. As the currents carried it leftwards and then outwards, Renar realised they weren't making for the fort at all. She felt a frosting of fear.

'I thought to rest after our journey,' she said.

'Shortly you shall,' Nimrit replied blandly.

On the shipfort's other side was a vast, waterlogged sandy plain, and beyond it the ocean. Their barge beached itself on the sand and the twins and their men jumped agilely ashore.

Amila held up a warning hand when Lanalan made to follow. 'Be cautious to step exactly in our footprints. The path is narrow. The rest is quagmire.'

Even the path was far from firm. Renar's feet sank above her boot-tops. The sandy mud was clinging and cold and her legs were soon coated in it. They grew heavier with every step. Despite her furs, she was shivering, although from cold or fear she couldn't tell.

She flinched when something brushed her hand, but it was only Lanalan reaching out for her. She clasped her fingers around his. They were the only warmth in this chilly place.

'There, to our left, do you see?' Nimrit said. 'The sands have a gift for us.'

It looked like a bush, stripped of leaves and drowning in the mud. As Nimrit slanted their path towards it, more and more became visible. There was a whole brittle field of them. But when the sun showed briefly through the clouds, it caught glints of metallic grey and gold, and Renar finally recognised what she was seeing. The glint of gold was a ring on skeleton fingers. What she'd taken for a stem was an arm bone, reaching desperately out of the mud. These were all bones.

'The mud sends them back to us, now and again,' Nimrit said.

Lanalan looked more enthralled than appalled. 'There must be hundreds.'

Renar crouched to examine one of the more complete corpses. It was armour-clad, all in metal. There was still flesh beneath, desiccated and pulled tight over the bones. It looked like the dried mutton that Nayan's household guard liked to chew. This man might have died a mere month ago. But the design of the armour was one she'd never seen among the Ashane, or any other people. The metal seemed to have a ceramic overlay, decorated with purple flowers. Sorghum, perhaps. And no one today spared that much metal on a mere soldier. 'These are old,' she said. 'More than old – ancient.'

The twins' men were already among the corpses, pulling off their rings and armour and prising their swords from the thick mud.

'Ancient indeed,' Amila said. 'Tell me, how much do you know of our history?'

Renar rose, futilely brushing at the mud on her woollen hose. 'I know your people aren't native to these lands. My people remember when yours first came here, across the ocean. The worm men killed them in their hundreds, until they learned that they must never build and always move on.'

'We who call ourselves shiplords were little more than brigands then,' Amila said, 'warring with each other. Seven times, a rival army was sent against Delta's Strength. But Delta's Strength still stands and here their bones lie among all the rest. Ashane himself was able to take the fort in the end, but only for one reason: the carrion mounts he found and bred could fly past our defences.'

'And the carrion mounts,' Nimrit added, 'are dead.'

*

When they returned to the shipfort, they were taken to separate rooms to wash and change their clothes. Renar didn't find herself charmed by the fort as she was led through it. Delta's Strength was made of very old oak, and years of staining and polishing had made it almost black. It looked more like iron than wood, and it felt like a cage.

The water in the bath the servants drew her was little more than lukewarm, and the mud had seeped into all her clothes. She was offered no others, so that when she entered the feasting hall that evening, she looked more like a vagabond than the envoy of a king. She and Lanalan were only able to exchange a brief, troubled look before being led to seats at opposite ends of the high table.

It was a long table, and Renar recognised a worrying number of those sitting at it. Lord Harjas of Greenshore was present. He must have left his fort moments after she and Lanalan departed and travelled some other route to beat them here. The lords of four of the Five Stars were seated beside Lanalan, and beside Renar, a colourfully tattooed group that must surely hail from World's End in the distant north. Only Nuwan, son and heir of sour old Nalin Nine Eggs, spared her a smile.

If the Lords of Delta's Strength had found conspirators from so wide a swathe of Nayan's realm, the Ashane King was in a very great deal of trouble. There was an ambush coming, that much was clear. All Renar could hope was that it would be metaphorical rather than physical.

When the huge stuffed fowl and suckling pigs were brought to the table, Renar's neighbour turned to her and smiled.

'You've had a difficult journey, I hear,' she said. Her face was hard to look at, with tattooed wolves racing each other across her cheeks.

'I've had harder,' Renar replied.

The woman laughed. 'So I've also heard. I'm Aadh, sister-daughter to Lord Balwinder of World's End. How strange this must all seem to you. I hear it's much different in your own lands. There's no lordship there at all, or so I've been informed.'

Renar shrugged. 'Customs change, but people are the same in every land. They want the same things.'

'Ah. You're asking what I want. They said you were cunning.'

'Not as cunning as I once was.'

'You think perhaps to find divisions between us,' Aadh said. 'A crack you can fit a wedge into. There is none. We're united in our thought. The rule of the Oak Wheel is over. King Nayan must content himself with being Lord Nayan of Ashfall only. I'm speaking very plainly, I know. The rest will talk you round in circles and never reach the centre of it. We don't have the time for that in the north.'

Had they agreed this approach between them beforehand? Renar trusted Aadh's straightforwardness about as much as she trusted her own. 'I appreciate your honesty,' she said. 'Let me give you some in return. You're united now in a common aim. When that's achieved? Then you'll remember all the differences between you. Lord Nalin will remember how much he's always coveted Lord Dimuthu's vineyards, and Lord Dimuthu will recall that Fort Daybreak has always monopolised the trade with the Wanderers of the Moon Forest folk. And there'll be no one left to keep the peace between them.'

Aadh widened her eyes in mock surprise. 'So King Nayan has been doing us a service all these years, and we so ungrateful. No, no. These problems may come, it's true. But they'll be *our* problems to solve. We must have our independence. Nimrit means to announce it at this meal. And then you'll return to King Nayan. If you and your brother stay silent, you'll return to tell him what we've done. And if you speak out against Nimrit, I'm very sorry, but Amila has said we'll send only your heads back to Nayan as their own message. We tried to talk her out of it, but she was quite adamant. Ah, look there – Nimrit is going to make the announcement right now.'

A hush fell as the Lord of Delta's Strength rose to her feet. Renar wondered how many people here had been told this announcement was coming. Her gorge rose as she caught her sib, on the far end of the table, gazing at Nimrit in puzzlement. If he spoke out, he'd doom them both, and he didn't even know it.

'Honoured guests,' Nimrit said, 'we are gathered on a momentous day—'

She broke off as the doors of the hall flew open and a man almost fell through. 'They're here,' he gabbled. 'They've come for us. They're in the sky!'

'Don't be absurd!' Nimrit snapped. 'The carrion mounts are dead. We all saw them.'

'Not birds, my lady,' the man said. 'Much bigger. Please, you must come. You must see.'

Nimrit looked like she wanted to silence him and continue her announcement, but her vassals decided for her. There was a rush to the door that swallowed up the messenger. Even half a dozen at high table had risen to their feet.

Aadh, still seated, studied Renar's face closely. 'Do you know what this is?' she asked.

'I can hardly know without seeing it.' It was a deliberate non-answer. If Renar could make them believe this disaster, whatever it was, was of Nayan's making, she might be able to guide the whole thing back onto its desired course.

'Sister, we'd best see,' Amila said in a low tone. It probably wasn't intended to travel as far as it did.

After that, there was no stopping the stampede. Renar shoved her way through the crowd towards her brother. His face was drawn when she finally reached him, his generous lips thinned with worry.

'Renar, the things they told me . . .' he said. 'I believe they mean to kill us.'

'Not if we keep our counsel. I can still work this in our favour, but not if you speak out of turn. We must find out what's going on.'

He took her hand so the crowd wouldn't separate them. The corridors of the shipfort were too narrow to accommodate so large a group. Elbows jabbed them and feet trod on theirs as everyone struggled to head upwards. Renar saw a stuffed boar's head knocked from the wall. Tapestries were torn down and trampled underfoot. This, it occurred to her, was a very good metaphor for what might happen if these people rejected Nayan's rule. But it was far too noisy to share the thought with anyone. And then at last there was a square of daylight ahead. The crowd surged through it and onto the fort's roof.

Up here, there was silence. Even in the thick of the battle for Täm, Renar had never sensed a terror so overwhelming.

The sky was crowded, but not with birds. Above Delta's Strength hung another fort, far larger, floating improbably in air. Its shadow covered nearly the entirety of the lake. And descending from it on ropes, an army.

9

They were singing one of their bloody dirges. Eric was sick of the sound of them, especially since Dae Hyo had added his bellowing voice to the chorus. He was drunk again. Eric didn't know how long they'd been here, in this place without seasons and nothing to mark the days, but he reckoned it would have to be somewhere near three years. About half that span of time ago, Dae Hyo had figured out how to brew a tipple from seaweed, and since then he'd been no company at all.

Eric shouldn't have come to Ozgur today. He should have stayed on their home berth, but he'd been desperate to stretch his legs. The great raft that was the centre of the Drifters' world was the only place a boy could do it.

The raft was big for something afloat, but small if you were looking for a change of scenery. The watery horizon circled them without a feature. He'd heard of ships becalmed at sea, helpless to move as their crews slowly starved. He'd thought it was a tale for the cullies. But here the Drifters were, in the heart of those still waters like a spider in its web, catching anything that floated past.

When they first arrived, Eric had a jolly old time of it touring the raft, spying bits of scrap from a thousand foundered vessels. Well, maybe jolly wasn't the word for it. He'd still been deep in his grief then. Now a shell had grown around his heart that mostly kept the pain from getting out, and anything much else from getting in.

He was on his third circuit of the raft when his eye caught something among the racks of drying fish and saltwater barrels of doomed lobsters. It was a fish too, only far bigger than the usual catch. Unlike them it hadn't been gutted and deboned but left whole. It was hanging from a wooden hook through its mouth.

Eric stepped closer. It was tucked away almost out of sight, meaning he had to push aside salt-crusted lines of fish-flesh to reach it. That was probably what had caught his attention, the way it seemed to be hidden. Probably some cully wanting to keep the whole catch for himself.

He'd heard about the big tunny that swum these waters. They were said to be three times the height of a man. This one wasn't in the best of nick. There was scarring on its left flank: a series of raised rings, some overlaid, all perfectly round. He couldn't imagine what had caused them.

A soft footfall sounded behind him and he sighed. It would be Zan Izel. It was always Zan Izel, who'd long ago latched onto Eric like a barnacle. He was ordinary enough looking for a Drifter: very short with muddy brown skin like an Ashaneman but the hooded eyes of the tribes. The Drifters seemed to be all the peoples of the world mixed together, the same way their rafts were a mix-up of all the world's lost ships. Zan's face might even have been called handsome, with its full lips and delicate bones, but Eric couldn't care for it. He hated the feel of the man's eyes on him, slimy like the underside of their raft.

'What are you doing, hiding here?' Zan asked. He used the Drifter word for hiding that had shades of 'lurking' and other nefarious deeds.

'I ain't hiding,' Eric replied in Ashane, just to annoy Zan.

But Zan had learned to speak their tongue as well as his own. He switched to it easily. 'You look like you're hiding. Come away. You don't want people saying you've poisoned the meat. Not after half the raft took ill three nights ago.'

'Half the raft took ill cause they ate fish what was too long in the sun.' But Eric followed Zan. He knew their situation here was precarious. He knew the cause of it too.

'He's been handing it out, you know,' Zan said, pointing his chin at Dae Hyo. Dae Hyo looked like he'd nodded off midsong. He sat with his head tipped back and a string of drool down his chin.

Eric shrugged and looked away.

'Ixchel was passed out drunk all last night,' Zan said confidingly, 'and Chaac vomited over his dinner. My people have never made fire-water like the landmen do. We don't have the stomach for it.'

'Then you shouldn't drink it.'

Zan sucked his lips together like an old scold. 'He shouldn't hand it out like feast-day roe. You know what they've started to say? They say he was sent here by the Eetlust to corrupt us all with the same hunger. I heard talk of sending him to the dolphins' care.'

'I'd like to watch them try.' Eric had seen Dae Hyo fight. He'd seen it too much recently, and drink had robbed the warrior of none of his strength. The Drifters were no match for him.

'There'll be trouble,' Zan insisted. 'We welcome land-livers here when they wash up. We give them raft-space we don't have to spare. But we expect good behaviour in return. They won't stand for it forever.'

'They've stood it so far. I reckon a person's responsible for his own actions, ain't he? It's Ixchel and Chaac they should be having a go at, not Dae Hyo. He's not the one vomiting everywhere.'

Insinuation having failed, Zan seemed to resolve to be ingratiating instead. His voice took on a wheedling tone that was like grit in Eric's teeth. 'Your berth is liked here, in general. Not just Dinesh – you too, Eric. You're young and strong, good fishermen. Even the Hunter is tolerated, though they fear her strange eyes. But Dae Hyo's a sun canker, growing every day. My people will cut out good flesh if they must, to scoop a canker out.'

'What have they been saying?' Eric asked sharply. 'What are they planning?'

'Nothing they'd tell me. I'm no berth mother. I haven't a voice here. But what do you owe him, anyway? He told me about his people once. He said they're all gone, all killed. Yet he still lives. Doesn't that hook questions? Was it Dae Hyo who brought doom on his own people? Why else would they all be gone?'

'Probably cause the Chun slaughtered them in their sleep,' Eric said coldly.

'Of course. I'm sorry I spoke out of turn.' But Zan didn't look sorry.

'Was there something else you wanted?' Eric asked, trying to ease away from him.

'No. Except only to ask if you plan to stay for the feast today.'

'A feast?' It was the first Eric had heard of it.

'Yes, the westward-path feast. Very important. An east wind bears us to the Eetlust's waters. We must eat and eat until there's no hunger inside us, nothing to draw the Eetlust here. But still, I think you shouldn't come.'

Eric was instantly suspicious. 'Why? I could do with some more grub.'

'But no one eats for free. You have to give to the common pot and your supplies are running low.'

'How do you know that?' Eric asked.

'Oh, Dinesh told me. The Eetlust knows if you eat food another man's hand took from the waters. That will draw it too.'

It seemed to Eric that if Zan wanted him away from the feast, he ought to be doing his best to attend it. Zan's eyes darted away from Eric like flies staying just out of reach of a flicking palm. It was clear he was up to something. But the truth was, Eric couldn't stand much company these days.

'I'm getting in an early night anyway,' he said. 'I'll give it a miss.'

Zan's pleased smile made him want to reconsider, but he squared his shoulders and headed for the raft's edge.

The water was as warm as soup. Swimming was the only way to travel between the individual berths and the great raft of Ozgur, and theirs was on the very outer edge of the fleet. Eric was exhausted by the time he got back there.

It wasn't much of a home, though bigger than it used to be. When they'd first washed up here, they'd been allowed no more than the ship wreckage they'd arrived on to make their own berth. They'd added to it since with a few lucky bits of driftwood they'd fished from the sea, and more that they'd bought and traded for. Or more precisely, that Eric and Dinesh had traded for. Dae Hyo was no use at all any longer and the Hunter – well, the Hunter rarely shifted from her arse beside their ever-sleeping companions. She always looked so deep in thought, Eric expected one day she'd leap to her feet and declare that she'd solved all their problems. But that day never seemed to come.

She looked up when he dragged himself on board, scraping his stomach on the rough edge of the berth. He could add it to the constant hurt of sunburn on his back and nose and neck. The sun was relentless here and clothing was in short supply.

'They have not woken,' she announced as he stood dripping.

'I'm shocked,' Eric said. She gave him the same grave report every time, as if she thought he expected something different. But Krish and Drut hadn't opened their eyes in all these uncounted days. They'd swallow water that was put in their mouths and even chew at food a little, if it was soft enough. But aside from that, they were as lively as sponges.

'The berth mothers came to see me again today,' she said.

'Complaining about Dae Hyo?'

'No. They wonder how much longer we mean to keep rotted wood with us.' She meant Krish and Drut, of course.

Eric shrugged. 'They've been asking almost since we got here. But they ain't got no say in it.'

'So I told them, but their questions have begun to sound more like demands. The fish have fled since we arrived and food is scarce. They blame it on Krishanjit and Drut.'

'How? They ain't done a single thing.'

'There is an emptiness inside them where their minds should be, and emptiness is like hunger, and hunger draws the Eetlust. So they believe.'

Eric sighed and sat beside her. 'Zan told me they're starting to say Dae Hyo's a servant of the Eetlust.'

'Zan is not to be trusted.'

'I know,' Eric said.

'I do not think you do. Zan does not want from you what you believe.'

Eric stared at her, startled. 'If you mean he ain't hot for me, then you ain't paying attention.' He'd known enough of men's lust to recognise it when he saw it. 'But I'd rather swim where they empty the shit buckets than let him anywhere near me. Besides, it ain't just me he's got his eye on. He's been making up to Dinesh just as much, hanging around him like a nasty smell.'

'You have mistaken Zan's interest, Eric. His desire is not for flesh, but for belonging. His parents were lost when he was very young, and their raft was breached and sunk by a sword-nose fish. He has no family among the Drifters, no berth of his own and few friends. Unlike you, he has not the gift of being liked. He lives a lonely life. He hopes for a place among us in our berth, and he believes you to be the one most likely to offer it to him.'

'Well, he's barking at a hole without a rabbit. Dinesh ain't interested in men that way. And I'd sooner *eat* the shit from the buckets than have him living here full time.'

'I think perhaps he is beginning to realise this,' the Hunter said, 'and that is what makes him dangerous. Be cautious around him, Eric.'

'I am,' Eric insisted. 'But I don't see what benefit he'd get from lying to us about Dae Hyo. And I've heard the chatter too. They ain't happy.'

'We could present the situation to Dae Hyo and ask him to amend his behaviour, although I do not believe he would listen.'

Eric almost smiled. Sometimes she seemed such an innocent, despite her thousand years of life. But more and more she seemed just like any other person, wise and foolish in balanced measure. The gold of her skin had long since flaked away, leaving her the glossy dark brown of an ordinary mage of Mirror Town. Her golden hair had grown out an unremarkable reddish-brown too. Last week, he'd noticed for the first time that she had the tiny creases of crow's feet around her eyes. Those golden eyes alone remained of what she'd once been.

'Do you think they'll ever wake?' Eric asked, looking at Krish and Drut.

She brushed a fleck of dust from Drut's pale cheek. 'I cannot say. But they have clung to life this long. Perhaps this world has a use for them yet.'

*

Dae Hyo woke with a pounding head and a taste in his mouth like a dead mouse. It looked to be around midday and Ozgur was quiet. Most of the Drifters had gone back to their berths to sleep through the hottest hours of the day. Only the salt cleaners remained behind, tending the contraptions that squeezed drinkable water out of the sea. Fully half of Ozgur's surface was taken up with them, conical sheets of silk suspended like upside-down hats above bowls of saltwater and mulched seaweed. At the centre of each bowl a cup caught the pure water that dripped drop by slow drop from the silk.

A full quarter of the rest of the surface was piled with the chewed wood nests of the insects that made the silk the contraptions used. The Hunter said they looked like the ancestors of the bugs the Ofiklanders had bred to giant size. Sometimes, if a person was very favoured, they were allowed to use a little of the silk to make a long, loose shirt. Dae Hyo hadn't ever been favoured that way.

Dinesh had, and Dae Hyo had a fair idea of where he'd be. He wove between the silk water-makers, heading towards the raft's nearest edge. A crowd was gathered there and the water beyond them was full of youths and splashes. They were playing their game again, the one they called tok-tok, that involved a ball and a lot of shouting and pulling as they fought over it.

A great cheer went up from half the crowd, a groan from the other half, and the players began to pull themselves from the water. Dinesh was among them, as Dae Hyo expected. He seemed to have been on the winning side. That wasn't a surprise either. He was clapped on the back and smiled at as he shook the water off and pulled his shirt back on.

Dae Hyo called out his name and Dinesh looked up. His

expression was cold. He turned his back on Dae Hyo and allowed himself to be led away by a group of pretty young girls, all vying to get his attention. Dinesh alone seemed to have found his place here. He seldom wanted for company either in his bed or out of it, and he'd been coming back to their berth less and less often.

Dae Hyo felt a tide of anger rise. His fist clenched and then relaxed as a tide of self-pity replaced it. He had no true friends here. Dinesh ignored him, Eric looked at him with contempt, and his brother couldn't even be bothered to wake up and keep him company. Was it any wonder he turned to drink to ease the pain? He turned a deaf ear to the small voice in his head suggesting that perhaps the drink itself was responsible for the coldness and the contempt.

He needed food to settle his stomach. Wasn't there a feast today? He had a fuzzy memory of Bacab complaining that he'd have to spend the day fishing for it. And now Dae Hyo paid attention, he heard laughter and raised voices from the direction of the moot. It was the one area of Ozgur that was always kept clear for when the Drifters all left their home berths to gather.

The first thing he saw when he reached the moot was Dinesh. He was seated on a low platform that nevertheless raised him above the rest. A few other Drifters were seated cross-legged beside him. All of them were young and well muscled, though much too short for true warriors. Why should they be honoured? Dae Hyo was stronger than any of them. *He* should be given the choicest fish and roasted sea birds that were being placed in front of Dinesh while the rest of them were handed smaller fry.

That weasel Zan stood behind Dinesh, leaning forwards to whisper in his ear. There was something about the expression on his face that Dae Hyo didn't like. It might almost have been triumph. When Zan spotted him, his face briefly betrayed dismay, before he rushed forwards to block his path.

'Get out of my way,' Dae Hyo said.

'You can't come here. You've brought nothing to the feast. You're not wanted.' Zan's voice was shrill with fear, but he stood his ground.

The babble of conversation stopped as everyone turned to watch with disapproving eyes. It bothered Dae Hyo that most of the hostility seemed to be directed at him. Zan was widely disliked. Dae Hyo had fallen too far if people preferred Zan to him.

'I've brought food enough to fill everyone's belly twice over this week,' Dae Hyo said. Though now he thought about it, it might have been a while since he'd bothered with fishing.

'Go, go, go home, Dae Hyo,' Dinesh said, rising to his feet. 'I'll bring food back to the berth later.'

Dae Hyo's teeth clenched at the condescending tone. Who did the boy think he was? 'And what if I want to eat now?'

'Hoi, Dae Hyo, come sit with us.' Tall, thin Ixchel smiled and waved Dae Hyo over. The plate in front of him was heaped with fresh fried fish, and Dae Hyo *was* hungry. He spared one last glare for Dinesh and sauntered to sit beside Ixchel.

The fish was tasty enough, but it couldn't dispel the sour taste of Dinesh's contempt. The boy seemed to be having a high time of it on that raised plinth with his friends, and Zan was always there, whispering in his ear. Dinesh didn't spare a single glance Dae Hyo's way, but Zan's eyes barely looked anywhere else. There was a man in need of a fatal accident.

He'd hoped to mine gossip from Ixchel, who always had a rich seam of it, but he shushed Dae Hyo as soon as the dancers came to the centre of the moot. The Drifters claimed their dances held their history. They always carried them out in precisely the same way, step for step.

Dae Hyo had seen this particular one a dozen times already. There was some writhing and clutching of stomachs at the start and later it would move on to what looked like rowing. Dae Hyo had tried asking what it all meant. The only answer he'd been given was to watch, as if the dance explained itself.

Now there seemed to be some kind of battle going on. One group was flailing at another, but slowly the groups moved apart, as if some force beyond their control was separating them. This must be when the Drifters took to the sea and left the land behind. Half the dance-warriors were now doing the writhing

thing, while the other slowly pulled away. Could there have been some plague the Drifters were escaping?

'After the dance will come the choosing,' Zan murmured in his ear.

Dae Hyo jumped half out of his skin. He'd been too caught up in the dance to see Zan coming.

'It will be Dinesh,' Zan continued. He leaned away at Dae Hyo's glare. 'There won't be a challenger. Everyone knows it must be Dinesh.'

Dae Hyo gritted his teeth. He didn't want to satisfy Zan by asking, but curiosity won. 'What will be Dinesh? What are they choosing?'

'The Coral King, of course. Our leader for the forty days of fear. It's a very great honour.'

'And what has Dinesh done to deserve it?'

Zan grinned, displaying his small, weed-browned teeth. 'Been the strongest and the best. The best at fishing. The best at tok-tok. The master of pok-a-tok too, but you weren't here to see it. You were sleeping fire-water sleep.'

Zan turned from Dae Hyo to the raised platform, and curse it, he seemed to be right. The other youths were laughing and pushing Dinesh to his feet. The painted dancers clustered around him, clapping a repeated, disjointed rhythm.

'I challenge!' Dae Hyo yelled across the feasting circle. 'I'm the strongest here, not him!'

Zan smiled as everyone turned to stare.

★

It was the noise that drew Eric, the roar of voices. He thought at once of Zan's face when he'd warned Eric not to attend the feast and barely waited to grab his boning knife before diving over the side.

To his surprise, another body dived in after his, and the Hunter was at his side as he entered the moot circle. Dae Hyo stood in the centre, as Eric had expected. He hadn't expected Dinesh to be there too. The pair were staring at each other, buck-naked and each clutching a fishing spear. Eric didn't think it would be easy to kill a man with them, but both of them looked like they meant to try.

Zan was nowhere to be seen. Even so, Eric had no doubt this was all his design.

While Eric hesitated, the Hunter pushed her way through the crowd until she stood between Dae Hyo and Dinesh. The tension in Eric's shoulders relaxed a fraction.

Her face was cold and stern. 'What is this madness? Are the ills of the world so few that you must visit more upon each other?'

Dae Hyo looked a little abashed, but Dinesh's scowl deepened. He raised his chin defiantly. 'He, he, he began it. It's his fault, it's all his fault. He's a curse on us – you know he is!'

Dae Hyo's expression darkened. 'A curse? You were nothing but a slave until I brought you here!'

'Don't talk nonsense,' Eric said. 'You ain't got nothing to do with Dinesh being back in his right mind. That was . . . the way the world changed what freed him. But Dinesh, you ain't got no call to be doing this. Back off, the pair of you. Stop acting like toddlers.'

The crowd murmured unhappily as berth mother Eztli stepped into the ring. 'Enough of this. A challenge made, a challenge accepted. It must be decided who is the stronger. There can be only one Coral King.'

There was a tense, expecting silence as the ring was cleared. Dinesh and Dae Hyo were made to stand ten paces opposite each other. The only sound that broke the quiet was the petulant crying of the scavenger birds that followed their rafts across the sea to eat their leavings. Eric had a horrible vision of them pecking at Dae Hyo's guts where Dinesh had spilled them across the wood. And then the fight began.

It was vicious. Dae Hyo charged first. He tried to use his greater weight to bear Dinesh down, but Dinesh was as slippery as a fish. He twisted away and rammed his spear in a thrust that would have taken Dae Hyo through the kidney if he hadn't dodged frantically aside. Even so, it left a bleeding cut the length of his rib.

Dae Hyo snarled and used his own spear, flicking his arm back and forwards with shocking speed to let it fly at Dinesh. Dinesh clearly hadn't expected Dae Hyo to let go of his weapon and the spear sank into his calf. He yelled in pain. Dae Hyo smiled, but Dinesh wasn't done. He pulled the spear from his own leg, leaving a ragged gouge behind. But now he had a spear in each hand and Dae Hyo had none. The crowd roared its approval.

Dae Hyo realised what he'd done. His expression was almost comical as he danced backwards, out of range of a double thrust from Dinesh. Bloody typical, Eric thought. He'd rushed in without a plan and now he was going to get himself killed. Eric was surprised that the idea upset him. Dae Hyo infuriated him on a daily basis, but he was a link back to home. A link back to a life that still had Arwel in it.

It looked to be almost over for Dae Hyo. Dinesh didn't seem in a mood to be merciful, even if the rules of this fight allowed it. He'd used his spears to herd Dae Hyo towards the edge of the ring and the racks of drying fish. It left him nowhere further to retreat without tangling himself up.

Dae Hyo stepped back as if he meant to try all the same. And then, quicker and lither than you'd possibly imagine him, he dived behind Dinesh's braced legs. Shocked, Dinesh turned too slowly as Dae Hyo surged to his feet. He grabbed the butts of the spears and pulled them back through Dinesh's hands – then angled them and thrust them forwards with brute force, pushing the points deep into Dinesh's flanks.

The crowd was stunned into silence. Even Dae Hyo seemed shocked by what he'd done. He stepped back, dropping the spears. Dinesh collapsed with a groan of pain while Dae Hyo shook his head and scrubbed his bloody hands against his thighs, leaving gory red streaks.

'The Coral King has been chosen,' Zan shouted.

He'd returned while the crowd watched the fight, slinking to stand beside berth mother Eztli. He was carrying something, almost staggering beneath its weight. When he flung it to the deck in the centre of the crowd, Eric recognised it as the dead fish with the strange, scarred rings.

At the sight of it, the crowd acted like they'd been stabbed themselves. They yelled and stumbled away. Eric couldn't make out much of what they were saying, except for one word that was repeated over and over.

'The Eetlust has come,' Zan said, not doing anything to hide his gloating smile.

'The Eetlust has risen,' Eztli repeated gravely. 'And the Coral King has been found. The Eetlust will be given the strongest of us to eat, and be sated.' She turned to Dae Hyo as a ring of men came to stand around him. 'When we reach the red seas, you will be crowned, and then the Eetlust will have its meal.'

10

Sang Ki found slavery unexpectedly agreeable. It wasn't an opinion that Jalena shared, despite not herself being subject to the condition. That disagreement had been the cause of some problems over the last few years. He could tell that today was going to present another of them.

He was already feeling irritable. After a successful month trading along the river, Bone Dancer had decided to head to Rah lands. They'd spent the last two miserable days trudging through the jungles that surrounded them. Sang Ki had long ago learned to tolerate heat, but the moisture that turned the air near enough to water was more than he could bear.

All that, and the pain in his ankle too. Bone Dancer had found a Seonu healer to fix rather than amputate it, for which Sang Ki supposed he must be grateful, but she hadn't fixed it well. He walked on it as little as possible. Alas, these lands weren't hospitable to horses or deer, and so here he was: in pain, hot and wet.

'Beautiful, isn't it?' Bone Dancer said. Her gaze had been caught by a huge white and blood-red orchid that Sang Ki wouldn't be in the least surprised to learn was poisonous.

'It's hard to say which are lovelier, the serpents or the insects,' Sang Ki said. An example of the former was wriggling its way down a nearby tree. Its virulently green and purple scales promised poison too. As for the insects, they were as thick in the air as the water, and far more prone to bite.

Bone Dancer laughed and clapped Sang Ki on the back. 'You're too dismal, my friend. When there's snow it's too cold and when there's rain it's too wet. There's no pleasing you.'

'Snow is quite widely regarded as chilly and no one has ever accused rain of being dry,' Sang Ki replied. That he could do so without fear of retribution or even reprimand was, of course, why he found his enslavement so easy to bear. It existed in little more than name these days.

A twig snapped loudly enough behind them to be heard over the buzzing of insects and the shrieks of the birds. They both turned, startled. Figures were barely visible through the dense foliage, at least half a dozen of them.

'Jalena's brought company this time, I see,' Bone Dancer said.

Sang Ki sighed. 'She's going to get them killed along with herself if she's not careful. I doubt she even knows what a venomous serpent is. There were none on the savannah. And look how bright their clothing is. The crocodiles will be on them before long.'

He and Bone Dancer had dressed far more sombrely, in the Rah style, so as not to attract the attention of the beasts that guarded their border. But Jalena resolutely refused to travel with them. She certainly wouldn't have accepted Bone Dancer's advice on how to dress. Either would seem to her an acceptance of a situation that, for three years, she'd tried all in her power to undo. Instead she'd followed along behind wherever they travelled, and staged 'rescues' of Sang Ki from his captor whenever she could. These rescues never succeeded and yet she never stopped trying. She had no idea how lucky she was that Bone Dancer found the charade amusing rather than irksome.

'Have no fear,' Bone Dancer said now. 'I've asked our hosts to shepherd her through. She'll face nothing worse than a cell. The Rah aren't fond of uninvited guests.' A sharp whistle sounded from up ahead, and then three short trills, not quite like bird calls. 'Ah, that's them now.'

*

The Rah lands, when they reached them half a day later, were far from what Sang Ki expected. He'd read travellers' tales and knew of the tribe's floating fields and houses. Those were still present, but there were many other buildings too, far more substantial and rooted in the earth. Some of the largest had curious clouds of pale steam rising above their roofs.

'Does the ground not cry out for sunlight?' Bone Dancer asked, eyeing the buildings.

Their guide was a close-mouthed, stern-faced representative of his people. 'The moon is dead. His servants too,' he said.

Sang Ki had begun to suspect so himself. In his years with Bone Dancer he'd heard a few others voice the same suspicion, but none had been certain enough to change a style of housing that had kept them alive for centuries. Here, the world was changing.

And yet, in other ways, it wasn't. Toiling in the floating fields, Sang Ki saw many poor, ragged souls who could only be slaves. Krishanjit had famously freed the Rah slaves, with the sort of disastrous consequences that habitually followed him around. In his absence, it seemed the tribe had returned to their old ways.

Although, when Sang Ki looked closer, he saw that the slaves didn't wear the dazed expressions of those who were in the grip of the drug bliss. Previously, the Rah had acquired their slaves from the mages of Mirror Town, who'd bred them from the peoples of many lands. Now, every fieldworker Sang Ki saw was of the tribes. Where their scant clothes exposed the skin of their backs, he saw marks of whippings and other physical abuse.

Their guide led them past several more of the strange, steam-emitting new buildings to one of the largest houses they'd yet seen. They were shown to their suite of rooms and told that their host would meet them at the evening meal.

'Well,' Bone Dancer said, once their guide had left them, 'what do you make of this? I smell riches, I'll tell you that much.'

'Riches,' Sang Ki said, 'and something somewhat more rank.'

'How so?'

Sang Ki shrugged. 'I couldn't tell you, but I've developed a nose for such things over my travels. What do you know of the Rah's leader?'

'Little enough. They've never been a sociable people, especially with their fellow tribes. It's rare to see a Rah face at the Spring Fair. But it's said the man is quite ruthless. When the war within the tribe ended, all who'd opposed him were killed, including his own kin. A man after your heart, Sang Ki!'

Bone Dancer laughed and Sang Ki managed a smile. It didn't make him easy to be the butt of this particular joke. Little Cousin's name was no longer spoken between them, but this sort of jab made it clear it wasn't forgotten. Not that Sang Ki would wish him forgotten: he'd been as fond of the man as one could be of someone so briefly known. It was Sang Ki's mother who'd killed Little Cousin, but in Bone Dancer's eyes that was enough for Sang Ki to share the blame.

'So there's to be a feast in your honour tonight,' he said.

'We'll meet the man then, no doubt. They've much coin to spend these days. Their clothing is the finest on the plains and it's said they've found a way to saw planks quicker and neater than any carpenter. If some of that coin makes its way into my purse, I'm sure I'll find a way to forgive their leader his past indiscretions.'

★

Sang Ki had expected the meal to take place in the grand dining chamber of this grand house, but they were led to another building, grander still, on the edge of the water. The water itself was blanketed by leaves and flowers of a startling bright pink. The fish that swam beneath them glittered like jewels. It was a very beautiful land, in its way.

The building itself could have swallowed Winter's Hammer whole. When he and Bone Dancer entered, it was to find hundreds seated at ranks of long, low tables. The walls were bare and the place had a feeling of austerity, belied only by the quantity and quality of the food. Sang Ki's father, a shipborn lord, had seldom put on such a feast, and never for so many.

Still, though his father's table might have been meagre, it had been substantially more jovial. There should have been a babble of chatter with this many people present, but the voices were hushed. They silenced completely when he and Bone Dancer walked in.

There was no dais, no clear table of honour. Sang Ki and Bone Dancer were waved towards the head of the leftmost, where three places had been saved. Sang Ki hoped the third was for Jalena. He worried for her, nuisance that she was. Bone Dancer had promised an escort to keep her out of danger, but the Rah might have felt less indulgent of her silliness. They guarded their territory fiercely.

Sang Ki studied the men and women he was seated beside. Although there was an aura of command about them, they were dressed the same as all the rest. He saw no jewellery on any of them. The Rah had once cared greatly for rank and wealth. Apparently that too had changed.

'I've heard much about the changes that new leadership brought to the Rah, and only believed a fraction of them,' Sang Ki said to a matronly woman who'd introduced herself as Haneul. 'I see now that many of them were true. Men and women dressed the same, and all equal to all.'

Haneul nodded. 'The leadership of the one over the many was a great wrong. Our former leaders gorged, while the poor starved. The change was a long time coming.'

'How are decisions made, when every voice must be heard?' Bone Dancer asked.

'Fairly.' Haneul smiled thinly. 'A People's Council is chosen every year to guide us.'

Sang Ki looked around him. 'You *are* that council, I suppose?'

'We are.'

'But only for a year.'

A thin, elderly man squinted suspiciously at Sang Ki. 'Most of us have sat on the council since its start.'

'I see. You must be very popular, to be chosen time and again.'

'There hasn't yet been a second choosing,' Haneul said. 'Times have been too troubled for a change in leadership to be wise. But naturally we'll take up our yearly choosings as soon as we safely can.'

'Naturally,' Sang Ki said. 'Because all among you are equal. Some, though, a touch less equal. I'd heard that the Rah dispensed with slavery. It appears the rumours were mistaken.'

Haneul frowned. 'Not at all. Slavery is no more. It was a vile institution and we abolished it.'

Bone Dancer's eyes, when Sang Ki briefly caught them, were

bright and amused. She enjoyed watching Sang Ki ask the questions that custom denied to her. It was nine tenths of his value to her.

'I see,' Sang Ki said. 'So those labourers in the fields . . .?'

Haneul shrugged. 'They're criminals – debt-bonded, not enslaved.'

'I confess I don't entirely comprehend the difference.'

'Slavery was an abomination. This is justice. In this manner wrongdoers spend their lives repaying the harm they did to the tribe.'

'What sort of harm?'

Her expression was hard. 'Any. Withholding the monthly tithe. Marrying without consent. Speaking ill of the new order.'

'Ha!' Bone Dancer said. 'If ill-speaking were a crime, kin-killer here would be a slave ten times over, not just the once he is.'

The thin old man beside Haneul looked shocked. 'You're a slave?' he asked Sang Ki.

Sang Ki shrugged. 'So I've been told.'

'And yet you bring him to table with you?' Haneul's tone was chilly. Sang Ki wasn't entirely sure whether it was him or Bone Dancer that she disapproved of.

'Tell me, would you use a chicken to pull a cart?' he asked.

'I'm not a fool.'

Sang Ki smiled. 'No indeed. You use each beast for its right purpose, and so does Bone Dancer here. Sending me to toil in a field would be as futile as hitching a bird to a wagon. The repayment of *my* debt for my crimes goes quickest when I'm used for what I do best.'

'And what's that?' the old man asked.

'His cleverness,' Bone Dancer said. 'It's more valuable than his body by far.'

'Cleverness?' a new voice said. Sang Ki had been so taken up in the conversation, he hadn't heard her approach. 'Yes, I remember you being clever.'

'Ah,' Haneul said. 'Here's the Chief Voice of the council now. But I see you've met before.'

It took Sang Ki a moment to recognise her. The woman who stood before him now had been so young when he'd seen her before, chubby-cheeked and quiet. She was young still, but the strong dark line of her eyebrows suited the firmer and more determined cast of her adult features. Some might have called her pretty. But then some would call the green-and-purple serpent they'd seen earlier pretty, and she had something of the serpent's quality.

'Ensee,' he said, speaking as evenly as he could while his heart raced. 'It's good to see you again.'

'You know this slave?' Haneul asked. There wasn't deference in her voice – no doubt it wasn't encouraged among the newly equal Rah – but there was a note of caution.

'He wasn't a slave when I met him,' Ensee said. 'I was his prisoner. He was the leader of the force that tortured my father.'

Bone Dancer looked shocked. 'Is this true?'

'Well, my army was allied with theirs. It was another who was guilty of that crime.'

Now Ensee smiled. 'Who called it a crime? My father was the criminal. The nails your people tore out of his fingers were barely healed when I had him stoned to death.'

*

After the meal, Bone Dancer wanted the full story from Sang Ki. He gave it. What choice did he have? And it was true that Cwen, the Hunter's hawk, had been the one responsible for torturing Ensee's father, in her quest to track down Krishanjit. Bone Dancer didn't seem to find Sang Ki any less culpable because of this, and he couldn't disagree. He could have stopped the torture if he'd chosen. But he was a different man now.

Then they went to bed, Bone Dancer perhaps to sleep and Sang Ki to toss and turn for the long hours until dawn.

When the sun rose, he was summoned. He found he'd been expecting it.

He arrived, though, to learn it was Jalena and not Ensee who needed his attention – a guard had been indulgent enough to pass along her request. She was locked in a room but otherwise unharmed. She'd been pacing before he entered, but when she saw him, she flung her arms around him.

He patted her back uncomfortably. 'I'm glad to see you well. But you shouldn't have come.'

She pulled back to stare at him. Her features had also firmed into adulthood over the past few years, but there was still something childlike in the intensity of her gaze. 'I'll always come,' she said fiercely. 'It's a very bad thing to keep a plant-speaker as a work-for-nothing person. I told her so the last time she stopped me from freeing you.'

'And the time before that, and the time before that.' He'd lost count now of the attempts she'd made to free him from a captivity he found perfectly acceptable. He was just grateful that Bone Dancer had instructed her guards to treat Jalena with gentleness. It was to the Ahn trader's credit that she hadn't chosen to take Jalena as her slave too. But there was no blood-debt between them and Bone Dancer was a fair dealer.

'This time is different,' Jalena said. 'This time you *have* to listen. You need to listen to the plants.'

This at least was new. 'I haven't visited the world-beneath-the-world since I left the savannah,' Sang Ki reminded her. 'I doubt it will be open to me. I doubt it's open to anyone so far from the grass.'

She looked mulish. 'It will be. You're the most powerful plant-speaker that anyone remembers.'

'Well, that may be true, but only because your people choose to forget the dead. I'm sure there were plenty just as good as me in years gone by.'

She'd covered her ears when he mentioned the dead, but now she uncovered them. 'No. You're better than any of them, even the forgotten ones. You must be. The plants showed you a very big, very bad thing in the world-beneath-the-world. And now the big bad thing has happened.'

Fear jolted through him, for the second time that day. 'What do you mean, it's happened? My hallucination – I mean to say my plant vision – was frustratingly vague. Anything could be seen as a fulfilment of it.'

'Not so,' she said. 'Not so. You said a worse thing was coming than the moon, and now I've been among the Ostatni Ludia I know the ill luck the moon brought. But now there are three new gods, *more* powerful than the moon. They've sent an army to the not-people land to the east.'

'To Ashanesland?' He heard his own voice shaking.

'Yes. And if they went east first, they'll come west next. A house-beast always needs to graze on fresh pastures. *Now* will you listen to the plants?'

★

Purple sorghum didn't flourish in Rah lands, but in recent years they'd made the attempt to cultivate it. They probably hoped to use it to pacify their debt-bonded criminals as bliss had once subdued the slaves. Sang Ki took the dried leaves they offered and allowed Jalena to brew a tea that at least slightly resembled the one he'd drunk in Juh Obec.

He braced himself for the terrifying fall into the fractured world that he'd experienced before. But this time there was nothing like it. One moment he was here, and the next he was there, in one triangular, translucent purple room of that endless honeycomb, pyramids piled on top of each other and side by side, stretching to infinity in every direction.

'You came back,' Krishanjit said.

He was standing exactly as he had been the last time Sang Ki had seen him, beside one of the windows that he'd claimed were eyes. His face and clothes were utterly unchanged, as if he hadn't aged a day. Could he really have been waiting years for Sang Ki's return? Or did time have no meaning in this place?

'I had to come back,' Sang Ki said. 'In the world above, I mean to say, the real world, there are forces stirring of a kind you might be familiar with. The evil that I sensed here . . . did you sense it too?'

Krishanjit's features shifted, not into a new expression but a new face. Now he looked much more like the clever, ruthless young man that Sang Ki had met in Mirror Town. 'I've seen them. Three new gods. I took my power out of the world, and someone brought it back and gave it to them.'

'A new moon, and a new sun?' Sang Ki asked. 'And some third this time, too – a star, perhaps?'

Krish shook his head. 'No. My power is back, but not the runes. I think . . . the magic is a language in a way. You speak a sentence in it and it makes it true. These gods speak a different language.'

'So, a new magic, a new language, but the same power?'

'Yes. It's always the same power.'

'But what is it?' Sang Ki asked. 'If it's returned to the world as you say, where has it returned *from*?'

'From here.' Krish frowned. 'I've been thinking. I've had a long time to think. It's hard to explain, but . . . have you ever dug up a patch of grass, or tried to pull a weed from the ground?'

Sang Ki raised an eyebrow at the change in conversational direction. 'Not frequently. As you may perhaps recall, I wasn't raised a farmer.'

'But you must have seen it happen. You know what plants look like beneath the earth, their roots all tangled, all of them connected. They're many, but they're also one. This is the place where they join.'

'They join in the soil. Are you saying that's where we are now, buried in the ground?

Krish's face twisted in frustration. 'No. You're thinking about that world – the world above – and this is the world below. It's not just plants. There's something in everything, in everyone, that has its roots here. Not made out of wood, or leaves or stems but . . . I don't know if there are words for it. Something else. The same thing that's in a person when they go to sleep and when they wake up. The piece that's missing when they die.'

Sang Ki glanced around, at the triangles piled on triangles. 'You're speaking of a place of spirit, I think. But this looks like a fortress.'

'Or a prison. It's been corrupted. Can't you feel it?'

Sang Ki realized that he could. It was absurd to imagine that this endless dream structure could feel pain, but it did. It had been stretched horribly out of shape.

'I think,' Krish said, 'that someone found this place. Long ago. There was great power here, but without shape or . . . or words or meaning. It just was. But a person can't use what they can't name. So he *made* it have a shape and a meaning. He wounded it to make it small enough for him to understand.'

'Why?'

'To make himself a god. He drew his power from this place. But he didn't want anyone else to use it. So he walled it off so that only he could touch it. And when he did, he cut people off from the part of themselves that lived in here, that connected them to this place, and through here, to each other. There's a spark that used to be in everyone and now it's trapped in here like a . . . like a hostage. And together all those sparks make a great fire.'

As if his words had summoned them, flames bloomed from the walls – an inferno. Sang Ki cried out in shock and fear, but the flames were heatless and a moment later they were gone. Only the endless pyramids remained. Each one, he supposed, one fragment of one person's spirit. 'But why does it look like this? Can spirit truly have a shape?'

Krish shrugged. 'Only because he forced it to. This must be how the one who made it imagined it. And he imagined it so strongly that he makes everyone else see it that way too.'

'But *who* made it? The Eternal Empire, I suppose, when they decided to bring Mizhara and Yron into the world.'

'No, they just used something they found, that was already here. And they – I think they put another meaning on it, their own meaning. The sun and the moon, order and chaos. I don't know why they chose that particular one. Maybe it was how they already understood the world. Or maybe they thought it would make the power easier to control. The meaning is how you use it. Do you understand?'

'I think I do,' Sang Ki said, though truly it hurt his head to think about it. 'That's what power is, I suppose. Making things mean the things *you* want them to. Making people see the world the way you choose.'

'Yes! There are others in here, you know – my sister, the servant who became Mizhara. We speak sometimes. There are the Yron and Mizhara from the Eternal Empire a thousand years ago, and before that again, when they were summoned to rule a nation that no one even remembers. Each time, people made gods to channel the power.'

'But it always came to ruin. The nations always fell.'

'I don't know why. Maybe because this place is sick. Everything in here is suffering. Or maybe just because they lost control of the meaning. The gods they made wanted to define themselves.'

Sang Ki smiled slightly. 'I suppose you can attest to that. I don't believe you were ever happy in the role that Olufemi forced on you.'

'I hated it, and then I loved it, but hating it was right. No one person, not even a god, should have all this power. He's still here, you know, the one who made this place to take the god-thing that lived inside everyone and use it for himself. He's trapped here. And while he lives, this place can't die. He's at the root of it. I've tried to find him, but however deep I go, he's always deeper.'

Sang Ki remembered what he'd felt, when he'd come here as he lay dying from his leg wound. 'I sensed him too. He was . . .' He shuddered. 'He didn't feel entirely sane. But I suppose one wouldn't be, after so long trapped in here.'

'I think he's outside too, somewhere,' Krish said. 'I know I am. My body, I mean. I've looked through Eric's eyes and seen it.'

'But this place is where your spirit is, the part that's truly you.' Sang Ki was beginning to understand. Being here made it easier. The irrational was rational here. 'Is that all being a god means? That you can be wholly here, or wholly there?'

Krish looked out through one of the window eyes. The view was nothing special: a spindle and the hands working it. 'Yes.

Whatever's missing from you, whatever part of you and everyone else is trapped here, I still have it. That's why this place can control you, and I can control it. Or I could, before I stopped being a god. Now someone else has found a new meaning with new gods and they're the ones who take power from this place. All I can do is watch.'

'Then how do we stop them?' Sang Ki asked. It was only in the moment of asking that he knew he meant to try.

'I don't know. It doesn't matter. I'm free of it all in here.'

'No, that's not good enough.' Sang Ki looked out through the window again, that singular view of the world that belonged to just one person. 'You freed yourself, Krishanjit, after doing great harm in the world. Now free them.'

11

It took Dae Hyo much longer than it should to realise that they were fattening him up. It was the fourth feast in as many days. As he picked at an oily fish he didn't have the appetite for, he saw the way they were all looking at him, with hungry eyes. They had a quarter as much food on their own plates.

He threw the plate to the deck, splattering oil on the guests to his left. No one reprimanded him. No one had said a bitter word to him since the day he'd made himself King of the Coral. No one denied him anything he wanted. He could have drowned himself in drink and they wouldn't have stopped him, but he'd lost his appetite for it. No drop of it had passed his lips since the day he'd speared the boy Dinesh in the gut.

Shame was a feeling he might previously have chosen to silence with drink. But it was the drink that had caused all these problems, and he couldn't pretend this was new knowledge. He'd never hurt an innocent before, though, someone with the fat of childhood still on him. A friend, or at least the friend of a brother. This was a pain he deserved to feel.

But the fattening up? The way they looked at him like a man condemned? He was less inclined to put up with that. It was time, he decided, to find out what exactly they had in mind for him.

The berth mothers were in their usual place. They sat on low stools near the frontward rim of the raft, sheltered from the relentless sun beneath a silk canopy. Wizened and very old, they looked at him askance, but didn't speak.

'Tell me about this Eetlust,' he said.

They exchanged looks, but didn't answer.

'I'm meant to be facing it, aren't I? I've a right to know what I'll be fighting.'

'The Coral King isn't meant to fight,' the youngest of them said.

'If I'm not meant to fight, why do you crown the strongest fighter?' Dae Hyo asked.

'The Coral King's courage sates the Eetlust,' another proclaimed.

'If it's a meal the beast's after, you ought to be sending down the fattest.'

They looked at him in silence. He'd impressed them with his arguments, he could tell.

'I tell you what,' he said, 'I don't care about the Coral Kings who came before. They were all stupid enough to drown. I mean to live. I'm going to kill this Eetlust for you.'

'No man can do it,' the first woman said.

'How do you know,' he asked, 'if they've never tried?'

★

When he asked around, hoping to get the measure of his enemy, he quickly found that no one knew anything. No one had ever actually seen the Eetlust. He might have wondered if it existed at all, if it weren't for the marks on that big fish. Something that lived beneath the waves had put them there.

He went to have another look at them. The fish was getting elderly by then. The smell was terrible, but the marks on its side, those strange rings, weren't that big. If they'd been made by the Eetlust's mouth, it couldn't be much bigger than a pony. Dae Hyo felt confident he could beat it in a fair fight. Although, if the fight was going to take place beneath the waves, it was true the odds favoured the fish.

He'd need help, that much was clear.

★

Now Eric had three invalids to care for. Krish and Drut remained as quiet as ever, but Dinesh tossed and turned and called out in his fever. Eric didn't think he was going to make it. His brow was slick with sweat and his clothes stank of it. There were red lines spreading from the two terrible wounds in his side. The Hunter had stitched them together with gut, but the flesh around the stitches was so inflamed that the gut string cut into it.

'He approaches again,' the Hunter said, looking seawards.

'Go away!' Eric shouted to Dae Hyo as he paddled through the water towards them.

Dae Hyo ignored him, as he had the first time he'd tried to come aboard, so Eric picked up one of their oars to push him away. He'd done that the first time too, but this time the Hunter placed her hand over his to stop him.

'I ain't got nothing to say to him,' Eric muttered.

Her eyes were fixed on Dae Hyo. 'Perhaps, but I believe he may have something to say to us.'

Dae Hyo didn't look at Eric when he climbed wet and dripping aboard their raft. It was smaller than it had been. Eric had been forced to sell five of their timbers to buy medicine and bandages for Dinesh, much good was it doing him.

Dae Hyo's attention was all on Dinesh. He had a face like a window, giving a clear view into his thoughts. Shame was shining out of him, but Eric didn't want to hear his apologies.

'You've seen your handiwork now,' he said. 'Now bugger off out of here.'

But Dae Hyo just tutted and knelt at Dinesh's side, drawing out a double-edged knife from his belt.

Eric dived to grasp his arm. 'What do you think you're doing? You think you can make yourself feel better, putting him out of his misery now?'

Dae Hyo frowned at him. 'Belbog's balls, did no one ever teach you how to treat a wound?'

He shook off Eric's arm, then placed the knife against the wound and cut through every stitch in one clean stroke.

Eric backed away, gagging at the foul stench of it. A noisome green-yellow pus was pouring out. It did the same on the other side when Dae Hyo repeated the procedure with the second wound.

'You have to let the evil out,' Dae Hyo said. 'Only a fool would think to lock the sickness in.' His eyes flicked to the Hunter. 'You've lived a thousand years and no one ever taught you that?'

'My hawks' flesh does not – did not – mortify, as yours does. I did not think.'

'Lucky for you that you've got me then.' Dae Hyo lifted an oiled bag that Eric hadn't noticed. He must have dragged it behind him in the water. There was amber-brown honey inside. 'We'll pack the wounds with this when the sickness is out of them. He'll be as fit as a spring calf in no time.'

There were only three hives on the whole raft. Honey was more precious than gold here. Eric knew enough to know that it was a wound-healer, but even every scrap of wood they owned wouldn't have been enough to buy some.

'They gave it to me,' Dae Hyo said to Eric's unasked question. 'I'm their king now. They'll give me anything.'

'Until they kill you.' Eric put some nastiness in the words. Dae Hyo might be helping now, but only to clean up the mess he'd made. He couldn't honestly expect thanks for it.

'I know,' Dae Hyo said. 'That's why I need your help. We're entering the red waters tomorrow, they say. That's the range where the Eetlust hunts. The day after they mean to feed me to it. I mean to see there's no monster left to eat me.'

★

The next morning, they reached the boundary of those red waters. Dae Hyo had thought it just a name, but they really were tinted a strange crimson, as if the light of the setting sun had taken to living underneath them.

'A weed that grows beneath the waves, I think,' the Hunter said. 'It will make what you plan even harder.'

'How do you even think you're going to find the bloody thing?' Eric asked. 'You gonna call its name and hope it's feeling friendly?'

The boy was angry with him still. It was beginning to annoy Dae Hyo. Dinesh's fever had broken late last night and the red lines on his skin were fading back to brown. The boy was going to live, so why was Eric holding on to the grudge? Yesterday's quarrels died with the dawn, that's what the elder mothers taught.

'I'll be taking fresh-cut meat with me,' Dae Hyo told him. 'Blood in the water. The razor-fish that live in the streams of the plains can smell it a mile away. The Eetlust will come to me. And I'll be ready.'

News of what he meant to do must have spread, as any novel thing did among these people who were so starved of anything new or interesting. Over the course of the morning, the other berths had been drifting closer and closer. By the time the sun was where Dae Hyo wanted it, a ring of boats and faces watched, none of them too friendly.

They didn't try to stop him, though. They didn't even protest when he swam to all the nearby rafts and picked them clean of rope. He was King of the Coral, and everything was his until the day he died for them. It seemed like a very stupid way to organise things, but he wasn't going to tell them that.

The Hunter and Eric tied all the bits of rope together, thick and thin, made of a dozen different fibres, until they'd made it into something very long. Then they tied one end to the raft, the other to his heaviest axe, and threw it over.

The unwisdom of what he was doing felt more pressing as he looked down at that rope and the fathomless depths beneath it. He'd hung his other weapons on a belt slung across his shoulder to weigh him down. He planned to use the rope to guide him. When he wanted to rise again, he'd lose the belt and float up. Of course, this would mean the loss of nearly all his weapons. Looking round at the watching faces on the other rafts, so grim and untrusting, that didn't seem particularly wise either.

'You wait much longer, they're gonna come and get their rope back,' Eric said.

It wasn't the words but the contempt in his voice that finally sent Dae Hyo over the edge of their raft and into the water.

He sank immediately. He hadn't expected that. He hadn't taken the deep breath that had been a tent peg of his plan, and he was ten paces from the rope. He kicked out frantically towards it, his eyes half-blinded by the salt water. He hadn't considered that either.

Finally, when his air was almost gone, his questing fingers found the rope and he pulled himself frantically up to the surface, where he gasped for air like a landed fish. When his breathing had steadied again, he drew in air so deep his lungs hurt, and let himself fall.

He had hold of the rope this time. He went down hand over hand, very, very fast with the weight of all that metal. He kept his eyes shut this time as he descended. Best to save them for when he needed them.

The water grew colder and the light shining through his eyelids paler as he descended. He was, he realised, dangling himself like bait on a hook, and yet no fish came to bite him. Could this Eetlust be no more real than the five Ashane prow gods, who were nothing but wood?

But then, very suddenly, he sensed it: something weighty moving through the depths. Water swirled in a caressing current against his arm and he opened his eyes.

It was there. Right there, in front of him. Or more accurately, all around him. No one had been able to describe the Eetlust, but Dae Hyo knew that this couldn't be anything else. It was impossible to tell its colour. Everything was dark red in this gloomy depth, but there was no doubt of its size. It was vast. It seemed formless.

Its tentacles undulated in the water like seaweed, each as thick as his torso. Worst of all was its mouth – its beak, absurdly like a bird's, but there was no bird this huge nor beak so vicious.

A shocked gulp of air came out of him. He watched the bubble float above him and break apart on one of the huge tentacles. His lungs were already aching with the need for air. He let go of the rope with one hand to fumble for his axe.

His weakened grip lost its purchase and he dropped abruptly. It was what saved him. The cruelly sharp beak lunged for the space where his head had been and caught the rope instead. It severed it as easily as a Smiler's Fair tailor snips a thread.

All reason left Dae Hyo. He was only panic. His hands pulled at the belt across his shoulder as he sank into the sullen red depths and the Eetlust spun in the water. It was far more agile than he'd guessed. Its tentacles streamed behind as it dived towards him.

Then the belt came loose and he was heading up. He was long past the point where he could remember not to breathe. He sucked in a lungful of water. The vast shape below him arrowed to follow his ascent, and he flailed towards the surface, his chest burning with agony.

He broke through, coughing up water in helpless gouts. When he opened his eyes, everything was darkness. Then a swell washed over him, nearly refilling the lungs he'd emptied, and he realised that he'd emerged under one of the berths. There must be only a handspan of clear air between its wooden bottom and the water.

The darkness above him was replaced by daylight in an instant so quick, Dae Hyo was blinded by it. The light shattered into rainbows through the water droplets that covered his eyes and when he blinked them away, he saw what had happened.

The Eetlust had followed him all the way to the surface. The raft that had covered him, small but not that small, was twined in one of its tentacles. The Eetlust raised it high overhead – and then brought it smashing down, straight towards Dae Hyo, as if it meant to squash him like a fly beneath a palm.

He dived desperately beneath the water, moments ahead of the raft. The water slowed it, just enough. It caught his shoulder a bruising blow but missed his head. And when he surfaced again, he saw that the raft had shattered and the Eetlust had moved on to other prey.

Its tentacles were all over the water, and everywhere they fell, another raft shattered. As the water cleared from his ears, Dae Hyo heard the screams of their inhabitants. Some dived to safety like he had. Others were less lucky. There was red in the water now, alongside the churning white of the Eetlust's thrashing.

It looked far stranger in the air than it had in its own home. Its skin couldn't seem to decide what it wanted to be. Colours flowed across it, grey turning to blue and then a bright wash of red, which in turn split into spots like blood and faded away. It wasn't just the colour, either. Even the texture of it seemed unable to settle on being just one thing.

Nearby, one of the monster's tentacles picked a young woman up from the water. It looked as smooth and dark as eel skin as it lifted her towards its hideous beak of a mouth. Dae Hyo watched, horrified, as it bit her in two. But when the tentacle returned, to throw the bottom half of her into the water, discarded like a chewed bone, it had changed. Now it was as wrinkled as a mammoth's snout, but the beautiful, iridescent white of mother of pearl.

It seemed to have gone mad, tearing apart rafts and people with equal enthusiasm. More than once, the morsel it brought to its own mouth was wood, not flesh, and it spat it out and reached for more.

A few of the braver Drifters swam towards the Eetlust. They hacked at its tentacles when they came within reach, but the blows of their bone knives were as pitiful as pins against its bulk. There seemed to be no pattern to the creature's attacks, only rage. As the moments passed, its movements grew jerkier and less sure, as if its rage was burning itself out. But its eyes were still open, and they seemed to be fixed on Dae Hyo. Him, it seemed to recognise.

A tentacle struck mere paces from Dae Hyo's head. Water fountained over him and when it cleared, he saw that the tentacle was wriggling through the water towards him like a snake. Just one axe still hung at his waist However monstrous and strange this thing was, it had eyes and a mouth. A head. That was the only place it might be vulnerable.

Dae Hyo had only an eyeblink to decide: fight now, or surrender to the tentacle's grasp and hope it carried him towards that head. He chose surrender. The tentacle, the colour of old ivory now, circled bonelessly around his middle and lifted. He was gasping for air when the Eetlust had him level with its huge flat eye, more alien by far than any creature of magic that Dae Hyo had ever seen.

Its tentacle gripped him as tightly as a lover in her climax and brought him towards its huge beak. Close up, it looked far less like a bird's than he'd thought, not even one of the huge dead carrion mounts. It was like a polished seashell, and looked as hard as rock. But as it gaped wide to take him, he drew his axe and struck.

The blade bit deep. Its beak gaped wider, but not to eat. It seemed to be a silent roar of pain. It almost pulled the axe from his hand, but he held on grimly and it came free, taking a ragged chunk of beak with it. The pressure of the tentacle around his waist slackened. It began to fall away, back towards the water.

Dae Hyo leapt, his free hand reaching for the Eetlust's beak. The shell-like surface sliced into his palm, but he held on. He swung his axe, as hard as he was able – not very hard, while dangling in the air – and it bit into the flesh beside the beak. A liquid oozed out, not a natural red but a deep, dark blue. There wasn't very much liquid, though. The cut wasn't deep. Not nearly deep enough.

Dae Hyo swung again, cut it another glancing blow – and on his third swing, his axe went deep. But it was too deep. By keeping hold of it, he lost his grip on the beak. All his weight was on the axe, and it tore a deep gouge downwards through the monster's flesh and then, when it reached the bottom of its dome-like head, fell away. Dae Hyo fell with it, into the sea twenty paces below.

The water was churning madly and he was almost out of strength. But there was a raft very close, by great good fortune still intact. He dragged himself over its side, stood on shaky legs and turned to face the Eetlust, ready to continue the fight.

But if he was ready, the monster wasn't. Its tentacles were still writhing, only far more slowly now. Its huge, unhuman eyes were misting over. The tentacles' movements, he realised, were no longer an attack. They were the creature's death throes. Had Dae Hyo injured it mortally after all, before he fell? He must have. What else could cause so monumental a thing to suffer so violent a death?

Dae Hyo watched as the Eetlust beat weakly at the water a few more times. Then it stilled. For a moment the bulk of it was sprawled over the surface of the ocean, and then, very slowly, it began to sink back beneath the waves.

It left behind the wreckage of its attack. Dozens of rafts had been destroyed by it. Driftwood floated among uncountable corpses.

Dae Hyo raised his arms above his head, his one remaining axe in his hand. 'Look!' he shouted. 'Is there any warrior mightier than me? The Eetlust is dead. I killed a god with my own hands!'

★

Eric thought it was a wonder they'd ended the day with every one of them alive. It seemed even more improbable that their raft was still whole. But plenty of others hadn't been so lucky.

The Drifters had a strange way with death, with no ground to bury a person in and no rocks to weigh them down. Eric had nearly vomited when he'd witnessed it the first time. The woman had been old. She'd probably died of disease. And they'd eaten her.

Of course, they made a song and dance about it, stripping the flesh from the bones while they sang one of their long songs. They left the heart and liver and kidneys to dry in the sun. They thought that was where a body's bravery lived. Eric hadn't partaken.

With so many dead, they'd have a proper feast tonight, but he didn't mean to attend that either. That left him stuck on the raft with the Hunter and Dinesh – bleary-eyed and silent, but clearly on the mend – and the two unconscious lumps who hadn't even woken to watch a monster bigger than Rii thrash out of the water.

There was Dae Hyo too, of course. He was cock-a-hoop, as pleased with himself as if what he'd done that day had somehow undone all the trouble he'd caused in the days before.

But still, Eric couldn't complain about what he'd done. From the day they'd washed up here, the Drifters had spoken of the Eetlust as this fearful thing. Now they were rid of it. If Dae Hyo would just stay off the drink, perhaps it could all be forgiven and forgotten, and they could make themselves a life here. He had to live to remember Arwel. There was no one else to do it.

Thoughts of his son chased Eric into sleep and followed him back to consciousness the next morning. The sky was a pale, pale blue above him and the waves were so still it was eerily silent. Even the seabirds that lived off the Drifters' leavings seemed to have decided to start the morning late. And Dae Hyo, sleeping on his side, for once wasn't snoring.

Except ... the silence was too much. It was too complete. Eric felt the rising dread even before he'd sat up.

They were alone on a vast, flat sea. The other rafts were all gone, as if they'd never been. They weren't even a blur on the horizon.

'They must have rowed all night,' the Hunter said. Her voice made Eric jump.

'But why?' he asked. 'We wasn't doing them no harm. We'd helped them. Well, Dae Hyo had I suppose.'

'Dae Hyo killed their god. How could you expect them to react? It had been their one constant on the shiftless sea, and now it is gone.'

'But they hated it. They was afraid of it.'

'Even so,' the Hunter said. 'Intended or not, Dae Hyo has done them a great wrong. We are fortunate that the repayment was so slight as this.'

The man in question was up now too. He spun in place, scanning the horizon, his face still stupid with sleep. Eric expected him to say something stupid to match. He usually did. But instead he pointed to their left and said, 'Look, there's land.'

Eric didn't trust in it, not at first. Over the last few years, there'd been wrecks and whales and tricks of his eyes that had led him to see rock and earth where there was only water. But as they frantically paddled nearer, it proved to be an island.

Closer still, and there was a spattering of green visible on its slopes. An island *and* water. Perhaps that was why the Drifters had felt free to leave them here. Or maybe luck had simply favoured them for once.

Eric's hands were red raw by the time their raft beached on the weed-clogged strand. He ran from the boat to stand on earth again, only to find it swaying beneath him as if he'd travelled in entirely the opposite direction.

Behind him, the Hunter lifted Drut in her arms, while Dae Hyo held Krish. Their raft was already being drawn back seawards by the current and he trotted back to do his best with Dinesh, passing Dae Hyo at the meeting point of water and land.

And when Dae Hyo crossed it, the moment his feet touched the sand, the limp figure in his arms stiffened and then stirred. Eric watched, astonished, as at long, long last, Krish's moon-silver eyes opened.

12

Olufemi had never intended to learn to cook. She'd never intended to be shipwrecked, either. She certainly hadn't meant to bring three new gods into the world after her abject failure with the first two. But all these things had happened, and now she must live with the consequences.

With an hour of daylight still left, the beach was empty. Most of the others were at work on the ship or gathering supplies for it. The cookpot wasn't as full as it once would have been. The hunters brought back less and less game these days. The small number of pigs and goats kept as livestock on the island had been slaughtered long ago.

They hadn't been the only deaths. It was more than two years since the Mortals' servants had turned on them, but Olufemi's gorge still rose every time she thought of it. It had been a slaughter, not a fight. She'd tried to warn the Mortals of the resentment that was brewing among those who'd once served them so loyally. She'd explained that on this island, away from Ofiklanod, and its beliefs and its ordered way of life, anyone might have wondered why those who were able to take care of themselves should wait on those who never could.

And then there were those Mortals who *hadn't* died. There were four in total. Three of them lay in their cage at the high point of the beach, on soiled dry-leaf bedding. The years of imprisonment and ill treatment had left them skeletally thin, blistered by the shadeless sun and utterly without hope. A few months into their imprisonment, two had tried to starve themselves to death. Their former servants, who'd once cooked and cut their food for them, ground it into mush instead and shoved it down their necks. Now their wills were broken and all three did exactly as they were told.

The Mortals' servants had possessed the wit to play at humble obedience long enough to extract all the knowledge of shipbuilding from their Mortal masters. Only when the plans were drawn up had they turned on them. And they knew enough, too, to doubt their welcome when they returned to their homeland and its new overlords. So they'd kept those pitiable three Mortals alive as an offering, a gift to buy their welcome.

Olufemi knew that she was lucky not to be among either the slaughtered or the imprisoned. But then, she'd sensed the direction of the storm and sought shelter among those she deemed likeliest to survive it. The choice hadn't delighted her. If the Mortals had only listened to her warnings, she'd gladly have pitched in with them instead. She'd found their company preferable.

But of course, one Mortal *had* listened. One was neither among the charred remains in their pyre nor rotting in a cell. Bruyar hadn't been found on the night of the slaughter, and *oms* hadn't been seen since.

It worried Olufemi. It *infuriated* Leverik, the man who'd made himself leader of the former servants. He still sent search parties into the forest to hunt for Bruyar and question what natives they could find. It was fewer and fewer these days. The Ofiklanders had hunted the island's game to near extinction and plucked and dried all of its fruit to store for their coming voyage. Most of them believed that the natives were as near extinction as their game, but Olufemi had her doubts. She suspected they'd merely grown better at hiding.

She didn't tell Leverik her thoughts. He was a man who preferred his plans to go smoothly. He was striding down the beach towards her now. The pink-orange sunset sky was behind him and most of the remaining Ofiklanders were at his side, fresh from tarring the ship's timbers and its rigging. The air was filled with the burnt-pine smell of it. The vessel was very nearly finished. And when it was finished, it would set sail.

Olufemi still wasn't entirely confident that she'd be on board when it did.

Leverik peered into the stew pot Olufemi was diligently stirring and frowned. 'A meagre meal, Femi,' he said, not aloud but with the finger-speech the servants used between themselves. The fact that the Mortals cut out their tongues when they took them into service had probably contributed to their resentment.

Olufemi wanted to tell him that the meal was only meagre because he'd supplied her so little to go in it. But instead she smiled ingratiatingly and said, 'I'll do better tomorrow.'

She filled all their bowls to overflowing, leaving only the dregs for herself and nothing at all for the captives. But then she and they were used to sleeping with an empty belly. She scraped out the pot with her finger and licked it all up greedily.

After the meal, the workers shared several flagons of the wine they'd learned to brew from the sour red fruit that had grown on the trees here, before they picked them all clean. They didn't offer any to Olufemi.

She rose from her crouch on creaky knees. 'I'm going to check on the ship's stores,' she told Leverik.

'That's the devotion I like to see,' he said. There was no tone to their finger-speech, but if there had been, his would have been gratingly patronising.

She turned away to hide her expression and headed for the ship. It was a hulking shape in the twilight, blotting out the newly risen moon behind it. The wind was high and silvered clouds scudded past, visible through its rigging, like a prophecy of the journey to come. The ship was well made, despite the inexperience of its shipwrights.

It wasn't floating yet. It rested on monumental logs on the sand. The ladder that led to its deck was very long, and Olufemi was very tired by the time she'd climbed it. She didn't go below to check the stores. She knew perfectly well that they were all in order.

She could have gone to check on the very small berth they'd assigned her in the hold. It was just one hammock between two others belonging to servants the Ofiklanders had recruited from the island's decimated tribe. She used to visit it often, to reassure herself that there really was a place for her on the ship. She couldn't shake the fear that they'd leave her behind when they didn't have any further use for her.

Instead of going below, she stood on deck and scanned the island's inland forest from this high vantage. There wasn't much to see. There was dense darkness between the trees, and a paler flatness here and there where the stony ground showed through.

There were also lights, high up in the tall hills at the heart of the island. Those hills were where the remnants of the tribe had been driven to starve to death. When Olufemi had first started looking, the lights had been scattered. She assumed they were family fires. The natives had only ever had a very loose sense of themselves as one tribe. Now the fires were clustered close together. In adversity, they'd found unity.

Or perhaps there'd been someone to unite them.

Olufemi reminded herself that the ship was very nearly finished. They had all the supplies they needed. If the tides and the winds obliged, they could set sail within days. She had a great deal to lose if she abandoned the servants now.

And yet Bruyar was out there, somewhere. Olufemi was quite sure of it. Sometimes, on foraging expeditions into the forest, she felt eyes on her. It was absurd to believe that she could know the identity of those unseen eyes, but she did. Bruyar was a plotter, a schemer.

Nearer at hand, the fire on the beach was far brighter. The noise of the Ofiklanders around it, drinking and laughing their strange tongueless laugh, drowned out any sound from the forest. They were so carefree and confident. But, however little they realised it, there was still another side to choose from, and the opportunity to choose would soon be gone.

Choose wrong, and Olufemi might be worse than merely stranded. Should she side with a single person who was handless and defenceless, not even able to eat without assistance? Or with the two-score healthy young fighters who'd built the ship with their own labour and knew how to sail it?

The answer, in the end, seemed very clear.

*

Olufemi didn't dare take a torch into the forest. They'd see it moving from the beach and know she'd gone. She had to rely on the light of the full moon to guide her, a bitter irony. It barely penetrated beneath the canopy and she shuffled forwards one small step at a time through the mulch. If she tripped on a root and broke her leg, no one would ever find her. She doubted they'd even look.

The moon did at least provide a beacon, towards the torchlight she'd seen from the ship's deck. But all sense of distance was lost beneath the trees.

She didn't know how far she'd gone when she realised that she wasn't alone. There were footsteps, paralleling hers on either side. They crunched the brittle pine needles And she felt eyes watching her, with that curious animal sense all people had. But every time she turned towards them, the footsteps moved away. She could only hope that these were Bruyar's people. Who else would be patrolling the forest at night? Perhaps when they'd finished whatever game they were playing with her, they'd approach. The game-playing made her think they must be Bruyar's too.

Then she had a second, far worse realisation. She was being hunted. Not by the people shadowing her – by a beast. She caught the reflection of its eyes, just for a second, eerily green in the underbrush to her left.

Panic overwhelmed her. Even as she ran, she knew it was futile. Worse than futile – it would only encourage the hunt. She heard the hunter's growls, now it knew it had been seen.

She chanced a glance behind her. The beast was almost on her. It was a panther, dark-furred and lithely muscled. The tree beside her had a branch at shoulder level. She grabbed it and pulled herself up with a strength she hadn't possessed since her youth. It was born out of terror.

A claw slashed and caught her arm. The agony was instant. She ignored it and grabbed the branch above, desperate to climb higher, out of reach of the beast. The growls and the hot, fetid breath of the panther pursued her. It seemed more at home in the tree than she was. But surely it couldn't climb as high or as fast as her? She reached for another branch.

Minutes later, she was running out of tree and the panther wasn't running out of strength. She pulled herself up again, to a branch so high and thin that she wasn't sure it would take her weight. The panther hesitated, perhaps with the same fear. For a long moment they stared into each other's eyes. There was more intelligence than she would have credited looking back at her. The part of her that was always thinking and not feeling took note of it. The feeling part knew this made the danger worse. The panther blinked, briefly shutting off the green glow of its eyes. Then it crouched low, tensing to spring . . .

And a whistle sounded from the forest, three short, sharp notes, like a hunter calling his hounds to heel. And just like a hound responding to its master, the panther swung its head towards the sound. There was the briefest hesitation, then it scrabbled back down the branch. It was far less elegant in its descent than it had been in the ascent.

'Well.' Bruyar's voice floated up from far below. 'The entertainment ends. You've found me, Olufemi. What is it you mean to do with me?'

*

They had to send men up to help Olufemi get down. All her strength was spent and she let them half-carry her to the ground. Bruyar had already departed and she was led in silence by the tribesmen to their encampment an hour's walk away.

She knew very little about the island's natives. They weren't mentioned in any book that she'd read. She could only assume that they'd come to this island from the same ancestral lands as the Ashane and the Moon Forest folk and the tribes. They looked like a mixture of all three peoples, tall and slender and swarthy with loosely curled hair and flat, expressionless faces.

The torchlight of the encampment was visible long before they reached it, turning the forest from midnight to early dawn. She smiled a little at that. She *had* been right about where Bruyar was. The panther that had so terrorised her was supine by one of the fires. Its eyes were half-lidded as its head was stroked by a child no older than five.

The Mortal leader waited for her on a stool by the largest fire. *Oms* had swapped *omas* robes for the clothing of the tribe, a leaf skirt that left *omas* bulbous breasts bare. Bruyar was thinner than when Olufemi had last seen *oms*. But *omas* mouth wore the same sardonic, amused smile.

'Well, well, what an unexpected delight,' Bruyar said. 'I assume it was me you were hunting, although I'd thought myself presumed dead. Whatever brings you here, Olufemi?'

'A gamble,' Olufemi told *omas*. There seemed little point in lying. 'I think you mean to steal the ship, don't you?'

'Why would I do that, when I'm quite incapable of sailing it?' Bruyar held up *omas* handless arms, but the superior smile was still on those plump lips.

Olufemi shrugged. 'I don't know. I only know one thing. You've had two years to plot and they're fools if they think they've bested you. I'm not such a fool.'

'No,' Bruyar said thoughtfully. 'No, indeed you're not.'

★

They let Olufemi sleep for what remained of the night, and at dawn Bruyar took her to see what *oms* had been working on all this time.

Olufemi stared at it in consternation. It was a replica of sorts, a model of a ship made out of rough tree trunks and palm-leaf cloth and hemp ropes. There was no deck, only the forest floor. Had she made a mistake after all? Had the slaughter of all *omas* companions broken Bruyar's mind?

Bruyar laughed at Olufemi's expression. Then *oms* turned to the tribesman standing at *omas* shoulder and issued what were clearly orders in the tribe's own tongue. Olufemi was startled to realise that she'd never heard it spoken before. The island's natives had seemed no more than another form of game to her, hunted to extinction by the newcomers from Ofiklanod.

Except they weren't quite extinct. Here in the rocky centre of the island, she could see that a good hundred or more of them survived. At Bruyar's words, more than half rushed into motion. They swarmed up the tree-masts to grasp the ropes. Quicker than Olufemi would have thought possible, the palm-leaf sails moved. Another order from Bruyar, and they moved again. Olufemi knew nothing of sailing, but it seemed to her that they were moving as a true ship's sails would, in response to a changing wind. Bruyar had must have spent weeks teaching them ship handling here, and all without stepping foot in the water.

'You've turned them into sailors,' Olufemi said.

'Indeed I did, my darling. They weren't easy to persuade. They've been quite angry these last three years. I'm sure you can imagine why. But I'd made contact with them already, when all that unpleasantness began. I'd been learning their tongue. And fortunately for me, they fear to harm the crippled. Their owl god forbids it.'

'But this . . .' Olufemi looked again at the training ground Bruyar had built here, the scale and the ambition of it. 'To persuade them of the need for this. To teach them how to do it . . .'

'Necessity is a sharp goad. And besides, their legends speak of a journey in just such a boat across the same ocean that brought us here. 'Tis plausible, is it not, that this is how they came? Although I doubt it was their owl god who guided them here, as their legends claim. They believe me an emissary of that god, come to guide them home again. It's been pleasing, Olufemi, to discover that I was right all along, about how useful gods could be if used correctly.'

'Yes,' Olufemi said. 'The seeds of it you planted in your homeland sprouted quite spectacularly. A shame the fruit was so bitter to the taste.'

Bruyar's mouth curved into a small smile. 'We have both bred the same fruit, to the same effect. If I'm to be judged for it, it won't be by you. And I hardly think I'm the villain of this play.

Strangers came to this island. They stripped it bare of sustenance and slaughtered its native people until only this remnant survives. A remnant whose own home is now so inhospitable to them that they are willing to flee it forever. So tell me, Olufemi, what made you come to me? When I can have no use whatsoever for you, and you've just spent the last two years working with those who murdered my companions?'

The tribesmen couldn't have understood Bruyar's words, but the tone of them was obvious. Olufemi felt the burn of many unfriendly eyes. Some of them were armed with stone-tipped spears. No one raised their weapon, but the angle of them shifted, until all the points were turned to her.

'It seems you can sail the ship,' she said. 'But how do you intend to take it?'

'Why should I tell you my plan?' Bruyar asked.

'No reason. Just tell me this: does it have a cost in blood?'

Bruyar shrugged. 'Most things worth accomplishing do, I've found.'

'And what if I told you that I could ensure none of it was your people's?'

'Then,' Bruyar replied, 'I would say that you should speak on.'

*

Olufemi returned to the camp on the beach near noon. She had a basket of wild mushrooms that Bruyar had gifted her. The excuse that she'd been gathering them was ready, but nobody asked. As Olufemi settled at her usual spot by the hearth, she realised that she hadn't even been missed. Why should she be? They saw her as no threat. Besides, most of them were absent, putting the final touches to their ship. Only two young women lounged on the strand, their feet bare and stretched out so that the waves lapped at them.

These were Dranal and Dredik, twin girls who'd once been among Bruyar's own entourage. They'd always been very pleasant to Olufemi. When Leverik chastised her, they sometimes argued in her defence.

Guilt was sour and unpleasant in her stomach. She reminded

herself that these girls had done nothing to intervene when the Mortals were murdered. No one on this island had hands untouched by blood. There were only hunters and prey here, and Olufemi knew which she preferred to be.

She threw the mushrooms she'd gathered into the stew pot, and then walked down to the sea herself, some distance from the girls. It wouldn't do for them to see what she was doing.

The sea was rich in life here. It might have sustained them, if so much of it hadn't been poisonous. A red-scaled fish that swam in profusion had cramped their stomachs for three days when they tried it. The white crabs that sidled from sea to rockpool had turned their stools to water. But worst of all had been the mussels. Leverik had grown cautious by then, and given it to one of the imprisoned Mortals to sample.

His death had been agonising but quick. Most helpfully for Olufemi, it hadn't occurred until three hours or more after the meal.

After she'd gathered her harvest, she pulled them from their shells and chopped them so fine that no one would ever know what they were eating. And then she threw them into the pot and set it to boil.

She found Leverik at the ship, supervising the final small pieces of work. She could tell him about Bruyar. The Ofiklanders were all armed with metal. The tribespeople outnumbered them, and they were angry, but the odds still favoured the Ofiklanders. Olufemi could throw the dice one final time, and bet on a different side.

'Your lunch will be cooked shortly,' she told Leverik. 'Come and eat when you're ready.'

*

At sunset, when there were only corpses on the beach, Bruyar emerged from the forest with the people *oms* had made *omas* own. The smell of vomit and shit was everywhere, but Olufemi made herself endure it. She had, after all, caused it. Bruyar looked briefly at the three Mortals dead in their cage, then moved on. Leverik had been in a generous mood and had insisted they be given half a bowl of stew each.

'That was sweetly done,' *oms* said. 'You've earned your place aboard, Olufemi. And truth to tell, I'll be glad of some civilised conversation on the long voyage.'

'To Ofiklanod?' Olufemi asked. 'Do you think they'll welcome us back?'

Bruyar shook *omas* head. 'That would be the height of foolishness, and of the many things I've been called, foolish has never been one of them. No, I have another destination in mind.'

'To Ashanesland? The land whose prince you killed?'

'Not there,' Bruyar said. 'Come, the tide's turning. We must board and be away before it does.'

'But away to *where*?'

Bruyar smiled. 'Why spoil the surprise? The journey will reveal itself soon enough, Olufemi, unless you mean to be left behind with these corpses? No? Then let's set sail.'

Olufemi was left with no choice but to follow Bruyar onto the ragged ship and the restless sea, for an unknown destination.

13

Bone Dancer's visit to the Rah, which had been intended to last only days, stretched on past a fortnight. After the first few days, she excused Sang Ki from her side. Haggling had never been one of his strengths and she hardly needed his help to tell her how to do it.

The Rah had always been masters of cloth-making, but now it seemed they'd extended their inventiveness to ship-building. Bone Dancer didn't share the details with him, but it seemed that they'd discovered some new means of locomotion that was neither wind nor sail. Sang Ki wondered if it was something to do with those strange new buildings of theirs, the ones that, day and night, emitted clouds of white smoke from their roofs.

He'd learned that the bulk of the debt-bonded criminals worked there, and not in the fields. The fields were reserved for those who'd injured themselves too badly in those buildings to continue. Injured themselves doing what, precisely, no one was willing to tell him.

He wasn't invited inside the buildings to study them. He didn't seem welcome anywhere, and wherever he went, he was watched. Bone Dancer had at least acquired some fascinating books recently from the Seonu, the most mysterious of the tribes, but he couldn't focus on their pages. Every time he tried, his mind instead chose to worry about the news Jalena had brought. Three new gods.

He'd told Krish that it was his duty to act. It had felt like a reasonable request, in the dream that was the world-beneath-the-world. Waking, he was less certain. What could Krish do without his powers against three gods? And what could Sang Ki do, who'd never even been a god himself? And yet he couldn't shake the certainty that the plants had sent him their visions for a reason. It was something to do with that hidden presence, the first god who was responsible for all the rest.

'Do you think we should go back to the obec, plant-speaker?' Jalena asked.

The two of them were walking the long, sandy beach that marked the western border of Rah territory. The day was overcast and the tide high. Every so often, a bold wave ventured far enough up the shore to tickle their feet. Sang Ki had been a stranger to the sea for his entire childhood. It still filled him with wonder.

'I thought you believed I should fight?' he said.

'Yes, but not for the Ostatni Ludia, for the ones who matter. Do you think the army of the three gods will come to the obec? I didn't think it could happen before. People know that a fight ought to be kept small and only at the borders of the land. Each obec has its own grass. But not-people aren't wise. I know what an army is now. Will they send one to the real lands?'

'They'll come to every land. That's the nature of armies, and gods. They always want more.'

'Then how do we stop them?' she asked.

'There are some things that can't be fought, only fled.'

'Not so!' she said. 'Not so. No obec would surrender a fight before it's fought. That would be the worst ill luck.'

'So would the entire annihilation of your people, Jalena. Bravery isn't always a virtue and cowardice isn't always a vice.'

She frowned, looking momentarily much younger. 'But where can we flee to? You said they'll always eat more land, and we're the furthest land from where they are. The time before last when I tried to free you, that kidnapper showed me her maps.' By *kidnapper* she meant Bone Dancer. 'Maps are a wonderful thing. People shouldn't copy not-people, but do you think we should learn to make maps too?'

'I don't think there'd be any harm in it.'

'Good, then. Good. When this is all over and we go back to the obec, we can teach them how to turn the world into lines. But anyway, I looked at the maps, and the grasslands are very, very far from where the three gods are. If they come to us, that will mean all the other land is taken. And people can't live on the big water, can they? So where can we go?'

'Across it. There must be land there somewhere. It's the place your people came from, though you choose not to remember it.'

'We had to forget,' she said. 'We did a great wrong there that caused a lot of death. We forgot how we did it, so we wouldn't do it again.'

In all his time in the obec, no one had ever told him this. 'Why have you never spoken to me about this before?' he asked.

She looked puzzled. 'Why would I? Every baby knows it. It would be like telling you that rain is made of water.'

'Well. Even so, those lands must still be there. The birds fly to them every year, or so we've always supposed. Look, they're doing it now.'

He pointed overhead, where indeed a flight of geese was arrowing over the waters to their unknown destination. Only one bird wasn't following the rest. It was winging low over the land towards them. Not a goose, he saw now. It had the wingspan and the blunt tail of a red hawk. But those birds weren't native to these lands. They were the messenger birds of Ashanesland. So what was one doing here?

Frowning, he watched as it overflew them and headed into the heart of the Rah's territory.

★

He returned from the shore to find everything in a tumult. Finally, it seemed, Bone Dancer was ready to depart. The prospect of leaving Rah territory raised Sang Ki's spirits considerably. And it was clear she wouldn't be leaving empty-handed. There was at least a score of wagons next to her house, harnessed to the huge, splay-legged lizards that the Rah used as beasts of burden. They had flat, evil eyes and wicked teeth.

Bone Dancer stood fearlessly between the beasts and their drovers, directing the packing of goods that, knowing her, she'd acquired at a bargain price. It was only as he came closer that he realised Ensee was also present, standing in the shadows of the house's eaves. She watched the procedure with sharp eyes.

'Your negotiations have been successful, then,' Sang Ki said to Bone Dancer.

Her smile was self-satisfied enough to be its own answer.

Sang Ki's eyes flicked briefly to Ensee. Her gaze seemed to be fixed on him. He could feel the prickle of it when he said, 'I hope our hosts won't be offended when I say I'll be glad to see the back of this land. It's a wonderful place, of course, but the heat and I aren't bosom friends.'

'I'm sorry to hear it,' Bone Dancer said, 'since you'll be staying.'

He laughed, even though he didn't think the joke was funny. He laughed because he was afraid that it *wasn't* a joke, and he hoped that by laughing he could make it one. 'I fear I'd make a very poor emissary for you in these lands,' he said. 'My wits are scrambled by the sun.'

Bone Dancer's expression didn't change, but the steel that was hidden beneath the surface of her affability was clear in her voice as she said, 'And what makes you think you have a choice? I own you, if you recall.'

'Yes, but—' he began.

'*Did* own him,' Ensee said. 'Now he belongs to the Rah. We clasped arms on the arrangement.'

'But you insisted that slavery here is abolished!' Sang Ki protested desperately. 'Only criminals are put in chains, and I've committed no crime.'

Ensee smiled thinly. 'Except for your part in the murder of Bone Dancer's brother. That's crime enough for a life of debt bondage.'

'Don't look so forlorn, kin-killer,' Bone Dancer said. 'You've had three better years than you expected with me, I'm sure. But coin is coin and Ensee offered a richer bargain than I could resist. She must be very keen to own you.'

*

Jalena was very clever about it. She knew the plant-speaker sometimes thought she was a child, a know-nothing and learn-nothing who still understood the world the way she had on the savannah. But she had learned, and she did know. So when the kidnapper said what she said about selling Sang Ki, Jalena kept her words behind her teeth and only watched as he was taken away by two of the Ostatni Ludia. The woman who'd bought him followed them.

That woman was important here. More important even than the conclave of the obec, who were very important indeed. And these were a war people, not a peace people. There'd be many spears and blades protecting the plant-speaker's new kidnapper, and Jalena had nothing bigger or sharper than her knife. She only had that because she'd strapped it to a sheath on her thigh, where they didn't think to search her.

So this was where Jalena was clever. She didn't go after the plant-speaker. She waited a few minutes, for the pack lizards that were a little like tiny house-beasts to waddle into the trees, and then she followed Bone Dancer.

Jalena didn't make the mistake she'd made before. Her own clothes had been filthy after her struggle through the trees to get here, so the not-people had given her their own clothes to wear while hers were washed. They were drab and didn't fit quite right, but she'd seen the way the creatures of the jungle looked away from anyone wearing these clothes. They must have been trained that way, just like food-beasts were trained to stand still for the harvesting.

She couldn't walk quietly in this place. She tried, but the ground was too thick with ugly green leaves and prickly trailers that snagged on her clothes. She snapped a twig with every step. One time she must have stepped on a frog because it let out an enraged croak that nearly made her jump out of her own body. So she kept out of sight and out of earshot of the convoy as she followed it.

It was easy to do. The trees were full of birds and the birds were full of things they wanted to say in very loud voices. And the trees were crowded far too close together. Only grass stalks were meant to stand side by side that way. Jalena didn't understand how anyone could stand to live here, with all that noise and no horizon to look at, but it was a good thing for her.

She knew she needed to wait for night. She'd always had excellent eyes for the dark. She'd been proud of it. She'd known that when it was her turn to be a hunter, she'd be chosen to go out under the moon and hunt the long-nose digging beasts that only came out at night and whose meat was much prized. She would have earned herself a great reputation with all the long-nose beasts she caught. But now she'd left the obec and that would never happen. The thought of never seeing her people again gave her a cold feeling, so she pushed it away.

The kidnapper and her guards stopped before dark. Jalena smelled the smoke of their fire and then of the food they were cooking on it. She hadn't had time to find any of her own and her stomach rumbled almost loud enough to be heard over the birds.

She hunkered down against the trunk of a tree taller than any she'd seen before. It probably needed to be that tall, to poke its head above all the others and see a little sun. The sun itself must have touched the horizon, because dark descended quickly. What had been the clear shapes of trees and bushes quickly became confusing shadows that her mind kept wanting to make into dangers.

But there *was* no danger. Bone Dancer hadn't even left a guard. The people who'd come to handle the burden beasts all slept beside them, huddled shapes in the darkness. One of them was snoring very loudly, louder even than the crunch of twigs beneath Jalena's boots. The beasts turned their heads to watch her approach, but their eyes were sleep-stupid. They didn't make a sound.

The dying embers of the fire showed Jalena the line of wagons and whatever they held that was hidden beneath rough sheets and tied down with ropes. She didn't care about those. It was the lead wagon she wanted. She knew that was where Bone Dancer slept.

She had a nasty moment when she stepped on the footboard of the wagon and it let out an awful creak, like an old woman's joints. But then some hidden creature in the jungle let out an even louder creak and Jalena used the noise of it to hoist herself the rest of the way in.

Bone Dancer was sleeping beneath a sheet and a blanket. Jalena didn't know how she could bear it in the heat. Her head was thrown to the side. In the darkness inside the wagon, it was impossible to see if her eyes were open or shut. For one horrible moment, Jalena thought they were staring straight at her. But then Bone Dancer mumbled and turned half over, twisting herself in the sheet, so everything was all right.

Jalena spent a further moment wondering how she would do this. Her first thought was to rest the knife against Bone Dancer's throat. But what if she moved too fast and Jalena ended up cutting it by mistake? That would be the end of her plans. So she decided just to kneel on the woman's chest and hold the knife in front of her eyes, so she could be very sure Jalena was serious.

Jalena crawled over – the inside of the wagon was very low – then shifted until she could press both knees onto Bone Dancer's chest at the same time, trapping her.

Bone Dancer didn't wake.

Jalena hesitated, not quite sure what to do with someone who could sleep through something like that. But just as she was wondering whether to slap her, Bone Dancer mumbled again, and this time her eyes opened. The whites of them were just visible in the ember light that shone through the wagon's open back.

Bone Dancer was clearly one of those people who woke all at once, and with her thinking sharp. Jalena's uncle was like that. Bone Dancer looked carefully at her, at her knife, and then she said, 'So you've succeeded at last. But I'm afraid you're a little late.'

'No. Not too late. You can free him. You think I'm stupid but I'm not. There's a paper, and you can put your mark on it, and then he'll be free.'

Bone Dancer smiled. It was a bit annoying, how not afraid of Jalena she seemed to be. It was like she didn't think Jalena would really hurt her. Jalena didn't *want* to hurt her if she could avoid it, but Bone Dancer didn't know that. 'It won't do you any good,' Bone Dancer said. 'He's sold already. The deal's done.'

'You still think I'm stupid. I know you sold him already, but what if you didn't own him when you sold him?'

'But I did.'

'Not if you make those marks you make, and one of them says that he's free and one of them says a time that was two weeks ago. Then you can't have sold him.'

Bone Dancer's eyes narrowed, as if she was finally taking Jalena a little seriously. 'If I did it, it would destroy my reputation as a fair dealer. And my reputation is my most valuable coin.'

Jalena shrugged, and now she did bring the knife down to Bone Dancer's throat. 'A dead person has no reputation. They've been forgotten.'

★

Ensee hadn't killed Sang Ki on the spot. He supposed he should be grateful for that, but he suspected she meant to make a spectacle of it. Death, he knew, could be drawn out a long time if the killer chose. He briefly considered ending it more quickly himself, but he knew he wouldn't do it. He'd always been a slave of hope.

He didn't sleep well, which he couldn't blame himself for, in the circumstances. And when the door of the shack in which they'd put him opened the next morning, he was already dressed to greet whatever awaited him.

He hadn't expected what was waiting for him to be Ensee herself. She was alone in the doorway. If she had a weapon, it was concealed. She studied his face, frowning. 'You look like you've sat on a viper.'

He made himself smile. 'No, merely been traded between them.'

Her frown deepened. 'Did you speak this way to your other owner?'

'All the time. That's why I was fool enough to forget what I was to her. I won't be that fool again.'

Finally, her face cleared. 'You think I'm going to kill you.'

'My allies tortured your father. I'm sure you remember; you mentioned it yourself.'

'And I told you that I had him killed.'

'Yes,' Sang Ki said. 'Another reason to suspect you intend for my remaining life to be short. A woman who murdered her own father is hardly likely to balk at killing the stranger who once imprisoned her.'

'My father had to die. The war would never have ended while he was alive. People would have rallied to him. Killing him saved a lot more lives.'

'How very rational.' He studied her. She seemed sincere, but that in itself was troubling. No one should be able to be so rational about such a killing.

'I heard that dream you had, when you took the sorghum,' she said. 'I had people stationed outside the room to listen.'

Of course she had. 'And you take them for the ravings of a lunatic, no doubt.'

She shook her head. 'A messenger bird came from Ashanesland this morning. It wasn't the first. We have people that we pay to send us news, people in every land. They told us that the whole kingdom's fallen in less than a month. And it's said the people who conquered it have cities that fly and bells that can shape metal and glass without forge or fire.'

'Having seen the workings of the former gods, I don't find it hard to believe.'

'Come with me,' she said. 'There's something I want to show you.'

The first place she took him was inside one of the building he'd so wondered at, the huge ones that made the white smoke. Inside, he was no closer to understanding its purpose. There was a contraption, very complicated, made out of metal and oakheart. A part of it was moving up and down, but he couldn't see any people or animals who were doing it.

Yet somehow, at the other end of it, cloth was coming out.

'It's water,' she told him. 'When you heat it, steam comes off.'

'Every child knows that.'

'But not every child knows how to harness the steam like a lizard-mount – how much power there is in it. Only the Rah know that. Come on, there's more I want to show you.'

She took him into building after building. One had a device that made written pages faster than any scribe could copy them. He saw a pile of books already finished and bound in leather. The cover of each said *The New Way* and then Ensee's name. He wondered who they could be meant for. And elsewhere there was a place where the yarn was spun and one where people appeared to be working with a vile, tar-black liquid.

When the tour was finished, he didn't know what he was meant to think or what he could say. He settled for, 'The Rah have a reputation for ingenuity, but I see it was severely understated.'

She smiled for the first time. 'Yes. Our cousin tribes are afraid of new things. We aren't. We know what they're worth. The new gods aren't a threat to people who welcome them. There's so much they could teach us, so many new ways to make things. My people are fast learners, and excellent craftsmen.'

'You mean to treat with the new gods,' he said slowly. 'That's the reason for the birds I've seen flying. You've been talking with them. Negotiating.'

'A rising tide can't be fought. But it can be sailed, in the right boat.'

'I wouldn't say it's wise, but what do you care for my counsel?'

She shrugged. 'I didn't expect you to understand. You're not Rah. You were raised to think the wrong things.'

'Then why did you buy me?' he asked.

'Your cleverness. I want you there with me when we visit them. I know you were an ally of the Hunter, and the sun. I think you know how to deal with gods. And with your visions, perhaps you can teach us how to make gods of our own.'

Her gaze, which had been intent on his, jerked suddenly over his left shoulder. For a moment he thought there must be an attack. But when he turned, it was to see Jalena approaching. He'd thought she might be gone. Hoped it, in fact. He hadn't wanted her to witness his death.

She smiled as she approached. There was a piece of paper in her hand, which she waved under Ensee's nose. 'I've got it! The paper-marks that say he's free. I got them from Bone Dancer, so now you have to let him go.'

Ensee snatched the paper from her hand and frowned at it. Sang Ki risked a peep over her shoulder and, extraordinarily, Jalena appeared to have produced precisely what she claimed she had. A document of manumission, backdated. He wondered what could have possessed Bone Dancer to produce it.

More importantly, would Ensee honour it? That wasn't a question honest Jalena appeared to have considered.

'This says you were a free man when Bone Dancer sold you to me,' Ensee said, still frowning. 'But if that was true, why didn't you tell me?'

'I thought it would mean nothing to you, when I thought you meant to kill me. But now I know your intentions are more honourable, I understand that you'll abide by the laws of trade and decency.'

For one moment their eyes met and held, and he wondered if he'd misjudged her pride. But then she blinked and looked away, as if he'd already been dismissed. 'Go, then. I'll send an embassy without you.'

Jalena grinned triumphantly and Sang Ki smiled shakily back.

He turned to go, hesitated, and then perhaps unwisely turned back to look at Ensee. 'You wanted my counsel?' he said. 'This is it. Gods promise everything, but their gifts are never worth the price. What you and your people have done here is extraordinary. All the more extraordinary because *you* did it, and it took work and thought. A god could do the same in an instant with a wave of their hand. All your achievements, all your work and thought will mean nothing in the shadow of a god's power. Is that truly what you want?'

He didn't stay to watch Ensee's reaction. He took Jalena's arm and walked away.

14

Krish had moments when he wasn't sure if he was waking or dreaming, but those moments had become rarer in the days since they had, he'd been told, come ashore from the floating land on which he'd spent the last three years. The time didn't feel that long to him. It felt like barely more than an eyeblink.

The fisherman who'd found them washed ashore on a desolate beach had given them a home of sorts in a large but ragged tent, leaky and multiply patched. Dinesh lay on a rough straw mattress to Krish's left, far more ill than him. Dae Hyo had lain to his right, vomiting and sweating and sometimes crying out. Krish, in his moments of clarity, had been afraid for his brother, until he'd learned that it was just the drink leaving him. His last dregs of sympathy had drained when he'd also learned Dae Hyo's role in Dinesh's injuries.

And then there was his sister-who-wasn't. She was as weak as Krish, but she'd chosen to leave the hut the moment her legs would hold her upright. Krish wanted to talk to her most of all.

She'd been present in his dream. She'd fled him at first. But after some time there, they'd spoken. She'd told him about what she remembered of her life before, in the city of ice. He'd told her about the goats, and the mountains, and his da – his father too. He'd told her his thoughts about the strange place in which they'd found themselves, his belief that it was the source of every god's power. She'd helped him to make sense of it. They'd shared everything. He thought they'd become friends. Perhaps she could tell him if it had been anything more than a dream.

He understood why she'd fled. It was Eric. She'd told Krish about him, too, about the way he'd come to the servants of Mizhara as one of their husbands, bound to all of them and special to none. Except he'd made himself special to her. He'd deceived her into loving him so that he could use her to escape on Rii's back, taking their newborn son with him, the one that she'd rejected for being a monster, because he'd been born a servant of Yron. Krish didn't know if it was anger at Eric or guilt at her rejection of her own child that tormented her most.

The real world was so full of knots and tangles and problems. Krish wished he could have remained in that other world. But it had been his choice to leave, or that's what he remembered. He remembered, too, that in his dream he'd been sure his body was now in the place it was meant to be, the place where he could do what Sang Ki had asked. He'd known that the task was vital, and urgent. If any of it had been real.

He tried, like he did every morning, to stand. He was weaker than he'd ever been, even in his youth, weaker than a newborn goat. A kid could find its feet within seconds of its birth. Krish had been left gasping for breath merely by sitting up. This time, though, he managed to rise.

He took one wobbly step, and then another. The tent had no windows, but a pale light shone through its canvas. It must be day, maybe early. Dae Hyo, when Krish looked down at him, was asleep. He twitched and mumbled, but didn't wake. Dinesh's eyes were open, staring blankly at the roof of the shack. He didn't look round when Krish shuffled to the entrance.

Krish was glad not to have to talk to him. The first time he'd looked over and seen the rune gone from Dinesh's cheek, he'd known that one memory at least was true. His power was gone. Krish had given it up. And with it, the power he'd had over Dinesh had gone too. The rune on his cheek had *forced* him to love Krish. Krish had done it to save him from bliss, or that's what he'd told himself. Now he was ashamed of the new form of slavery he'd forced on the boy – the man, now. He didn't know what Dinesh would want to say to him, with his mind finally his own. And he had no idea what he'd say in reply.

The sea was very close, sliding up and down the narrow beach, and leaving behind a strange, purple-green weed when it withdrew. The weed had little hard, golden seedpods on its strands. Krish didn't recognise it. He didn't recognise anything.

It was a bleak place. Behind him, the land rose into low hills, covered in close-cropped grass. The white dots of the sheep who'd done the cropping were visible in the distance. There were patches of purple there too. The whole place seemed to have been splashed with the colour. But it was muted by the overcast sky.

A figure was walking towards Krish along the beach, slender and fair-haired. 'Not much to look at, is it?' Eric said when he was close enough.

'Where are we?' Krish asked.

'An island. That's all the cullies here seem to know. They ain't even able to say what land it belongs to. If they sail to the next island over, they reckon they've taken a long trip.'

His words were light, but the tone wasn't one Krish remembered from him. There was an undercurrent of bitterness. His face was also different from the one Krish remembered. He'd been a pretty youth. Now he was a handsome man, but he didn't look like a happy one.

Eric frowned. 'What are you staring at?'

'Sorry,' Krish said. 'It feels like I've jumped from the past into the future. You look very different from what I remember.'

'You and me both.' Eric studied Krish's face. 'Ain't you been shown a mirror yet? I suppose not. Come to think of it, I doubt there's one on the whole island. Come over here and have a gander.'

He led Krish a little further inland, to where a cluster of rocks had trapped some seawater. Eric stood beside Krish as they both looked down into the pool.

Krish's reflected face was dim and rippled. It was also terribly thin, but he'd expected that. He hadn't expected it to be so changed. He looked worn, older than his years. The reflection wasn't clear enough for him to see his own eyes, the moon eyes he'd been born with. Had they been changed when he threw away his godhood?

'Ah, don't worry,' Eric said, seeing Krish's expression. 'Few solid meals will have you looking right as rain again.'

'What about my eyes? Are they . . .?'

'The same. Same for the Hunter. She says our hair grows and our skin gets shed – just like a snake, only not all at once. That's why they can change. But the eyes you're born with are the eyes you'll die with.'

So Krish would always be marked out as different. But then he supposed he was and always would be. He might no longer be a god, but he had been one. That was something only one other person in the world could understand, and she didn't seem to want to talk to him.

Eric touched him cautiously on the shoulder. 'Whatever you're thinking, it probably ain't as bad as all that. Most problems can be fixed. And the ones that can't . . .' His face twisted with a pain Krish didn't understand. 'Well, they ain't worth dwelling on.'

There was a noise behind them, as Dae Hyo stumbled out of the hut. Krish watched him fall to his knees on the water's edge and retch.

'Speaking of unmendable problems,' Eric said.

The bitter look was back on his face, and Krish finally remembered the question he should have asked the first time he and Eric spoke. 'Where's your son? Did you leave him in Ofiklanod?'

It was like a shutter came down over Eric's face. It was completely blank as he said, 'Dead.'

'Oh. I'm sorry. How . . .?' He cut himself off. Why ask the question? It wasn't a wound that needed reopening.

Eric answered it anyway. 'He was flying on Rii's back, when the magic left the world. We was in that great battle – do you remember that? And so I sent him off to be safe.' Eric's smile had absolutely no humour in it. 'Should have remembered, there ain't no safety where gods are concerned.'

Krish had done this, then, without meaning to. It was one more guilt to add to all the rest, though it felt the heaviest of all of them. 'Do you hate me?' he asked.

Eric shrugged. 'Hate's too much effort. I don't care too much about anything these days. I've tried to tell Drut, but she ain't speaking to me, nor listening neither. Course I don't imagine she'll mind too much. She wanted him dead the second he was born.'

'I can tell her, if you want,' Krish said.

Eric shrugged again, and turned his face away. 'Do as you please, you generally have. Only don't call her Drut. That's the name I gave her, and she ain't fond of it.'

*

They took their lunch with the fisherman who'd rescued them, on rough rugs outside his tent. Wherever this place was, life here wasn't so different from the one Krish had been raised to. It was only him, Eric and the Hunter there.

The fisherman's four children were at the meal. They made a shy, silent audience to the conversation. Krish looked at their twig-thin arms and sunken cheeks and thought that these people knew hunger like he once had.

'Thank'ee for the taters,' the fisherman said to the Hunter. He was as thin as his children and so weathered by his work that his age was hard to guess. He was Ashane though, Krish was fairly sure of it.

The Hunter nodded gravely.

'You harvested them?' Krish asked her.

'It was the least I could do for the kindness we have been shown.'

'And for the bream too,' the fisherman said, now looking to Eric.

'I ain't spent the last three years at sea for nothing,' he said, and smiled slightly.

The fisherman's gaze, though, seemed most reserved for Krish.

He kept darting curious glances his way. When he realised that Krish had noticed, he said, 'So we've a fisherman here, and a farmer, and the two as is still resting in my tent are warriors, I've been told. What trade have you?'

'I'm a goatherd,' Krish said, then thought to ask, 'Do you have goats here?'

'Aye, on the bigger isles. I saw one once when I journeyed in my youth. Strange creatures with strange eyes.'

'They're gentle when you know them,' Krish told him.

'You've been asleep a long time, I hear.'

Krish nodded. 'For years. Me and . . . my sister both.' It was only after he said it that he realised how very different they looked. In the dream place he'd felt a genuine kinship with her.

'Your sister?' The fisherman frowned, but then said, 'I reckon things are different on the land.'

Krish guessed by that he meant the mainland. These people were as isolated as his own had been. Would he have once believed that the people of the Ashane lowlands birthed siblings of different races? He didn't know. He felt so very different from the boy he'd been then.

'We have to leave the island,' Krish said, without quite meaning to. The urgency he'd felt at the end of his dream seemed to have followed him into the waking world.

Eric shot him a sharp look and the Hunter a thoughtful one. 'Our host has no boat to spare,' the Hunter said. 'And we have no coin to buy one.'

'Don't you worry,' the fisherman said. 'The Queen's been told of your coming. She asks to learn of all newcomers here. I sent word on the packet boat that takes food between the isles.'

'The Queen?' Krish asked. He hadn't heard of any land that was ruled by one, and he'd travelled a good portion of the world.

The fisherman nodded. 'Aye, she's a hard one, but fair, or so we're told. If you petition her, maybe she'll find a ship for you.'

'And why does your monarch wish to know of every visitor?' the Hunter asked.

The fisherman chewed stolidly, and spoke with food still in

his mouth. 'Because there's some as come here for bad purposes. They come and say these lands belong to them, when the Queen is who we've chosen. Others come to steal our root.'

Eric looked at his plate of tubers. 'They come all that way for these?'

The fisherman laughed. 'Not that root. The other, the purple one that gives you dreams, though not as long as yours.' This was directed to Krish.

'Oh,' Eric said, eyes widening. 'You mean the purple sorghum. There was those in the fair what took it. But then I know where we are. These are the Hundred Islands. They're Ashane.' He looked at Krish. 'Part of your kingdom – I mean to say the one what you come from. But ain't the King here Nayan?'

'There was a king, I think,' the fisherman said. 'But we told him we'd rather our Queen. She'll not harm those who come here in all innocence.'

But just how innocent, Krish wondered, would their group seem to anyone who knew who they really were? And who could this new Queen be, who'd displaced his father?

*

The meal gave Krish enough strength that he felt ready to explore. Though the island didn't offer much in the way of elevation, there was one hill higher than the others and topped by a tumble of rocks. It was hard to tell the position of the sun with the sky so full of clouds, but Krish thought that it was close to setting.

When he reached the summit, he saw that the stones were square and moss-covered, some piled on top of each other, and others lonely in the grass. They might almost have been the ruins of a building, though it would have to be an ancient one. No one would build with stone in a land where the worm men – where Krish's servants – lived beneath the earth. It occurred to him for the first time to wonder if they'd died along with the magic. But he hadn't created them, and it wasn't his actions that had driven them mad. The guilt of that, at least, was a burden he didn't need to bear.

From up here, it was clear how small the island really was.

He could see the full, jagged circle of it. There was nothing even like a village here, just a scattering of other tents exactly like their host's, and rude fishing boats still out to sea, hunting for the flounders and trout that bit in the evening.

Krish walked a circle round the stones, and when he'd nearly finished it, he found her. His sister. Perhaps he'd been looking for her. She was seated on one of the mossy stones. Unlike Krish, her eyes were on her own shoes and not the view. But she looked up at his approach.

'I'm sorry,' he said. 'I didn't mean to disturb you. Do you mind if I sit?'

She gestured, wordless, for him to do so.

He watched her, but she didn't seem like she was about to speak and there were things he wanted to know. 'Do you remember it?' he asked. 'The other world, I mean.'

She hesitated, then nodded.

'We were friends there, I think. Do you remember that too?'

There was a longer hesitation, then she said, 'We were. I didn't ask to be her, and you didn't ask to be him. The things we did to each other, we didn't choose.'

That should have been a relief, but he thought the words weren't really about him. They were about Eric, the one who *had* chosen the harm he did her. 'What Eric did to you was wrong,' Krish said. 'But what your people did to him was wrong too, when they took him as a husband. He didn't have a choice to come to the ice. And once he was taken there, all the choices left to him were bad ones.'

'He could have submitted to the Oroborus,' she said fiercely. 'That was the right thing to do.'

'Was it? You've been Mizhara now. A part of you still is, the way a part of me is still Yron. Do you think the law you lived by was right? You were only given bad choices as well.'

Finally she smiled, tentatively. 'I remember why I forgave you, in the dream.'

'I've got something to tell you,' he said, reluctantly. 'It might upset you. Or . . . it might not.'

'My son is dead,' she said. Then, at Krish's startlement, 'I looked out of that place through Eric's eyes many times in my first year there. I heard him speak of it.'

'And . . . how *do* you feel?' Krish asked cautiously.

'I don't know. For all my life in Salvation I was taught to feel nothing but love for Mizhara. And then, when Eric came, he tricked me into loving him. So I became Mizhara. And when I was her, I felt nothing except hatred for you. I've never felt any of the in-between feelings. I don't know what they are.' She turned to pin him with her golden eyes. 'Will you teach me, brother?'

He took her hand, pale and white now where once it had been gold, and threaded her fingers through his. 'Of course. Would you like me to give you a name, to replace your other one?'

She smiled. 'Yes, I'd like that very much.'

'Thilini,' he said. 'It is . . . it was my ma's name. I remember searching for her, when I was in that place. I looked for her eyes and I never found them. But if we'd really both been born of her, maybe she'd have given you her name.'

'Thilini,' she said – and then her words cut off as she stood abruptly. She was looking out to sea, using her hand to shade her eyes from the diffuse light of the clouded sun.

'What is it?' Krish asked.

'Boats, three of them. Galleys.'

'Galleys? Those are big, aren't they? Bigger than any fishing boat here.'

'These are war boats,' she said, still staring at the horizon.

They retraced their path as quickly as they could, through the rocks and back down the hill. But the ground was rough and the going slow. The galleys were perilously near shore by the time Krish reached it.

They found everyone in the tent the fisherman had given them. Dae Hyo was pale but sitting up and drinking broth. Dinesh was awake too, his back turned to Dae Hyo. When Krish walked in beside his sister – Thilini now – Eric tensed but didn't flee. Thilini's gaze only swept over him to settle on the Hunter.

'Three warships are approaching,' Thilini said. 'I saw the gleam of metal on them. I believe there are warriors aboard.'

'They are coming for us,' the Hunter declared.

Eric shook his head. 'Ain't necessarily so. We don't know who else is on this island. Could be a fugitive what's wanted by this Queen of theirs.'

'We are the only newcomers here that I have heard of,' the Hunter said.

Dae Hyo turned his haggard face to Eric to add, 'I tell you what, with the luck we've had, we're bound to be their quarry.'

'Half the bad luck we've had was courtesy of you!' Eric snapped.

But it very soon became clear that Dae Hyo and the Hunter were right. After not many minutes, they heard the shouts of the sailors as they prepared to beach their boats. They couldn't have been more than a moment's walk from the tent where they were all huddling.

'We should run,' Krish said.

Dinesh turned to him, his expression unreadable. 'To, to, to where? We're on an island.'

'We could hide, then.'

'Where, brother?' Dae Hyo asked. 'Svarog's cock, I may be weak but I'll not run or hide like a child. Where's my sword?'

'You sold it for drink a year ago,' Eric said.

And then it all became irrelevant anyway, as the flap of the tent swung open.

There must have been at least a dozen warriors crowded behind the first. They were Ashane, but they weren't wearing the uniforms that Krish had seen on his father's men. These were black, and they had a crescent moon for a crest. He took a step back into shadows, not sure what it meant.

The troop leader's eyes touched him. 'You,' he said, then his gaze moved until it was on Eric, 'and you will come with us.'

Dae Hyo moved to stand in front of Krish. 'They won't take a step until you tell us what this is about.'

'If one goes, we all go,' the Hunter said. She, unlike Dae Hyo, seemed to have no intention of fighting, though she was in a better condition for it. Krish was glad. He'd seen enough spilled blood to last for all his remaining years.

The troop leader studied them all, then shrugged. 'Very well then, let you all come. We're bound for the Graveyard. And then the Queen can say what she wants done with you.'

15

Bruyar's island tribe sailed the ship competently, even through the storm that blew over them on their fourth day at sea. Olufemi stayed inside for it, unlike the contents of her stomach, and when she finally dragged herself out of her hammock and on deck the next morning, it was to find only one sail torn and a few spars snapped. The spars were repaired and the journey wore on, but the further they travelled, the more Olufemi's patience with Bruyar's secrecy about their destination wore thin.

'Wherever you mean to take us, we need to find land soon,' she told *omas*, standing by the wheel of the ship on the seventh day. The waters were slack at present and the wheel had been roped into position.

'How fortunate we have you aboard to tell me so,' Bruyar said scathingly.

Olufemi bit her lip to stop her sharp reply. The sailors looked to Bruyar and not to her. They wouldn't balk at throwing her overboard if Bruyar ordered it.

'We've been drifting eastwards,' she said, as pleasantly as she could. 'The currents all tend that way at this time of year.'

'La, I'm no navigator, as perhaps you've observed, but even I can see the position of the morning sun. I'm aware of our course.'

'You *mean* to sail east? But why? What do you think you'll find there?'

'It surprises me that one so well travelled as you doesn't know,' Bruyar said.

'Of course I know!' Olufemi snapped. 'The lands that the Ashane and the Moon Forest folk and the tribes once came from lie to the east, the place they once called the Motherlands. But they fled for a reason, though no one remembers it. There are no maps of the land, no knowledge. We don't even know if we'll find a harbour.'

'There are no maps that *you* have seen, my dear.'

'Bruyar, what have you not been telling me?'

'Oh, a very great deal,' Bruyar said. 'Did you never wonder why I first thought three gods could be made in place of two?'

'You told me you sought three because of the stability a base of three provides. Two can only ever be in opposition.'

'Yes. But if two were all there'd ever been, why would I believe any other configuration was possible?'

'Because it's been done before, is that what you're saying? Were there three gods in this land? Are these the people that ours learned the making of gods from?' Now that Olufemi said it, it seemed obvious. She'd made Krish in imitation of what came before. She'd never thought to question what Yron and Mizhara might have been created to mirror.

'Yes,' Bruyar said, 'that was the source of the idea. You Exiles of Nkankan-lati-Ohunkohun took the knowledge of the runes with you when you fled our lands, a millennium ago, but did you really think you took it all? There were certain books, very ancient, that my agents found in the City Below. The Ashane and the tribes and the Moon Forest folk all came to our lands, but the people of the savannah came before them, and they brought their god with them. Just one god, Olufemi – the first.'

'But that god is gone, long gone. Surely you can't mean to resurrect them?'

'La, 'tis not the resurrection that interests me. It's the reverse. How was the first god got rid of to make way for the moon and sun? If we can learn that, perhaps we can learn how the Three may be disposed of too.'

'It's a very slender hope to have brought us all this way.'

Bruyar's expression was entirely unreadable. 'It's the only hope we have. My own home is closed to us. The Ashane lands, as you so astutely observed, are likely to be hostile. And the tribes of the far north are said to eat those who trespass on their territory. But on the unexplored continent to the east, who knows what we might find? Thrilling, isn't it? Don't tell me you've lost your thirst for adventure, Olufemi. I won't believe it.'

Olufemi had lost it entirely, sometime after she'd first met Krishanjit. But she didn't see any benefit in saying so.

And, on their ninth day after leaving the island, they finally sighted a dark line on the horizon that could only be land. A few hours later, when they'd drawn nearer, Olufemi began to make out the shape. There were buildings, clustered on a promontory. She swept her eyes over the waters, but she couldn't see a single other vessel afloat. For the first time in a long time, she felt a burn of excitement. She'd always been a woman who sought out the novel and the strange. It had been, in many ways, her undoing. But what could be more novel or more strange than this?

Not much later, Bruyar came to join her on the deck. The coastline had grown clearer by then. Olufemi could see that the city was vast, at least a hundred times the size of Mirror Town. And in the heart of it there was a building far larger than all the rest and constructed in the shape of a pyramid. Its sides shone bright white in the sunlight, with geometric traceries of what looked like gold on patches here and there.

'Well,' Bruyar said. 'What sort of welcome do you think we'll find here?'

Olufemi frowned as she studied the place. They were near enough now to begin making out its streets, but like the waters around it, they seemed to be empty. Some of its buildings were tumbled into ruins. 'No welcome at all. Can't you see this place is deserted?'

'Perhaps, or perhaps merely fallen from greatness. I'd always wondered why no more invaders came to our lands from these. The tribes were the last and they sailed the other ocean hundreds of years ago. I wonder if this was why.'

Olufemi couldn't tear her eyes away from the nameless city. Some of the distant shadows in the streets seemed to move as she watched. 'When great things die, smaller and more savage things often come to feast.'

'Indeed,' Bruyar said. 'Just as well, then, that our sailors have brought their bows and spears.'

*

As soon as a gangplank was put to shore, the sailors rushed across it. Bruyar shouted something to them in their own tongue, but whatever it was, they didn't listen. Olufemi was amused to watch their lurching gait. Several of them fell. Sea legs were another thing they'd had no prior experience of.

The heat here was intense. Bruyar mopped *omas* brow with a cloth as *oms* and Olufemi walked across the dock. There were large but rough buildings on its far side. Olufemi guessed they were warehouses. If they'd ever had doors, they'd long since crumbled to dust. It was impossible to say what goods had once been stored there.

'Where should we go?' she asked.

'Why, we must introduce ourselves to those in power,' Bruyar said, 'or else risk being taken for invaders.'

Olufemi nodded, even though they'd yet to see evidence this city had any inhabitants, let alone rulers. 'That building, then.' She nodded over at the marble-faced pyramid. It towered above the skyline of the city, even though by her reckoning it was at least a mile from the docks. It must be vast.

The streets they walked through at first were narrow and the houses that lined them tall and crudely built. If they'd been made of wood instead of brick, they wouldn't have looked out of place at Smiler's Fair. In the third street they walked down, Olufemi stopped to peer through the missing door of one of the houses.

It took a moment for her eyes to adjust to the gloom, but slowly, the wreckage of tables and chairs resolved from the darkness. And, sitting on one of the chairs, a shrivelled corpse. She jerked back, shocked.

'What is it, dearest?' Bruyar asked.

'It seems not all the inhabitants here fled.'

Bruyar looked inside, but didn't flinch. 'Perhaps invaders came unexpectedly and slaughtered them. Invaders frequently do.'

'Perhaps,' Olufemi said.

They saw more dried-out corpses as they progressed through the city. Most were inside their homes, but a few lay scattered on the streets. In other climates they might have been disjointed bones, but here the dry heat seemed to have mummified them almost intact. They were whole enough for it to be clear that none were carrying weapons. It was possible they'd rusted away with the untold years since their deaths, but Olufemi didn't think so. She felt an uneasiness she couldn't explain. Bruyar seemed not to share it. But then Bruyar's face was hard to read.

After some while they came to a high wall with an arched gateway in it. This seemed to mark the boundary of the poorer district. Beyond it, the buildings had plastered sides, many of them covered with tiny, coloured stones. Olufemi saw images of warriors in metal armour, the metal enamelled and painted with flowers. The style was nothing she recognised, but the people themselves were more familiar.

Bruyar stopped to look at a mural that appeared to show two lovers, twined together in bed. Their faces were both turned towards the observer, as if they'd been caught in the act. 'Pale-skinned, but not one of the Moon Forest folk,' Bruyar said. 'These are the ancestors of the savannah tribes.'

'They appear to be.' Olufemi felt a sharp twinge of something that wasn't quite grief. Guilt perhaps. The woman in the mural had a face very like Vordanna's.

'If they came from here, they would have landed in the east. And yet they've made their home in the far west of our lands. Why not settle where they first came ashore, I wonder?'

There were many images of two particular figures, both wearing jewel-encrusted robes. There was little to distinguish them, aside from the fact that one seemed male and the other female. But after a while, Olufemi noticed that the man was always shown with a circlet of leaves around his forehead. The woman always held a spear. Frequently she was shown in a chariot and the spear was being thrown at a tiger, whose like Olufemi had once seen in the Menagerie of Smiler's Fair.

Beyond this district was another high wall, curving to encircle the innermost area of the city. This one was covered in a flaking but startlingly bright blue paint. Once they'd passed through it, they found themselves walking through broad streets and past marble-faced houses of enormous size.

'My children would love this place, I think,' Bruyar said.

'You have children?' Bruyar had never once mentioned them.

'Eight of them. Three birthed of my body and five of my wife's. Ah, I see I've shocked you. You wonder how I could have left them behind.'

Olufemi *had* been wondering that, and how any parent could have murdered those other children so easily, but she didn't think it wise to say so. 'They weren't in the Cinderlands, were they?' she asked instead.

Bruyar shook *omas* head. 'I left them safe in Täm. I love my husband dearly, but he's a man with very firm principles. He wouldn't have cared for my work if he'd seen it. And my wife is an innocent. I thought it best not to shock her with the truth of my research. And when the new gods came . . . I knew they'd be safer without me. No, don't give me your pity, Olufemi. I don't care for it.'

Olufemi thought of Vordanna, whom she hadn't quite loved, but had certainly cared for and also left behind. 'I'm sorry it became necessary for you to part from them,' she said cautiously.

Bruyar smiled, the brief melancholy shrugged off. 'The situation was entirely of my own making, though you've been too kind to say it.'

The islanders had been following behind, cautious-eyed and whispering among themselves. But now one of them gave a glad cry and ran towards the courtyard of the nearest building. It had grown wild long ago, but Olufemi saw that there were still fruit trees there, with ripe fruit on them. The islanders' sullenness dissolved as they filled their mouths with it. It had been many days since they'd had fresh food.

The trees in that courtyard couldn't feed them all, but there were other courtyards as they progressed, and more trees. Bruyar spoke sharply to them, but they didn't listen. After the third time of being ignored *oms* sighed and said, 'Well, it won't hurt to have them well fed if we venture out of the city. And bringing a guard with us to see the ruler here might be taken amiss.'

'If there *is* a ruler here. Bruyar, surely you can't believe we'll find anyone in that palace? This is a city of the dead.'

'We can't be sure until we visit it.' Bruyar's eyes were bright, and Olufemi realised that *oms* felt the lure of the novel just as strongly as Olufemi. The pair of them were more alike than she enjoyed. It was painful to see her reflection in a child-murderer. But then, was what Olufemi had done to bring her own god into the world any less shameful?

And then, at last, they reached their destination. Each face of the building was a triangle with their tips meeting at its top. It looked like a vast, half-buried jewel made of marble.

The ground around it had been paved for fully five hundred paces. The heat of the sun-warmed stones was intense even through the soles of Olufemi's shoes. And she saw many dark slits in the side of the building where archers could sit. This would be a very hard place to take by force of arms. Her shoulders stiffened at the thought of those arrows finding her, but no attack came as they crossed the paving. And when they reached the huge, wooden doors of the place, carved all over with images of tigers and leaves, they were hanging open. She and Bruyar exchanged a look, then stepped through.

There was no living person inside. She'd known by now there wouldn't be. But there were corpses, and some of these were armed. Their rusted swords and the tips of their spears lay beside them, the wood of their hafts no doubt rotted away long ago. Even so, Olufemi didn't think they'd died in battle. There was no other sign of violence in the building, no burn marks or blood stains. But as they climbed the stairs from floor to ever more opulent floor, there were many more bodies.

It was, she realised, a little like the fields outside the Garden of Yron that she and Yemisi had once walked through. They had been full of corpses too, although those had been fresh. She'd eventually learned what had killed them: the meeting of two irreconcilable magics. Had the same thing happened here? But what magics might these lands have held?

'What extraordinary wealth,' Bruyar said, pausing to run *omas* eyes and then *omas* fingers along the plates and knives and cups still set on a marble table. They all appeared to be made of solid gold.

'It doesn't seem to have done them much good,' Olufemi said.

Bruyar turned away from the table. 'No indeed.'

On the seventh floor, or perhaps the eighth, they found the map room. The war room, Olufemi thought, when she studied its layout more thoroughly. There was a central table ringed by chairs, and on the table a model of the world, two continents facing each other across an ocean of lapis lazuli. Like so much else here, it was made of gemstones and precious metal: gold for the deserts, and jasper for the mountains, which had been sculpted into peaks and valleys to match, she supposed, the contours of the land.

One continent, the eastern one, had been rendered in far more detail than the other. Olufemi was sure it must depict the land in which they currently found themselves. There was a strange, rounded script carved into the model here and there. Names, perhaps, but Olufemi couldn't read them. It was no language she'd seen before.

There were small models of ships too, and soldiers, scattered around the map. Olufemi had seen something similar in King Nayan's chambers, when she'd still been in his favour. This was how he'd planned his skirmishes, when he'd been putting down a minor rebellion in the south. But it wasn't the toy soldiers or the jewels and precious metals that interested her; it was the map itself.

'It's not hard to guess which city this is,' Bruyar said, pointing at the coast of the eastern continent.

The tiny model houses clustered round a bay were the exact shapes of the ones they'd just walked past. On the promontory, the building in which they stood was reproduced in miniature, although on this model the geometric golden inlay covered the whole structure.

But it was the other shore that drew Olufemi's eyes, the western one, on the far side of the lapis lazuli ocean. There was another building shown there, the mirror of the one they were currently climbing. But alone of all the structures on the map, it was made from base material, not precious. It appeared to be brick, as if a primitive attempt had been made to copy the wonder of the original.

She ran her fingers along the contours of the coast on which the building sat. 'According to the map, this lies west across the ocean from here – it should be Ashanesland. But the shape of the shoreline is all wrong.'

Bruyar's fingers traced another path, a little inland from that coast, where the ground began to rise. 'The Ashane call the waters around the Hundred Islands the "Inland Sea", I believe.'

It took Olufemi a moment to realise what *oms* meant. 'You think the land was drowned. The coastal plain flooded to become the Inland Sea, and what was left above the waters became the Ashanesland we know.' She looked again at the map. The border of the plain did indeed match the borders of present-day Ashanesland. 'Yes, I think you may be right. I wonder what could have caused such a flood.'

'Only time, perhaps. Our oldest records show that the land was cooler once than it is now. Why, there are records of snow in Nesevadan, centuries ago. The world is not as unchanging as we think. 'Tis strange to think, is it not, of such a monumental building as that lying beneath the waves that wash up on Ashanesland?'

They left the map behind and returned to the stairs. And when they finished the climb, they found two bed chambers. Each was the size of a house. The walls of the first were covered in paintings of trees and flowers – no, not paintings. Every image was made out of jewels. All the wealth of Mirror Town in its prime couldn't have paid for half of them. This must surely be the place where the man or god in all those images had lived. But the room was empty. Its inhabitant hadn't died here.

The second room just as clearly belonged to the second figure. The walls were embossed with figures of tigers made of a metal that was surely pure gold. And this room wasn't empty. The corpse wasn't on the bed like so many of the others had been. It was huddled in one corner of the room. Olufemi thought she must have been standing or perhaps kneeling when she died. When Olufemi looked closer, she saw a sword, caught between two of the body's ribs. It was possible that she alone in this city had died by violence, but Olufemi guessed that it was by her own hand.

Beyond the corpse was a balcony. It offered an extraordinary view of the bay and the harbour and the sprawling, beautiful, empty city.

'What could have brought so great an empire low?' Bruyar asked.

Nothing that Olufemi wanted to encounter, she was sure at least of that. 'We should sail on,' she said. 'If we hug the coast, we might find a friendlier harbour. And with the fruit from the courtyards and our unspoiled rations we'll be able to keep to the water for a week, if we need to.' She had no desire to make landfall in any other places like this one.

'No, wait,' Bruyar said. 'Over there – do you see it, or are my eyes deceiving me?'

Olufemi followed *omas* pointing arm past the harbour and along the tree-fringed coast to their north.

'Is there another city?' she asked. 'I don't see it.'

'Not a city.' Bruyar's voice was tight with excitement. 'A ship. And I swear I see people by it. There, by the grove of red-gold trees beneath the highest peak.'

Olufemi looked again and yes. Yes! Bruyar was right. She laughed with a sudden, giddy relief. 'You have sharp eyes, Bruyar.'

'The design is nothing I recognise,' Bruyar said, 'and I've had spy reports from all across our lands, even as far distant as the Moon Forest. I think these must be people of the Motherlands.'

'If we find them,' Olufemi said, 'we can ask them.'

*

Their return journey was far quicker. The riches they'd marvelled at on the way up had become commonplace to them, and of far less value than other living people. They soon came to a street that Olufemi recognised, lined with pillars made of a marble that was oily black, almost pearlescent. She and Bruyar had walked down it when they first parted from the crew.

'Down here,' she said.

It was only as she turned the corner that she noticed quite how silent it was. Had the islanders gone back to the ship without her and Bruyar? Had they sailed without them?

She glanced around the street and saw the fruit trees she'd remembered but no sign of the crew. Worry gnawed at her – then turned to shock, when she finally realised where all of them were. She shouldn't have been looking around, but down.

Two of them were in the courtyard to her left. She hadn't seen them because their bodies were half-buried in the grass. She allowed herself to hope that they were merely sleeping. But when she crouched down to touch their necks, she felt no pulse. One of them had a virulent green froth around his mouth. The other had fallen with the peach she'd picked still half-eaten in her hand.

'Poison,' Bruyar said. 'It can be nothing else.'

'Perhaps this tree was tainted in some way,' Olufemi said. 'We need to find the rest.'

'Yes. They'll be close by, gorging themselves without a care, no doubt.' Olufemi could hear in Bruyar's voice that *oms* no more believed *omas* own words than Olufemi did.

It didn't take long to find the others. Five were in the same street, lying lifeless beneath the apple trees they'd plucked bare. They found another single dead islander in the shadow of what appeared to be a plum tree. After the fourth group, a little further on, lay dead with the figs they'd eaten smeared around their mouths, Olufemi stopped looking.

Her earlier question, she thought, had been answered. Now they knew precisely what had killed all the people of this fabulously wealthy empire.

16

Renar and Lanalan had fled Delta's Strength. No one tried to stop them, no doubt because the invasion they were currently undergoing had taken precedence. As a servant of King Nayan, Renar should perhaps have stayed to fight for his realm, but she'd never handled a weapon and she didn't feel she would have contributed much to the shipfort's defence.

What had that great, floating thing been? Even now, days later, Renar couldn't begin to guess. But only a day after it had arrived, it had begun to send out other vessels. They'd been of a more reasonable size. The largest had the dimension of one of the Ashane mammoths, if those mammoths had somehow learned to fly. And it soon became clear that these outrider forces were heading north-west. Their destination must be Ashfall. Along the way, wherever they saw armed people on the road, soldiers descended to overpower them.

So Renar had been forced to revise her plans. There would be no point in racing to warn King Nayan. The danger would clearly arrive before they could. Nor was that the worst thing. On one occasion, Renar had been close enough to see the faces of these airborne soldiers. The invasion force appeared to be composed entirely of Ofiklanders.

It was baffling. When Renar and Lanalan had left their homeland, it had been in a shambles. The power of the sun was gone, Täm was in ruins, and the Mortals who should have led them through this trouble had fled. How had Ofiklanod gone from *that*, to this? Renar could think of only one answer: it must be Bruyar's doing. And Bruyar wanted Renar dead.

The invading forces were focused on the richest, inland areas of Ashanesland. In their efforts to avoid them, Renar and Lanalan had been driven to its marshy rim.

'La,' Lanalan said, 'this land lacks charm. Renar, if we continue much longer this way, we'll be in the ocean.'

'I know,' she snapped. He made a pleasant enough travelling companion in good times. In bad, he was more vexing. 'We're making for Fell's End. If any shipfort remains unconquered, it will be that one. It sits in the centre of a swamp and has almost nothing to recommend it. And it lies east even of Delta's Strength. If I were leading an invasion force, I wouldn't spare the people to take it, at least not in my first offensive.'

'But you aren't leading the force. What if whoever does is less wise than you?'

'Then we'll carry on,' she said grimly. 'Unless you have a better plan?'

He shook his head, of course. She couldn't argue with him about the charmlessness of the terrain. They were on the outer edge of the swamp, where there were many small hillocks of dry land to walk on. There were also many muddy channels to cross, and both she and Lanalan were filthy from the waist down. The smell was vile. Some miasma seemed to be released by the waters here that resembled the output of a troubled bowel.

Lanalan smiled sunnily at her. 'I'm sorry to complain, Renar. You haven't led us astray yet. We haven't seen one of those flying houses for more than two days now.'

She was reminded, once again, why she loved her sib. 'That's true. And look – I believe that may be Fell's End on the horizon. Do you see? A brown structure on the largest of the lakes.'

'What if the invaders are already there?'

'The skies are clear,' she said. 'We'll keep our eyes sharp as we approach, but I think we may finally have found our refuge.'

'Who's lord here? Is he an ally of King Nayan's?'

''Tis a lady, not a lord. Imesha. She has a reputation as a hard and ruthless woman. Both those qualities seem desirable in the current circumstances.'

*

After another hour's trudging they were at the borders of the lake on which Fell's End sat. The only way to reach the shipfort was by boat, which a small amount of haggling procured them. It sat so low in the water that they were drenched with every oar stroke.

'Do you ever wonder,' she asked Lanalan, 'at how far we've fallen in these last years?'

'Not at all. We're on an adventure, so we must expect some hardship. And imagine the tales we'll have to tell when it's done. We'll be the toast of Täm.'

'Täm isn't currently at its peak. 'Tis in fact a ruin.'

'It was a ruin. But it must have been rebuilt, mustn't it, for our lands to have launched an invasion like this? We'll be returning home one day soon, Renar. I know it.'

Once upon a time, she would have scorned him for his naivety. These days she found a certain comfort in clinging to his unshakeable optimism, when she had so little of her own.

And despite her pessimism, they were allowed inside the fort with very little persuasion and taken to meet the Lady Imesha in her receiving room.

Renar had met the woman before. She had a glancing acquaintanceship with nearly all of Nayan's vassals. Imesha's long grey hair had shaded a little further towards white since Renar had last seen her, but her expression was as sharp as ever.

The chamber they'd been brought to was plain and functional. Nothing in it seemed designed to impress. Even the rug was threadbare. This might have spoken of poverty, but Renar suspected it spoke instead of a woman so secure in her power she felt no need to demonstrate it.

Imesha eyed the pair of them in thoughtful silence for a long moment, before saying, 'So, Nayan's foreigners have come to me. How unexpected.'

'I hope you'll forgive us for our unannounced visit,' Renar said. 'We come bearing grave news.'

'The invasion?' Imesha smiled thinly at Renar's surprise. 'News travels faster than you, it seems.'

'But not the enemy?' Lanalan glanced around the room as if invaders might be hidden in its darkest corners.

'Who would want to conquer these lands?' Imesha asked.

It was precisely what Renar herself had been thinking, but even so it made her uneasy. She noticed that Imesha had neatly avoided answering the question.

Imesha fixed her eyes on Renar. 'Ashfall itself has fallen, did you know?'

'We suspected. And King Nayan?'

'Fled. It seems word of the invaders reached him before he could be taken. So, have you come to beg for soldiers for your fugitive King? Let me be honest with you: I'm not inclined to offer any. The Oak Wheel did little enough to help us while Nayan still held it. I can't see any benefit to aiding him now power is out of his hands.'

'We don't ask for aid,' Renar said. 'Only shelter.'

'Ah, a selfish motive then.'

Renar chose not to be affronted by the criticism. 'And will you provide us it, my Lady?'

'You may stay if you desire,' Imesha said.

★

They were each given rooms of reasonable comfort. Renar knew that she and Lanalan should discuss their position and their options. She trusted Imesha as little as she liked her, but the last few days had exhausted her, and she took to her bed instead.

In the morning a servant woke her, then lowered her eyes when Renar groaned, rose and began to dress. Renar always found the meekness of the Ashane servants disturbing. She was even more troubled by the way in which the shipborn were so unnaturally able to ignore them. It was as if they saw those lower born than them as objects rather than people.

When Renar was ready, she was led to a meagre breakfast with Lanalan.

'Well,' he said, as he polished off the last withered slice of apple, 'if this is to be our new life, 'tis not too unpleasant.'

'We can't stay here,' Renar said.

'Whyever not?'

Because she'd very much disliked Imesha's smile. But the servants were still in the room and she, unlike the Ashane, could never forget their presence nor who they'd be reporting to. As if summoned by Renar's thoughts, a moment later Lady Imesha herself walked in.

'Good, you've eaten,' she said. 'I don't like guests to leave me on an empty stomach.' Then she stepped aside to reveal the four men of Ofiklanod who'd been standing behind her.

Renar's stomach made a very strong effort to return her breakfast to her. 'But why? Why betray your country?'

'Have you not heard? There are new gods to replace your moon.'

'From Ofiklanod?' Lanalan asked, incredulous.

Imesha shrugged. 'From Ofiklanod and from the Moon Forest and thirdly from these lands. Lucky for me, the third is well known to me. In his mortal days, he was my son.'

'Your *son*?' Renar said incredulously.

'Gods are born of woman before they become divine. And Marvan was born right here. As a consequence, he's given orders for my lands to remain untouched. The least I can do in return is send him one who'll soon be plotting against him, if left to her own devices. I know your reputation.' She nodded at Renar and then at the soldiers. 'You may take them now.'

'You,' the frontmost said to Renar and Lanalan in their own language, 'you'll come with us. The God-Triumvir wishes to speak to you.'

★

They were marched upwards through the shipfort. As ever in this place, the decaying smell of the marsh accompanied them. Lanalan looked at Renar as if he wished to say something. He was twisting his hands together as he'd done in his youth when he knew he'd displeased their parents and was anticipating his punishment. But for once in her life, Renar had nothing to say.

God-Triumvirs? Was it a new scheme of Bruyar's? Was *oms*

one of this new Triumvirate? But it didn't seem like Bruyar's style to step so firmly out of the shadows. Besides, what to make of this Ashane shiplord who apparently now held sway in Ofiklanod? That felt very little like something Bruyar would do, either.

Renar studied their guards as discreetly as she could. Her first impression had been of normality. They were bare-chested and white-skirted in the manner of Ofiklanod men. But now she looked closer, she saw that each had a piercing in his left ear. Every man wore the same earring, too: a little charm made out of three bells. If Renar listened very closely, she heard their tinkle. It was an odd sound. It seemed to make her head buzz, and she quickly stopped listening for it.

Was this some new Ofiklanod fashion? Her people had always been servants to it. But the instinct for trouble that had served her so well over the years told her it was more than that.

When they reached the shipfort's highest floor, their guards opened a hatch in the ceiling and placed a step-ladder to climb higher still. It was clearly a move they were familiar with. Renar thought they must be frequent visitors here. What a fool she'd been.

On the roof, she craned her neck and gasped. She'd been expecting one of their smaller air vessels, but it was the monstrosity they'd seen above Delta's Strength that floated less than twenty paces above the highest tower. Renar had to stop herself instinctively ducking. It was so impossible that something so big could stay in the sky that her mind only seemed able to understand it as being in the process of falling.

Nothing but its base was visible, almost blotting out the sky. It was made of some curious matt grey metal that wasn't lead. The whole thing appeared to have been cast in one vast sheet of it. Renar couldn't see a join anywhere. She couldn't even see a flaw. There was a vibration in the air around it, so deep it was more feeling than sound.

'There must indeed be new gods to have made such a thing,' Lanalan said.

A hatch opened in the metal, where no seam had been visible. The stairs that were lowered from it were, reassuringly, ordinary rope. Renar struggled to climb them. Her limbs had been weakened by fear.

There was a short tunnel, sloping up, and then they emerged into air and sunshine.

Their guards allowed them a few moments to stare in shock. They were, improbably, in a city. There were houses and streets and carts pulled by oxen. For a disoriented second, Renar wondered if she'd returned to Smiler's Fair, but these houses were far less ramshackle. The people walking the streets were very different too. There were hundreds of them, strangely silent. Smiler's Fair had been a jubilantly noisy place. These people were all, she saw, wearing the same belled earrings as their guards. They were all Ofiklanders too.

There *was* one sound, reverberating ceaselessly through the place. It was so omnipresent it took Renar a little while to locate its source. It was only when she looked up that she saw another structure, also metal and as round as the sun, but with an opening on its lowest side. And suspended at the very highest point of the city, beneath that opening, were a dozen vast bells. Renar couldn't begin to guess how the whole thing worked, but she was sure that in some way those bells were the means by which the city flew.

Lanalan, she realised, was staring across, not up. The road they were on ran straight, but ended two hundred paces away in simple blue. The horizon here was very close with only empty sky beyond it. What must it feel like, to live so high and so precariously?

They were marched quickly through the streets towards a tower that broke the skyline not very far away. The shape of it looked familiar. As they approached its door, Renar realised why. It had the same flared base and tapered top as the windmills of Vien. It was even made of a similar white ceramic. Only the amber lacquered vanes were missing.

Here, for the first time, there was an ordinary babble of voices.

As she and Lanalan were marched along a broad corridor that spiralled upwards around a central hollow in the building, people stopped to stare. They weren't wearing earrings. Was that the reason they were so much more lively? On the journey from Täm to the sea, Dae Hyo had explained about the rune that had once bound the boy Dinesh to Krish's service. Did these bells function in something like the same way?

Finally, they reached the doors that led to the very uppermost chamber. They were ceramic, too. White vines twined around a white tree on each door, all with threefold leaves.

Renar looked at Lanalan again. Her sib smiled at her. 'Beautiful, isn't it?'

The door opened before she could reply, and they were pushed in. There was one figure inside, seated on a white throne. Renar tried to keep her surprise from her face. The figure on the throne was inter, but little more than a child, and no one at all that Renar recognised.

Their guards all bowed so low, the tight curls of their hair brushed the ground. 'The emissaries of King Nayan,' their leader said.

'Why, they're two of our people!' the inter replied, peering at them. 'I thought you were bringing me godlanders. Oh, but I shouldn't call them that now, should I? Well don't just stand there, bring them closer.' *Omas* voice was very young too, as was the open expression on *omas* face.

Renar chanced a bow, then said, 'I'm very glad to meet you, but I fear there's been a mistake. My sib and I *were* in the King's employ, but we parted—' She cut off, as the inter leaned forwards suddenly.

'I know you, don't I?' *oms* said.

'I don't believe we've met. This is my sib, Lanalan, and I'm Renar—'

'Renar the Fox!' the inter exclaimed. *Oms* looked unexpectedly delighted. 'I've read so many news-sheets about you. There was even one with a picture, although . . . I don't think your eyes were yellow then.'

'You mustn't believe all that you read in the sheets. The scoundrels who write them don't have an honest bone in their bodies. I should know – I've bribed enough of them.'

The inter clapped *omas* hands in delight, looking even more childlike. How *had* this person come to this power? Krish had been young too when he was a god, but he'd never seemed a tenth this innocent.

'You're exactly as I expected you to be!' *oms* said. 'The newssheets didn't lie at all. But what are you doing in this place? And dressed in those ridiculous robes, just as if you're one of *them*?'

'God-Triumvir, what would you like us to do with them?' their guard asked.

'Leave them with me, of course,' the inter said. 'They're going to work with me – why, nothing will be beyond me, if I have Renar the Fox guiding me.' *Oms* frowned at Renar, looking briefly unsure. 'You will help me, won't you?'

'In any way I can,' Renar said. It was the only possible reply in the circumstances.

'Triumvir—' the guard said.

'Be quiet!' There was a sudden, shocking viciousness in *omas* face and voice. 'Get out, you're boring.'

The guards left without another word, and the inter turned back to Renar. *Omas* face was once more carefree and cheerful. The lurch from happiness to anger and back again was more alarming than any more consistent emotion could have been.

'Look at me,' *oms* said. 'I've no manners at all! I haven't even introduced myself. I'm Nabofik, and I'm a god now, even though I was always told gods are a bad thing. But I'm not going to be like those other ones were. I want to make the world perfect. You'll help me with that, won't you? Oh, and you too, of course.' The last was directed at Lanalan.

Lanalan had the wit to say, 'La, I can think of no greater pleasure.'

'Wonderful,' Nabofik said. 'Wonderful. Things didn't go very well in Ofiklanod, I'm afraid. We didn't know what we were doing back then and we made a bit of a mess. But that's all right. Alfreda and Marvan stayed behind to fix it. And I came here to start again with a whole new country. With your help, I'm bound to do much better this time, aren't I?'

Renar nodded and smiled and didn't ask just what kind of mess her homeland had been left in.

17

'You have been a long time coming home,' the Hunter said, taking her place beside Krish at the railing. The soldiers had given them all the freedom of the ship, even if not the freedom to leave it. They were treated more like guests than prisoners, and no one stood any obvious guard over them, although he'd seen them looking at his moon-silver eyes, and at Thilini and the Hunter's gold ones, and muttering. But then they'd looked at Eric's pale skin and muttered too. Krish wondered how often outlanders ever came to these islands.

'I've never been here before,' he told the Hunter. 'I don't think even my father had. These islands were at the outer edge of the kingdom. He told me nothing ever came from here except fish and the root of dreams.'

'If an invasion fleet came from Ofiklanod, this might be where it first touched land.'

'But why would they invade?'

'You took the magic from the world, and magic was the source of that land's health and its wealth. They may covet the greenness and fertility of Ashanesland, if their own is now barren.'

'I didn't mean for that to happen. I thought I was doing the right thing when I let the power go.'

'You were,' the Hunter said firmly. 'Rightness and easiness are often mistaken each for the other, but they are not the same.'

Krish turned his gaze back to the sea. He couldn't yet see their destination, the island that the sailors called the Graveyard for all the ships that had foundered on its reefs, but the view still drew him. It was now almost as much land as water. The islands here clustered far thicker than on the outer reaches of the chain. A few of them were ringed by jagged peaks, and one had a mountain at its centre, white-tipped, but most were low and gentle, covered in a coat of green and muted purple. Seagrass and purple sorghum, he now knew. And on several there were more stone ruins, moss-covered and more monumental than anything else in this land.

Even here, in the heart of the archipelago, the tents of its inhabitants were widely scattered. He hadn't seen a single structure that resembled a shipfort. One of the sailors told him that most people lived aboard their boats. It didn't look like anywhere that had suffered an invasion. It certainly didn't look like a place that was under occupation. But then the people didn't seem to chafe under their new Queen's rule. He'd heard only love for her from anyone who'd been willing to talk.

'Do you think my father might be dead?' he asked.

The Hunter turned from the rail to study him. 'Would it grieve you if he were?'

'Maybe.' Krish was surprised by his own answer. 'He's all the family I have left.'

She looked from him down the length of the ship, where the rest of their group was congregated. 'I think you have more family than that.'

Eric was staring at Thilini, but when she looked in his direction, he looked away. Dinesh and Dae Hyo were arguing again, their faces twisted with anger. 'A broken one,' Krish said.

The Hunter smiled a little. 'Families frequently are.'

★

Night-time was the worst on the ship, Dae Hyo found. It was spent below decks, where everyone was packed as tight as fish in a net, and there was no avoiding the others. Worse, that was when his gut reminded him how much it wanted a drink. But every time he looked at Dinesh, he remembered why he'd decided to stop.

Krish had tried to talk to him, but Dae Hyo shrugged him off. He didn't know what to say to his brother, when it was Dae Hyo's fault he'd slept through three years of his youth. Worse, Dae Hyo had stolen his power from him without asking leave.

Dinnertime was worst of all. They were seated round a small galley table in the lantern-lit gloom and forced to stare at each other. No one could have called the food good. The hard biscuits were full of worms and the meat was on the point of spoiling.

'We're very nearly there, I think,' Krish said. 'That island with the flat top, that's where we're headed. It can't be more than two days' journey.'

We're running out of time to escape was what he meant. Only he couldn't say it, not surrounded by their captors like they were. That was the worst thing about supper. They might at least have found common cause if they could talk about the one aim they all shared, but instead they were forced to make nothing-talk, when every word was like a shoal, waiting for someone to founder on it.

'I think this land is beautiful,' Thilini said. She always seemed to want to smooth things over.

'That's cause your home's carved from ice,' Eric replied. 'Any place is more beautiful than that.' The smoothing over wasn't going so well with him.

'Where we were was beautiful.' Dinesh's tone was even but his eyes were angry. 'The, the, the Drifters had a good life. A free one. But because of Dae Hyo, we're here.'

Dae Hyo had felt some guilt when he thought the boy was dying. But Dinesh had lived. He was fit as a five-year-old stallion and bearing a grudge wasn't reasonable. It had been a fair fight. 'I tell you what,' Dae Hyo said to him, 'if you liked it so much there, why don't you try swimming back?'

'Enough,' Krish said. 'What's done can't be undone. There's no use picking over the corpse.'

'Why should I forget the wrong that was done me?' Dinesh's tone was now as heated as his eyes. Some of the sailors were looking over at them. And he was looking at Krish now, not Dae Hyo. 'No one's made amends to me. No, no, no one's even said sorry!'

'No one's ever said no word about my son being dead, but you don't catch me complaining!' Eric snapped. 'All you got is a couple of scars in your side. You ain't got any idea what pain is.'

Dae Hyo looked at everyone glaring at everyone, and at the sailors watching it all with interest. And for the first time in a long time, he had a good idea.

★

Krish shared a berth with Eric. It was small, their beds nothing but two hammocks strung side by side, but at least there were timber walls between them and every other person on the ship. Even the illusion of privacy was welcome. Krish had spent a solitary childhood and he couldn't plan when he was so surrounded by people. It was as if the noise of them got inside his head and drowned out his own thoughts.

'I don't know what to do with them,' he said quietly, when he was lying in his hammock alongside Eric. Their bodies weren't quite touching, but were close enough that he could feel the heat of Eric's.

'You don't need to do nothing,' Eric said. 'They ain't your responsibility. You ain't no one's god no more. Don't take on a burden that's someone else's to carry. My mum told me that, before she sold me to the thegns.'

There was an edge of bitterness to all Eric's words, but he wasn't wrong. And yet, 'If you break something, it's your job to mend it,' Krish said. 'My da taught me that, before I left. Nobody would be here, nothing would be the way it is if it wasn't for me.'

'That's true, brother,' Dae Hyo said, and both Eric and Krish let out yelps of surprise. Neither of them had heard him enter the cabin. For such a large man, he could be silent when he chose.

'Get out,' Eric snapped. 'Ain't we seen enough of each other to last the day?'

Dae Hyo ignored him, and spoke to Krish. 'If it weren't for you, Dinesh would still be a slave to that rat-fucker Uin. And I'd have drunk myself into a grave, or fought myself into one.'

Eric's face was a pale circle in the moonlight shining through the porthole. 'He's right,' he said grudgingly. 'If it weren't for you, Rii wouldn't have helped me. And if Rii hadn't helped me I'd have still been stuck up on the ice, tupping women I didn't get no pleasure in tupping. I'd never have had a son.' His face twisted with a pain that didn't seem to have aged with the years.

'And you would never have lost him,' Krish said quietly. 'I've done more bad than good.'

Dae Hyo shrugged. 'You can only turn a life into a tale when it's over. Yours isn't yet, brother. And I mean to make sure it isn't over soon. I've got a plan. All it needs is a boat, an oar, a rope and a knife.'

Krish hoped his own face wasn't as openly dubious as Eric's. He didn't want to hurt his brother's feelings. 'What plan?' he asked cautiously.

'Well,' Dae Hyo said. 'I tell you one thing, I don't think anyone's going to find it a struggle to do the first part of it.'

*

There were a million things that could go wrong with the plan. Eric had thought of half a dozen by the time the sun had risen. But since he didn't much care if it succeeded or failed, the same way he didn't much care about anything these days, he decided not to speak up.

His part was easy, anyhow. They were on a ship, so a coil of rope wasn't hard to come by, nor to stow near where they'd need it. The Hunter filched a carving knife from the kitchen when the sailors weren't watching. They tended to stay out of her way. Eric didn't think it was just her gold eyes that put the fear in them. There was something about her that wasn't like any other person. Eric knew it was because she was a thousand years old, and had once been god to his people. The sailors didn't know that, but perhaps some part of them sensed it.

The boat was easiest of all. The ship had three and the smallest was hung from the side by a device whose name Eric had learned was a davit. It was made to lower the boat into the water by two winches at either end that held it suspended horizontally. They couldn't let it down into the water all in one go. The sailors could hardly miss that. But each time one of the six of them passed, they moved the winch a turn or two.

By lunchtime, the boat was only a few hands off the water. A fellow who wanted to reach it would have to slide down the ropes by which it was suspended, but Eric reckoned he was up to the task. Krish he wasn't so sure of. Even despite the time that had passed since his waking, the Ashane prince was as thin as a reed and looked as ready to snap.

'They ready?' Eric asked quietly, when Krish approached.

Krish nodded. 'They're waiting for my sign. But I don't know if I should give it. It's not right that it's just me and you escaping.'

Eric sighed impatiently. They'd had this conversation before. 'Dae Hyo and Dinesh can't come, or we can't do it at all. Drut prefers to be wherever I ain't, and who knows why the Hunter does what she does.'

'Yes, I suppose you're right. We'll have to go back and rescue them once we're free.'

Eric had been sick of the sight of these people for years now. The faster he got away from them, the better. But he didn't see any profit in telling Krish that. The prince had seemed far softer since his waking than Eric remembered him being before. 'Send the signal,' Eric said. 'We're as ready as we'll ever be.'

Krish hesitated only a moment before scratching his left eyebrow, the signal they'd agreed. Then he scratched it again for longer, because Dae Hyo hadn't been paying attention the first time. The plan was off to an impressive start, and that was only the first stage of it.

It took a while to see whether the second stage was under way. He and Krish were at the far end of the ship from the others, and the conversation was impossible to hear. But Dinesh and Dae Hyo *were* standing very close to each other, and their faces weren't at all friendly. After a while, Dae Hyo shoved Dinesh's chest to push him away, and that seemed to do the trick, because now some of the sailors were rushing over to stop what looked to be brewing into a fight.

Krish glanced around to check they weren't being watched, then said, 'Let's get to the boat.'

They still had to move nice and gently. Not every eye was on Dae Hyo and Dinesh yet. A lot were, though. Like Dae Hyo had predicted, he and Dinesh didn't have much trouble making their fight look convincing.

'They'll have to do it soon,' Krish said tensely. 'Otherwise the sailors will break them apart.'

It did look like a couple were making a grab for Dae Hyo. He must have seen it too. He shouted, finally loud enough to be heard, 'I should have put the spears through your heart!'

Dinesh, equally loud and with every appearance of real anger, shouted back, 'Killing's all you were ever good for, and you're not good for that any more!' And Dae Hyo roared and charged.

The sailors were too taken by surprise to stop him. Every eye on the ship was watching the fight now.

'Not yet,' Krish said. 'Not yet . . .'

Then Dae Hyo's hands met Dinesh's chest. They shoved him back, then back again. And with the last shove there was no more deck, only the rail at Dinesh's back, and the force of Dae Hyo's hands pushed him over it.

There was a shocked stillness, until the splash of Dinesh landing in the ocean jerked everyone into action. A man overboard was about the most serious thing that could happen at sea. And none of them here knew that Dinesh could swim. All the sailors rushed towards the rail. Eric met Krish's eye, and they each grabbed one of the ropes supporting the small rowing boat and shimmied down.

When Eric's feet hit the deck, it swung on its ropes, nearly toppling him over. He sat down before he could fall into the water, then looked across, expecting Krish to have done the same. But he was still hanging near the top of the rope, his legs wrapped around it.

'Quick,' Eric said. 'We have to cut free soon.'

Krish nodded, but his throat bobbed as he swallowed. The prince, Eric knew, *couldn't* swim. It had been near number one on Eric's list of things that could go wrong with Dae Hyo's plan.

Krish's legs slid tentatively lower, clasped around the rope, he released one hand – and a moment later he was falling.

Eric flung himself forwards without thinking, arms outstretched as if he could catch Krish. But he was too heavy, even now, and falling too fast. He fell on Eric and Eric fell to the floor of the boat. All the wind was knocked out of him, or else he would surely have cried out and given their position away. His back would be one big bruise. But one good thing had happened. The force of the collision had snapped the suspending ropes. The rowing boat was free and floating on the water.

Krish scrambled off Eric, then hovered above, his hands not quite touching, as if he didn't know what to do with them. 'Sorry, sorry,' he said. His dark cheeks flushed darker. 'Are you hurt?'

'Not so bad I won't live.' Eric couldn't help groaning as he sat up. He looked around, fearful they'd been heard, but the ship was already its own length ahead of them.

Krish was peering not there, but at the waters behind it. 'I think they left Dinesh behind. I suppose they think he's drowned.'

'He won't. He swims like a dolphin,' Eric said.

'Could he swim to shore from here?' Krish asked.

Eric looked to the west, where the sun was setting behind a long, low island. It had looked a lot closer from up on the deck of the ship. He shook his head.

Krish frowned. 'I didn't realise that things are so hard to see when you're in the water. The waves get in the way.' They were gentle, but getting busier. In the distance they were streaked with white.

'Then I suppose we'd better find him,' Eric said.

★

The next thing Dae Hyo knew, he was waking in the deep gloom of some below-decks room. The only light came squeezing thinly through the planks above. He'd been flung onto a heap of lumpy sacks. When he fumbled one open, an earthy smell leapt out. Potatoes, then. They'd put him in the ship's stores. And there he stayed, for hour after dull hour. A beer would certainly have made them pass quicker. He wondered if that would ever stop being his first thought, when things went badly. Would his hand always reach for a drink?

He was still wondering it when there was the rattle of a bolt being shot, and then the door opened and Drut – no, Thilini – walked in. She was carrying a lantern that lit her pale face and gold hair in a lovely light.

She sat daintily on the pile of lumpy sacks. 'They didn't want to let me in. They're very angry with you,' she said.

He laughed. 'Well, I didn't expect them to be singing my praises.'

'I told them I was your wife. They're not angry about the escape. They haven't noticed that Eric and Krish are gone yet – we've told them they were feeling sick and went to their cabin. Your plan worked very well. They're angry because they think you killed Dinesh. They don't like murder.'

'Show me a man who does,' Dae Hyo said. 'But that boy is harder to kill than a tortoise. My brother will find him.'

'They're talking about hanging you,' she said.

That shook him, he wouldn't lie. But when he thought on it some more, he found it didn't trouble him too much. The idea of not being was easier than the idea of being. A Dae Hyo who wasn't there couldn't crave drink as badly as slaves craved bliss. He couldn't be eaten up by guilt or shame or anger or any of the other, uglier emotions that he'd come to know so well over the years. So he shrugged and said, 'If the other two are free, that's all that matters.'

'Yes, I understand,' she said. 'I've felt that way too. I used to know my purpose, every day, and for all my days. But Salvation is gone, and my sisters, and Mizhara is . . . not inside me any more. She's gone too. There's nothing left. So why am I still here?'

'I was the one who killed your sisters. I didn't mean to. It was the price of my magic.'

'No,' she said, 'I killed them, by bringing them to that battle. Or . . . Mizhara did, when she was me. I loved her entirely for so many years. Then I betrayed her, for Eric's sake. And when he betrayed me, then I became her. And now . . . now I think I hate her.'

She looked very young in that moment. 'I'm the last of my people too,' he said. 'I don't know why they all died and I lived. Belbog's balls, it wasn't because of my worth. There were a thousand warriors of the Dae worth more than me, and all the elder mothers. If something survived of the tribe, shouldn't it have been the best of us?'

'Do you think we survived so that we could remember? So that someone should remember them?'

'That would be a fine joke, when I've spent every year since trying to forget. I've drunk enough beer to fill a lake and enough spirits for another, and the memories are always there waiting for me when the drink leaves.'

'Then remember,' she said. 'I know you regret what you did to Dinesh, and . . . and my sisters. If this is our penance, should we not accept it?'

He was spared the need to find a reply when the door opened and the captain walked in with two sailors behind him. Thilini wasn't wrong. They looked like men who'd swallowed a honeycomb and shat a bee.

'I know what you did,' the captain said. 'They've gone.'

'Don't hurt him,' Thilini said. 'It wasn't his plan alone. It was all of us.'

Dae Hyo glared at her, because what was the point of them all dying when he could do it on everyone's behalf and spare them the trouble? But the sailor only nodded, as if he'd known that already.

'Hang me for it if you want,' Dae Hyo said.

'We won't hang you,' the captain said. 'We've sent out the alarm. Every boat in these waters will be looking for them.'

'So you'll let us free?' Thilini asked.

'We'll take you to the Queen,' the captain said. 'She'll have questions for you about where your friends have gone. And then she'll hang you.'

18

Nabofik didn't understand why Alfreda had chosen Täm as her home, and Marvan didn't care, but it seemed to Alfreda like a fitting place for her work. There were two cities here, or there had been. The City Below, the home of the sun god, had died a millennium ago, been brought briefly back to life, then died again. Täm had been thriving until very recently, but it too had died. The city's crumbled remains had fallen through fissures into the calcified bones of the one below. There was death everywhere.

Alfreda's home gave her a good view of it all. She'd constructed it on the highest remaining hill in Täm. The Mortals told her this was close to where their own grand hall had once been. She'd offered to rebuild it for them, but they'd claimed not to need it now that their three gods had come to them.

They always told her what they thought she wanted to hear. She hated it. But when she told them to stop, it only scared them. She enjoyed their fear even less than their lies. It wasn't needed. She had no anger in her, not these days, since she'd been made a god. She felt her incompleteness sometimes, the missing pieces of her where some of her feelings should be.

People were an alloy, she thought, made of many things. But gods needed to be made of a purer metal and so their feelings, hers and Nabofik's and Marvan's, had been refined and split between them. Marvan had the anger, Nabofik the innocence, and as for Alfreda? Sometimes she thought she'd been given only the grief.

She thought of Algar every waking moment. She wasn't sure who she missed most: him, or the person she'd been when she was with him. There'd been such joy in him, some of it had spilled over into her. He'd taken so much with him when he'd gone. And then Cwen's death and Jinn's had stolen what remained. Her laughter and her hope and her trust all lay in their graves beside them.

But for all that she'd lost, there were things she'd gained. She was still learning the extent of her own powers. The Mortals weren't keen on her experiments, but they wouldn't stop her. They seldom visited. Only Yemisi regularly kept her company as she worked. Among so many worshippers, it felt good to have a friend. And maybe one day Yemisi could come to mean to her what Cwen had. Maybe, if she succeeded – *when* she succeeded – the three of them could all be friends.

Yemisi had been running errands elsewhere in Ofiklanod these past few weeks, but today Alfreda found her waiting in the laboratory when she walked in.

'You've had some success in my absence, I see,' Yemisi said. She was staring into one of the glass cages that lined the back wall of the place. The thing inside it had been a dog before it died.

Alfreda joined her, but could hardly bear to look at the thing. 'I wouldn't call it a success.'

'It's animate, at least.' Yemisi put a hand against the glass, but the thing inside didn't react. It merely twitched. That was all Alfreda had been able to craft it to do.

'Only through my will,' Alfreda said. 'Not its own. See.' She withdrew her power from the thing and it was once again a corpse, a little way into the process of decay. The jagged hole from the spear that had killed it remained unhealed. Three years, and Alfreda still hadn't learned the trick of making dead flesh regrow. What was the use of being a god, if she couldn't do that one simple thing?

She exerted her will again, and something else shambled from a dark corner of the room. Yemisi gasped in shock before schooling her features back to calmness.

Alfreda hated it when she tried to hide her feelings. If even she couldn't forget that Alfreda was a god, couldn't treat her quite like a person, then Alfreda really was alone. She missed Algar's teasing so much, and Cwen's forthrightness. But maybe it would be different with Yemisi when Alfreda gave her back her memories.

Although she often wondered if Yemisi would be glad of it when she finally got them. Alfreda's head was full of memories she'd rather not have. But how could she wish them away? To forget the moment of Algar's death, or the sight of Cwen's body, or Jinn's, would be to throw away a part of them. Every hour she'd had with them was precious, even the bad ones. Unless her experiments succeeded, she'd never be getting any more.

The point was moot, anyway. She'd no more been able to grant Yemisi's wish than her own. She couldn't return Yemisi's past to her, and she couldn't make something living from something dead. All she could make were decaying marionettes like that dog, or empty vessels like the one that now stood in front of them.

Yemisi was staring at it in fascination, circling the body to see it from every angle. It was at least in the shape of a man, and it was made of the same stuff. Alfreda was sure of that. She'd dissected enough corpses, both physically and with her newly opened mind, to know what flesh and bone were made of.

Recently she'd been studying it layer by layer, then building each layer on this thing. She'd started with the bones, and moved on to the muscle. The veins had been a new addition since Yemisi last saw it. She watched them throb and pulse as Alfreda forced blood through them. There was no spark of life. It was all her.

There was another system, though, one she'd only just begun to study and whose purpose she didn't understand. It led from the brain to every furthest reach of the body. When Alfreda had pulled it apart, it formed a tracery as delicate as lace, or like a system of roots. Alfreda was increasingly convinced that this was what it was: the root system of the mind. Somewhere in it was the thing that allowed her body to contain *her*, that meant there was something looking out from behind her eyes.

Nothing looked out from behind the eyes of her creation. She withdrew her will from it and it collapsed to the ground, where it looked like nothing more than a flayed corpse. It *was* nothing more than a flayed corpse, although it was of a man who'd never lived.

Yemisi stepped hurriedly away from the thing, and Alfreda saw a splash of red on her white sandals. A vein must have ruptured in the fall. She'd repair it later.

'Will you come and eat?' Yemisi asked. 'Even a god needs food.'

'Do I? I amn't sure.'

'A rest at least.'

'That I don't need. Nor sleep neither.'

'But I do,' Yemisi insisted. 'I've been on a long trip and I'm tired. Won't you sit and have a cup of rice wine with me?'

'Aye, fine then,' Alfreda said, if only because Yemisi wanted it.

'I've just come back from Makat,' Yemisi said with a strange note in her voice.

Alfreda paused with a fork of food halfway to her mouth. 'Aye, and what of it?'

'The stib and sof and luc bugs are all dead.'

Alfreda shrugged. 'They were made with the old magic. They were bound to die without it.'

'But they were the source of Makat's wealth.'

'Why should I care about that? If they want new coin they need to make new things.'

'Indeed yes. But after the war there was . . . a shortage of people to work the fields. And much rebuilding to do.'

The war she meant was the one the Mortals had waged on their new gods' behalf to take control of Ofiklanod. The Ofiklanders hadn't been as receptive to the gods as the Mortals hoped. The war had a been a bloody and drawn-out thing, but Alfreda didn't think about it often. It wasn't her concern.

'I'm sorry for them then,' she said, and maybe meant it a little. 'But there's nothing I can do to help. Should I bend my back in the fields with them? A little work and time will see them fine.'

Yemisi leaned forwards, her eyes intent. She seldom pressed

a point this far. 'All well and true, if the crops grew. But they don't. It seems the climate there, the rain and the fertile soil were products of the old magic too, and they're all burning away. Before too long the whole region will be as dry as the Silent Sands. Perhaps the whole country. And when there's only scraps, people will fight over them like hounds. There'll be war before there's starvation.'

'Oh.' Alfreda could grant that this was a problem. But, 'Well then, my work here's even more important. When I've learned how to bring back life, I'll bring back life to them. I need their . . . their bodies though. Algar and Cwen and Jinn. We sent out our sil-nafön days ago. Why have they not come back? I told them where to dig.'

'You told them a general area. Be a little patient, the search is bound to take some time.'

Alfreda nodded reluctantly, unsatisfied. 'I suppose.'

'And the country needs governing in the meanwhile,' Yemisi said.

'Nabofik and Marvan can keep order until I'm ready.'

'Nabofik has gone to Ashanesland. Don't you remember? You built *oms* an entire fleet of sil-nafön for the invasion. Not to mention that great flying city. I believe Nabofik's called it the City On High.'

'Oh, oh yes.' Alfreda had in truth forgotten. The making of the fleet had taken two months she'd very grudgingly spared from her own work. 'Marvan then. He'll be in charge until she's back and I'm finished. Go to him, Yemisi. Tell him that.'

★

Yemisi chewed over the conversation for the entirety of the flight east. She'd taken one of the smaller sil-nafön. The globe that held it in the air was only the size of a house, and the basket beneath it barely bigger than a wagon. She clung to the centre of her bench seat while the steersman sat more easily in his opposite. He was belled, so had nothing in the way of conversation. It left Yemisi too much time for her own thoughts.

Tell Marvan to take over the rule of Ofiklanod? It was absurd.

The man could barely rule himself. He *didn't* rule himself, not now he was a god. His dark passions were entirely his master. Yemisi avoided him as far as was humanly possible while working beside his sister-god. Talking to Marvan was always a chancy endeavour.

Was there something she could have said that would have moved Alfreda? Probably not. Yemisi had tried every argument to convince her to take up the reins of power that were lying so dangerously slack. Every argument but one: that death was a door that opened only one way and Alfreda's efforts to force it would always be in vain. Alfreda was her friend and she'd never given Yemisi cause to fear her, but she feared her response to those words.

And besides, maybe they weren't true. Maybe there *was* a way to give Alfreda back her happiness, and then Yemisi her memories.

It was why she'd begun her own researches, the ones she hadn't yet told Alfreda about. Because if Alfreda couldn't solve the problem of death, Yemisi had decided that she needed to solve it herself. The Mortals wouldn't be able to help her. They played with the new magic, but she didn't think they truly understood it. Bruyar might have, though. The entire scheme had been *omas*. Oms fled Ofiklanod years ago, of course, but *omas* notes remained. Yemisi had had them all transported from the Cinderlands to the ruins of Täm.

Unfortunately, the more she understood, the less probable it seemed that she'd find what she wanted there. The new magic had a great deal to say about matter, but nothing to say about mind. It was entirely silent on the subject of spirit. She would keep searching, though. What other choice did she have?

She sighed and looked down at the country passing by beneath them. But that only led to gloomier observations. The reversion of fertile land to desert was happening even faster here. Hundreds of paces below the sil-nafön there were patches of cultivated green, but far larger patches of yellow. The network of canals which had once brought water to most corners of this country still stood. Yemisi saw the long, perfectly straight line of one running almost parallel to the horizon. But there was no glint of water from it. They'd dried out long ago.

Yemisi sometimes wondered why she concerned herself with it at all. This country wasn't her home. These weren't her people, or her gods. But Alfreda was the loneliest person she'd ever met, and Yemisi felt great fellowship in that loneliness. She'd always been a woman with many friends, never short of people to drink or eat or fuck with. But every friend she remembered so vividly had died decades before. Alfreda thought she'd lost a lot, but Yemisi had lost everything.

And there was so much power here, if it could be harnessed. Then Yemisi could show Olufemi what a woman of knowledge could really do with a friendly god. Then, perhaps, the Olufemi in her head, that little nagging voice, would stop telling her she'd made a terrible mistake by staying.

The sil-nafön began its descent. Once it had covered half the distance to the ground, Marvan's home became visible. It was a great mansion, fifty rooms or more and lavishly decorated on the inside. The decoration was always visible, because Marvan had chosen to have its walls and ceiling fashioned entirely out of glass. Alfreda had made the place for him. Marvan himself seemed little interested in using his powers, except in so far as they allowed him to act precisely as he pleased.

There were, Yemisi saw once they were a mere two hundred paces above the scrubby ground, two figures moving through it. She was sure that one of them was Marvan. She wasn't close enough to see his face, only the dark top of his head. But even from this height it was clear that one of the figures was hunter and the other prey. It was something in the stalking way that the figure at the rear moved, and the hunched shuffle of the other. There wasn't much space between them. The hunter was moving in for the kill.

Yemisi girded herself, then said to the steersman, 'Don't head for the house. See those figures up ahead? It will be best if you land by them.'

Lower still, and the base of the sil-nafön obscured Yemisi's view of the ground beneath it. She was glad of it. She had no desire to see the hunt reach its bloody conclusion.

But, once they'd landed and she'd dismounted, she realised that it hadn't concluded yet. Marvan stood, knife in hand, in front of a kneeling figure. The figure was alive. It was a man, of course. Marvan never hunted women or children. It was hard to say that made him admirable.

The man in front of him was very young, and well muscled. A farm labourer perhaps. He might have taken Marvan in a fight, if the fight had been fair. His face, Yemisi saw when she'd walked cautiously closer, looked oddly blank. He wasn't pleading for his life, the way she'd seen Marvan's other victims do. He barely seemed to care that his death was here for him.

Marvan spun to face her when Yemisi crunched a dried stalk of grain beneath her sandal. Had this wasteland been a wheatfield, not very long ago?

'Oh,' Marvan said. 'It's you.'

'I'm sorry to interrupt your hunt, God-Triumvir. Please, continue.' It cost Yemisi a lot to keep her face still and her voice indifferent.

Marvan looked back at the man. He raised the knife for a killing blow – then lowered it with the blow undelivered. 'What's the point? Where's the joy in it?'

'The same place it's always been, I would think.' Yemisi quickly slammed her lips shut. That wasn't the tone to take with him.

He didn't seem to notice. 'Hardly. The pleasure's in the hunt and in the fight. Look at him. He barely bothered to run. And now he won't even raise a hand to me. I offered him a knife and he won't take it.'

The youth in question didn't seem to be listening. His eyes were glazed, as if he'd retreated into a place deep within himself.

'Perhaps he realises the futility of fighting you,' Yemisi said cautiously.

'But I might even release him if he puts up a good enough fight. I've told him that.'

Perhaps he doesn't believe you, Yemisi thought but didn't say. 'Perhaps it's time to focus on other pleasures,' she said. 'There are enough available to you. Will you return to Täm? I believe Alfreda would be glad of your counsel, and your company.'

His eyes warmed at Alfreda's name. It was strange to see something so like a normal emotion on that face. It more usually showed only mockery and perverse pleasure. 'How is she?' he asked.

Yemisi shrugged. 'Still at her experiments.'

Marvan sighed. 'Then there's little point my returning, is there? And little point my remaining here, either.' With shocking quickness, he turned and slashed his knife across the kneeling youth's throat.

Blood gushed in a fountain that barely missed Yemisi. The stink of it filled her nostrils along with the stink of his released bowels. But the youth himself remained silent even in his last, twitching moments. It was as if the most essential part of him, the part that Alfreda was trying so fruitlessly to reanimate, was already gone.

When Marvan turned back to Yemisi, the light of the murder was still in his eyes. The knife was slick with blood.

She forced herself to stand her ground. Fear would only draw the hunter. 'Perhaps you need to vary your pleasures,' she said. 'Have you thought to make them fight each other for you? If they knew that the winner would be spared, they'd be less prone to despair.' Her own words disgusted her even as she said them. But Marvan would kill either way. It was his nature.

'Don't you think I've tried that?' His voice was dangerous now. 'I've watched a hundred others fight to the death. I felt nothing. I've taken a father with his children and told him they'll be spared if he puts up a good fight, and suffer if he doesn't. He used the knife to slit their throats himself, then turned it on himself. I've travelled to every corner of this cursed land and I can't find one person whose death will give me any pleasure.'

'Then you need to go elsewhere.' The plan was forming only

in the moment Yemisi said the words. She had no chance to judge if it was a wise one. 'God-Triumvir Nabofik has conquered Ashanesland. That was your home, wasn't it? And a land in total ignorance of who you are now, and what you're capable of. If you go there before they've had a chance to learn, you might find victims more to your liking. You'll have a whole nation of them to choose from.'

She could tell from the narrowing eyes that she'd hooked him. But then his expression twisted into something sly. 'Keen to get rid of me, are you?'

'Far from it.' She could tell that neither of them believed her words.

'I know what you've been doing,' he said. Then, at the alarmed expression she couldn't hide, 'I have spies among the Mortals. I know you've been digging through that inter's research, the one who made us.'

'I have. There's nothing nefarious in it. I'm looking for another way to help Alfreda.'

He studied her with narrowed eyes and her heart raced. Then he relaxed. 'I suppose you might be. And anyway, Alfreda can swat you herself if you give her trouble. But have you found the most interesting part yet?'

It took her a moment to fathom the implication of that. 'You read Bruyar's notes yourself?'

'Before I let you have them. I'm not a fool. But there were too many to read them all. It was only by chance I saw the note. Perhaps you haven't reached it yet.'

'I can't say, unless you tell me what it is.' She kept her voice carefully neutral.

'The bells, the music, this is the third magic. That's what the note said.'

Yemisi frowned. 'This isn't news. Yron and Mizhara weren't the first to embody the sun and moon.'

'No, not them. They were merely different incarnations of the same magic. I'm talking about an earlier one, the first magic. That's what the inter's note said. But then nothing more. Intriguing, isn't it? I think *oms* may have been trying to keep it hidden, even from *omas* own people. But *oms* had a house in Täm, I've heard.'

'Buried with the city,' Yemisi said.

He smiled. '*Omas* husband and wife weren't buried with it. Perhaps you should talk to them. After all, who does one confide in if not one's family?'

19

After the events of the last few weeks, Renar had never expected to find herself again in the purple-red, spiral corridors of Ashfall, or in the familiar hall beside the wheel that was the symbol of its sovereign. She certainly hadn't expected to be at the right hand of that sovereign. She'd have been correct, however, to predict that the ruler would no longer be Nayan. Another had taken the helm of the Ashane people.

Nayan had been gnarled and diminished by age, like an apple left too long on the tree. Nabofik had all the energy and beauty of youth. Where Nayan had slumped in the austere, too-large chair on its raised dais, Nabofik leaned forwards, frowning as *oms* listened to the petitioners who'd come to plead for aid from their new ruler.

The pleas were quite familiar to Renar too. The solutions that Nabofik offered, however, were nothing that she could have guessed.

The queue of those waiting to speak to Nabofik stretched to the back of the long hall. At its front there was a weaselly looking young man whom Renar had informed Nabofik was called Dulaj. He was the first cousin of the second remove to the former ruler of Fort Victory. The ruler himself had fallen beneath the swords of Nabofik's conquering army and was yet to be replaced.

'Wheelking,' Dulaj said, then blushed and faltered. 'I mean to say . . .'

'You can call me Nabofik,' *oms* said. 'I don't care about titles. They're a silly thing that only primitive people use.'

He bowed very low, perhaps to hide his reaction to being called primitive. 'Nabofik, the current . . . the current difficulties have left the spring planting far too late, and now half my landborn farmers have fled. I would like – my gratitude would be enormous if the Oak Wheel, I mean to say – that is, if some hands could be lent to get the potatoes and beets and broccoli in the ground. Or else I'm afraid there'll be starvation come winter.'

Nabofik laughed. 'La, what a silly thing to worry about. Don't you know that you have gods now? You haven't met Alfreda yet, but she's very clever. She's working on a way to bring the dead back to life. You won't need to plant. Alfreda will come and make everything all right.'

This time, Dulaj bowed too late to hide his expression of dismay. Nabofik frowned at it.

'If I could make a suggestion?' Renar said hurriedly.

Nabofik's frown cleared. 'Why of course. 'Tis why I brought you here. What counsel could be more valuable than that of the Fox of Täm?'

'I think Dulaj's concern is with his landborn. They're unworldly people and prone to irrational fears.' Renar had no idea if this was true, but it seemed plausible. 'If they see no crop being planted, they're likely to panic. Dulaj doesn't doubt your powers. Who could, after such a conclusive demonstration? He merely wants to forestall such foolishness on the part of the ignorant but good-hearted people who look to him for leadership. In your name, of course.'

Dulaj shot her a grateful look as Nabofik said to him, 'Do you really think so?'

'Yes,' he said. 'Yes, that's exactly what I meant to say.'

Nabofik sighed. 'Oh, well in that case I'll send some of my soldiers to help with the planting. They haven't needed to fight much anyway. When we came, most people just ran away. I think my soldiers were a little disappointed.'

'Perhaps our people didn't fight because they recognised the rightness of your cause,' Dulaj said. Relief seemed to have made him more eloquent.

Nabofik smiled. 'Yes, I suppose that might be it. And for the ones who don't, there are the bells. We can always bell your farmers, if they keep complaining. Then they'll be quiet and do whatever I say. Belled people are boring, though, so I hope they don't need it. Maybe you could tell them that? It's obedience or belling. In Ofiklanod most people chose obedience, once they knew what belling was, but I know things are different here.'

Nabofik's face brightened suddenly, as if with a new thought. Renar hid her dismay. In her short experience, Nabofik's thoughts were seldom good ones. 'I can help even more than that, now I think about it,' *oms* said. 'I can make the crops grow so fast they'll catch up all the time that's been lost. You can make bells to do that, can't you?'

This last was directed to the gaggle of Mortals that Nabofik had brought with *omas* to Ashanesland. Renar had barely had a chance to talk to them. Nabofik kept them endlessly busy, designing new bell-songs to work whatever magic Nabofik demanded on a passing whim. Their leader, a gaunt old man, nodded and said, 'The potential exists within the magic, yes.'

Nabofik looked momentarily irritated. Renar knew that *oms* found the details of the magic dull. *Oms* barely even seemed to understand its workings.

'Are you satisfied?' Renar asked Dulaj, before Nabofik could come up with an even more wildly impractical solution.

'Deeply satisfied, my lady.' Dulaj bowed again – he'd spent more time in the hall bent than upright – then wisely left before Nabofik's fickle temper could shift.

Nabofik looked at the line of people stretching out through the doors of the hall. *Oms* had a petulant expression that Renar knew presaged trouble.

'Perhaps you've heard enough petitions for the day,' she said quickly. 'These can wait for the morrow. Your time's too precious to spend long on such trivialities.'

'Oh yes, yes you're right,' Nabofik said with relief. *Oms* turned to the hall and made a shooing gesture a little like a farmer herding cattle. 'Get out now, I'm done with you for the day.'

A few of those who'd been waiting for hours to see their new ruler looked disgruntled. More looked relieved. They'd already learned to fear *omas* temper.

When they were all gone, Nabofik stretched like a cat, then said, 'It's wonderfully savage, the way these godlanders live, isn't it? I'm glad you persuaded me to come down from the City On High. If I'm going to rule these people, I need to understand them. Now I think I do.'

'It was indeed a wise choice,' Renar said carefully. At the time she'd suggested it, she'd simply been desperate to feel the earth beneath her feet again. She'd found sleep a stranger in the impossibly floating city. She spent every hour of the night waiting for it to plummet to earth.

'That went well, didn't it?' Nabofik asked, the slightest hint of uncertainty in *omas* voice.

Renar bit back the immediate urge to reassure *omas* that it had gone wonderfully. It was easy to assume that Nabofik was a fool, and also dangerous. Nabofik was merely young. *Oms* eyes, intent on Renar, saw more than some people supposed.

'You did as well with them as could be done,' Renar said. 'It will take time before they're at peace with their new situation. Conquests are rarely easy and seldom so quick. 'Tis to be expected that the new soil will take some time to settle.'

*

Freed from duty for the rest of the day, Renar found that she wanted Lanalan's company. There'd been a time when she might have avoided it as assiduously as she wished she could avoid Nabofik's, but that time was long past. She'd learned, later than she should have, to appreciate his honesty and fine spirits.

She found him in the sanctuary. It was the place where the Ashane kept their gods, or at least the images of them. It had taken Renar some time among the god-sick people to understand that they made a distinction.

'I'm glad you persuaded *omas* to keep them,' Lanalan said. He was standing in front of the figure of the Crooked Man. His fingers lightly traced the plane of the idol's face. It was an old sculpture, carved with wrinkles and with what seemed to be cankers on its face and hands. The age of the wood itself, surely many centuries, made the figure seem more decrepit still. It was said the five prow gods had come over with the ships that brought the very first Ashane.

'Burning them was only a passing fancy of Nabofik's,' Renar said. 'I told *omas* to leave them here, so the Ashane could contrast the dead wood with the real power that now rules them.'

Lanalan moved on to inspect the next figure, Lord Lust. The paint on it had flaked away long ago, but the huge phallus that stood proudly from the body was still stained red. 'Do you think these were ever real, Renar? The moon and sun were, and now the Three. Were these the gods before?'

Renar studied the largest of the images, the Smiler with his rolls of wooden fat and untrustworthy smile. 'I've never heard that they were. There are no tales of them walking the land. I think perhaps the Ashane preferred gods who couldn't speak back.'

'I can hardly blame them.' Lanalan turned to face her. 'Renar, what do you think is happening in Ofiklanod?'

''Tis hard to speculate.'

Lanalan was at the Fierce Child now. This image, thin and crouched, had always reminded Renar a little of Krishanjit. They both seemed to contain the same wildness. 'I want to go home,' Lanalan said. 'We can now, can't we?'

'Nabofik values my counsel.'

'But it's like counselling a child of five!' Lanalan's voice was far too loud. 'People are just toys to *omas*. I fear what Nabofik will do when *oms* tires of them.'

Renar grasped his arm, hard enough that he winced. She put a finger to her ear, and then pointed at the wall.

'Oh,' Lanalan said. 'Oh yes. Of course, when I say a child, I only mean *omas* youth compared to us.'

She drew him towards the figure of the Lady. She was the only one of the prow gods to lean against the outer, lakeward wall of the fort. 'They believed that this one could quicken their bellies,' Renar said.

'And was it true?'

'Why, not that I've ever heard, and yet their prayers continued. Lanalan, you must be careful.' She leaned in to murmur the last in his ear. 'I have *omas* under control. I can't have you upsetting the cart it's cost me some effort to set on a better course.'

'Is *oms* under your control?' His face was unusually serious. 'It seems to me *oms* does exactly as *oms* pleases.'

'Nabofik is a child, as you remarked, but not a stupid one. *Oms* can be taught. Can be trained, in time.'

'I believe you could train a cow to sing, truly I do, Renar. But Nabofik frightens me.'

'I worked for Bruyar for years, and *oms* was far cleverer and more dangerous than our new god. If I could survive that, I can surely survive this.'

'And yet *oms* wasn't a god. We haven't seen Nabofik's power, Renar. You've kept *omas* from using it. We were both there for that battle between sun and moon. We've seen the powers gods have, when they aren't made of old wood.'

'I don't believe Nabofik has such power, not in isolation. Theirs is a threefold godhead, and two thirds of it is back in Ofiklanod. There are the belled, of course.' She shuddered at the thought of that mindless slavery. 'But beyond that, what evidence of Nabofik's power have we seen?'

Lanalan smiled sunnily. 'Why, you're right, of course. Thank you, Renar. You've put my mind quite at rest.'

Renar smiled back. But she wished she found herself as easy to convince as her sib.

*

The next day, Renar was woken by a servant and summoned to see Nabofik in King Nayan's pleasure gardens.

There were others in the garden too. From a distance, Renar had taken them for Nabofik's soldiers, or *omas* compliant, belled servants. But when she walked the gravelled path towards them, she saw that they were Ashane. And when she was close enough for Nabofik to see *her*, she recognised exactly which Ashane these were. The last time Renar had seen them, they hadn't look half so cowed.

Standing in front of Nabofik, surrounded by keen-eyed guards, were the shiplords of Ashanesland. Not all of them. Renar might have found that less alarming. It was only those whom she and Lanalan had supped with and been threatened by and finally run from. That had only been weeks ago. It felt far longer.

Nimrit looked every bit as haughty as when Renar had last seen her, and her sister Amila every bit as smug, but there was a bloodstain on the shoulder of Nimrit's blue-and-green shirt, and Amila's curly hair was in wild disarray. Lord Harjas walked with a noticeable limp when the guards pushed the group closer at Renar's approach, and handsome young Nuwan had no smile for her now. From the way he cradled his arm, Renar guessed it might be broken. What could Nabofik mean by bringing them here? Most crucially, what did it mean for *Renar*?

'Renar, you're very slow sometimes. I was expecting you half the hour ago,' Nabofik said, but *oms* sounded excited rather than angry.

'My most sincere apologies.' Renar made every effort not to stare at the assembled Ashane notables. She kept her eyes on Nabofik, as one would on a venomous insect that had skittered too close. 'I don't have your youth or indeed your godhood to speed me.'

Nabofik laughed. *Oms* loved, Renar had learned, to be reminded of *omas* own power. 'But you're here now and that's what counts,' *oms* said. 'And look, I've brought a present for you.'

Renar finally allowed herself to turn to the Ashane lords. They looked as if they loved her even less now than they had at their last meeting. No doubt the way in which Nabofik had spoken to her was responsible. The familiarity and friendliness of it would be telling them its own tale.

'I see the Ladies Nimrit and Amila of Delta's Strength, Aadh sister-daughter to Lord Balwinder of World's End and two dozen others of lesser or greater nobility,' Renar said. 'Half the shipforts in Ashanesland must currently be unled, with these people here. Far be it from me to scorn such a generous gift, but a new horse might be of more use to me.'

Renar saw Nabofik's frown and berated herself for failing to judge *omas* mood before she spoke. It was never wise to irk *omas*.

'Look again,' Nabofik said. 'What do all these people have in common?'

Renar considered lying for only a second. As she'd told her sib, Nabofik was not to be underestimated. 'Lanalan and I attended a dinner with them on the eve of your arrival,' she said. 'It was a jovial meal, but I don't feel an urgent need to recreate it. Why are they here?'

The gathered lords shifted at her words and some of the looks cast her way were now nothing short of murderous.

Nabofik stamped *omas* foot, making no sound at all in the grass. 'It *wasn't* jovial, don't lie to me! You know I hate that. These people all threatened you. I heard Lanalan talking about it. They were going to kill you if you didn't do what they wanted.'

'If I may speak,' Lord Harjas said.

'No you may not!' Nabofik shouted. 'You're not here to speak. None of you are.'

It had been some time since Renar had cursed Lanalan in her mind. She did it now. 'My sib exaggerates,' she told Nabofik. 'There were hard words at the meal, but that is the nature of the political game. They said no worse than Bruyar said to me upon occasion.' This, at least, was true.

Nabofik's mouth was set in a thin, stubborn line. 'But Bruyar ran away and they're here. And anyway, I don't think they were lying. I've read about the godlanders. They have swords and soldiers rather than politics, that's what my father said. And my maker told me they're as vicious as hyenas and nothing like as trustworthy.'

'Your parents were wise people,' Renar said. 'Perhaps these shiplords did mean what they said to us. But they had no time to act on it, and now they can't. I thank you for your gift, truly it's very thoughtful. My anger with them, however, is quite spent.'

'Oh, you're too kind,' Nabofik said. 'And too soft. You're my counsellor – my chief counsellor – and they almost killed you. If I let them go, it will make me look weak. I didn't learn that from my father or my maker, I learned it from the Ashane. I've been reading some of their old kings' writings in the library here. Some of the things they say are shocking, Renar, truly.' In that sudden way of Nabofik's, *omas* attention had been diverted and *omas* temper had softened with it. 'I'll send them to your room so you can read them too. You wouldn't believe some of the things they did to people. Did you know a man could have his guts pulled out and still live for hours and hours? They used to do that here.'

Someone in the group of Ashane lords whimpered at those words.

'Those do sound fascinating,' Renar said. 'Perhaps we could discuss them further on the walk back to Ashfall. As for these, if you want my counsel, you'll send them back to their shipforts. The reason they threatened my life and my sib's was that they wanted their freedom. Sending them back to rule in your name and under your command – and mine – will be a far worse humiliation than any barbaric practice of an ancient king.'

Nabofik laughed delightedly. 'Don't be silly, I don't care about humiliating them. I'm going to kill them. I just thought you'd like to watch.'

Before Renar could speak again, before she could even react, Nabofik acted.

Oms opened *omas* mouth and a sound emerged that was neither music nor speech but somehow both combined. There was a meaning in it, but not one Renar could hope to understand. She could only experience the force of it, inescapably strong. It resonated in every bone in her body and every corner of her mind. Nabofik's magic, now that Renar was at last experiencing it, touched places inside that should have belonged only to her.

She fell to her knees, covering her ears in a futile attempt to block it out. There was no evading it. It was everywhere.

But she was spared the worst of it. As she watched, helpless and on her knees, the lords of Ashanesland died where they stood. She didn't know what caused it. Some terrible pain twisted their faces and wracked their bodies. Their mouths were open in screams she couldn't hear. There was nothing to be heard but the inhuman sound that Nabofik was making.

And then, all at once, it was over. The note ended. Renar fell forwards onto her hands, gasping for breath as if, in its going, that awful chord had taken all the air with it. Around her, the corpses of the shiplords of Ashanesland were scattered, their faces forever locked in their final paroxysms of pain. Blood leaked from their mouths and noses and their wide, terrified eyes, not quite clouded yet with death.

'I made the blood boil inside them,' Nabofik said. 'It's really simple with the music. Alfreda showed me how to do it with water, to make all the little tiny bits of water move faster and faster, but I've never tried it with blood. Oh, Renar, do get up. There's loads I want to talk to you about. I want you to advise me, so I don't have to do to lots of other people what I just did to these ones.'

20

They only just made it to the cave in time. If Eric hadn't seen it when he was combing the beach for the tiny shelled creatures that had been the bulk of their food for a week now, they wouldn't have escaped their pursuers at all. It reminded Krish horribly of a time right back when all this had started, and he'd been fleeing for his life from his own father's men.

It was very damp and very cramped in the tiny side chamber they'd squeezed themselves into. None of them had been smelling too fresh when the escape began. By now they were all as pungent as billy goats. Krish had one side pressed up against Eric's shoulder and his legs somehow tangled with Dinesh's.

'What, what, what if they look inside?' Dinesh asked quietly.

'I don't think they will,' Krish said. 'They saw our boat. They didn't see us, not up close, and they didn't see where we went when we got out of the boat. They'll think we've headed further inland.'

'*How* did they spot our boat?' Eric asked. 'They was halfway to the horizon when they turned tiller to us. We scrubbed the name off the side days ago. There was half a dozen boats in sight no different from ours.'

'But none of them had you in them,' Dinesh said. 'You're the problem.'

'I ain't the one what nearly got us caught trying to pilfer dried haddock on that last island!' Eric replied fiercely and too loudly.

Krish shushed him. Eric scowled, but shut his mouth. Their tempers had all been stretched to breaking point by the last few days. Getting away from the boat had been easy enough. Getting far enough away from their pursuers was more of a problem.

The outer islands were too sparsely populated, and Krish, Eric and Dinesh were too distinct a group. With word out about them to every fisherman on the sea, the only hope of hiding was in more crowded waters, where a few outland ships and their crew could be found. And so they'd been driven inexorably inwards, until finally they'd been forced to come to the Graveyard, the island at the heart of the archipelago, the capital of the Hundred Islands. It was where Dae Hyo and Thilini and the Hunter were being taken, so it could have been useful. But it would do them no good to come to the same place as their friends if they were captured in the process.

'Dinesh is right,' Krish said to Eric. The indistinct voices of their pursuers outside the cave were growing ever fainter. They were moving away. 'It's your fair skin and your hair most of all. It's the same problem we had in Ofiklanod.'

'I'm sorry to be such a trouble to you,' Eric said.

He hadn't been so sharp-tongued when Krish had last known him, what felt like the blink of an eye ago. But it had been three years for Eric, and in those years one of the worst things that could happen to a person had happened to him. Krish reminded himself of that, and waited the few moments until his own temper had cooled to say, 'You're not trouble, you're a problem, and problems have solutions.'

'You think I should give myself the pox again?' Eric was frowning, but thoughtful now rather than hostile.

Krish shook his head. 'That would draw even more attention. We need to change the colours, that's all.'

'You, you, you don't have your power any more.' As usual when Dinesh spoke, Krish couldn't tell if there was a hidden meaning in the words, or if it was just his own guilt that made him hear one.

'I don't need power,' Krish said. 'I just need my memory. When I was a boy my . . . my da had me dye the goatskins for market sometimes. And this land is my home. Here on these islands, it's more like the mountains than Ashfall or anywhere else I've been in Ashanesland. I think I can find what I need.'

*

Two hours later, he'd gathered enough horn-root to do the job, and they'd been lucky enough to find a sweetnut tree, heavy with nuts. A farmer nearly saw them stripping its branches, but Krish hugged the bole of the tree until he passed. Then they found a fast-moving creek in a gully whose overhanging bushes would hide them from anyone who passed.

Eric looked dubiously at the plants Krish had gathered. 'You sure you ain't gonna make my hair green with that?'

Krish laughed. 'It's the root, not the leaves. You'll see.'

Eric didn't look much less dubious at the sloppy brown concoction Krish spent an hour boiling, but he used the time to smear his face and arms and neck with the husks of the sweetnuts they'd picked. The results didn't make him look much like an Ashaneman. His features were wrong. His nose was too small and his eyes a blue-green that was very seldom found in the country. But Krish's eyes would always mark him out too, and from a distance it would be good enough not to draw attention.

When the dye was ready and cooled, Krish took it to Eric.

'What am I supposed to do with that?' Eric asked. 'Dump it over my head?'

'I'll help you,' Krish said. 'Sit forwards, and lean your head over or I'll get it all over your clothes.'

Eric looked at him askance, then did as he'd been told. Krish wasn't sure of the best way to do it. It wasn't very much like dyeing a hide. In the end, he scooped the bitter-smelling liquid up a handful at a time, and trickled it into Eric's hair, then used his fingers to massage it in.

It was an uncomfortably intimate act. In his youth, Krish had known only his mother's gentle touch and his father's harsh one. Since then, there'd been the whore in Smiler's Fair, years ago now, that Dae Hyo had hired for him. That had ended with Krish being beaten into unconsciousness. And there had been the time Dinesh came to him, while Krish was sleeping, but he preferred not to think of that. Dinesh had been enslaved and not acting of his own will. After that, there'd been only the battle to survive. Krish hadn't realised how hungry he was for another living thing's touch.

He thought Eric might feel the same, from the way he unconsciously leant into Krish's hands as he rubbed in the dye. Eric had been a whore once. He must have been touched a great deal. Krish hadn't understood at the time how a man lay with another man, until Dae Hyo had told him what the men of the tribes did with knife women. Eric had been as pretty as a girl back then, but now his face had the firmness of a man's, though a more handsome one than most.

Krish pulled back, startled, when Dinesh stepped out from between the bushes. He'd been moving very silently. Or perhaps Krish had been too lost in his thoughts to hear.

'Are you finished?' Dinesh asked.

'I think so.' Krish took Eric gingerly by the shoulders to turn him towards Dinesh. 'What do you think?'

Dinesh studied him critically. 'I, I, I think we shouldn't go too close to anyone.'

Eric shook his head like a dog, sending droplets of brown-dyed water everywhere. 'I wasn't intending to go doing cartwheels in the streets. We can stay hidden by this stream for a while. Then there'll be hedges we can hide in, or ditches.'

'No, that will make us more noticeable,' Krish said. 'They're looking for three men who are trying to hide. But they're looking for two Ashanemen and a Jorlith. If they see the three of us walking along like any other islanders, we won't draw their eyes.'

'But where are we going?' Dinesh asked.

'The chief town of the Islands,' Krish said. 'They call it Fleet. That's where their Queen is. It's where they'll have taken the others.'

Dinesh looked mulish. 'So we're going back for *him*.' It was clear 'him' meant Dae Hyo.

'And for Thilini and the Hunter,' Krish said.

'It ain't just because we owe 'em,' Eric said, unexpectedly. Krish hadn't been sure he approved of this plan. 'We'll be stronger if it's all of us. The Hunter's a fighter and Dae Hyo too, especially now he's sober.'

'I'm a fighter,' Dinesh said. He looked it again, finally recovered from the injuries Dae Hyo had inflicted, and strengthened by the last week spent at the oars.

'Fleet is where you'll be able to hire a boat to take you to the mainland, if that's what you want,' Krish told him. 'You don't have to stay with us.'

Dinesh gave him another of his inscrutable looks and didn't reply. Krish couldn't guess what choice he'd make, if they managed to reach Fleet.

The roads here were busy, unlike on any other island they'd visited. There were many wagons loaded with produce and others with fish packed in ice whose origin Krish couldn't guess. There'd been no snow in their time here. There was only the almost constant, salt-laden wind from the sea.

There were more of the ruins here, the scattered, monumental slabs of rock they'd seen on many of the islands they crossed. Krish almost thought he could make out the shape of the buildings they'd once been. And near the island's coast, outlined against the sky, was a hill. That surely wasn't natural, with its squared-off sides and flat top. Perhaps this island had held the chief city of that ancient civilisation, as it held the islanders' now.

An hour into the journey, Eric exclaimed, pointing to their left, 'Look, up there. Do you see them birds?'

Krish saw three of them, but he couldn't see what about them had attracted Eric's interest. 'There's a thousand kinds of gull and heron here,' he said.

'But those ain't none of them. They're too big. I reckon they must be carrion mounts, with the size they are, and I could swear there's someone sitting on that one's back.'

Krish looked closer. He thought Eric might be right. The humped shape on the leading bird's back definitely looked like a person. 'But the carrion mounts look to the Oak Wheel,' he said. 'Or the loyal shiplords. If there's been a rebellion here, there shouldn't be any.'

'Maybe things ain't exactly as we suppose,' Eric said.

Another cart was approaching along the road, this one seemingly loaded with rough round loaves of bread. Krish met the driver's eye as he passed, and risked asking, 'Can you tell us the way to Fleet? We're a little lost.'

The wagoneer pointed ahead and a little to their right. 'She'll be in Horseshoe Harbour now, not but three miles away.'

Krish nodded his thanks, and when they came to the next crossroads, they took the right-hand path.

'I'm hungry,' Dinesh said.

Eric rolled his eyes. 'I wouldn't say no to a nice roast and a syrup pudding myself, but we ain't been invited to any feasts.'

'We can't risk stealing food,' Krish told Dinesh, then spotted a very familiar sight on the scrubby slope to their left and smiled. 'I can get us something, though.'

The small herd of goats seemed to know they'd been seen. Their golden eyes turned towards the road and the billy lifted his brown-and-white head and bleated. The memories that sound woke in Krish were still clear, despite the years between. Some of them even had joy in them.

'You can't mean to slaughter one of those?' Eric said.

'Not slaughter, no.'

It wasn't hard to separate a nanny with milk-gorged teats from her kid. Eric laughed when he saw what Krish was doing, then lay down to rest. Dinesh came to help, though. He held the nanny's head while Krish sat on a low rock beside her. He put the same pot he'd used to dye Eric's hair beneath her, freshly washed. The sound of the milk hitting the pail, squirt after squirt, was familiar too. It was strange how these little things could bring the past back so vividly. Often, Krish's childhood felt more like a dream to him than the impossible place he'd been trapped in for these last three years.

'You've done this before,' Dinesh said.

Krish nodded. 'I was raised to be a goatherd. It was all I knew, until my father's men came for me and I had to run.'

'And then you became a lord.'

'That makes it sound as if I changed, from a goatherd into a lord. But I'm still the same boy who was a goatherd. I still know how to milk a goat. And when I milked goats back then, I was already a lord. I was always my father's son.'

'And then you were my owner,' Dinesh said.

Krish froze, with his hands on the goat's teats and her strong smell in his nose. He made himself continue. This conversation was easier when he didn't have to look Dinesh in the eye.

'I wanted to save you,' he said. 'All of you. But I couldn't free you from the bliss. I'm sorry.'

There was a long silence and Krish thought that might be the end of it. When he looked up finally, the job done, Dinesh was staring at him. Krish dipped a cup into the still warm milk and offered it to him. 'It's not food, but it should ease the hunger.'

Dinesh hesitated, then took the cup. The face he made when he took his first sip made Krish laugh.

'It's a strong taste,' Krish said. 'I suppose the Rah don't have goats, or cows. Do they drink milk at all?'

Dinesh shook his head and passed the cup back to Krish. He emptied it thirstily.

'You, you, you tried to free me,' Dinesh said. 'And you couldn't. You tried and you couldn't. That isn't your fault. But then you used me. You used all the slaves of Mirror Town. That *is* your fault.'

'Yes,' Krish said. 'The only way to free you from bliss was to bind you to me. But once you were bound, I didn't have to send you to war. I didn't have to use you as my army. That was a choice I made.'

Dinesh rubbed at his cheek under his eye. It was a habit he had, when he was thinking. It only occurred to Krish now that he was rubbing the place where the rune that once bound him had been inked onto his skin. 'I don't know what I feel about you,' Dinesh said. 'I can't make up my mind.'

Krish smiled. 'I think that's freedom.'

*

Another hour's walk, along the winding, hedge-lined mud road, and they reached the coast. There was no town, though. There was only a long beach messy with wet weed, a mass of ships out to sea, and one very long wooden pier.

'Oh!' Eric said, after a moment. 'The ships *are* the town. Just like the Drifters.'

There must have been two hundred or more, great and small, floating just beyond the pier's end. Each one was attached to another. Some were only tied on with ropes. For others it was gangplanks and, in the distance, Krish saw an arched bridge wide enough for a horse to cross between a galleon and what looked to be the largest vessel of them all, a vast flat-bottomed barge. A bridge led between the end of the pier and the nearest ship.

'Make haste,' an old woman said, elbowing past him, 'else we'll miss our chance. Can't you feel the wind?'

They walked over the bridge to the first ship, a small sailing boat, and then across two galleys, all of which seemed to be given over to living quarters. The next was a wide raft crammed with market stalls. Hawkers shouted their wares and other people yelled and pushed at each other to get to a stall stacked with fresh cakes or one that was piled with fruit. In the centre of it all, a juggler in bright purple and red struggled to keep his balls in the air as he was knocked first one way then another by the crowd. He had a hat at his feet, but no one stopped to fill it with coin.

'No,' Eric said. 'It ain't the Drifters at all. It's the spit of Smiler's Fair.'

Krish had thought once they reached here that it would be clear where to go. He thought he'd see the ship that held the others captive docked in the bay, but this chaos offered him no directions.

'Up there!' Dinesh said. 'It's one of those big birds again.'

But, closer to, it didn't really look like a bird at all. It took Krish a moment to understand what it actually was, because the scale was all wrong. It was the size of a carrion mount, if not the shape, but it should have been either far smaller, or much, much larger.

Eric let out a gasp that was half a sob. 'Her children!' he said. 'That's one of her children.'

He said something else, but his voice was drowned by a sudden chorus of horns. They sounded all at once and seemingly from every ship. When their echo died down, a voice shouted, 'Wind's a blowing, weigh anchor, set sail.'

The people who'd one moment ago been selling produce, or haggling for it, all rushed to left and right. A sea of sails were raised all around them – and the town made of boats began, very slowly and ponderously, to move.

The boats weren't all fixed in their position relative to each other. Some were tied by many ropes, others only to their neighbours. As the town itself moved, the boats moved around each other. And two sailing vessels slid apart to reveal, beyond them, the great barge at the centre of the floating city. And on it: Rii.

Eric stared at her, wide-mouthed, for one long moment of shock. Then he took off towards her, heedless of the danger of running over the moving ships. Krish grabbed Dinesh's arm and pulled him along in pursuit. They sprinted up a steeply tilted plank that ran from their raft to the deck of the sailing ship. The plank wobbled and they teetered perilously on its edge. Then it righted itself and they leapt onto the deck, dodging ropes, and then down another ramp, until all three of them were standing, staring at the monster they'd never thought to see again.

'*Thou hast come at last, morsel,*' Rii said. '*I have kept thy son safe for thee as I promised.*' She peered down, huge half-blind eyes blinking as Eric fell to his knees in front of her and wept.

21

Olufemi and Bruyar had been eight days in the woods. They'd taken as much food from the ships as they could carry between them, but Olufemi was old and Bruyar unused to hard labour. They hadn't been able to carry much, and they'd eaten the last of it three days ago.

They'd passed at least a score of streams in their journey, pouring their waters through rocky gullies into the ocean, but they hadn't dared drink. If every tree here was poison, and their roots drank from this water, who was to say the water itself wasn't death? But the water they'd taken from the ship had run out yesterday.

Currently, they were in the dense darkness of the woods. 'I believe,' Olufemi said, 'that I hate the forest most of all.'

'So you told me yesterday, my darling,' Bruyar said. 'And the day before it was the beach that you most loathed. But the last headland we passed was very familiar to me – the shape of it, like a rearing horse. I'm sure the ships we saw lie just beyond it.'

'So *you* said yesterday, of the rock shaped like an apple, and the day before it was the stand of trees in the shape of a heart. I wonder what landmark will be familiar to you tomorrow.'

Bruyar made no reply to this. Neither of them said the most obvious thing: that they might have failed to find the ships because they'd sailed away.

Olufemi kept her head down, watching her own feet. There were venomous insects here, too. A creature that had looked like a grasshopper had sunk its fangs into her ankle yesterday. The bite had swelled to the size of a plum and was weeping a thin yellow fluid.

A loud cry sounded ahead of her, and her feet stumbled. When she looked up, she realised that Bruyar was no longer in sight. Had that cry been *omas*? She lifted up her robes and hurried as best she could along the path of trodden-down vegetation that Bruyar had left.

When she finally found Bruyar, Olufemi let out a cry of her own.

'Did I not tell you that I recognised the headland?' Bruyar said.

They had, at last, found the ships. There wasn't just one but an entire fleet, swaying on the waters of a great, half-moon bay several hundred paces below the clifftop. They were sailing ships, clearly ocean-going vessels, but not of any design Olufemi had ever seen. The ships were three-masted, with sails not just square on the mast but angled to run the length of the ship, and all a bright crimson. A banner with the head of a wolf in a similar blood red snapped from the foremast of each.

The bay itself was a black desolation. There'd been a fire here that had consumed all the vegetation for at least a mile in each direction. It had clearly been recent. No green shoots were showing beneath the soot, and Olufemi saw wisps of smoke curling from its furthest reaches.

'Did they set it, do you think?' Olufemi asked. 'Or were they drawn by it?'

'I can think of one way to find the answer.' Bruyar stepped onto the narrow path that curled down the cliffs towards the sand.

★

Their feet were crunching through the charcoaled branches before they were spotted. It was a young woman, with the curled hair and milky skin of the Rhinnanish folk of the Moon Forest, although the cast of her features looked more like the tribes. She was raking the coals aside, to what purpose Olufemi couldn't guess. When she saw them, she shrieked, dropped the rake and ran.

'Well,' Bruyar said, 'I suppose we must look quite a sight by now.'

Olufemi had caught her reflection in a pond yesterday afternoon.

Their clothes were little more than rags and their hair was dusty and wild. She knew that her years were sitting very heavily on her.

Before they could move, more footsteps crunched through the soot and a moment later they were faced with a line of five men. Their faces were drawn and the skin seemed too tight over the bones of their arms, but each of them carried a sword.

'We mean no harm,' Bruyar said in the Moon Forest tongue.

The men's faces were uncomprehending.

Olufemi repeated the phrase again, in Ashane and then the dialect of the tribes. Finally, she tried the language of the savannah people she'd once learned from her lover, and their faces cleared.

'How came you here?' the lead man asked.

Olufemi had to concentrate hard to understand him. His accent was heavily distorted. Was it time or distance that had changed it from the one she knew? 'Our ship was blown off course,' she said. 'Is this your home?'

'This is home to nobody,' the man said. 'These are the Deadlands.'

'All this area?' Bruyar asked.

The men eyed *omas* askance. Olufemi thought they might be trying to work out if *oms* was man or woman. Inter weren't known outside of Ofiklanod. It had taken Olufemi herself some time to make her mind accept the in-betweenness of them, the both and neither of their nature. Her mind kept trying to fit them inside neat lines.

'All the land,' a younger man said. 'All of it.'

'The whole country?' Olufemi asked.

'All the land,' he said again. 'Any earth that touches this earth is poisoned. The seed of every plant and every tree. All poison.'

Bruyar and Olufemi exchanged a glance. They'd been right, it seemed, to forgo all food. 'How can it have happened?' Olufemi asked. 'We saw a city – a great city. And we know that people came from these lands. Many different peoples. This earth wasn't always dead.'

Now it was the men exchanging glances. 'People came? Came where? What people?'

'Perhaps,' Bruyar said, 'we might discuss it over food and drink? We've been without for days. I have no coin to pay you, but there's gold on my ship, if you can return us there.'

This, Olufemi knew, was most definitely a lie.

One of the men laughed, a high squawk that didn't sound quite like amusement. The others frowned him into silence.

'Yes, of course,' the first man said. 'Come, follow us. We have bread and soup for your gold.'

The encampment was ramshackle, part canvas tents and part huts made of old, warped wood. But there was metal everywhere: in the men's swords, the blades of shovels and hoes and the thick needles that Olufemi saw a small group of youngsters using to repair a sail. Whatever land they came from, it must be free of Yron's servants, if metal was so easily mined.

They were kept waiting, while the inhabitants of the camp stared at them out of the corners of their eyes while trying to seem indifferent. There were at least fifty people here. None of them looked better fed than those who'd found them. Still, when the meal arrived, it was generous. They were given dried fruit and round, flat bread to dip into a soup with a little meat in it.

Bruyar drew eyes again, this time when they saw the stumps where *omas* hands had been. Olufemi had grown so used to the task of feeding *omas* that she barely noticed now the way in which she took one mouthful for herself and gave another to Bruyar. But these people didn't know what the Mortals were.

The strangers were full of questions. It took a little time for them to grasp that Bruyar and Olufemi came from a great continent across the ocean from this one. They found it even harder to understand that many folk had come there from here.

'How long ago?' a woman asked. She appeared to be their leader. She was the eldest by far, white-haired and unsteady on her feet. They'd been told her name was Atlani.

'Different times,' Bruyar told her. 'Longest ago were the Fourteen Tribes, around eight hundred years past. Two hundred years later, the shipfolk came, and a further two hundred years, two folk together, the Jorlith and the Rhinnanish people. As for the people of the savannah – those who resemble yourselves most closely – no one can say. They've chosen to forget their own past.'

Atlani leaned back, seemingly satisfied. 'Yes, so the histories say. But none ever returned. We thought that every one of them had perished. If they had found a fertile place, a good place to live, why did they not return to us?'

'The lands we come from are poisoned too, though not as comprehensively as these,' Olufemi said. 'There's a death that lives below the ground, if the ground is kept in shadow.'

'And how long ago,' Bruyar asked, 'did the death of this land occur? Not a one of the peoples who came to us spoke of it.'

'Two thousand years past,' Atlani said.

Bruyar frowned. 'But surely that cannot be? The last people came to our lands from these a mere few hundred years ago.'

'*This* portion of the land died two thousand years ago, as the seeds of poison spread. But at first it was contained. When the people here knew the death they'd made, they built a great canal from sea to sea at the narrow neck of the promontory to keep that death from spreading. They died, but the other people of this continent lived. And for centuries, all knew not to step foot here. But the truth turned into a legend and the legend came to be believed false. And so, when an empire rose four hundred years ago that was hungry for land, the canal was crossed, letting the seed of poison free to spread to the wider land.'

'I see,' Bruyar said. 'The Ashane and the Fourteen Tribes must hail from corners of the continent where the poison hadn't yet reached.'

Omas eyes were intent on Atlani, so perhaps *oms* didn't notice what Olufemi did. They'd been given food to eat, but no one else was partaking. Her stomach knotted and she had to fight the urge to spit out what was in her mouth. If they'd been given poison, she'd already eaten enough to doom her. And their hosts seemed too keen to question them to want them dead. Perhaps it was merely a courtesy, to feed guests before themselves, but Olufemi couldn't quite make herself believe it. The people here were all too thin, and their eyes were all too desperate.

'And so eventually the death came for all of you,' Bruyar said. 'But what *is* the death?'

Atlani shrugged. 'A hating in the plants for us. We do not know its cause. It's said an angry god did it, in revenge against his sister. Is there truth in this? I cannot say.'

Bruyar nodded. 'And where have your people lived, in all the years since? An island, I presume? It must be land cut off from other land.'

'Cold islands in the far north. It has been a hard living. Many died. We are a remnant of a remnant of those who fled the death in these lands. And so my people came, to see if the death itself had died after so many years, and thus we could return.'

'But the poison is still here,' Bruyar said.

Atlani made a gesture with her hand that Olufemi didn't understand. She thought perhaps it meant a warding off of ill luck. 'My people came three years past, ready for the poison. A colony was planted. We thought to visit them again in ten years' time, and see how they fared. But the next year in our home, there was a murrain among our cattle. The year after, a fire mountain that buried our chief town, and after that a year without a summer. Many died and many more are starving. And so we have returned, to see if our colony is thriving.'

'And is it?' Olufemi asked. She and Bruyar had seen no sign of one.

'No, not thriving,' Atlani said. 'We will show you on the morrow.'

The day had waned into night by the time the meal and the conversation were finished. Then they were rowed aboard one of the ships and given a berth in its lowest quarters, cramped but dry.

'Well,' Bruyar said, as *oms* lay down to sleep, 'a very generous people and a far kinder welcome than we could have expected.'

The tone was entirely sincere, but Olufemi had been with Bruyar long enough to sense the currents beneath the surface. She understood that Bruyar had, in fact, noticed what Olufemi had. Throughout the meal, not a single bite of food had passed their hosts' lips. Either these were the kindest folk that walked the earth, or there was something that they wanted of Bruyar and Olufemi. And if their hosts had failed to ask for it, it was probably something they wouldn't be happy to give.

★

In the morning, Bruyar asked if they might be allowed to see the colony. They were told to inspect it at their leisure. Their hosts left them to guide themselves along the broad path that led inland from the ashen area around the ships.

It was a beautiful setting. There were mountains in the distance, jagged and snow-capped, and the trees were in spring bloom. The eyes of monkeys peered at them through the leaves while insects feasted on the flowers. Whatever this poison was that so afflicted the place, these animals must be immune to it.

'They were too glad to let us go,' Bruyar said, once they'd turned a corner in the path and were out of sight of the ships and the ramshackle camp on the shore.

'Glad of a chance to talk without us present,' Olufemi said.

'But what is it you think they're discussing?'

'Nothing that we'll enjoy, I'm sure of that.'

Bruyar frowned. 'Are you, my darling? I'm sure they meant us harm when we first met, but after we exchanged our tales? Our news was as fresh to them as theirs was to us.'

'Do you think the poison here could be the work of the sun or moon? They said a brother created this poison in revenge against his sister. Or was it this progenitor god you spoke of?'

'If we returned to the city, we might learn more. There were books there, did you notice? I saw a library in a house we passed. The whole place seemed like an insect set in amber on the day of its death. 'Tis certain there'll be knowledge there that shouldn't be left to rot.'

'We'll ask our hosts to sail us back,' Olufemi said cuttingly. 'I'm quite sure they'll oblige.'

'Dearest, there's no need to take that tone with me. I'm well aware of the fragility of our position. But any hand may be played to advantage if it's played well.'

Olufemi snorted. 'So speaks a person unskilled at cards. Some hands should only be thrown away and the game conceded.'

'No,' Bruyar said, 'some hands require that the game be changed, to one that the cards can win.' *Oms* stopped as voices became audible through the trees ahead.

The village was surrounded by the stumps of the trees that had been felled. But here too a fire had been set in the land around it. There was ash in all directions but the one from which they'd come, stretching far further than the burning around the beach. Olufemi wondered if the flames they'd set had blazed beyond their control.

'Ingenious,' Bruyar said. *Omas* eyes were on the fields that surrounded the village, the only place where green shoots still showed.

But they weren't fields, Olufemi realised. They were wooden trays of earth, laid on the ground. Had the newcomers brought their own soil with them? The plants were young still, but she saw one tray of tomatoes close to ripening and another with pea pods just developing.

'Perhaps they're not as poorly off as we thought,' she said with relief. 'They're merely waiting for this crop to bear fruit.'

'All things are possible,' Bruyar murmured.

There were children in the fields, some little more than babes. When she and Bruyar walked closer, they stopped to stare, mouths agape. They were skeletally thin. Some looked too weak to work.

'Weeding,' Bruyar said. 'A more vital task here than in most lands. If one seed of this land takes root, will it poison the rest? I suppose they must think so.'

'Where are their parents?' Olufemi asked, but then caught sight of her answer. In the distance, a train of cattle was being herded across the ash towards the village. They were milk cows, she saw once they were closer. Their teats looked full.

'And animals put out to pasture on the local grass,' Bruyar said. "Tis well thought through.'

But when the adults had reached the outskirts of the village, Olufemi saw that they were worse than thin. Some had faces raddled with pox, fresh sores weeping. One cradled a hand that was more black than pink. And there was a hopeless look on all their faces.

'If they came to see how their colony is faring,' Bruyar said dryly, 'the answer would appear to be: not well.'

'And the people on the boats chose to remain by the shore. They've kept themselves apart from this colony. Something is iller here than I understand. We must leave. We can return to our ship.'

'And sail it on our own, I suppose?'

'We can find a way. Bruyar, the meat in the soup they gave us, I think I know what it was.'

'It was human,' Bruyar said calmly. 'I guessed so on the first bite.'

Olufemi swallowed the bile that stung her throat, even though she'd suspected the same. 'Then surely we must run away? What choice do we have? I'd rather starve than be eaten.'

'La,' Bruyar said, ''tis quite simple. We change the game to one in which we need suffer neither fate. But we should return before they've made up their minds whether to boil or fry us.'

★

The men were waiting for them on the beach when they returned, weapons drawn. They didn't look hateful or angry. They merely seemed resigned. Atlani stood in the centre of them, leaning wearily on a young man's arm. She saw their faces as they emerged from the forest and nodded.

'You understand, then. The colony can't sustain itself. The poison is changed by passing through a beast, but it's poison still. Slower, only. Seeds travel on the winds. The fields can't be kept clean, no matter how hard they try. Even the bees bring the poison with them when they move from flower to flower.'

Olufemi didn't understand how Bruyar could look so calm. Her own chest was so tight with fear she could barely draw breath.

'So the flesh of your colonists is poison too,' *oms* said.

Atlani nodded.

'You've had to eat each other.' Olufemi's horror grew.

'We drew lots,' Atlani said. 'Twenty have been chosen to feed us on the journey home. Until then, all the food we have left is theirs to eat. It is the only justice we can give. But now you have come, and you are healthy and there is still flesh on you. Because of you, three, maybe four of our own may be spared.'

'Or,' Bruyar said, 'you could set sail for the lands from which we came.'

'You said those also are poisoned. We cannot travel from death to death. Our home is bad, yes. The crops have failed, but there is still life there to be had.'

Bruyar smiled. 'There's life to be had in our lands too. There's a very good one, for those who know how to take it. Those such as myself and Olufemi. We can teach you how to live there, if you put some other unfortunates in your cookpot.'

'Why should your people welcome us? Are you leaders there?'

'You won't need their welcome,' Bruyar said, 'if you come as conquerors. Metal is scarce there and weapons primitive. But your swords are steel.'

22

Arwel was playing with Rii's children, the seven Eric now knew had survived. They were frolicking in a meadow to the east of where Fleet had made anchor. One edge of the meadow was a fence, and beyond it a long white cliff down to the sea. There were cows in it, brown-and-white and stupid-eyed, who'd scarpered to the far end when Rii's children showed up. Her pups weren't much bigger than them, but Eric was sure they made an alarming sight if you were a cow. The cows probably didn't much like the scent of them either. They smelled of mouldy cinnamon, just like their mum. They looked like their mum too, but in miniature. Born into a world without magic, they'd grown to a normal size, small enough their wings could hold them aloft without any other power to help.

Arwel was as happy as a dog with a marrow bone. His high, piping voice wasn't much different from Rii's pups. They chattered and ran about like any group of children might, playing chase and wrestling and laughing, only sometimes they did it in the air. The first time Eric had seen Arwel leap on one of the pup's backs, he'd close to died of fright. Arwel had only been clinging on by one arm as they rose a hundred paces above the field. But Arwel held tight and giggled with a joy so pure it hurt Eric's heart.

He didn't think Arwel knew he was there, watching from the shadow of the hedge. He wasn't sure his boy would have cared, even if he did know. When Rii had introduced Eric to him, Arwel had hidden behind Rii's leathery wings. He hadn't said more than two words to Eric since, despite every effort Eric made to talk to him. Arwel was close to four, and no memory he still had held Eric in it.

The pain of it was terrible. But there was also the giddy

Moon's End

pleasure of the knowledge that his son had lived after all. Eric had been a stranger to happy feelings for so long that he found the joy even harder to manage than the pain.

Rii had fallen in the sea, just like he'd been told. But she'd floated, and the currents had carried her to the shores of the Hundred Islands with her surviving pups, and Arwel. Eric was still unclear how she'd gone from driftwood to monarch here. But the islanders were odd coves. They seemed to prefer a Queen of their own, however strange, to their distant ruler on the mainland. She was flightless now, without the moon's magic to hold her up, so there was no chance of her picking up and leaving. The locals probably liked that too.

A footstep crunched on twigs behind him, but he didn't turn around. Unlike Arwel, he was quite conscious of who'd been watching him from up the path a bit. Drut, or Thilini, as he was supposed to call her now. And there was another strange mix of feelings, shame and anger all jumbled together. There was a little affection too. He'd cared for her once, and she for him, even if it wasn't the sort of caring he'd let her think it was. That part of the memory was pure shame.

'You should go to him,' she said quietly.

He glanced at her and then away. 'He don't know me from a boulder.'

'Then we're both in the same position.'

He looked at her again, to see if that was meant as a barb, but she seemed serious.

'He's happy. I don't want to stop his play,' Eric told her.

She stepped forwards again, until she was half in front of him, and he was forced to meet her eye. 'He doesn't know you, but his happiness is because of you. He wouldn't be safe here if it weren't for you.'

'If I'd let you kill him, you mean,' Eric said, and there was the anger.

She hung her head.

'It weren't right, what I did to you,' he added more softly. 'I'm sorry for it.'

She smiled, a tiny bit. 'It was so long ago. Since then I've been a different person.'

'Yeah. I think I have too. I've spent so long mourning him, I've forgotten how to be his dad.'

'I never learned to be a mother,' she said. 'Perhaps we can discover it together.'

She made it sound simple, when he knew it never could be, but he nodded anyway. It was better to have hope, wasn't it? And Arwel was alive. He was alive, so nothing else truly mattered.

'I think—' she said, and then broke off, her gaze on the horizon.

'What is it?'

She looked a moment longer before saying, 'Ships.'

He laughed. 'You'll be finding sand on the beach next. There's always ships in these waters.'

'Not such as these. They aren't fishing vessels. There are marks of battle on them.'

He peered where she was looking, shading his eyes from the sun, but they weren't as sharp as hers. All he could see were a few distant dots. 'Is there any banner on them? Anything to say whose they are?'

'There is a flag. I believe . . . there's a wheel on it, with spokes that extend past its circumference. Does this symbol mean anything to you?'

'It's the Oak Wheel,' Eric said. 'The King of Ashanesland. Looks like he's come to take back the islands what Rii stole off him.'

*

It was impossible to have a private conversation with Rii. Her bulk was too great to fit anywhere in Fleet but on the raft that the people of the Islands had made for her. She'd lost the ability to fly when the power of the runes left the world. Krish thought it might have done her other damage too. Her breaths rasped in and out as if they caused her pain, or required great effort.

It was a strange court she kept in the open air. The gulls overflew it and the sound of the sea breaking on the shore accompanied every word. Any inhabitant of Fleet was free to come and speak to her, and they seemed to do it without fear. His first day here, Krish saw a fisherwoman draw up her coracle at the edge of the raft and shout to Rii, 'There's tunny in the waters east,' before sailing off.

But there were a few who seemed to have made themselves her courtiers. Krish wasn't sure if Rii had chosen them or they'd chosen themselves. She seldom seemed to consult them, but they were there every time Krish came. They were there when Rii told him there was war on the mainland. There'd been an invasion from Ofiklanod by people following some strange new gods. Krish thought he knew the ones she meant. He'd felt them in the dreaming world. But that wasn't what he'd come to speak to her about today.

When he and Eric and Dinesh had arrived, they'd found Thilini and the Hunter imprisoned in the bowels of one of the bigger ships, and Dae Hyo raging but impotent. He'd told Krish that Rii had sentenced them both to death.

'You can't kill her,' Krish said, to Rii and the interested audience of islanders. 'Bachur isn't our enemy, not any more. She and Eric are friends.'

'Then he is too easy with his friendship. The Hunter bound me with magic through a millennium of servitude. I will not suffer her to live a day longer. Thou art lucky, that I allowed the one who was once Mizhara to go free. I did it only for the sake of Eric's son. For Bachur, there is no cause to spare her.'

'What if I commanded it?' It was the first time Krish had dared to ask. He didn't know if it was him, or only the dead moon she served.

'I am not thine to command,' Rii said.

There was his answer, then. It troubled him how little he minded it. He would have spared Bachur if he could, but the letting go of power? There was a freedom in it. He'd used authority when it was given to him. He wasn't sure if he'd ever done anything good with it. And he was just a mortal man now, not even one who'd been trained to rule. Goat-rearing was the skill he'd been born to. Why couldn't he go back to that, and let the world care for itself?

He had his answer to that, too, when a moment later Eric ran, gasping, onto the great raft. His eyes flicked between Rii and Krish as he struggled to regain his breath, as if he wasn't sure which of them to speak to. When he could talk, he made his choice and looked at Krish. 'Ships are coming, flying the flag of the Oak Wheel. I think your dad's here.'

★

Krish waited on the pier for the lead ship's arrival. The closer it got, the more battered it appeared. Eric had been right. The figure standing in the prow was his father.

When the ship finally docked, he strode down the gangplank to clasp Krish's shoulders in his withered hands. He'd been an old man the last time Krish saw him, but he was even more diminished now. His grasp on Krish was weak and his hands were shaking. It woke the gentlest emotion in Krish that he'd ever felt around his father. It wasn't love – it would probably never be that – but it was a sort of fondness.

'I thought you were dead,' his father said. 'Renar told me that you'd drowned.'

'I thought *she* drowned,' Krish replied, startled. 'She's with you? And Lanalan as well?'

Nayan shook his head. 'They were. She told me you were no longer . . . what you used to be.' He stared into Krish's eyes, whose pupils were still crescents.

'I'm not a god.'

'But you remain my son, and Wheelheir to a kingdom that's under attack from Ofiklanod. Why now, after all this time? Was it something that you did there?'

'No,' Krish said firmly, but then added, 'or I suppose it was, in a way. When I stopped being a god, three new ones came. I don't know how it happened. That's who the Ofiklanders are following now, or at least that's what Rii told me.'

'Rii,' Nayan said flatly. 'The usurper.'

'They love her here. Da, don't pick a fight with her too.'

His father smiled faintly. 'I don't mean to, Krishanjit. I mean to make an alliance. I can take back our lands; all I need is an army.'

★

Eric went to see the Hunter. The cell in the ship's hold was clean, at least, and they'd given her food and a chair and water. Her eyes were very calm as the guard grudgingly let Eric inside.

'You look well,' she said. 'I am glad your son has been returned to you.'

'I've talked to Rii,' Eric told her, 'but she ain't listening. She's hated you so long, she can't remember how not to.'

'She has every right. I made her a slave. That is an evil thing for any living thing to do to another. And she my husband's mount and friend.'

Eric sat on the bed beside her. 'Tit for tat then. But ain't you sick of it? It just goes on and on.'

She smiled. It caused the little crow's feet in the corner of her eyes to wrinkle, the marks of age that hadn't been there when they first met. 'So it has always been, and I am content with that justice. I am very tired, Eric. I have lived a great many years and seen every corner of the world. I have watched a thousand of my hawks die. There is nothing left for me to do but this one thing. I am satisfied with its conclusion.'

'Well I ain't! I want it to end. I want all of it to end.'

'All of what, Eric?'

'The killing. The vengeance. All the ugly things I seen so much of these past years. I've got a son. I don't want a world of war for him.'

'Do you wish for it to end, Eric? Or do *you* wish to end it?' She took his hands in hers. It was the first time she'd ever touched him in that way, and it shocked him into stillness. 'Nothing will change unless someone changes it. I did my part, when I took Mizhara from the world, but my day is over. It is your day now, yours and Krishanjit's and all the rest, the children's children of those for whom I once fought. The world is yours now. You must choose what to do with it.'

★

Krish sat in the war council for as long as he could bear. It went on a whole day, and then halfway into another. Rii had a mind for it, and his father was born to it. It was strange to see them so allied. But Krish's hope that this would distract Rii from her plan to hang the Hunter was fruitless.

'*I would drink her blood with mine own teeth,*' she told Krish, at the end of the second day's council. '*But my island people do not kill thus, so for their sakes I will hang her.*'

He didn't imagine the manner of the execution would make much difference to Bachur. Dead was dead. But it seemed too ordinary an end for a being who'd led such an extraordinary life. For a thousand years she'd pretended to be a god, and now she'd die like a common criminal.

The ships of Fleet hadn't moved since Nayan and his people came. The waters around them were full of the shit and piss and spoiled food that people always left behind them. It reminded Krish of Smiler's Fair more than ever, and he couldn't stand it. There were too many people and too many of them seemed to be talking about the Hunter's death. They were looking forward to the spectacle.

On shore, he found Dae Hyo pacing near the thick ropes that moored Fleet to the land.

'I tell you what,' he said, as soon as he saw Krish, 'I'd like to hang all of *them* and let the Hunter go.'

'Me too.'

'You're not in the war council, brother.'

Krish shrugged. 'They're plotting battles. My father and Rii and every Ashane lord who made it out after the conquest.'

'*They're* plotting it, but not you?'

'What do I know about armies, or war?'

Dae Hyo laughed. 'More than them. You beat Nayan at Mirror Town.'

'I had my magic then. Now I'm just a man.'

'Men win wars too,' Dae Hyo said. 'You're no warrior, brother, but you have the wisdom of an elder mother.'

'If I was wise, I'd be able to figure out how to stop Rii killing Bachur.'

He went to watch the hanging the next morning. He felt he owed her that. Dae Hyo came too, and Eric, all her travelling companions. Her eyes met each of them in turn before she began her walk to the gibbet.

Dae Hyo let out a growl of anger. His hand was near his sword, and Krish placed his own on Dae Hyo's arm as Bachur reached the scaffold. A fight here could only lead to one thing. There were a thousand in the crowd who'd come to watch the execution. All of them seemed to know what Bachur had done to their Queen, and there was bloodthirst in their expressions.

Bachur's back was straight and her face calm as she climbed the wooden steps. The crowd didn't like that. They wanted her fear, and she wasn't giving it to them. But then her face had always shown very little of what she thought. Krish couldn't believe she felt nothing at all in these last moments. She'd lived such a long life. She'd been born un-ageing, made so that she'd never face death. Surely the prospect of it now must daunt her.

He wished he'd asked her about it. He wished he'd had more time to speak to her. There was so much she knew and could have told him. Without meaning to, his own feet took him forwards, until he was at the edge of the crowd that surrounded the scaffold. The folk of the Islands were too focused on Bachur to mind him, but she saw. She turned her eyes to him as her head was placed in the noose.

Now his own hand was on his own knife and it was Dae Hyo who was looking at *him* with alarm. But he was the Wheelheir. What could they do if he cut the rope away?

Bachur's eyes flicked down to his hand then back to his own eyes, and she smiled and shook her head. He released his hand from the knife. In the end, this was her choice. She waved away the sack that was offered to cover her eyes. Rii's own big, black, half-blind eyes were fixed avidly on her as the hangman took his position. And then the trapdoor was dropped and the deed was done.

Krish walked away at that. He didn't need to see her death dance. He'd seen enough deaths already. After a few paces, he realised that Eric was walking beside him. There was a tear forming in the corner of Eric's eye, but he swiped it impatiently away. 'She died for nothing,' he said.

'For vengeance.'

'For nothing,' Eric repeated. 'I think she was my friend. I ain't got many, and now there's one less.'

'I'm sorry,' Krish said. 'I hardly knew her.'

Eric nodded, and they walked in silence for a while. They headed by unspoken agreement to the coast path that ran a complete ring around the island, sometimes high on white cliffs and sometimes low in the salty weeds at the beach's edge.

'I ain't angry with Rii,' Eric said after a while. 'She was only acting according to her nature. She's been the way she is for a thousand years and more. I expect she's too old to change.'

There was a meaning beneath his words that Krish didn't fully grasp. 'But you aren't?' he tried.

Eric looked uncertain and briefly a lot more like the young man that Krish had first met. But then his expression firmed. 'I changed when I thought Arwel was . . . when I thought he was gone. I always thought my nature was sunshine. That's what Madam Aeronwen told me. She was the madam in the place what I worked. She told me I was a dreamer. She didn't mean it nice, but I was proud of it. I saw other people so full of anger or bitterness. I never said it, maybe I never thought it clear in my own head, but I reckoned I was better cause I never gave in to those things. I thought I didn't have that darkness in me. Then Arwel was took away from me, and I learned it was there all along.'

'I killed my father,' Krish told him. There was a release in saying it. He'd kept it hugged close to himself for so long. 'My da, I mean – the man who raised me. That's when I saw the darkness in myself.'

'I suppose we was only acting according to what's in *our* natures.'

'Yes. All I used to know was my village. I didn't understand anything then. But I've met a lot of people since. I've seen a lot of evil. I've seen good too. I think maybe everything is in everyone.'

'You're different since you woke, you know,' Eric said. 'Less . . .'

'Angry?'

'Yeah, I reckon. Do you think that's cause the moon was taken out of you?'

Krish looked out across the sea. It was very still today beneath a white sky. 'It would be nice to think so, wouldn't it? To blame everything on him. But he was me. The moon comes and the moon goes. Wars are fought and won and lost and fought again. What's the point of it all?'

'I don't know,' Eric said. 'But I know one thing. It only ends when we end it.'

23

Yemisi spent a few days simply ignoring what Marvan had told her. Her fruitless research continued, as did Alfreda's experiments. Her horrifying, reanimated dog had been joined by a cat, a beetle mount and a whole nest of serpents. But none of them was anything more than a meat puppet of her will. The man she'd slowly built, layer by awful layer, was now in possession of skin. But he wasn't, and would almost certainly never be alive.

Then, a week after Marvan had departed for Ashanesland, the sil-nafön crew that Alfreda had sent to the Moon Forest to fetch her brother's remains returned.

It was only luck that had Yemisi present when they did while Alfreda was off obtaining more dead flesh for her experiments. She found the crew still waiting below their grounded sil-nafön, its bells silent. There were five of them: four men with their ears belled and their expressions blank, and one woman leading them. She wasn't belled, and *her* expression was fearful as Yemisi approached.

'Well?' Yemisi said. 'A failed mission, I presume? You won't be punished. It wasn't likely you'd be able to track down one body in the whole forest.'

'No, not a failure,' the woman said.

'You found him?' Yemisi peered over the side of the wagon. There was indeed a cloth-wrapped bundle on its floor. It looked smaller than a corpse.

'We found what remained of him.' Grim-faced, the woman lifted the bundle out of the wagon. She laid it on the ground in front of Yemisi and knelt to open the cloth.

Inside, there was nothing but bones. Yemisi saw a skull with a ragged hole in its left side, a shin bone, a clavicle and four finger bones. There was nothing more.

The woman's look of fear had intensified. 'La, 'twas not our fault. We did all that we could, I swear. We put people to the spear until they spoke and dug a hundred pits. But the body was buried too shallowly. Beasts had at it, and who can say where they went to gnaw the bones? Should we go back and hunt for each wolf or lynx that prowls the forest?'

It took Yemisi a moment to realise that the woman meant the suggestion quite seriously. 'No,' she said. 'There's no need for that.'

'Then we should take them to the God-Triumvir?' The woman now looked on the point of fainting from terror.

'There's no need for that either. Go about your duties. I'll see that Alfreda is told.'

She waited until the sil-nafön had vanished into a cloud before she picked up Algar's remains. Then she sat and drank rice wine until her own fear was sufficiently dulled. Alfreda was a gentle person at heart, she reminded herself. A good one. And she was Yemisi's friend.

But every time she had that thought, her mind insisted on presenting her with her another one: an image of Alfreda's face, if Yemisi were to show her the pitiful bag of Algar's bones.

She couldn't do it. It would destroy Alfreda's hope. But maybe Yemisi could find another way to give it back to her, before she had to show her what remained of her brother. Marvan had spoken of an older magic. A more powerful one, perhaps, and Bruyar had known its secrets. *Omas* family were still in Ofiklanod, and Yemisi had a fair idea of where to find them. And with the knowledge of the old gods, surely even ... even remains such as these could be made flesh again.

She tossed the bag into the bottom of a chest, where Alfreda couldn't stumble over it. Then she went to find the Mortals in their new hall.

She wasn't a welcome presence in this place. The Mortals resented her for her closeness to Alfreda. But because of that closeness, they didn't dare turn her away when she strode through the door.

'Bruyar's family?' Rorön asked. 'Why should we be interested in them?'

'Because they're Bruyar's family and one day Bruyar may return,' Yemisi said flatly. 'Don't pretend to be an idiot, Rorön, when I know you aren't. You know where they are.'

'And if I did, why should I tell you?'

'Because if you don't tell me, I'll send the God-Triumvir to ask, and you can pretend ignorance to *her* instead. Or maybe I'll send Marvan. He told me he's in need of entertainment.'

Rorön couldn't hide his shudder. The Mortals didn't love the gods they'd created. 'We've kept them with our other guests,' he said grudgingly. 'They're in the Garden of Yron. Or what remains of it.'

★

What remained of it, Yemisi discovered, was very little. When she and Olufemi had stumbled on it, it had been ringed by a vast wall inscribed with runes. The wall was shattered and the runes obliterated. Only scattered heaps of brick and crumbling stone told where it had ever stood.

Inside, the marble paths and statues remained, but they wound between bare-branched orchards and a dry stream bed. It reminded Yemisi of the fields around Mirror Town, leached of the sun's power. And yet, in its very centre, there was a paradise. It was as lush as the Garden of Yron had once been, but no plant that grew here now would have grown there. Every one of them was three-leafed, and each leaf different.

Yemisi followed the path through the woodland, until she came to a meadow, noisy with the shouts of cicadas. Sitting at his ease in the middle was a fat man in a reclining chair. A thinner inter lay on *omas* back on a blanket beside him. The scattered remains of a substantial picnic were all around them, already attracting wasps.

When the man saw her, he frowned. 'And who are you? Another of our gaolers?'

'Are you Bruyar's husband, Dastief?' she asked.

'What do you want with him?' the inter demanded. 'Don't you think you've hurt him enough?'

Yemisi studied the man, but he didn't appear to be the slightest bit injured.

The man seemed to understand her look. 'I'm *not* Dastief. I'm Siamo and my spouse there is Prasic.'

So these were Nabofik's parents. 'I'm not here to hurt anyone,' she said. 'I serve your child's sister-god.'

'So does everyone in this wretched place,' Prasic said. 'They serve her and us too, in everything we want, except our desire to leave. We haven't even seen our own child since the season turned.'

'*Oms* is in Ashanesland. The God-Triumvir has conquered it.'

Siamo laughed. 'Our Nabofik, a conqueror? Why, *oms* can barely rule *omas* own life. *Omas* female-parent still has to wake *omas* every morning, else *oms* would sleep till noon.' His expression sobered. 'Or at least, Komot *did* wake *omas*, when we were allowed to see our child.'

'You're kept here against your will?' Yemisi asked.

'We're told it's for our safety,' Prasic said. 'We're told there's a war.'

'There *was* a war. It's long over. But I suppose you are safer here. Any ruler has enemies, and a conqueror even more.'

Prasic's face remained untrusting, but Siamo gave Yemisi instructions on how to reach the area where Bruyar's family were kept. And she hadn't lied. It *did* make sense for Nabofik's family to be guarded. But she didn't believe that was why the Mortals had done it.

Only Nabofik of all the Three had living folk *oms* cared about enough for them to be used as leverage. And here they were, safely in the Mortals' grasp. But the Mortals were fools if they thought they could control their gods.

And with that thought, Yemisi finally admitted to herself what she'd always known: she was as much a fool as the Mortals if she thought Alfreda was her friend. You could no more befriend a god than you could a hurricane. Yemisi hadn't come here to help Alfreda, as she'd told herself to quiet her conscience. She'd come here to find a way to end her. She had, she realised now, been searching for it for some time.

Because Alfreda's never-ending grief was a form of madness, just as much as Marvan's love of killing. He'd murdered hundreds, maybe thousands, since being made a god. But Alfreda understood her powers far better than him. She'd mastered them. If *her* madness were given free rein, the cost in blood would be much, much higher.

The place Yemisi came to at the end of the forest path was built of dark marble and its only windows were high and barred. Inside there was gloom and a surprising chill. There was only one cell, and only two people in it.

'Who are you?' the man croaked. He must be Dastief. He was painfully thin, but that wasn't what made him look so wretched. There were the half-healed wounds of torture on his bare arms and legs, and his left hand was held crooked against his chest. She suspected all its fingers had been broken. It was possible the nails had also been removed.

'I'm not a Mortal,' Yemisi said.

The woman shuffled forwards. Her name, Yemisi had been told, was Dono the Light-Hearted, although she wasn't currently living up to it. There were no injuries visible on her, but she was also far too thin. 'If you aren't a Mortal, who are you?' she asked. Then, with a pitiful note of hope, 'Did Bruyar send you?'

'No, but my business does concern *omas*.'

Dono shuffled back the two steps she'd taken forwards. Dastief flinched and turned his face to the wall.

'We'll tell you nothing,' Dono said. 'Haven't we shown that already?'

'You remain loyal to your joiner,' Yemisi said. 'Even though *oms* left you behind to suffer this?'

'What could Bruyar have achieved by staying, except to suffer it too?' But there was a quaver in Dono's voice. Perhaps she felt more abandoned than she'd admit.

'My questions aren't to hurt you, or Bruyar,' Yemisi said. 'My only concern is *omas* research. I need to find it.'

'We've been asked about that too.' Dono reached out a hand towards Yemisi, then let it drop. 'The price of an answer is our freedom.'

*

Yemisi spent the journey back home trying to figure out how to obtain it. She'd have to use magic to snatch Bruyar's wife and husband from under their guards' noses, that much was clear. The bells required to make the chords wouldn't be a problem. She had a vast stock of them, from her many futile attempts to help Alfreda in her work. But the tunes themselves would take a lot more thought.

The secret of this magic, she knew, was its threefold nature. No single note had power. Only the harmony of three together brought results. So she needed to find three concepts, related but distinct, and intertwine them to produce the desired effect.

Secrecy was the answer. To stay hidden. So what threefold concept could she find in that? To be hidden you must be unseen. That was one. And you must also be unheard and, she supposed, unsmelt, so there she had her three. But that would be a very weak working of magic. Much as with the runes, complexity brought power.

So, to be unsensed was one braid of the tune she needed. To be forgotten could be another. And for the third . . . perhaps not to be cared about. Were the bonds between those concepts true and tight? She thought that she could make them so. As she circled the rim of the chasm that had once been Täm, the excitement began to fill her. The intellectual challenge was stimulating quite apart from its practical use. Was this how she'd once felt about the runes?

She was so consumed with her plans, she didn't notice at first that her room was already occupied when she entered it. It was only as Alfreda shifted on the stool in the shadows of one corner that Yemisi became aware of her. She placed a hand against her racing heart. 'You startled me. It's a wonder a person as tall as you can be so inconspicuous.'

Alfreda leaned forwards. Half her face was caught by the afternoon sun shining through the window. The other half remained in shadow. 'Why did you do it?' Her voice was terrifyingly flat.

'Do what?' Yemisi made her own tone as innocent as possible. She wondered how Alfreda could possibly have learned of her visit to the garden so quickly. And then she finally saw what was sitting at Alfreda's feet, its lid flung open. The bones inside it were jumbled together. It was impossible to make out the shape of the person they'd once been. It was only now, when it was too late, that it occurred to her how disrespectful it seemed, to keep the bones of Alfreda's brother like that.

'They were only brought this morning,' Yemisi said. 'And you were nowhere to be found.'

'Is that so? And when were you intending to tell me about them?'

Yemisi reached out a hand towards Alfreda, but dropped it at the expression on her face. 'It was for your own sake. I couldn't bear to take your hope away from you.'

Alfreda stood. The height that Yemisi had moments ago made into a joke was purely menacing now. 'No, I suppose you couldn't. You need me to hope, or else why would I do the work you want?'

'No.' Yemisi backed away a step, and then another as Alfreda advanced on her. 'That wasn't it. I've been researching the oldest magic, the one that came first. I believe it can help you – it can bring them back. You just need to give me more time.'

Alfreda looked back at the pitiful box of bones. 'What's in there will never be a man again. My brother's gone. I'll nae be seeing his face in this life.'

'You might. I've found Bruyar's—'

'Be quiet,' Alfreda said. She spoke softly, but the words had her power in them. They snapped Yemisi's mouth shut. 'I was a fool. I thought you cared about me, that we were friends. But there's only two people left who care for me and not what I can do for them. Nabofik sent me a message. Things aren't going well in Ashanesland. *Oms* has asked for my help and I'm going to give it.'

'Yes!' Yemisi said, her mouth freed again. 'Yes, I can help with that.'

'No,' Alfreda said, 'you can't. It's time for you to die now.'

Yemisi had one moment to wonder what form her execution would take, before she realised that the words themselves were it. And then the colour went out of the world, all in one go, and a moment later her life with it.

24

Nayan came to see Eric when he was having his breakfast. It was kipper again, like it had been for the last three mornings. The juices were smeared round his mouth when the King entered his small berth on one of Fleet's many ships. He was only half dressed too, and he was so busy holding his shirt closed and wiping his mouth that he forgot to bow.

Nayan didn't seem to notice. There was a distracted expression on his face as he said, 'Admiral, I have a task for you.'

It was a while since anyone had called Eric that. He didn't really see how he could claim the title, seeing as how his vessel – if you could call Rii that – was grounded for good. Still, it was never wise to say no to a king.

'I'm game,' Eric said. 'What is it you want?'

'Those . . . children of the beast's, they're large enough for a passenger, aren't they? I've seen your son on their backs.'

'He's only a tiddler, but the lot of them are growing like radishes.' He eyed Nayan up and down, trying to figure the weight of him. 'Yeah, I reckon they're strong enough now. Where is it you want to go?' It was a funny image, Nayan with all his pride, clinging to one of the pups.

'Nowhere,' Nayan said. 'I hope to use them as scouts. The enemy's forces travel by air. We can't track them by land and we need to learn their current disposition. I've spoken to the beast about using the pups, but it's stubborn.'

'It might help if you called Rii by her name,' Eric said, then added, 'Wheelking,' when he realised how sharply he'd spoken.

Nayan's mouth twisted, but he bit back whatever response he'd been about to make. He must want this favour badly. 'Rii, then. She says there's only one person she'll allow on their backs.'

'Me?' Eric asked, flattered by it. He'd barely had a chance to speak to Rii since coming to this place. She was so tied up in war councils and the business of ruling. He hadn't been sure if she still much cared for him.

'You,' Nayan said. 'Will you do your duty?'

*

He went to check with Rii, to be sure the King hadn't been having him on. None of his dealings with toffs in recent years had made him any more trusting of them. The bargains he'd made in Smiler's Fair had been more honest: coin for his flesh. He'd known where he was with that.

Rii wasn't hard to find, seeing as she never moved these days. He went to market first and bought a nice juicy trout for her to suck on. He knew how to keep her sweet.

The great raft she lived on rocked when she reached for the fish, and Eric saw several of her courtiers look away as she sucked it dry of blood.

'Thy gift is pleasing, morsel,' she said.

It was a blustery day, and the wind blowing through her greasy hair spread the mouldy cinnamon smell around. Eric found it a comfort. So much had changed since he'd first ridden her to the far north, but that had always been the same.

'Nayan came to see me,' he said. 'He wants to use your pups for spies and me the rider on them. That ain't what you want for them, is it?'

'I trust in thee to keep them safe.'

'Course I will, I'd give my life for them,' he said, and meant it. 'But this war ain't truly your business. Why do you want to go and get mixed up in it? The invaders haven't come here. You're safe as a spider in its web on these islands.' And Arwel was safe with her.

She sighed. It came out as a breathy sort of whistle from her huge fanged mouth. *'I am dying, morsel. My flesh is heavy on me. It cannot abide long in a world without the moon. Before I leave, I must make it safe for my children, and thine.'*

'And you're certain war's the way to do that?' he asked, swallowing past the lump in his throat that the thought of her death gave him.

'I see no other path,' she said.

*

Krish had walked a dozen circuits of the island since he'd come to it. His father had asked him to join the war councils, and he'd come to some, but he did his thinking best alone.

It was raining that afternoon, slanting sheets that had soaked him through within minutes of leaving Fleet. He liked the feel of it, the freshness. The walking had put muscles back on his legs and he felt stronger than he had since waking. He liked the view, too: the frothing waves breaking on some unseen rocks far out from shore. He'd lived eighteen years before he'd set eyes on the sea. He didn't think he'd ever tire of it.

He spied Rii's children from a distance. They were black dots against the sky, growing into hairy blobs on bat wings as he walked closer. The rain that had grounded the sea birds hadn't kept them from the air. It was only when he was within shouting distance that he realised Eric was with them too. The dye was slowly fading from his pale skin and gold hair but he still didn't look quite like himself. He was fixing a saddle to the largest of the pups, tying leather straps beneath the creature's chest to keep it on.

The pup was as big as a bull now. They'd grown even in the fortnight since Krish had come to the island, though Rii seemed certain they wouldn't grow much further. The power of flight would never be lost to them like it was to her.

'Are you leaving?' Krish asked. He was surprised to find that the idea pained him.

Eric shook his head. 'Just popping out. Your dad's asked me to do some scouting for him. Figure out where the Ofiklander soldiers are.'

'He thinks if they're garrisoned in all the shipforts, they'll be spread too thin to guard every inch of the coast. He's hoping he can land an army without setting off an alarm.'

'But you ain't sure,' Eric said, peering at him shrewdly.

Krish shrugged. 'He might be able to land the army. But what then? He came to Mirror Town with an army too and it didn't do him much good. He wasn't ready for the magic. He didn't understand it.'

'And we don't understand this new magic.'

'We know a little bit. We know it's made with music, somehow. We know when people are fitted with bells, it makes them like the slaves of Mirror Town, after I put the rune on them.' Krish winced with shame, even now, at that memory. 'We know there are three gods, but we don't know what they stand for. How can we defeat something we don't understand? How can we even protect ourselves against it?'

'It ain't just music,' Eric said, 'it's chords.'

'I don't know that word.'

Eric grinned. 'And who said my time in the fair was a waste? Chords are how music's made. I learned that off a lad from the Queen's Men. He taught me how to play the pipes, though I weren't ever much good at it. When you play three notes together – if they're the right notes – they make a new sound. It's always gotta be three. So I reckon that's how it works for these three gods.'

Krish smiled cautiously back. 'Yes, that makes sense. But *how* do the three notes fit together? How do they know what music does what magic? With the runes it was the glyphs and how you put them together. If we could find a list of the notes they play, if we could even get hold of some of their bells, maybe we'd know how to fight this magic.'

'Well,' Eric said, 'I'm heading for the mainland right now. How about you come with and have a gander?'

*

Krish had flown on Rii before, but flying on her children was very different. She'd been so huge, when you were on her back, you could almost pretend you were on land. The pup beneath his legs felt far too slight and there was far too much sky all around him. He clung on tighter to Eric's waist as Sii tilted nauseatingly sideways. Eric's warmth was comforting in the chill wind that whipped past them as they flew. They were moving very fast, taking moments to travel what would have been a day's ride on a horse.

'There!' he shouted into Eric's ear. 'See, that's Delta's Strength down below.' It was no more than a dot on a grey expanse of water, but Krish had spent a lot of time studying his father's maps. 'That was one of the first places that was taken. We should see if there are invaders still there.'

Eric relayed the message to Sii and they dropped, so quickly that Krish couldn't help letting out a yelp of alarm. But when they were no more than a hundred paces above the fort and the vast maelstrom it circled, Eric yelled, 'Back up, back up!'

The invaders *were* still there. There were four of their strange sky ships on the shore of the lake and a fifth taking off from it. People with the very dark skin of Ofiklanders were milling around them. A thin residue of their voices followed Sii up as he rose, and for a moment Krish thought they'd been seen. But the rising sky ship didn't turn in their direction and was soon lost in the greyness of the sky.

They visited Fort Greenshore next, which turned out to have at least a dozen sky ships near it, and then Ashfall itself. The ancient shipfort was beached, the mammoths that had once pulled it let loose from their traces. It made a sad sight, tilted at an angle where its base rested against the shore, but Krish was more troubled by what had put it there. It would have taken a great force to lift such a monumental thing. And it was the same story, everywhere they looked: a country conquered and strongly guarded, all its centres of power fallen and secured by the invaders.

'We'll have a sorry report to make to your dad,' Eric said, when they'd stopped to rest in a grove of ancient oaks far from any shipfort.

Krish stretched his cramped legs. 'Maybe. He wanted their forces scattered, and they are.'

'Yeah, but only scattered till they get the call. With those bloody sky ships of theirs they can be anywhere they want quick as a five-coin shag.'

'It's my father's old advantage turned against him. He used to be the one with carrion riders. I wish we could get closer to one of those sky ships. Maybe if we can figure out how they fly . . .'

'You reckon we can learn to use them ourselves?' Eric looked dubious. 'The moon's magic only worked for those what worshipped the moon. And we ain't too fond of the Three.'

'But that was the old magic. This isn't even the same game. It's like we were playing knucklebones and now they're playing cards. Maybe the rules are different.'

'So if we got ourselves one of those ships of theirs, you think you can figure it out?'

'I don't know. I could try. But we can't take on a whole fleet of them. We need one on its own to capture it. And they always seem to be in groups at the forts.'

'Yeah,' Eric said, 'bigger groups for bigger forts, ain't that right?'

Krish nodded.

'I think I know a fort so small it would only have one ship there, if it's got any at all.' There was a note in Eric's voice that Krish didn't understand, and a look on his face he couldn't read.

'Which one?' Krish asked. It was strange that a foreigner like Eric would know his own land better than him.

'Smallwood,' Eric said.

★

The place looked different from the air. The dead white trees that surrounded it were flattened by distance into a complex white tracery, as if someone had scribbled on the ground with chalk. The muddy lake on which the fort sat was little more than a puddle. The mammoths that drew it seemed to move at a snail's pace seen from this distance. Or perhaps they really were moving that slowly. They'd been elderly even when Eric first saw them.

It was funny, Eric could barely remember the person he'd been when he came here: the careless boy with a hopeful heart. He wasn't ashamed of who he'd been then, but he couldn't imagine how he'd ever been so naive.

'There it is,' he shouted into Sii's ear. 'You can bring us down.'

'Circle it first,' Krish said. 'Let's see what's there.'

That was just like the prince, cautious and careful. He'd given Eric a sharp look when Eric suggested coming here, but he hadn't asked any difficult questions. That was like him too. He wasn't one to probe.

Sii swooped lower, and the shipfort came into focus. It looked to be in an even worse state of repair now than when Eric had first seen it. The tower that had been leaning when Eric visited all those years ago was now broken off completely. Had a storm done that, or war? Eric could guess why it hadn't been repaired. With its lord lost, the shipfort must have slipped even further into poverty.

There was no sign of the Ofiklanders, though. There was nothing around the fort but a few round-bellied fishing boats.

Sii found a grove where he could set himself down, and then Eric fussed with taking his saddle off – he didn't want him to get sores – and rubbing the sweat off him with grass before it could cool and chill him.

'All is well, all is well,' Sii said, when Eric had been rubbing him down a while. His voice was far higher than his mum's, more of a trill than her deep piping.

'Are you sure you're gonna be OK all on your own here?' Eric asked. 'We could be gone a while.'

Sii butted Eric with his hairy head. *'I saw a fox. I will eat.'*

So then Eric had no more excuse not to go.

The stunted, dead white forest was leafless even in summer. Before long, he began to spy glimpses of the shipfort between the gnarled trunks.

'You've been here before?' Krish asked, when they were approaching the edge of the forest.

'I lived here a short while,' Eric admitted. 'Years ago. Had a bit of a fling with the man that was the lord here.'

'Was?'

'He died in the war at Mirror Town.'

'Fighting my forces,' Krish said.

'I fancied myself in love with him.' Eric wasn't quite sure why he was confessing this. Maybe it was because Krish was so earnest that he seemed to invite honesty. 'Wept a little, when I found out what happened to him. But it was like a little brook compared to the ocean of feeling when I thought my boy was dead.'

'How did it end?'

'The lady here – Babi, they called her – found out what me and Lahiru was up to. She didn't take too kindly to it. Sold me off into slavery. That's how I came to be on the ice with the servants of Mizhara.'

Krish smiled very slightly. 'So neither of us is likely to find much of a welcome here. We could turn back if you'd prefer.'

'No. I wanted to come. Don't know why. It just . . . feels like business that weren't never shaken on. Unfinished.'

Eric took one last careful look up and around, to be sure there were no sky ships here, but the sky held only clouds. One solitary man stood guard over the bridge to the fort, slouching in his woollens, and very definitely an Ashaneman. 'The lady isn't taking visitors,' he said. 'Especially the likes of you.'

'She'll see me,' Krish told him. 'Or else answer to King Nayan for turning away the Wheelheir.'

Eric was impressed with the authority he'd managed to put in his voice. He sounded like a proper toff, even though Eric knew he was no more noble-raised than him.

It did the trick with the guard. He saw them over the bridge, but before they could reach the rickety front gates, they squeaked open and a man and a girl fell out.

No, not quite a man. He was a youth, with the sort of beard a young man grew to prove he could. The girl wasn't wearing bunches like the first time Eric had met her. She'd sprouted another whole foot, but he recognised her all the same. 'Yo-yo!' he said.

She drew herself up with the dignity of a ten-year-old. 'No one calls me that any more.'

'I recognise you,' the boy said.

'I knew your dad,' Eric told him, which was about as diplomatic as he could put it.

The boy scowled, so he probably already knew exactly *how* Eric had known his dad. 'You're not welcome here. Get out.'

They must have been making a bit of a commotion, because a woman's voice called out from inside the fort to know what was going on. A moment later, Babi herself appeared in the door.

Her face paled at the sight of Eric. He supposed he must be a bit of a spectre to her. He tried to find some satisfaction in it, but he could only manage shame. What she'd done to him hadn't been right, but the first wrong had been his.

Krish's gaze flickered quickly between them, taking it all in. He stepped in front of Eric. 'I'm Krishanjit, Wheelheir to King Nayan. Will you let me enter?'

The children were dismissed and Babi brought them through to what Eric knew was the poshest room in the fort. It was richly furnished, but the rugs were faded and the carvings on the wooden chairs half worn away. Eric had seen far posher in the years since he'd first come here.

They were served beer and small, star-shaped cakes. Babi shooed away the servants who'd brought them and turned to Eric. 'You've come up in the world, I see.'

'Since you sold me for a slave, you mean.' He bit his tongue. He hadn't meant to bring any anger to this.

She smiled thinly. 'If you've come to pay court to my husband, I'm afraid you're too late. He died a thousand miles away, along with my father.'

'I know,' Eric said. 'I was there.' And then, because it was true, 'I'm sorry, for that and all the rest. I was only a boy. I didn't know no better.'

She looked at Krish. 'And now you've baited your hook for fatter fish.'

It took Eric a moment to realise what she meant. 'No, that ain't it at all. I'm an admiral now, in the King's Army. I got a boy of my own.'

'You have a child?' She eyed him up and down, looking the

tiniest bit less like a prickled-up cat. 'Have you mended your ways, then?'

'Not as such, though I ain't been much interested in that sort of thing these last few years. You know how it is, when you got little ones. Nothing else matters.'

'No, nothing else does.' She wiped a hand across her eyes, and he realised suddenly how old and tired she looked. 'It doesn't matter now.' She turned to Krish. 'You call yourself Wheelheir, but Ashfall's conquered. By flying soldiers from the Eternal Empire, or so the rumours say.'

'It's all true,' Krish said. 'But my father is on the Hundred Islands. He means to take Ashanesland back.'

'And why should I care about that? Why should I care about anything except my children and what little is left of my wealth?'

Krish paused and Eric could see him figuring how best to reach her. He could see the prince's mind at work. When they'd first met, Eric had found Krish a tough nut to get into the meat of, but he knew him better now.

'There's no reason at all you should help,' Krish said at last. 'I'm not sure if you can, anyway. We came looking for one of their sky ships, to figure out how it works. We thought they might have posted one here. We were hoping that we could ambush it.'

'And bring trouble to my door,' she said.

'Yes. It might have.'

'And you think it would have been my duty anyway?'

'No, I don't,' Krish said. 'The invasion, taking back Ashanesland. That's the business of kings. I don't think anyone else should die for it. I saw the battle of Mirror Town. I saw a worse one in Ofiklanod – the Eternal Empire, you'd call it. I don't want to see another.'

She tipped her head to study him. 'You're nothing like your father.'

Krish leaned forwards, staring into Babi's eyes. 'If this was just a war between countries, or kings, I'd say sit *here* and let it happen *there*. But this is the business of gods, and gods are always bad for everyone.'

'I see no gods here,' she said, though her gaze kept getting caught on Krish's strange silver eyes.

'Not yet. But they'll come. They can't help themselves. I think it's in the nature of gods, to want everything. They're like water, squeezing into every crack. You can put cloth in the cracks and pitch on the door, but it will find a way in. Better to stop the flood at its source.'

'And how do you mean to do that?' she asked.

'I don't know. I don't know if I can. But I know I'm going to try. I think . . . that *is* my duty.'

She looked at him for a long time in silence. Eric was tempted to speak, just to fill it, but Krish shook his head at him. And finally she stood.

'Follow me,' she said.

She took them through the hallways of the fort, much narrower than they'd been in Eric's memory, and then to a door he'd never used.

His heart lurched and he wondered if she was leading them to a quiet place for murder, or a kidnapping. It wouldn't be the first time, as he well knew. Krish must have thought it too, because Eric saw his hand move to his knife.

The door swung open, and he tensed still further, but it was only a storeroom, dark and musty.

'You thought a sky ship might come here,' she said to Krish, holding out her lamp, 'and you were right.' The yellow light played over shapes that Eric couldn't make out, a mess of dull grey and flashes of bronze. And then, as his eyes grew accustomed to the gloom, he saw it for what it was: a sky ship, tipped on its side, the strange ball that held it up collapsed beside it, and a pile of bells of different sizes, jumbled up together.

Babi moved the torch around, so that each part of it in turn became more distinct. 'There were three of them riding it. Two had bells in their ears and nothing to say. But the third spoke our tongue. He told me it had been a fashion among his people, to learn the languages of the god-sick folk. He was very proud of it.'

'What happened to them?' Krish asked.

She smiled, the same little ruthless smile that Eric had seen once before. 'I invited them to dine with me. I asked if they expected more to join them, or had told anyone exactly where they were heading. I said I'd buy more food in if they had. And when they said no, I bid them stay the night and had my servants slit their throats in their sleep. Then I took their ship and hid it. I even took the bells from their ears. It's all yours, Wheelheir, if you want it.'

'Thank you,' Krish said. 'I don't . . . I didn't expect this.'

She raised her chin and looked down her nose at him. 'I'm a loyal Ashanewoman. I don't care for others to come and take what's mine. All I ask is that you remember me, when this is over. Your last war took my husband and my father. I'll expect a fitting recompense.'

25

When he and Jalena had left Rah territory to head across the vast grasslands that were home to the bulk of the Fourteen Tribes, Sang Ki hadn't had very much of a plan. His main concern had been leaving before either Bone Dancer or Ensee reconsidered the legality of the manumission that Jalena had secured for him. After a few days of directionless and horseless travel, he'd procured rides and decided on a destination: the Tribes' spring gathering. He'd hoped at the very least to warn them of what was coming. But by the time he and Jalena arrived at the meeting ground in the territory of the Four Together, the gathering had already ended and something else was there.

The sun had only just cleared the horizon as they approached. Jalena squinted against it. Her face, always so open, told Sang Ki she wasn't impressed.

'It's Smiler's Fair,' he told her. The last time he'd seen it, it had been aflame. He'd hardly expected to see it again, especially not in almost exactly the same place he'd first encountered it. The travelling city's circuit of the lands was supposed to take longer, but it probably moved more easily now it was so much smaller. The blot on the horizon was barely a third the size of the place he'd once watched burn.

'It's very ugly,' Jalena said.

'It certainly is. Physically and in its spirit.'

She turned her eyes on him. 'Your head's hurting. It's making you not-happy, and when you're not-happy you're not-nice to be with.'

His head *was* hurting. He'd used up the last of the purple sorghum last night, on another trip to the world-beneath-the-world. He'd been searching fruitlessly for the first god. Krish had claimed he was imprisoned at the heart of the place, and Sang Ki believed him. He'd sensed the same thing that the prince had: a presence, a power at the root of it all that was malign, and not quite sane.

If Krish was right, that first god was the anchor that held the world-beneath-the-world in place, and the world-beneath-the-world was the wellspring of every other god's power. If Sang Ki wanted to stop these new gods, he could think of only one way: to find and somehow destroy the first god, rip out the roots of the world-beneath-the-world, and with them the very idea, the very possibility of gods.

But no matter how far down he went, he could never find the bottom. He could never find the root because he could never make the world-beneath-the-world *be* a thing that had roots. Something far stronger than him, that had lived in that place much longer, wanted it to be the shape it was. The first god, most likely. Perhaps he'd sensed Sang Ki as Sang Ki had sensed him, knew his purpose and was putting all his power towards preventing it.

And, as Jalena had so astutely pointed out, the journeys were taking a physical toll on him.

'My head feels like the anvil of an overeager smith,' he admitted. 'But even if my temper were as sweet as honeysuckle that place would still be a den of villains.'

'So we shouldn't go there?'

'On the contrary, it's precisely where we need to be. All rumours find their way to Smiler's Fair eventually. If we want to learn what's happening in Ashanesland, that's the place to do it. And besides, they're bound to have more purple sorghum for sale there.'

She looked doubtful. But when they were closer, close enough to smell the stink of the place, Sang Ki saw something that put any doubts to rest. He thought it was a bird, at first, hanging in the sky above the fair. But no bird left living was that big. And when they were in sight of the gates, he realised what it was.

'Is that a normal thing the Ostatni Ludia do?' Jalena asked. 'Hang up in the air like that?'

'Well, we once had carrion mounts big enough to carry a person. All dead now. But that thing is a working of a different magic.'

'The Three?' She squinted at it. 'But what's the point of it? Look, it's coming back down again.'

It was. Soon it was close enough for him to make out the shape of it: a silver canopy above something a little like the bed of a cart, in which half a dozen people were standing. Then it was lost to sight, descending to land somewhere near the centre of the fair.

Had the rule of the Three stretched so far already? But though he scanned the sky, he saw no more of the things. And when they came to the gates, the same gaggle of Drovers waited to take charge of their mounts and the same bored Jorlith warriors stood guard.

'Halt, stranger, and speak your name,' one of them said, just as the guards of the fair always had.

'Is there any need for that now?' Sang Ki asked. 'The worm men are dead, every one of them. They've been gone years now. You've no more need to watch for the First Death from the ground.'

'The fair will always watch for the First Death,' the other guard said. So Sang Ki gave both their names and they were let through.

Jalena stopped and stared at the sight that greeted them: the filthy, straw-lined streets littered with discarded animal bones, and the jostling mix of people from the whole breadth of the land. Sang Ki had to admit he stared a little too. It had been a long time since he'd been in such a crowd. They'd entered the district that was home to the Queen's Men, one of the more disreputable of the fair's companies.

Jalena gawped at a troupe of acrobats outside the nearest whorehouse, who'd arranged themselves into a pyramid four persons tall. She was so engrossed that she hadn't noticed the young woman in the process of rifling her pack. Sang Ki shook his head at the thief, and she slunk away.

Behind her, a bell-ringer grinned and winked at Sang Ki. The guard hadn't been lying, then. They still kept watch for the worm men. The bells remained ready to warn the fair if they came, though for three long years they never had.

'I saw that strange contraption floating above the fair,' Sang Ki said to the bell-ringer, since he seemed friendlier than most. 'Those are the people who conquered Ashaneseland, aren't they? Have they sent forces to the plains now too?'

The bell-ringer laughed. 'Itreig is no soldier. His god sent him to the Moon Forest on the hunt for old bones, it's said. He stopped at the fair for food and found other entertainment. Now he serves only himself. He isn't the first and he won't be the last to find Smiler's Fair more appealing than whatever life he came from.'

'I see,' Sang Ki said.

'Two glass feathers for a ride in that contraption of his, if you're interested. They say the view's spectacular, though I've no head for heights myself. Itreig's been taking in more coin than a fresh young sellcock since he arrived.'

It didn't take long to find the Ofiklander. The contraption itself guided them, rising once more above the fair. They watched its ascent and followed its descent into a broad, muddy square surrounded by gambling dens. And the bell-ringer hadn't been wrong that Itreig's service was popular. The grounded vessel was surrounded by people clamouring for a turn.

Sang Ki pressed two glass feathers into Jalena's palm. It was her money, anyway, proceeds from the furs of animals she'd trapped or hunted on their journey. 'Get a ride,' he told her. 'Try to see how the thing works while you're at it – and what this Itreig is about.'

She looked uncertain. 'You're not coming?'

'I have other business. And besides, he's more likely to be forthcoming with you than me.'

'Why? You're the plant-speaker. I'm not even a gatherer. I have no place.'

The sentiment startled him. It was the first time he'd heard her express it. 'You've an honest face and a guileless air,' he said. 'Those are worth more than you know. And you *have* a place. It's with me. Who else would look after me when I visit the world-beneath-the-world?'

His own task proved easier than he could have hoped. The first procurer who came to offer Sang Ki a girl proved equally able to supply purple sorghum, or at least point the way towards someone who could. For the price of another of their dwindling supply of coins, the procurer gave him directions to an Eom apothecary and instructions to claim that the drug would be used for medicinal purposes.

The Eom's house wasn't hard to make out, once Sang Ki had found the narrow street that held it. It was wooden like all the rest, and rickety, but it was the only one that had been painted a truly hideous lime green.

The apothecary himself – it took Sang Ki a moment or two to be sure he *was* a man – had long, purple-dyed hair and a face that was orange on one half and lime green on the other.

'Do I know you?' the Eom asked, the moment Sang Ki stepped into his shop. And then, before he could reply, 'I *do* know you. The mixed-blood lordling. The one who wanted to cure a woman and then kill her.'

The memories were so deeply buried, they took Sang Ki a moment to retrieve. 'Min Sun, was it? I do remember you. You saved Mahvesh – I suppose I would have called her Nethmi then – but you'll be pleased to hear I didn't hang her.'

'Min Soo,' the apothecary corrected. 'And what do you want this time? Is there a second person you hate enough to hang and love enough to treat?'

'Nothing so difficult. I'm merely on the hunt for some purple sorghum.'

'The root of dreams? Have you really fallen so far?'

'Not a fall so much as a change of profession—' Sang Ki said, then stopped as he registered exactly what Min Soo had said. 'The root of dreams? Is that what you called it?'

'Why? Do you think a different name will make its effects less harmful?'

'No,' Sang Ki said. 'You can be assured I don't think that. In fact, I now suspect quite the reverse.'

★

It took Jalena a long time to do as the plant-speaker had told her. She tried to push to the front of the people clustered around the flying craft, but there were so many of them and they behaved like beasts. Finally she was forced to use her own elbows until she was face-to-face with the man.

He stared at her, looking startled. She tried not to stare back. His skin was very, very dark and his hair hung in braids down his back, just like an old woman's. She'd heard of the mages of Mirror Town – the obecs that were most to the north sometimes dealt with them – but it was still strange to look at a person so unlike any other person she'd ever seen.

'I've finished for the day,' the man told her.

'But it isn't even lunchtime yet.'

He shrugged. 'Business was good, and I have an appetite.'

'But I have the coin,' she said. 'And it's taken me all this time to get to you. And I might not be here tomorrow. This is a not-good place and I'd like to leave it soon.'

He laughed, then seemed to realise that she wasn't joking and smiled a more private smile. 'I'm rather fond of it myself. Did you know, if you have the coin, you can pay a man or woman to have sex with you? Extraordinary. If I ever go home, you may be sure I'll be sharing the idea. The poor of the park would be glad of the money.' His expression darkened. 'Or . . . they would have been. There are no parks now, let alone poor unfortunates in them.'

'Why would you need to pay those people to have sex with you?'

'Alas, I fear my charms would be lost on them otherwise.'

She frowned at him. 'But why would you want to make babies with someone who didn't want to do it? That would be no fun, and then what would you do with a baby whose mother didn't want it? That's why coin's an ill thing. It makes you behave stupidly.'

'And yet I see you using it.' He deftly scooped the two glass pieces out of her hand, still smiling a secretly amused smile. 'Get in then, but it will only be a quick trip.'

The sky ship, she saw now, was made of wicker – or at least the bit you sat on was. It was what real people made their baby baskets from. But a baby weighed a lot less than she did.

'Won't the bottom fall out?' she asked.

'It hasn't yet.' He went to a little board that hung from the side of the basket and from which pieces of metal hung on strings. When he shook a section of the board, three pieces of metal sounded at once, different sounds that blended together into one.

'I didn't pay for music,' she complained. 'I paid to fly.' And she made her eyes very wide, because Sang Ki was right; not-people thought she was stupid. Sometimes she was afraid the plant-speaker did too. But she understood the job she'd been given.

'The bells are how you fly,' the man said. Then he went into a great long explanation even as he made more music and the basket began to rise, up and up until the ground looked very far away. It was almost like a rug with the green grass everywhere, but she knew it wouldn't be anything like as soft as a rug to fall on.

'That's as high as I'll go,' he said finally, then tipped his head, studying her. 'I've not seen your kind before, and I've seen every kind of person at the fair.'

She almost said, *That's because I'm a real person and none of you are*, but she'd learned that the Ostatni Ludia didn't like it when you told them that. 'I come from the south,' she said instead, 'beyond the yellow no-water place.'

'From the savannah? La – then I know your history. Your people's history, I mean. You were the very first to come to our shores, did you know that?'

'I can't know it,' she said. 'It's been forgotten.'

But he didn't seem to understand that she meant it *should* be forgotten, and he told her things she wasn't supposed to know for the whole journey back down.

★

Sang Ki found Jalena in the seventh gambling den he looked in. She was watching in fascination as people too drunk to decide wisely lost money they couldn't afford to lose.

'Oh, you're back,' she said. 'These people are very stupid.'

Several of the gamblers glowered at her. Others looked as if they secretly agreed. He took her elbow and guided her out, before she could say any more.

'I did it,' she said. 'Just like you asked. I went up and then down, and I watched what he did. I asked him all about it too. He said, "The bells are the source of the power, do you see? But they must be worked—"'

Sang Ki held up his hand. 'I believe you can recite every word of it. But I've learned something of interest myself. You call purple sorghum the dream-flower, but do you know what the Eom call it? "The root of dreams." Intriguing, isn't it?'

'Why? The not-people have their own words for lots of things.'

'But names make meanings and meanings matter more than anything, or so Prince Krishanjit says. The purple sorghum is the path a person takes into the world-beneath-the-world. What if that's because it was at the root of its creation?'

She frowned. 'Creation? No one made the world-beneath-the-world, except the plants.'

'But someone found a way to bend it to his will, to use it. What if purple sorghum were the key? The Hundred Islanders might know more. That's where it grows in the greatest profusion.'

'Oh,' she said. 'That's a funny thing. The man with the flying ship said that's where people came from. Real people, I mean, not the Ostatni Ludia. Or . . . no, he said we came across the sea, but that's where we landed. He said *his* people were here first, so they remember, even though they shouldn't. But maybe what he said wasn't true, because he also said we used to build cities and be very powerful and have a god of our own. But we don't build and we don't believe in gods. That's as important as forgetting.'

He stared at her, so startled he was momentarily speechless. Startled and then filled with the tense excitement of a man whose puzzle had almost, at long last, reached a solution. 'You came to the Hundred Islands first,' he said slowly. 'The land where the sorghum grew. Or perhaps it didn't grow there at all, before you came. Jalena, I fear I may have been too clever by a half, which has always been my fault. I was working in metaphors, looking for a spiritual root to tear out, because that's the language of the world-beneath-the-world. But we're in the world above, and here things are literal.'

'I don't understand any of that,' she said.

And he realised that he couldn't explain. He wasn't sure how he would do what he intended. Perhaps the solution would be as simple as razing the fields of purple sorghum. But however he achieved it, he meant to destroy the world-beneath-the-world and the power of all the gods with it. Yet the world-beneath-the-world was the very thing that made her hold him in such high regard. He couldn't begin to imagine how she'd react if he told her his plans. 'We must go to the Hundred Islands,' he told her instead. 'The story began there. If there's to be an end, perhaps it's there too. It's a very long way from here, but I believe there may be a way to make the journey shorter.'

She trotted after him as he left the gambling den, asking questions he didn't attend to. Because yes, there at the boundary with the Merry Cooks was exactly what he'd been looking for. It was another bell-ringer, sitting on his high chair, or more accurately slumped in it. By the smell of him, Sang Ki was sure he'd drunk himself into a stupor. And he'd left his bell unattended.

Sang Ki put his hand on it, then turned to Jalena. 'When I ring this, there'll be panic. People will be running. I suppose some might scream. Don't pay any attention to it. Just follow me – no, better, keep hold of my hand – and go where I go.'

She opened her mouth, probably with another question, but he pulled the bell rope before she could ask it.

A few people looked round at him, frowning with either puzzlement or annoyance. Other than that, nothing.

He waited a tense moment for the reaction that should have followed. It didn't come, so he rang the bell again, longer and louder. And this time he shouted, 'The First Death! Death from the ground!'

Some people still looked only puzzled. It had been a few years and many newcomers wouldn't know the ways of the fair. But enough people had lived here before the fall of the sun and the moon. They remembered the worm men. The other bell-ringers were slow to respond, but they *did* respond. And everywhere the call echoed: 'Death from the ground. Smiler's Fair must move!'

Even with his warning, Jalena almost lost her grip on him as the crowd surged and panicked. His bulk was of benefit here. It made him more immovable than most, and he was able to forge ahead, like a ship making headway through treacle.

To left and right, some were already at work dismantling the houses and inns that had seemed so permanent moments before. The streets began to fill with carts, gradually piling high with the disassembled walls and ceilings of the fair. Sang Ki bent his route around them and kept moving. Until, when his arm was becoming numb from dragging Jalena, they came to the square and the strange flying vessel.

It was barely a square any more. Half the houses were gone. A mammoth stood disconsolately eyeing the muddy ground as if searching for a blade of grass. But the vessel was still there – and, most importantly, its Jorlith guard had gone. They were probably taking care of their own departure. There was no sign at all of Itreig. Sang Ki had counted on that. As a newcomer to the fair, Itreig wouldn't know this particular tradition.

'Oh, I see,' Jalena said.

'You told me you remembered how to make it fly.' Sang Ki fiddled with the wicker sides of the thing until he found the catch to the door. He pushed Jalena in and snapped it shut. Some of the surrounding people had begun to eye the vessel as soon as

Sang Ki went into it. They'd probably realised that this was the quickest of all possible ways to depart.

'I told you I remembered what he told me,' Jalena shouted above the racket of the crowd. 'Not that *I* know how to do it.' But her hands were already working at the bells that, somehow, seemed to be the source of the thing's motion. And when she rang three together, the basket juddered like it wanted to throw them out, and rose.

'I did it!' she said triumphantly. Then her face fell. 'Oh, but I don't know if I can steer it. He didn't explain that part very well.'

Sang Ki's looked east, towards the distant shape of the mountains that had once been his home, growing clearer as they rose. 'Well, I dare say we'll have time to work it out.'

26

Marvan directed the sil-nafön to pass over Fell's End. The shipfort looked no more lovely from the air than it did from land, although from this height at least he couldn't smell the putrid swamp gases that surrounded it. He'd thought he might descend and visit his mother, Imesha, who ruled the fort and was the last remaining member of his family, but he found he didn't want to. He felt only the faintest glimmer of affection for her. Alfreda mattered to him far more. Even before she'd become his sister-god, she'd been his sister in spirit, the only person he'd met with a void inside her that was greater than his own.

A little further on, above Fellview, he saw the first evidence of Nabofik's presence: the grey circles of grounded sil-nafön. When he adjusted the bells to lower his own, he began to make out their riders, darker-skinned figures among the brown-skinned Ashane who were toiling in the fields. But it was the fields themselves which interested him.

Here in Ashanesland, spring wasn't far under way. The remnants of the morning frost lingered in silver bands beneath the hedges. The fields themselves should still have been winter-brown, but they weren't. They were verdantly green.

On a whim, he brought the sil-nafön to land on the edge of one of the fields, where a group of Ofiklanders were supervising the work of a score of landborn Ashane. The landborn were, he realised, trying to harvest the wheat, their sickles moving in the endless, rhythmic, tireless motion of those who were belled.

'The crop's green,' he said to the Ofiklanders as he strode up to them. 'You won't be making any flour out of it.'

'It's that or let the cold kill it in the ground,' the nearest

Ofiklander said. Then his eyes widened as he recognised Marvan. He dropped to his knees, pressing his forehead to the ground as those around him saw their visitor and did the same. Most of them, Marvan saw, were handless: former Mortals who'd once scorned gods and now served them.

'Get up,' he said impatiently.

They scrambled to obey. And now they each had a circle of mud on their forehead, where they'd pressed it to the ground. When this had begun, he'd enjoyed the fear he inspired and the way people humbled themselves to him. Now it just irritated him.

'Well?' he said. 'Why are you planting wheat to sprout in winter and be harvested unripe in spring?'

They exchanged glances. Unlike the Ashane workers, they were unbelled. Marvan preferred people that way. It made them able to experience fear and pain. But it also left them capable of ignoring his commands.

'It's been days since my last kill,' he said pleasantly. 'My knife is thirsty.'

'It's the bells,' one of them said hurriedly. 'The God-Triumvir commanded us to devise a magic to help the farmers here.'

'Most generously, most wisely,' the first man said, until Marvan glared him into silence.

'We thought we had,' another said. 'The crops grew as the bells commanded. But they grew too fast.'

Marvan looked at the fields with their green, brittle, useless stalks. 'So my sibling-god has hindered instead of helped.' He laughed. 'How very like *omas*.'

The man looked directly at Marvan for the first time. 'My lord, we've no more seeds to plant another crop. And besides, this one has leached all the goodness from the soil. What should we do?'

Marvan looked at the earth, which did indeed seem pale and barren, and then back at the Ofiklanders. 'Why in the world should I care?'

*

Renar took the report in her room. It was a habit she'd developed as the reports grew darker and Nabofik's mood with them. Her mansion was on the edge of the City On High and its entire upper floor was ringed with windows, some of which looked over the roofs of the city, and others into the clouds and sky and, far below, the land. It was yet another in a succession of dismal, rainy days. The raindrops fell across the great canopy that held the city in the sky, and something in its design amplified the sound. It drove Renar to distraction.

Nabofik's attempts to help the Ashane farmers had been a disaster. Renar was able to keep that information from *omas*, but not news of the sporadic acts of sabotage. One sil-nafön had been burned as it rested on the ground and a group of five Mortals ambushed and killed. No one knew where the attackers had come from or to where they'd disappeared. Nabofik had raged for an entire day about that. Two more Mortals had died, not at the hands of their enemies.

But the biggest problem was one Nabofik didn't even seem to appreciate. *Oms* had shrugged when Renar risked telling *omas* that the landborn were fleeing Ashanesland in their thousands, pouring through the Blade Pass towards whatever future awaited them on the plains. Without those people to work the fields and tend the cattle, the shipborn would starve.

Moments after she'd finished reading the report, Lord Dimuthu of Sword Star was brought to see her. He bowed, which he'd never troubled himself to do when she was in Nayan's service, and his smile when he straightened again was oily. Renar had never much cared for him. His gaze, however, was pinned to her windows, with their excellent view of the sky and the very distant land.

'We haven't fallen yet,' Renar said dryly. 'It's unlikely that your weight will be too much for the City On High to bear.'

'My trust in our God-Triumvir's power is absolute. I was merely marvelling at the view.'

It took a wearying half an hour of ingratiation and subtle sparring for him to come to the point, but when he did, Renar sat up straighter in her chair.

'King Nayan survives?' she said. 'You're sure of it?'

Dimuthu nodded. 'I have spies on the Hundred Islands. And not just him, all the absent shiplords and their men. And' – here he smiled the smile of a man who knew he held a trump card – 'also his moon-eyed son. The missing Wheelheir himself.'

'*Krishanjit* is alive?'

'So they say, and all of them plotting treason, no doubt.'

A mere two months ago, Dimuthu would have considered his current behaviour treasonous. But he was that rare thing: a lucky gambler. It was said he'd obtained half the wealth of Sword Star at cards. He'd always been a man who knew which hand to bet on.

'So,' he said, 'this is news the God-Triumvir will be grateful for, don't you think?'

'Very grateful,' Renar said, although she had no intention whatsoever of telling *omas*.

When she was finally rid of Dimuthu, she considered going to see Lanalan. She dearly wanted to discuss this with him. But she couldn't risk sharing with him what she was contemplating. His face gave everything away. Nabofik would take one look and know that something was amiss. And besides, Renar had no desire to put her sib in that kind of danger.

She wasn't sure she wanted to put herself in it, either. Betray Nabofik? It was lunacy. And yet it was perhaps a worse madness to stay in *omas* service. Renar was accustomed to being in the employ of a dangerous person. Bruyar had been ruthless, but *oms* had never been capricious. Not so Nabofik. One day Renar, or more likely Lanalan, would say the wrong thing entirely without realising it, and then . . . The memory of those murdered shiplords was always with her, screaming as the blood boiled in their veins.

She'd thought of fleeing, too. What was Ashanesland to her? But that was an even greater risk. Nabofik, for all *omas* childishness, had the terrifying power of a god. *Oms* could find Renar and Lanalan wherever they fled. The image of the dying lords presented itself to Renar once again.

But Krish? The youth had a cunning that matched Renar's own. And who was to say? Perhaps he'd woken from his long sleep with his own god-powers still intact. If Nabofik was to be stopped – and *oms* had to be stopped – the prince was the one who could help Renar do it.

The Hundred Islands weren't a part of Ashanesland that Nabofik had yet troubled with. There was no outpost there that Renar had any excuse to visit. Sending a message of any kind would be difficult, and it took her a day and much pacing to devise a plan.

She decided to implement it on the morning set aside for deciding the disposition of Nabofik's fleet of sil-nafön. Renar knew that *oms* found that task especially tedious. The moment she'd been waiting for came when she and Nabofik were bent together over a map of Ashanesland.

'I shouldn't need soldiers at all,' *oms* said petulantly, scowling down at the map. 'I'm helping them. They should be grateful.'

'Most are,' Renar replied. 'It's the shipborn who are the problem. They're jealous of your power. They know they could never rule their people as well as you, and they resent it.'

She worried she might be spreading the praise a little thickly, but Nabofik grinned. 'Do you really think so?'

'Yes, I do.'

They'd been using dice to represent Nabofik's forces, scattered over the country as they were. Renar moved one group east, another west, half of a third to the coast and the other half towards the mountains. She had no idea if that was a sensible deployment of forces, but she was fairly sure that Nabofik didn't either.

'I think that will shore up World's End and leave enough to crush the growing rebellion in Blue Bird,' she said. Then, with studied casualness, she turned to one of the belled guards and said, 'Fetch juice and sweetmeats for the God-Triumvir – this is thirsty work.'

He ignored her, as she'd known he would. His pose remained rigid as he stared stiffly into space.

Nabofik turned *omas* scowl on him. 'Are you deaf? Do as my counsellor said!'

He complied immediately, as Renar had also known he would.

'He's not to blame,' she said to Nabofik. '"Twas my fault for forgetting that the bells compel service only to you and your sister- and brother-gods.'

'Do they?' Nabofik looked surprised.

'Why yes, and so they should. You are the masters of the magic that rules them. If it wasn't so, I wouldn't need to waste your time with trivialities like this.' Renar gestured at the map. 'I could assign the troops myself and save you the bother.'

'Oh, well then,' Nabofik said, 'I'll just tell them to do as you say.'

Omas face was utterly guileless. But Renar had seen other people underestimate Nabofik. 'There's many in Ofiklanod,' she said, 'who'd warn you not to put such trust in the Fox.'

Nabofik shrugged. 'But you won't let me down. You know what happens to people who do.'

*

Over the next four days, Renar did precisely as she'd promised. She sent troops hither and yon, chasing the saboteurs and rebels that she now suspected were being controlled by Krishanjit or his father. The soldiers always arrived too late, and Renar dutifully and penitently reported their failure to Nabofik. It was clear the situation in Ashanesland was worsening. The crop failures were fanning the flames, driving more landborn from the country or into the arms of their former King. But that simply made Nabofik lean on Renar more heavily.

And on the fifth day, Renar sat at her desk and composed a long and careful letter to Krishanjit. She added a sketch map she'd already drawn of the City On High and rolled it into one of the leather tubes that he must surely know by now were used for official communications between the Ofiklanod forces. Then she sat and stared at it for nearly an hour, trying to summon the nerve to send it.

It was the receipt of a report from the High Water Fastness

garrison that finally drove her to her feet. A hundred landborn had attacked the fort. It wasn't clear if they'd been acting on Nayan's orders, or had simply been starving and desperate for the food that was hoarded in the shipport. The end result was the same.

She gripped the leather tube in her hand and hurried to the sil-nafön port, where three of the vessels were docked and another was arriving. She strode up to the leftmost, whose crew were still loitering, and held out the leather tube.

'A message from the God-Triumvir. *Oms* requires it to be delivered immediately.'

'Where to?' the woman asked. The bells in her ears jingled as her head moved and her empty eyes met Renar's.

'Little Parvat,' Renar said. It was the easternmost of the Hundred Islands and anyone going there would have to overfly all the rest. That should give Krishanjit more than enough opportunities to bring the sil-nafön down. Renar had come to strongly suspect that the prince had aerial forces of his own. It was the only way to explain the geographical breadth of the recent attacks.

The woman frowned. The bells rendered their wearers docile but not stupid. Renar sometimes forgot that. 'Who am I giving the message to?' she asked.

'Our spy on the island,' Renar said. 'Look for a red cottage on the smallest bay.'

'A red cottage on the smallest bay.' The woman nodded, then bowed. 'It will be done, Lord Counsellor.'

Renar watched her mount the sil-nafön, then watched it leave the dock. And when it was on its way, she finally sagged in relief and turned away – only to find herself staring into the eyes of a man she'd never met before. He was Ashane, with a narrow face, a long nose and eyes that were far too sharp.

'And who are you?' he asked.

Renar opened her mouth to reply, then snapped it shut again. Power emanated from him like the note of a bell too deep to hear. She felt it in her bones. 'God-Triumvir,' she said carefully, bowing very low. She'd been with Nabofik long enough, and spent enough time among her Mortal entourage, to know the stories about Marvan. 'I am merely a servant of your sister-god.'

'A servant who has command of the belled, I see.' His voice was bland, but his eyes retained their cutting edge.

'La, 'tis the manner in which I serve her,' Renar said.

He gave a final smile, as sharp as his eyes, and strode off. He was probably going to Nabofik. If Renar went with him, she could attempt to steer the conversation down her favoured paths. But every second in Marvan's company felt unsafe. And she had to warn Lanalan of his arrival, lest her sib's loose tongue land him in trouble deeper than even she could dig him out of. He'd be in his quarters. He seldom ventured out of them these days.

Her sib frowned when she told him. He looked, remarkably for him, almost as concerned as he should. 'But he's a killer, is he not, Renar?'

'And worse,' she said. 'Stay away from him, Lanalan.'

But when the summons came from Nabofik as the day waxed towards evening, it came for both of them. They walked together to *omas* white tower in an uneasy silence.

'You'll never believe who's come, Renar!' Nabofik said, the moment they stepped through the door. 'It's my brother-in-power, Marvan! Marvan, say hello to Renar. And Lanalan too, I suppose.'

'Renar and I have already met,' Marvan said, 'when she was commanding one of your sil-nafön.'

Perhaps he hoped to catch Renar out in a lie, but Nabofik nodded dismissively. 'Yes, that's her job for me. She does all the boring things so I can concentrate on ruling.'

'And you've given her power over the belled?'

Nabofik looked uncertainly at Marvan. 'She couldn't help me if I didn't. Do you think it was wrong to do it?'

Marvan studied Renar for a moment, head tipped and smiling a little. Then he shook his head. 'It was wise. But now I'm here, there's no need of it. Best to take that power away from poor Renar. It's too much for one who isn't a god to bear.'

'Oh, I'm sorry, Renar,' Nabofik said. 'Of course I'll take the burden off you now Marvan can help me. You will help me, won't you? Only things have been very difficult here. The people are so ungrateful. I've thought about killing them all and starting again with people from Ofiklanod who know how to behave. But I don't think Renar would like it, would you?'

Renar's skin had shivered with an icy chill at Nabofik's words. But, very conscious of Marvan's eyes on her, she made herself shrug and say calmly, 'It seems premature. And Ofiklanders wouldn't know how to work this land as well as local people do. I'm sure they can be broken to the whip.'

Nabofik was frowning again. 'The trouble is, they've got a leader who's encouraging them to rebel. That really boring man Dimuthu came to see me. I would have told you to meet with him, but you were busy, Renar, so I let him speak. He says the people working against me are based on the Hundred Islands. Did you know?' There was the tiniest hint of suspicion in *omas* eyes when *oms* looked at Renar.

'I'd heard rumours,' Renar said immediately. When lying, it was always best to answer fast and work out the details as you went. 'I wanted to investigate them further before bringing them to you.'

'Well, Dimuthu is sure they're true.' Her attention switched to Lanalan. 'They say it's King Nayan himself, and his son. They told me his son has silver eyes just like you.'

'Why, they're speaking of Krishanjit,' Lanalan said. His expression looked both shocked and pleased. Nabofik could hardly fail to notice it, but it was Marvan who reacted.

He stood abruptly, his hand curled around the hilt of one of the tridents at his belt. His gaze was like a hawk's, or perhaps a wolf's. A hunter, either way. 'Krish is alive? And here?'

Nabofik shrugged. 'If that's his name. Why, do you know him?' Her eyes drifted again to Lanalan, untrusting. 'It seems that Lanalan does.'

Marvan's hand clenched, once, white knuckled on his trident, and then he released it. 'I've made his acquaintance, yes. This is news we must share with Alfreda. I *can* help you, Nabofik. You concern yourself with governing. You have a worthy adviser here.'

His eyes on Renar were mocking. 'And while you do, I'll concern myself with your enemies. I'd begun to tire of the hunt, but here's a quarry who'll truly test my skills. The prince escaped me three times before. He won't again.'

27

Today was when Krish would find out if he'd got it right. His father had given him parchment and he'd filled sheet after sheet of it with notes. Not words – he'd not yet mastered them – but his own system for marking the shape of tunes.

They'd given him a grand cabin aboard one of the biggest ships in Fleet, but he'd taken to living in a tent on shore. It was easiest to perform his experiments there. And he found it easier to sleep under the cowskin roof, not very different from his childhood home.

Rii had ordered a forge made for him, and his father had supplied him metalworkers. Neither of them seemed much interested in his work, though. They'd been sending men to cause trouble for the invaders on the mainland. On several nights he'd heard loud laughter floating from Fleet towards the shore. He thought it probably meant a victory. The sky craft that Babi had given them had proven to be very useful. But Krish knew those battles weren't the ones that mattered.

The captives they sometimes brought him had been more use. Two refused to talk and Krish refused to have them tortured. They were probably mouldering in a hold somewhere. But the third had been belled and very angry about it when the bells were removed and she had her mind back. She'd been a Mortal, too. She understood the magic of the Three and she'd been more than willing to tell Krish about it.

There came a time, though, when ideas had to be tested. Krish left his tent as the sun cleared the horizon on an unusually bright day for the Hundred Islands. The ceaseless wind whipped through the trees and Krish's jerkin as he took two steps towards his forge and his stock of bells. Then he hesitated, before turning and walking towards Fleet instead. He wanted Eric there, who had a quick mind as well as a quick tongue. His opinion would be useful.

Eric's cabin was on the same ship as Krish's unused one. When Krish entered it, he was just rising from his hammock. He slept shirtless and Krish found his eyes lingering on the lines of his bare chest. It was broader than Krish remembered it in his three-years-outdated memories.

'Trouble?' Eric asked, grabbing a silk shirt.

Krish shook his head. 'I think I've figured it out. The bells, I mean. Do you want to come and see?' It felt strange now he said it. Why should he need Eric as a witness?

But Eric grinned and nodded and they went back to the forge together.

There were four dozen bells there, carefully crafted to each give a single, pure note. It had taken Nayan's smiths almost as long to figure out how to make them as it had taken Krish to figure out how to use them. If he *had* figured it out.

'The magic's made out of tunes, right?' Eric said. 'It ain't like the runes at all.'

'The power is in the music.' Krish gathered the bells he'd need. 'But it *is* like the runes. In the large idea, anyway, not the small one. I think that the heart of every magic is the same, doesn't matter if it's the moon's or the Three's. It's about finding a way to describe things that's so . . . absolutely true, it makes them be real. It's about knowing something's nature.'

Eric laughed. 'I ain't so sure things have got just the one nature. Everything changes.'

'Yes. That's how the moon's magic worked, and the sun's: the glyphs of being and becoming. What something is and what it could be.'

'Makes sense,' Eric said. 'So how is it with them bells?'

'For the new magic, you have to break down a thought into pieces, and then those pieces into more pieces.'

'Three pieces?' Eric guessed.

Krish nodded. 'Three ideas that, linked together, make another.'

Eric flicked his finger against the smallest bell, making it sound. 'For the moon's magic, didn't you have to be a moon worshipper to use it?'

'Yes,' Krish said. 'I think it's different with the Three.'

'But you ain't sure?'

'No. That's why I'm going to try it out today. Something simple but useful. The idea of going down. Of bringing something down.'

'You mean to crash those sky ships of theirs.'

'If I can. I'd like to crash the flying city too, the one my father's spies have been talking about. But for today, getting this to drop would be enough.' As Krish was speaking, he was tying one of the bell-trees to a rope and the rope to the branch of a tree.

'What are the ideas inside falling?' Eric asked.

'Depth.' Krish showed Eric the deepest bell, then fitted it to the tree. 'Movement.' That was the middle bell. 'And loss. For the lost height,' he added at Eric's puzzled look, and fitted the final and smallest bell to the tree.

Eric looked at it dubiously. 'And that's all? If it's that easy, why ain't everyone doing it?'

'I think it's in the mind, too. You – me, I mean, the person doing it – has to understand the bells to mean those things. You have to hold the three-part idea in your mind at the same time as the three-part note rings.'

'Reckon you can do it?'

'Let's see,' Krish said, and shook the rope to ring all three bells together.

The effect was instant and shocking. Krish had hoped the rope holding the bells would snap with the downward force of them. It did, but it didn't stop there. The bells hit the ground and kept going, *burrowing* beneath it, lower and lower. And still somehow, impossibly, ringing.

It was only when Eric fell to his knees beside the ever-deepening hole that Krish realised the effect hadn't been limited to the bells themselves. Eric's knees dug into the earth as if they too wanted to vanish beneath it. He cried out in pain and fell prone, his face pressed into the earth. It was sinking in, all of him was sinking as the bell's ringing grew fainter and fainter but never quite disappeared.

Krish's stomach lurched in fear. There was no way Eric could breathe with his face pressed into the earth that way. Krish dropped down beside him and grabbed hold of his shoulders, but they were immovable. It was as if he had an invisible mammoth sitting on his back. And now his arms were spasming. His feet were already lost beneath the earth.

It was the bells. Krish had to silence them. When he looked at the hole they'd left, he couldn't see its bottom. But there was earth, piled up all around it. With frantic haste, Krish used his boot to shovel the earth back into the hole after the disappearing bell. Until, finally, the sound of it was gone.

There was a desperate gasp behind him, and he turned to see Eric rolling onto his back, clawing the mud away from his nose and mouth and eyes.

Krish's legs felt suddenly weak. He thumped down on his bottom beside Eric and, after getting his breath back, Eric sat up beside him.

'Well,' he said. 'It definitely worked.'

Krish laughed in helpless relief. 'I didn't mean for it to do that.'

'Maybe that's like the runes too: the stronger the mage, the stronger the working he can do. Ain't that what Dae Hyo said?' Eric frowned in sudden realisation. 'It didn't work on you, though. Do you reckon it's cause you made the magic?'

'I don't know,' Krish said. 'Maybe. Or maybe it's because I used to be a god. I've seen . . . when I was asleep, I saw . . . I can't explain. A place that was and wasn't real. All the gods were there, all the ones that had ever been. I knew, I don't know how, that that place was where our power came from. And the place was full of windows and every window was a set of eyes. When you were in there, you could look out through the eyes of anyone in the world.'

Eric shuddered. 'You mean a person – a god – could use that place to take a gander inside my head?'

'Not into it. Out of it. I didn't know what other people knew, or feel what they felt – but I could see what they saw.'

'I still don't much like the thought of it.'

'That's because it's unnatural. You don't know it, you can't feel it, but there's a part of you that's always trapped in there. They took a piece out of everyone and used it to warp that place, to turn it into somewhere a person could use.'

'You're saying it's made out of corpses?' Eric looked simultaneously intrigued and appalled.

'Not bodies – minds. Something that was inside everyone, that everyone used to be able to use. Now it's inside that place, and only gods can use it, or people in service to the gods. I don't know what it is or if it even has a name. But it was stolen, and everyone is poorer and less free without it. Except us. Except the gods. We were born with the missing piece still in us, that's what I think. That's what makes us different. Even now I've lost my power, I still have the god-thing inside me. I'm whole, in a way that nobody else is.'

Eric played with his fingers, the ones that were intact and the ones that weren't. Krish had learned it was a thing he did when he was thinking. Then he looked up at Krish. 'If it was stolen, it ought to be given back.'

'Yes,' Krish said. 'It ought.'

*

Dae Hyo had no patience to sit through the endless war councils. He needed a place away from people, somewhere he could be alone with his thoughts. Sometimes he lay for hours on the flat top of the hill they called the Barrow, that sat on one side of the bay housing Fleet. Other times he walked along the ragged coast of the island. Looking at the empty sky and empty sea, he hoped to find that emptiness that had been inside him, the one that gave him peace. He hadn't yet, but he meant to keep trying.

Or he would have, if Dinesh hadn't chosen to trail along behind him on today's walk.

'What do you want?' Dae Hyo asked, after about an hour of it. He turned around to glare at Dinesh. 'I tell you what, you should either keep a man company or go away. And I'd prefer the going away.'

'You ought, you ought, you ought to be nicer to me,' Dinesh said. 'You nearly killed me.'

Dae Hyo sighed and turned back to his walk, resolving to ignore Dinesh like you would a horse fly.

Dinesh didn't seem to want to let him, though. He trotted up until they were walking side by side. Ahead of them, black shapes dipped and twisted in the sky: Rii's children and probably Eric's boy with them. Dae Hyo wished he could be so carefree.

'They're useful,' Dinesh said, looking at Rii's pups.

'Useful for what?'

'For the war.' Dinesh switched his gaze from the big bats to Dae Hyo. 'You're not.'

Dae Hyo agreed, but that didn't mean he liked to hear it. 'You're less use than I am.'

'I know. I was useful with the Drifters, not here. I think I'll leave.'

'Leave?' Dae Hyo stopped to stare at him. Useless as he felt, it hadn't occurred to him to abandon Krish. 'And go where?'

'To Mirror Town.'

Now Dae Hyo was beginning to wonder if Dinesh had lost his wits. 'Why? It's seen two battles in a decade. There's not much left of it but rocks.'

'The other slaves are there,' Dinesh said. 'And they're free now and they have no one to lead them. I'm good at leading. That's what I learned when I was with the Drifters. I'd be useful there. And I don't have to fight Krish's war, not any more.'

Dae Hyo might have made an argument, if a different shape in the sky hadn't caught his eye. 'Look there,' he said. 'That's no pup of Rii's.'

Dinesh glanced up, then shrugged. 'A flying cart. King Nayan has two of them now. They captured another one yesterday.'

'But that's neither. Nayan's keeping his close by him in Fleet, not in the sky. Those rat-fuckers on the mainland have sent it to spy on us.'

'Do, do, do you think we should tell someone?'

'I think we should stop it. That's something we can both be useful for.'

Rii's children were further away than they looked. Dae Hyo was breathless by the time he and Dinesh had run across the hill to them and the flying cart was drifting seawards.

'Spies!' Dae Hyo gasped, pointing up. 'We have to stop them.'

The pups were used to passengers now – they'd been on twenty outings or more for Nayan – but they weren't used to ones as heavy as Dae Hyo. It was only when he was a hundred paces above the ground and rising that it occurred to him he had no saddle. There was nothing but the pup's greasy hair to cling to.

Dinesh was a little ahead on the pup he'd chosen, the largest of the girls. Seeing how precarious his perch looked didn't make Dae Hyo feel any better about his own. But they were gaining on the flying cart. The pups were far faster in the air.

'What are we going to do?' a high piping voice asked, and it took Dae Hyo a moment to realise that it was the pup itself speaking. In truth, he'd forgotten they were more than mounts. And in remembering that, he remembered they were only children and far too young to be risked in war.

'Take us above,' he told the pups and Dinesh. 'We'll drop down into the cart, and then you fly off. If there's fighting to be done, me and Dinesh will do it.'

It didn't take the pups long to reach the level of the cart's bed. Dae Hyo saw the two occupants, staring down at the distant land. And then one of the pair jerked his head up, alerted by some sound or the shape of the pup's wings against the sky. He shouted to his companion – thin words that didn't travel intact as far as Dae Hyo – and then the pair of them were reaching for their weapons.

There was a crack, like a whip snapping. Almost at the same time, a line of pain scored his ribs.

'Get away!' Dinesh shouted just as Dae Hyo bellowed, 'Get

closer!' and Dinesh's mount fell away as Dae Hyo's swooped towards the cart.

He could see both weapons now, long thin tubes of metal, pointed at him. Krish would be angry if Dae Hyo got Rii's pups injured. Rii would probably eat him. And so he released his convulsive grip on the pup's fur and stood. Instantly, the wind seized him in its icy grip and he flexed his legs beneath him and jumped.

He'd misjudged the distance. Rather than landing inside the cart, he thumped against its side. There was a sharp crack that might have been another volley from those weapons or might have been a rib cracking. Either way the result was pain. Dae Hyo slid down the wicker wall of the cart, and reached out desperately to grab its rim.

A moment later there was an agonising blow against his fingers. The cart's riders were trying to dislodge him. But this was no different from flinging yourself on another man's pony in the heat of battle. He'd done that a hundred times and always ended up the one in the saddle. He tensed his fingers despite the pain in them and hauled himself over the side and in.

The men inside stared at him in shock. The tube weapons were still in their hands, but the things were too long to bring them to bear on Dae Hyo now he stood beside them. Before they could reach for their knives, he grasped the cloth of one man's jacket at the shoulder, put another hand between his legs and heaved him over the side of the cart and into the sky.

The man didn't even scream as he fell. The other stared at Dae Hyo, wide-eyed. The fool *still* didn't reach for his knife, so Dae Hyo took out his axe and chopped halfway through his neck.

The blood gushed everywhere. His face was splashed and the copper taste of it was in his open mouth. He wiped it away with his sleeve and grinned. That had been a good fight. He took a moment to enjoy the view, the islands spread out below him just like outlines on a map.

It was only a little while into the enjoyment that it occurred to him he had no idea at all how to make the flying cart move where he wanted. The land he'd thought so pretty was already sliding away beneath him, leaving only the endless sea. He was surprised to discover that he wasn't afraid. If a man had to end his days, floating away in the sky after a good fight didn't seem like a bad way to do it.

Then there was a shout from nearby, human, and the high piping call of the pups, and he realised that they'd returned for him.

'Can you take this thing down?' he said to Dinesh, as the boy scrambled aboard from the pup's back.

Dinesh looked at him as if he'd taken leave of his senses.

'Oh well, I suppose Nayan can send someone after it if he chooses. My brother will want a look at this new weapon, though.' Dae Hyo knelt to prise it from the dead man's grasp. He searched him while he was at it, but there was nothing more interesting to find than his smalls.

When he was done, he whistled the pups back over. 'Take us to the man who fell,' Dae Hyo told them both as he pulled himself on board the first, hoping that pulling at the thing's hair wasn't hurting it too badly.

'Why?' Dinesh asked. He'd already found his seat on the other pup's back, more agile than Dae Hyo.

'The man's a spy,' Dae Hyo said. 'We'd better make sure he's dead.'

It took a while to find him, even from the air. But when they did, there wasn't any doubt that he was done spying. He'd landed on rock, face-first, and now there wasn't much of a face left. Blood was seeping out of his clothes. It was possible his clothes were the only thing holding him together.

Dinesh knelt by his head. He ran his fingers gently along the bells that hung in a cluster of three from his ear.

'That's like the mark Krish put on you,' Dae Hyo said. 'I heard it from one of Nayan's people. It robs a man of his will. I tell you what, if it's slaves you're worried about, there's a few of them in Ashanesland that need freeing. The elder mothers always said, "Cut the meat that's on the plate – the meat on the rabbit can wait."'

Dinesh didn't look at Dae Hyo, but the stiffness of his body said he was listening. He pulled his fingers back from the bells as if they'd burned him.

Dae Hyo had almost given up on the body when he felt something tucked inside the man's belt. It was tube-shaped, and at first he thought it was another of the strange weapons, but when he pulled it out, he saw that it was a parchment case. He drew out and unrolled what was inside, then frowned at it. Reading was women's knowledge and he'd never learned it.

'Oh!' Dinesh said, staring at it. Of course the boy would have learned what wasn't a man's to learn.

'Well, what does it say?' Dae Hyo asked, as Dinesh read in silence.

Dinesh, probably just to spite Dae Hyo, continued reading every word. On the second page there was what looked like a map. Dinesh frowned as he studied it. Then, finally, he looked up.

'This, this, this is written to Krish,' he said. 'It's from Renar.'

*

Krish received two things, one straight after another. There was the parchment that Dinesh and Dae Hyo had somehow recovered from a spy, and there was a messenger from his father.

He was poring over the first when the second arrived.

'I'm sorry, Wheelheir,' the messenger said, 'but King Nayan thought you should hear this. It's the leader of the invaders – the other leader, not the one who's been here.'

'The other god,' Krish said and the man flinched. Even now, people seemed unwilling to admit that this was what they were facing.

'Yes, Wheelheir. The second of the Three. They say his name is Marvan.'

Krish's skin shivered with remembered pain. When he'd been little more than a boy, visiting Smiler's Fair with Dae Hyo, Marvan had captured him and tortured him for sport. He'd meant to torture him to death and he would have succeeded if the fair hadn't burned to a cinder around them. Later, when they were in Mirror Town, Krish had imprisoned him, but even when he'd been in Krish's power, Marvan had taunted him. He'd asked what sort of heritage ran in his blood, when his own father had tried to murder him.

'Are you saying he's come to Ashanesland?' Krish asked.

The messenger nodded, and swallowed nervously.

'The news won't get better the longer you keep it.'

'Wheelheir, they say he's been travelling from shipfort to shipfort, asking after the moon-eyed lad. Your father thinks he's hunting you.'

*

After that, Krish went to Eric. 'I think I can bring that flying city down,' he said, as he walked through the door of Eric's cabin, then stopped short. 'Sorry, I didn't realise.' Eric's son was there, Arwel, the child Krish remembered as a grey-skinned baby. He was a pink-skinned young lad now, sitting in the curl of Eric's legs, playing at jack and ball.

Eric had been grinning as they played, and he turned the same grin up to Krish. Eric's happiness seemed so great, it warmed Krish. But he saw the delicate, almost tentative way Eric was holding his son, like a man might hold an untamed bird.

'I'll come back later,' Krish said.

Eric shook his head. 'I heard what you said. That's good tidings, ain't it?'

'But another of the three gods has come here. Or to Ashanesland, anyway. And he's someone who knows me. Hates me, probably.'

'That's less glad news.'

'The trouble is,' Krish said, 'if I bring the flying city down, the people in it might die, but the gods in it won't. And then I'll have two angry gods on the ground. It won't make things any better.'

Eric frowned, as his hands continued to guide his son's on the jacks. 'You weren't there when the Eetlust came,' he said at last.

'Dae Hyo told me about it. It was why he and Dinesh fought. That's what he said, anyway. They fought over the right to battle it.'

'In a way . . .'

'But the Eetlust died, didn't it?' Krish asked. 'I know the Drifters thought it was a god, but I don't think it was. Or no more than one of the moon's leftover monsters, anyway. A thing of the deep waters.'

'Yeah, that's the point I'm trying to make. It was a thing of the deep, and it died when it was brought up. To hear Dae Hyo tell it, it was him what killed the beast. But you should have seen the size of the thing. His little axe couldn't do much more than tickle it. It died all of its own accord, as soon as it hit the surface. And there's another thing too. I've flown on Rii's back, all the way to the top of the world and back again. Sometimes we went so high I couldn't find my breath. She said the air gets thinner, the higher up you go.'

Krish smiled, very glad that Eric was on his side, and not on anyone else's. 'So you're saying I shouldn't try to bring the flying city down at all. You think I should send it *up*.'

*

The war council was in full session again when Krish went to it. Tables had been set up on Rii's raft for all the notables. Krish recognised shiplords he'd fought against at Mirror Town. There must be many here who'd lost friends and family in his wars.

'I was a goatherd once,' Krish said, loudly enough that all the heads turned to him and Rii's furry ears swivelled. 'A long time ago. I lived in a tent with my ma and da and tended the herd. My da beat us, and I was too weak to fight back. There was a sickness in my chest. Being a god burned it out, but back then I thought I could die of it.'

His father was frowning at him, his expression a mixture of puzzlement and embarrassment. 'Krishanjit, that's in the past. You're Wheelheir now.'

'No, listen.' Krish swung his gaze around the room until it was clear he was saying it to everyone. 'I was weak, so I used poison to kill my da. I tricked him into eating it. And I had no letters, but I figured out a lot of things. When I was weak, I was clever. I had to be to survive. Then I became a god. And because I was strong, I forgot how to be clever.'

He heard one of the lords whisper to another, 'Why is this goatherd at our council?' but his father frowned the man into silence.

'I'm not a god any more,' Krish said. 'I'm weak again. We're all weak, because it's gods we're facing and people can never be as strong as them.'

'He's talking defeat before the battle's even fought!' another of the lords said, a little too loudly.

Nayan glared him into silence too, but barely softened his eyes when they turned on Krish. 'We're not so weak as you think. The tribes and the Moon Forest folk are no more pleased with these gods than we are. Alliances have been made.'

'With who?' Krish asked. 'People on the far side of the White Heights? They'll never make it to us in time. We'll be trodden into dust before they get here.'

'If you'd bothered to attend this council on any day before this, you'd know that our new allies are due to reach us within the month. And they promise weapons even a god will fear. Sit down, Krishanjit. This is a time to listen and not to speak.'

Krish shook his head, and didn't sit down. 'You can gather your armies and march to war, but you'll lose every battle. You'll spend lives and never buy what you want with them. We can't be strong, so we need to be clever.'

'And I suppose you are here to present me with a superior plan,' Nayan said cuttingly. 'With all your many years' experience of ruling.'

'I've never ruled,' Krish said. 'I don't know how to command armies or carry out raids. I've never been much use in a fight. But I do have a plan.'

PART 3
A Different Path

28

The hedge gave Krish and Eric a good view of the circled wagons which comprised the village. Every one of the villagers who was working the fields, or sitting outside the wagons in the spring sun, spinning yarn, laboured methodically and slowly and without pausing to speak or even rest. They were all belled. More and more villages on the mainland were similar now, even ones like this on the wild eastern edge of the continent.

'What if she ain't coming?' Eric asked, shifting restlessly beside him. The hedge was full of prickles, but the foliage was dense enough to hide them from casual eyes.

'Then we'll do it anyway,' Krish said. 'We've got no—' But then he saw it: a black dot in the sky, rapidly swelling as it descended. 'It doesn't matter. They're here.' He got his knees beneath him, ready to rise, but Eric grabbed his arm.

'*Someone*'s here, don't mean it's Renar.'

Krish shrugged. 'Then I'll pretend to be working the fields until they've gone.'

'If they don't recognise you. If they ain't come here especially looking for you.'

'If I'm taken, you'll go back to the Islands to tell my father – that's why you're here to watch.'

'And then what'll he do? Those allies of his he was crowing about hadn't showed their faces when we left. I ain't sure they're coming at all, and without them, what sort of force has he got? Most of his best men are here on the mainland, doing as you tell 'em. If this fails, we may as well throw in our cards. The game'll be over.'

'But the plan can still happen without me. And anyway, look, it *is* Renar.'

The sky ship was only fifty paces above the ground. There seemed to be at least a half dozen people inside, but only Renar was peering over the edge. Looking for him, probably.

'We don't even know we can trust her,' Eric insisted, his fingers still warm around Krish's arm. 'She weren't exactly our friend in Ofiklanod. She tried to murder you!'

'I remember. And maybe she sent me a message to bait a trap, but I don't think so. The things the spies have been telling us, the way Nabofik behaves . . . no one sane would want to serve *omas*, and Renar isn't mad. You don't need to fuss, Eric. I'm not Arwel.' But he didn't mind the fussing. It was still a strange feeling, to know that anyone cared. Dae Hyo did, of course, but his caring generally took a rougher form than Eric's.

He waited for the commotion that came with the sky craft's landing to step out into the field, where the crop of wheat was already golden-ripe, far too early in the year. He picked up a scythe left lying spare and took a swing at the stalks, trying to keep time with the dead-eyed workers around him. The field was ringed with bells. He knew their ringing meant something, but he hadn't mastered the magic well enough to know what it was.

He risked a glance towards the newcomers, though none of the other belled fieldworkers seemed to have even registered their presence. It took him a moment to pick out Renar's narrow face among the rest, and in the moment he did, she must have seen him too. Their eyes met and locked and then he looked away. She knew he'd come. Now it was up to her.

When he was starting on his second sheaf, he heard footsteps behind him and a voice that wasn't Renar's saying, 'It all looks well to me. A fine harvest, and early too. La, what's there to complain of?'

'Look at the ground, you fool,' another voice said, and this one *was* Renar's. 'It's dry as a summer in Ofzib and about as fertile. The wheat's grown unnaturally and it's taken all the virtue of the soil with it. There'll be no crop next year, I'll tell you that.'

She was right. Krish noticed for the first time the hard surface of the earth beneath the wheat, cracked like a shattered pane of glass.

'You!' Renar said, and a moment later, 'You there, working by the hedgerow!'

She was, Krish realised, talking to him. He looked up, his heart speeding. Now he'd learn if she meant to betray him, when it was too late to do anything about it.

'I want you to show me the rest of the fields,' she said. The crowd around her stirred. They were all Mortals, though no longer black-robed now they served a different master. 'Try to get some sense out of the villagers while this one shows me round,' Renar said to them. 'I want to know how much they've harvested already and whether it will last an extra year. Perhaps this won't be as bad as I fear.' Then she snapped her fingers at Krish, turned her back and walked away.

He trotted obediently after her, across the field and into another before he dared draw level. Still looking forwards rather than at him, she hissed, 'Your ruse was idiotic. A single spy sent to find me in all of the City On High? And the clappers in his bells removed. Anyone could have noticed. There were a hundred ways it could have gone wrong.'

'But it didn't,' Krish said. 'And you came.'

He was shocked by the change in her face. There hadn't been a single line when he'd last seen her, nor any grey in her braided hair. Now the hair was more white than brown and her cheeks were scored with care and worry. Three years couldn't account for a change that big.

'Well?' she said. 'What do you want? I can't be away for long – the others will wonder what I've found to entertain me among the hovels. Why did your message insist I bring so many with me? It's made this ten times harder.'

'I thought it would help to have them as witnesses.'

'Witnesses to what?'

'You'll see when you leave.'

She huffed in irritation and quickened her pace. 'Is that why you summoned me? To send me away again?'

'No. I have a plan and I need your help.'

'I hope 'tis better thought-out than the scheme that brought me here.'

'It is,' Krish assured her, even though it depended on just as much luck as that one had. 'We're attacking that city in the sky tomorrow. The City On High, is that what it's called?'

She stopped to stare at him. 'With what?'

'It doesn't matter. You don't need to know.'

'Worried I'll betray it?'

'If you're caught, yes.' He didn't know her well, but he knew that lying to her would be a fool's game.

She snorted and resumed walking. 'Perhaps I've grown more stupid as I age, but I can't see why you've bothered to drag me all this way, if the plan can proceed so splendidly without me.'

'You're Nabofik's chief counsellor, aren't you? The rumours say you're the only one *oms* listens to.'

'Would that *oms* listened to me more. Nabofik is as ungovernable as a swarm of wasps and considerably more dangerous.'

'But if you tell *omas* there's an attack planned, that King Nayan has found a way to build his own sky carts—'

'Sil-nafön,' she corrected.

'Sil-nafön, then. If Nabofik believes that my father has his own and plans to attack *omas* in the floating city, can you persuade *omas* to call back all the sky carts to defend it? It will be no use destroying the city if its army is elsewhere.'

'Maybe.' Renar frowned. 'It will be hard to convince Nabofik of the existence of the attack. *Oms* believes the magic that moves the sil-nafön to be wielded only by *omas*.'

'Yes,' Krish said. 'That's why I asked you to bring the others. And when you go back, you need to make an excuse to head west first, towards the Five Stars. Only ten miles or so. And stay high in the air, but not so high you can't see the ground.'

She was looking at him incredulously. 'Any other orders for me, my prince?'

'No, that's it. If you can do that, you'll see all the evidence you need.'

★

Dae Hyo climbed the nearest hill to get an overview of the camp. The hill wasn't very high – the area around the Five Stars was almost as flat as the plains – and the view wasn't very impressive. He saw nearly a hundred tents below him, but he knew that barely a tenth of them were occupied. The rest were only for show. And on one edge of the camp there were two dozen big wooden boxes with circular canopies suspended above them, all dyed a muddy grey. They looked, Dae Hyo thought, very little like the flying carts of the Three that they were attempting to impersonate.

The two real ones they'd managed to capture were elsewhere, hidden under branches. They couldn't risk *those* being attacked, not before Dae Hyo, Dinesh and their small contingent of Ashane soldiers had flown them to the city in the sky.

The Ashane soldiers themselves were crouched on the ground below him, waiting for his command. They were chatting among themselves as they waited. He sighed and went down the hill to them.

'Svarog's cock,' he said, when he was in earshot, 'I thought my orders were clear. You're not to take the wax out until the job's done. How are you going to get used to it, if you don't keep it in?'

They muttered rebelliously, but did as he'd asked, pressing the thick tubes of candlewax as deep inside their ears as they'd go. Dae Hyo didn't much enjoy the feeling either, but he did the same. The shout and clatter of Nayan's men was immediately muted.

Muted, but not silenced entirely. The plugs were meant to protect them against the influence of the music that had turned so many into slaves. It was a good idea of his brother's. Most of his brother's ideas were good, but quite often they didn't work out the way Krish meant them to. Dae Hyo had a bad feeling this would be one of those times.

Still, he drilled the small group in the signals they'd worked out. One of Nayan's lords had been born deaf and he'd taught the idea to them, but they hadn't had long to learn it. Half the time, when Dae Hyo signalled them to crouch, they stood, and when he signalled them forwards, they held back. That was another way Krish's plan could go wrong.

As he was on the point of ordering them to take the wax out again so they could hear him shout at them, he saw what he'd been waiting for. They were approaching from the west, just as they were meant to. And they were flying high, but not too high, just as Krish had said they would be.

'They're coming!' he shouted to the rest of the camp. 'Make ready!' He only hoped the boxes and awnings and tents looked better from the air than they did from the ground.

Everything *was* going to plan, except that Dinesh wasn't back yet. He and Dae Hyo were meant to do the next part together. Dae Hyo wondered what was keeping him.

*

Marvan left the shipfort with half a dozen corpses mouldering behind him, but no new information. He'd hobbled his horse by the shore of the lake, where it could crop the withered grass and admire the rocky scenery. It was a fine tall roan, the pick of Lord Nayan's stables, and it whickered when it saw him. He could have travelled by sil-nafön, but he preferred to be closer to earth. The spoor was easier to find that way.

Or it should have been. He always seemed to be two days behind Krish. When he went to Ashfall, it was to find that the prince had been sighted in Fort Daybreak, and when he went to Fort Daybreak, it was to pick up rumours of Krish among the Five Stars. It was clear Krishanjit had some way to move that was faster than a sil-nafön, but Marvan hadn't been able to find out what it was. The carrion flock were all carrion themselves now. And no one had seen that monstrous bat of his since it had flown out to sea and, it was assumed, drowned.

Marvan was no longer enjoying himself. He relished the chase, but the kill was the true thrill. It was clear he needed a way to get ahead of the prince. Alfreda should be in Ashanesland soon. He resolved to ask her to forge something for him: a compass, perhaps, that always pointed to Krish's location, although the truth was he didn't know if the power he wielded was capable of that. The Mortals who'd tried to explain it to him had been very tiresome. Several of them left his company short more than two hands, and him none the wiser. But Alfreda would be able to tell him.

He was so caught up in these thoughts, he almost ran the youth down before he saw him. He almost ran him down after, too: what was the fool doing, standing in the middle of the road? But then he registered that the man was waving his arms as if, improbably, he meant for Marvan to stop.

'Lord Marvan,' the youth said. 'Lord Marvan, please, I need to speak to you.'

Marvan stared at him in silence for a very long moment. He enjoyed how much fear he could instil, just by doing that. But the youth looked disappointingly unmoved. Closer to, Marvan saw that he was of mixed blood, Ashane and the tribes probably, but strikingly handsome despite his sickly pale skin. There was a confidence about him, too, a sureness of his own strength and beauty in the way he held himself. Marvan disliked him immediately.

'My title is God-Triumvir,' Marvan told him, remaining on his horse.

'I'm, I'm, I'm sorry,' the boy said, and at his words, and more particularly the way he said them, a memory sparked in Marvan.

'I know you,' he said. 'I've met you before.'

The youth nodded. 'You met me among the Rah. We travelled together to Mirror Town.'

'You're Krish's slave! Dinesh, that was your name.' Now this was interesting.

'I *was* his slave,' Dinesh said, and Marvan couldn't mistake the bitterness in his voice. 'Now I'm, I'm, I'm free. He can't command me any more.'

'And why have you sought me out, Krish's slave-no-more? You can't have thought it would end well for you.' Marvan's body was already stirring at the thought of the pleasure he'd find in this boy's blood.

'I want it to end badly for *him*. I can tell you his plans. I know all of them. He thinks I still serve him.'

Marvan slid from his horse's back. He seized Dinesh by the shoulders, hard enough to hurt, and stared into his face. 'And you want me to believe that you don't? Why in all the world should I trust you?'

'Because I hate him,' Dinesh said, and Marvan saw the truth of it in his eyes. 'I want him dead, but I can't get near him. Now he's a prince he has guards, but they wouldn't be able to stop *you*. You can kill him. I heard that you were hunting him, and so I came.'

Oh, this was a lure it was hard not to bite. Could it really be true? Marvan watched every twitch of Dinesh's face as he spoke. 'Tell me then, what is the prince's plan?'

'To attack the flying city.'

Marvan released his shoulders, both disappointed and relieved: he'd have a kill now, but not the one he wanted. 'A feeble attempt.' He drew the trident from his belt and pressed the long central prong to Dinesh's throat. 'I know the prince is no such fool.'

Even now, Dinesh didn't flinch. 'He isn't,' he said. 'That's why you have to send me back to him. So he won't suspect you know the truth. The, the, the attack is a trick. His real target is Fell's End. He wants to take your mother captive and use her as a hostage. *That's* where you'll find him, tomorrow. And that's where you can kill him.'

29

There was, Renar found, very little that she wanted to take with her. What was there left that she cared about, except her sib? She'd once owned a small but much-admired collection of sculptures by Jal the Butcher. She'd also acquired the original manuscript on which Cäf the Open-Hearted had penned her most famous play, *The Aquater's End*. Renar had been offered an estate in Makat in exchange for it and turned it down. But those and all her other possessions were gone, lost in the wreckage of Täm.

From Nayan she'd had a gold-braided torc, but she'd thrown that into the sands during her flight from the invaders. It marked her too clearly as a woman of rank. He'd also given her some of the finest furs his huntsmen could supply. The last of those had been ruined by mud during the same journey.

Nabofik had offered her the spoils of Ashanesland. *Oms* had proposed setting Renar up as shiplord of Delta's Strength. Renar had remembered the fate of the fort's last lords and declined. She hadn't wanted anything from Nabofik, when it was all so steeped in blood. So she found that all she had to pack was one fresh dress and the oil she used in her hair.

Lanalan walked into her chamber just as she was fastening her pack. It saved her the trouble of going to find him.

He hovered near the doorway, frowning. 'Is all well, Renar?'

'Everything is . . . everything is going as it should. Shut the door, Lanalan, and come in.'

'Oh,' he said, noticing her pack. 'Are you leaving?'

'*We're* leaving. Immediately.' It was already past sunset. Too much time had been eaten up since her meeting with Krish: first by their return to the City On High, and then by the news they had to report on their arrival. The prince's ruse had certainly worked. The Mortals she'd travelled with had been convinced that the fleet of sil-nafön they spied on the ground were an attack force. Renar wondered what they'd truly been, but she wasn't interested enough to stay and find out. Let the other Mortals deal with Nabofik. She had her own skin and her sib's to save.

'Has Nabofik sent us somewhere?' Lanalan asked. 'But why? *Oms* has barely let you leave *omas* side in a month.'

'Nabofik doesn't know, and mustn't find out. Marvan may have taken away my right to command the belled, but I've watched a sil-nafön flown often enough to grasp the trick of it. We'll take one and be away before anyone notices.'

He sat on the bed beside her, his friendly face tight with concern. 'But what's happened, Renar? Why must we leave now? You must know Nabofik will pursue you. And—' He shuddered. ''Tis not pleasant to think what *oms* might do if *oms* catches us.'

'Nabofik will be otherwise engaged. I hope.' He looked unconvinced and she knew that she'd need to tell him what was going on. He deserved the truth, anyway. She leaned in to whisper, 'Prince Krishanjit means to take the City On High. Tomorrow. We must be away before then. If we stay, once Nabofik knows there's trouble, it will be just as you say. *Oms* will want me by *omas* side and then there'll be no escape.' This had occurred to her mere minutes after the prince had left. He'd asked her for her help, but he'd made no mention of any plan to rescue her.

'The prince told you this himself?' Lanalan asked.

She nodded.

He studied her, his head tipped to one side. The gesture was a little too big, an actor's performance of curiosity, though she knew he was sincere. 'But he must have had a reason to tell you. Was he asking for your help?' Because her foolish sib must show a moment of intelligence at the worst possible time.

'He asked me to ensure that the sil-nafön remain aboard the city when the attack comes.'

'La, you can hardly do that if you've left already.'

'And I won't be able to leave if I stay long enough to do as Krishanjit asked. Were you not listening to me, Lanalan?'

His mouth thinned with disapproval. He had, she knew, very firm ideas of right and wrong. It was yet another way in which they differed. 'Without you, will Krish's plan fail?'

She shrugged. ''Tis hard to say, as he wouldn't tell me it. I'm not sure if you recall, but I once attempted to murder him. Ours has not been a close relationship. We owe him nothing. Well, I have everything I need here.' She stood and shouldered the pack. 'Let's go to your room and take whatever you require. We're running out of time.'

But he didn't rise. She remembered, as she should have done before, that he'd once conceived a passion for that boy Eric who served the prince. It would be just like him to worry about the boy's fate and not his own if Krish's plan failed.

'Lanalan, please,' she begged. 'If you've ever loved me, come.'

'I can't. Renar, you're right, you should go before you're trapped. But Nabofik has never much cared for me. I can carry out the plan and then leave. Why, if Krishanjit had thought of it, I'm sure he would have suggested it himself.'

'Nabofik doesn't trust you. *Oms* is as likely to kill you as let you go.'

'Then *oms* will kill me,' he said, with a steely finality that was very unlike him. 'I suppose you're right. We don't owe the prince our lives. But what about the people of Ashanesland? Or Ofiklanod? My ears aren't so closed as you think. I've heard Nabofik threaten to raze the whole country if it continues to defy *omas*.'

'That was nothing but talk,' Renar said, but with little conviction.

'Nabofik is a monster. I know you know it. I've seen you, Renar, trying to rein *omas* in. 'Tis a fine face you put on, of not caring, but I see beneath it. *Oms* must be stopped. And we're the only ones who can do it.'

Renar dropped her pack to the ground and sat beside him again on the bed, lowering her head into her hands. He put his arm around her and squeezed tight, as he'd done when he was a boy.

'Very well,' she said. 'I'll stay. I'll see Krishanjit's plan through to the end. There's no need for you to remain with me.'

She looked up to see his loving smile. 'But you know I will.'

★

They found Nabofik in *omas* white tower. There was a map of Ashanesland spread out on the large table in front of *omas*, and a corpse, bleeding from its eyes, at *omas* feet.

Renar recognised the man. It was Salmun, one of the oldest of the Mortals that Nabofik had brought to serve *omas*. The expression fixed on his face suggested he'd suffered before he died.

'Renar, there you are!' Nabofik spun to face her. 'I thought you'd deserted me, and then I would have had to kill you, and you're the only person here who talks any sense.'

Oms didn't mean it as a threat, Renar knew. It was no more than an offhand statement of fact. 'I've been speaking with the sil-nafön captains as they return,' Renar said. 'It seems the force of Nayan's that we saw wasn't the only one. There are at least three others, all within a few hours' flight of here.'

'But how could this happen? It's not right! The sil-nafön are mine. How did they know how to make them?'

'Why, there must be spies inside the city,' Lanalan said, widening his eyes theatrically.

Fortunately, Nabofik wasn't looking at him. 'Yes, that makes sense,' *oms* said. 'That explains why Salmun wouldn't tell me where Nayan's army came from so suddenly. I thought he was just being useless, but actually he must have been working against me.'

'All is not lost though,' Renar said. 'The King may have his own fleet of sil-nafön, but we have the greater numbers. The important thing is to protect this city, and you most of all. We should concentrate our forces here. If you'd like my advice, it's to summon the sil-nafön back to our defence. We'll repel Nayan's attack with ease and send his whole fleet to the ground.'

Nabofik smiled. 'Yes, that's a good idea. And we'll only need to do it for a little while. Once Alfreda arrives, she'll destroy them all.'

'Alfreda?' It took everything Renar had to keep the alarm she felt from her voice. 'The God-Triumvir is coming here?'

'Yes, of course. I thought I told you. Oh, but maybe I forgot because I was so worried about all the crops failing, and you know how I can't keep two things in my mind at once. I sent her a message weeks ago, telling her I needed her. And now she's coming. She's the strongest and cleverest of the three of us by far. So everything is going to be all right, isn't it?'

'I believe it will be,' Renar said, bowing to hide her face. Because here was the thing Krish couldn't have accounted for in his plans. And Renar had absolutely no way to tell him.

30

Krish crouched over the map, with Dae Hyo beside him and Dinesh opposite. He'd arrived in the encampment near the Five Stars only moments before, but time was of the essence now. Time, and everyone conducting their part in his plans exactly as he'd designed them. He worried that Dae Hyo and Dinesh would veer from it just to spite each other. It was gloomy under the canvas even with two lamps lit, and stifling. The stink of badly cured hide filled the whole space.

Dae Hyo frowned at the parchment. 'Can the place really be this big?'

'You've seen it in the sky,' Dinesh snapped. 'You can see how big it is.'

'Renar gave us a plan of it when she contacted me. And since then we've managed to get three spies aboard,' Krish said. 'This was as accurate as they could make it. You can take it with you, but it's better if you memorise it. You might not have time to stop and look at it.'

'We know.' Dinesh sounded equally impatient with Krish. It was strange to hear him speak so sharply and with such little affection. Before Krish's long sleep, there'd been nothing but love in Dinesh's face when he looked at him. 'The bells are above the tallest tower, the white one in the middle. I remember everything.'

'Good then.' Krish stood, rubbing his thighs where they'd cramped.

'*He* shouldn't come,' Dinesh said, just as Krish reached for the tent flap.

Krish sighed and turned back to him.

Dinesh's expression was mulish. 'He's not Ashane. He'll stand out. It will be easier without him.'

'Dae Hyo is my brother. It's right for him to lead,' Krish told him firmly, and left before Dinesh could say anything further.

He heard a footstep behind him, but it was too heavy to be Dinesh.

'I tell you what,' Dae Hyo said as he moved to Krish's side, 'that boy is asking for a beating.'

'Please don't. There are enough other people to fight.'

Dae Hyo grunted, which was probably as close to agreement as Krish could expect.

'There's something I wanted to show you anyway,' Krish said. 'I think it should be ready by now.'

He'd set up the firepit a little way from the camp, behind the cover of a grassy hill. This was private, something between just the two of them. Dae Hyo frowned as he approached the blaze with the stew pot suspended over it. 'There's food enough in the camp, brother.'

Krish sat to spoon the stew into the two bowls he'd left ready. 'This isn't for everyone.'

Dae Hyo crouched opposite him, still looking doubtful, but he took the bowl when Krish handed it to him.

'It's lion's balls,' Krish said. 'For strength and courage.'

Dae Hyo laughed. For a moment he didn't look like a warrior in his middle years, scarred and disappointed by life, but like the young man he must once have been.

'I didn't hunt it myself,' Krish admitted. 'I didn't have time. I sent some of my father's men to find one in the mountains. Do you think that will still work?'

'I think it's close enough.' Dae Hyo took a large mouthful and swiped at the juices as they dribbled down his chin.

They ate in companionable silence for a while. It was a bright day, the sky blue and only a little speckled with clouds, and the warmth of the coming summer was in the air. The copse of trees on the hill's flank was all in bud. It was a hopeful-feeling day, but Krish knew it might be his last. It might be the last day for all of them.

'Dinesh is right,' Dae Hyo said, when he'd licked his bowl clean. 'I can fight better than any man, but I haven't got an Ashane face. What if I'm the reason your plan fails?'

'You were the first person to help me who wasn't kin to me. You were my first friend. I'd rather fail with you than succeed without you.'

Dae Hyo studied him thoughtfully. 'You aren't that boy any more. You've changed, brother.'

'Doesn't everyone?'

'Not me. I think I lost the knack for it when my people died.' Dae Hyo's eyes were on the horizon, narrowed against the sun, but Krish knew that his mind was in a long-distant time. Then he shook his head, stood and offered Krish his hand to pull him up. 'Come on. A man shouldn't sit around when there's work to do.'

★

Eric had seen Krish take Dae Hyo aside; he didn't know for what. He felt a jab of jealousy that he didn't expect. It was daft, anyway. He knew there was nothing of that kind between Krish and the warrior. And besides, if there was, why should he care?

Still, he had little to distract him from it, as he watched the final preparations being made. Dae Hyo and Dinesh would be taking a clutch of warriors with them to the city in the sky. Enough to help but not enough to draw too much attention, or so they hoped. They were all arming themselves and readying the sil-nafön that Babi had given them and another they'd captured later. They ought to blend right in with the Three's forces when all sil-nafön were summoned back to the city. *If* the design hadn't changed. *If* Renar had done as Krish had asked.

There was a whole heap of ifs. Eric didn't like it. He'd seen too many gamblers lose what they couldn't afford in Smiler's Fair to enjoy a wager himself. And this was playing against very long odds. But Krish had decided, and all Eric could do was his part. It was an easy enough one, anyway, seeing as how he was no warrior. His job was only to tell Rii's pups where to go as they sent messages between the divided force. He was in little danger himself, but that just made it harder to bear that others he cared about were in so much.

Then Krish and Dae Hyo came striding back to the camp, side by side, and Eric knew it was all about to start.

Krish saw him looking and beckoned him over. 'We'll send a message once they've taken to the air,' he said.

Eric nodded. 'Sii's ready. He'll let Lord Suraj know to start the fake attack.'

Krish clasped Dae Hyo's arm. They exchanged one wordless look, and then the warrior strode away. He gestured to Dinesh, loitering with the rest of his men, and all of them began climbing into the sil-nafön. Krish gave the signal, the bells rang and the sil-nafön began to rise in that unnatural way of theirs. After all the planning, this was finally happening, and there was no more calling it back.

Krish stood, grim-faced, watching the departure. Eric knew that he understood the seriousness of what was happening. Looking at his face, Eric wondered if Krish truly thought it had any chance of succeeding, or believed he was sending them all off to die. But he wouldn't play them for cullies that way, and Eric couldn't dally. He had his own job to do.

He went to Sii, who was hopping from foot to foot, excited by the action and the task he'd been given, and too young to understand its gravity.

'Now, you remember the message, don't you?' Eric said to him, grabbing hold of one of his leathery wings to stop him taking off in his enthusiasm.

'*Tell Nayan's general the sky boats have set sail,*' Sii said obligingly.

'Boats is close enough, but you ain't supposed to just call him Nayan. It's King Nayan to you.'

Speed was important and so Eric let him go, watching him grow smaller in the distance just like Krish had watched the sil-nafön containing Dae Hyo, and with just as much concern. He didn't like that Rii's pups were caught up in this. He'd never let

Arwel within a mile of danger if he could help it. But they were faster than the sil-nafön and far more agile, and besides, Rii said they were more than ready for action. Who was Eric to argue with their mum?

When he could no longer tell Sii from the swallows and swifts that had returned to Ashanesland with the spring, he turned away and went to the now-deserted campsite. Krish was at one side of it, saddling his horse. Or trying to. The piebald gelding was dancing sideways away from him, its skin shivery with the tension it must feel from the prince.

'Breathe in and out slowly, like you're about to nod off,' Eric said to him. 'The horse gets his mood from the rider. I learned that off the Drovers, years ago.'

Krish nodded, but it was hard to say if he'd followed Eric's advice. Every line of him was taut as a harp string.

'You're off to Fell's End, then?' Eric asked, even though he knew the answer. It was another part of the plan he didn't care for. Maybe the part he was least happy with, if he was honest with himself. 'Sure you don't want me coming with?'

'There's nothing you could do. I'm the only one—' He cut himself off, frowning at something over Eric's shoulder.

It took Eric a moment to pick it out in the sky. It was Sii: hurtling back the way he'd come, even faster than he'd left.

'He can't have reached Lord Suraj that quickly,' Krish said.

'Maybe he saw something—' Eric began, then cut himself off too as the pup grew closer still. 'That ain't Sii. Look at the dark brown streak on her wing. That's Pelii. But she's supposed to be back on the Islands.'

Pelii was flying so fast she overshot the campsite by a house-length. She was already speaking as Eric and Krish ran towards her, gabbling in her panic. *'Attack, attack, you must come. Mother says you must come!'*

'Slow down,' Eric told her. *'Who's* attacking? More important, where are they doing it?'

'A fleet,' she said. *'Many ships.'*

Eric looked at Krish. 'That means the sil-nafön. They think

everything's a ship, on account of how they grew up on the sea.'

'*No,*' Pelii said. '*No. Ships, on the sea. Dozens of them coming from the sun-side.*' By which she meant east, Eric knew.

Krish didn't curse. Eric admired him for that, because this sounded like his plans unravelling. 'They're counter-attacking,' he said. 'Why didn't I think of that? They're trying to draw us away from the City On High.'

'But we ain't gonna be drawn. We only get one roll of these dice. You been saying that to us for weeks. If we get rid of the city, there won't be nobody left to lead the attack on the Islands.'

Krish still looked doubtful.

Eric dared to rest a hand gently against his tense forearm. 'You trust me, don't you?'

'I trust you,' Krish said, and despite everything, that gave Eric a warm glow. Krish wasn't a man who trusted easily.

'Then go to Fell's End,' Eric said. 'I'll ride Pelii back to the Islands. Back in Smiler's Fair we used to say: it ain't over until the King's Men draw the curtain.'

★

While Dae Hyo watched the sky, he could feel Dinesh watching him. The boy's eyes prickled between his shoulder blades in that way a person's eyes did when he intended to follow them up with a knife.

'A man knows when another man doesn't care for him,' Dae Hyo said. 'When this is over, I'll be happy to take a pair of knives and decide which one of us gets to walk away. But today we've got another pony to ride.'

Dinesh didn't reply, but he moved to stand beside Dae Hyo at the railing.

Dae Hyo pointed north, where there were three swelling dots against the blue. 'Those sil-nafön are moving closer.' He pointed left and then behind him. 'Those ones too. At least a dozen. They're all heading this way.'

'Heading for us or heading for the City On High?' Dinesh asked. The impossible place was hanging in the air only a little way ahead, like a huge rock that had started falling and then forgotten to finish the job.

Dae Hyo shrugged. 'If we wait, we'll find out.'

The time passed in that slow way time tended to before a fight. As the other sil-nafön drew closer all around, Dae Hyo kept his face pointing down. Dinesh wasn't wrong that he stood out. His hand reached out to touch his own ears, to check that the clapperless bells still hung there. They were the best disguise they had.

There was a horrible, tense moment when the other carts were like a swarm around them and Dae Hyo thought for sure they'd be attacked and taken down. He flinched as darkness swallowed them, turning the day to twilight – but it was only the vast shadow of the city, hiding the sun. The sil-nafön were heading there and not for Dae Hyo's force.

'Follow the others,' he said quietly to the man who was at the strange, bell-strung construction that told this thing how to move. 'Dock where they do. We want a big crowd all around us.'

The swarm of ships veered, and their two followed, rising above the city's rim – and the motion which had seemed leisurely when they hung in the air was suddenly revealed to be very fast. The city seemed to be hurtling towards them.

'The left-hand bell!' Dinesh yelled at the steersman when they were twenty paces and closing from what seemed to be the dock, with its wooden pontoons stretching into air instead of water. There was a bone-jarring impact as their vessel came to rest beside a score of others, whose crews rushed immediately from the dock towards the City On High itself.

'Out and after them,' Dae Hyo hissed, then realised that one of his crew was sitting groaning on the floor of the sil-nafön.

'You broke my leg, curse you!' the man shouted at their steersman.

'Just as well your task is to remain behind,' Dae Hyo said. 'You need to cut all the other sil-nafön loose – it won't do us any good to get rid of the city if everyone escapes it. You can cut rope with a broken leg, can't you?'

He didn't wait for an answer, just shoved three other men towards the injured one and the rest out of the sil-nafön and onto the dock.

The injured man shouted something after them, but Dae Hyo didn't attend. His attention was all on the city. It was strange how like a real place it was: too orderly, its streets laid out in perfect lines, but with only the silver canopy visible above it, you could make yourself believe you were still on the ground. At least until the ground lurched, and dropped.

'What happened?' Dinesh asked. 'Is the city sinking?'

'Just the currents of the air,' Dae Hyo said with a confidence he didn't feel.

In the rush to leave the sil-nafön, he hadn't thought to ask if they'd brought the bells, but he saw now that they had, slung in sacks over the men's shoulders and stuffed with cloth so they wouldn't ring until it was time. He turned to Dinesh, who was frowning at the map, hidden from curious eyes at the centre of their little group.

'This isn't right,' Dinesh said. He turned the map sideways, as if that might somehow change what it said. 'None of the roads are in the right place.'

'Maybe we came to the other dock,' one of the men suggested. 'There are two on the map.'

'Then, then, then how do we know which one we're at?'

Ahead of them, in the heart of the city, a white tower rose hundreds of paces above every other building. There was, now Dae Hyo paid attention to it, a resonance in this place so deep it rang inside his flesh. He sensed its source, somewhere ahead and above him, like a flower senses the sun. And above that white tower was a sequence of shapes that looked very much like bells, suspended from a frame that arched over the roof.

He pointed at the tower. 'I don't need a map to tell me that's where we need to go. Now put the wax in your ears, and follow me.'

The streets were teeming, but not like the streets of Smiler's Fair, where every person was busy taking care of their own business and nobody much cared if that got in the way of anyone else's. This was more like one of the termite colonies that Dae Hyo and his friends had liked to cut open when they were boys. There was order to it, but he couldn't guess what that order was.

As they pressed on, towards the flared white tower, the crowd thinned, and those that remained weren't belled. Dae Hyo and his men began to attract glances, at first annoyed and then suspicious. Until at last a tall, thin man with Ofiklander dark skin and a haughty expression stepped in front of them, raising his handless arms.

He said something to them – Dae Hyo could see his mouth moving, but only a faint mumble made it through the wax. And then his eyes narrowed. Dae Hyo thought that it was him the man had noticed, that he'd given them all away just as Dinesh said he would. But the Ofiklander wasn't staring at him. He was staring at their vanguard. He was looking at their ears, at the bells in them. The bells that were, it must be obvious from so close up, without clappers.

The Ofiklander's mouth moved again, wider this time, yelling something as he backed hurriedly away. Dae Hyo didn't need to hear the words to know that he was raising the alarm.

Dinesh's knife took him through his chest, but others would come looking in moments, and the streets were empty save for Dae Hyo's small force. They were bound to be found.

Dae Hyo drew his axes. Now was the time for him to prove that his brother had been right to send him on this mission. Now there was no choice but to fight.

31

Marvan visited his mother first. His family had always kept a cold table, with little conversation and infrequent guests, and it hadn't grown warmer since the deaths of his father and brothers. He and his mother ate the salted fish and marsh greens in a chilly silence. She didn't ask him his reasons for being there and he didn't offer any.

He watched her as she ate: her narrow face and knowing expression. He toyed briefly, as he had before, with the thought of killing her. *That* would be a death that made him feel something. He could imagine the betrayal in her eyes and his pulse sped up at the thought of it. He reached for his knife – but used it only to cut his meat. With his mother gone, there would be no one else left to remember his childhood. The memories felt too heavy to carry alone.

The half-blood boy, the traitor, had told Marvan that Krish intended to lead an attack force through the network of streams that covered the landscape to the north of the fort. The prince had travelled them once before, when he'd joined the hunt for a sea serpent. He would be leading a force of only a dozen men, hoping so few would go unnoticed.

Marvan could have taken a dozen men of his own to oppose them. He could have taken a thousand, but he wanted Krishanjit to himself. He planned to take his time about that particular killing. The rest of the prince's men were a mere nuisance that Marvan could swat as easily as he did the midges that plagued this place.

He took a small fishing vessel from the fort's dock. The fisherman was old, wrinkled and hunched, his eyes so rheumy it was a wonder he could see from them. But he must have recognised Marvan. He watched, unprotesting, as Marvan rowed the boat away, across the green-smeared water of the lake and into the broadest of the streams that drained into it.

He'd come this way before, years ago, with Alfreda. She'd been leech-bitten and sick with fever, and he'd been afraid that she might die. He'd enjoyed the fear, an emotion far sharper than those he usually felt. That was gone too, now. There was nothing left in the world that could hurt Alfreda, or him, no wound they couldn't heal from or mortal blow they wouldn't survive.

The rushes grew tall on either side of the boat, their heads bobbing in the sea breeze that sometimes blew here and cleared, if only briefly, the miasma of the marsh from the air. He would have been lost in minutes if he hadn't known this place as well as he knew the lines on his own palm. The prince might think that this was an impossible place to guard against attack: too many routes winding towards the fort. But Marvan knew that every one of them passed by the low, squat mound that he and his friend Ishan had called 'the toad' when they were children, for its hunched shape and the two white rocks on one side of it that might have been eyes.

Marvan moored his boat between them, then went to sit, cross-legged, just beneath the brow of the hill. He wouldn't be visible from the western side until it was far too late for Krish to escape. And if he didn't come? Well, then Marvan would enjoy hunting down the boy who'd lied to get him here. He settled down to wait.

An hour passed and Marvan rested back on his elbow, his face turned to the midday sun. The air was thick with the familiar calls of water birds: the small, plaintive cheeps of ospreys, the squawking of herons and the low grunts of pelicans.

And then, at first quieter than them, and then louder: the splash of oars in water.

Marvan lowered himself to his belly to watch through the cordgrass as a boat nosed through the reeds towards him. There was just one boat and just one figure rowing it, slender and shaggy-haired. Could Krish truly have come alone? Marvan looked left and right, where far narrower channels led towards the hillock, but they contained only a small cluster of ducks, bright green against the more faded green of the grass.

When the boat was only two oar-lengths away, Marvan stood. Krish glanced up at the movement, looking momentarily startled. But only momentarily. He shipped the oars and let the boat glide nose-first into the mud on the shore of the hillock.

'You were expecting me,' Marvan said.

The prince stood, wobbled as the boat tipped leftwards into the mud, and stepped ashore. 'I was expecting you.'

'So the boy was no traitor after all. Interesting. I thought his hate for you was real.'

'It was. It is. That's why I sent him. But people are complicated. Most of us feel more than one thing.'

'Not me.' Marvan drew the twin tridents from their sheaths on his belt. The weight of them felt good in his hands. He felt his hunger stirring, that very old companion.

Krish frowned, thoughtful but still not afraid. 'Yes. That's true, isn't it? I wondered what it was that was so wrong about you, and maybe that's it. I think there's something broken inside you.'

An unexpected needle of anger pricked Marvan, but he made himself smile. '*You* call *me* broken? The landborn boy who poisoned his own father? Tell me, how did you contrive to lose your godhood? It was very careless of you.'

'I didn't lose it, I gave it up. Being a god takes more than it gives. I'm sorry I can't give you the time to learn that.'

Marvan studied him, so strangely confident. 'Where's your fear? Do you think you're in control?' He looked around, but there was still no sign of any other person, no sound but the birds. 'If this is a trap, it's a very poor one.'

'Not a trap,' Krish said, taking another step forwards. 'A duel.'

Marvan laughed. 'A duel? Why don't I just finish the job I started in Smiler's Fair and kill you?'

Krish drew a knife from his belt. The blade was as long as his hand, and hooked at its tip. A knife meant for gutting. 'You liked to duel when you lived in the fair. Eric told me. You could have killed in the dark and no one would have known. But you preferred to play with the people you murdered.'

'Let's play then,' Marvan said, and launched himself at Krishanjit while the words were still in the air.

Krish was a little slow to react. He dodged to the side, but the mud was loath to release his feet and Marvan's knife sliced through his shirt. It nicked his flank, making a red flower bloom on the white cotton.

'You're right.' Marvan spun out of the way of the prince's return swipe. 'I do enjoy drawing out the kill.' He retreated a step, tempting Krish to follow him onto the firmer ground that lay higher on the hillock. Firmer but rockier, as Marvan knew and Krish didn't.

Krish took the bait. His feet danced forwards, more agile than Marvan had anticipated, but not agile enough to evade the round stone that twisted his ankle. He stumbled, almost fell, and now Marvan had scored his flesh again, this time across his chest, cutting deeper than before. Marvan felt a moment of resistance as the blade jarred against Krish's collar bone. It slid out as Krish regained his footing and darted away, towards the peak of the hill.

Krish had the advantage of the high ground now, and Marvan advanced more cautiously, but Krish seemed to have given up on attack for now. He was in a defensive crouch, his knife held out in front of him. His eyes darted from Marvan's face to his tridents and finally to his feet.

'I'm not going to kill you, you know,' Marvan said conversationally, enjoying the contrast of his controlled voice with the prince's gasps. 'I'm going to hamstring you, and then I'm going to take you to Alfreda and let *her* kill you. Sometimes I used to think that hating you was the only thing that kept her drawing breath.'

Krish's stance relaxed a little, lulled by the shift from fight to talk. Marvan hid his smile and surreptitiously shifted his weight, getting ready to spring.

'Is she the woman who attacked me here, three years ago?' Krish asked. 'But why does she hate me? I didn't even recognise her.'

'You killed Cwen, the leader of the Hunter's hawks. She was Alfreda's only friend. Well, before she met me. And you killed the child she loved. She's probably found a way to blame you for her brother's death too.'

Krish frowned. His entire concentration seemed to be on the conversation now, rather than their duel. 'I haven't killed very many people.' His face darkened. 'Except in Täm, when I wasn't really me. I remember all the rest, and I've never killed a woman or a child. Dae don't do that.'

Marvan had forgotten the boy's insistence that he was a man of the tribes. It seemed even more pitiful now he'd been shown to be such a poor duellist. The tribes were savages, but they knew how to fight.

'Maybe you didn't kill Cwen yourself, or Jinn,' Marvan said. 'But your people did. They died in the battle your father brought to you. Your presence in the world led to their deaths. Maybe the reasoning seems convoluted to you or I, but Alfreda is cleverer than both of us. She understands the making of things, and the root causes. And you were the root cause of all her suffering.'

'I don't think—' Krish said. And then, without having seemed to gather himself, without warning, he sprang.

Marvan was lethally unprepared. His tridents were in his hands, but his hands flew to the side as Krish landed on him and bore him backwards and down. His back fell against the rocky ground. He cried out helplessly in pain as a sharp rock jabbed his kidney and another struck a blow to his head that made lights sparkle behind his eyes.

He struggled mightily, trying to free his arms, trying to strike back, but Krish was on top of him, his knees pinning Marvan's arms and his thighs holding his body fast. Krish was far stronger than Marvan had guessed and far quicker. He twisted his body, trying to buck Krish off, but his weight was too great. He wasn't getting away from Krish's hold. Not that way, anyhow.

'This is boring me now,' Marvan said. And then, using the voice that godhood had brought him, the one that no mortal could resist, he added, 'Get off me.'

Krish's legs didn't move, and his knife was still descending.

'Drop the knife!' Marvan commanded, putting all his power into it. The words boomed out, echoing across the water, and though he couldn't see them, he heard the flap of a hundred birds taking flight. But still the prince didn't move.

'That doesn't work on me,' Krish said. 'I think it's because I was once a god myself. But I'm glad to know that you're what I thought you were.'

'And what's that?' Marvan asked. He tried to sound contemptuous, but his voice was too rasping to carry it off. He'd forgotten what fear felt like these last few years.

'You're a coward. You're only interested in fighting fair while you're winning.'

Marvan tried to shrug, but the weight of Krish's body denied him even that. 'I'm not a fool. And you've not got the victory you think. You should have learned the lesson yourself when Alfreda put a knife in your heart. You can't kill me.'

'I don't need to kill you,' Krish said. 'I just need to bury you.'

His knife moved in a flash of silver, across Marvan's throat. The agony was instant and overwhelming. He tried to scream, but blood gargled in his throat, and now Krish's fingers were in his mouth. They were pulling at Marvan's tongue. And Marvan realised, in this moment when it was too late, that he could have commanded the trees to fall on Krish. He could have commanded the water to drown him or the birds to throw themselves on him. But now the knife was against his tongue, it was sawing into it, and all he could do was writhe and gargle as more and more blood gushed down his throat.

Krish leaned back to look at him, then very calmly used the knife to cut his hamstrings and sever his hands at the wrist. That took a while of sawing. The blade wasn't made for it. Marvan would have liked to pass out from the pain, but that seemed to be something his godhood denied him.

Only his eyes were left him. He didn't know if that had been meant as a mercy or a further cruelty. He stared up at the blue of the sky as Krish worked somewhere to his side. Marvan didn't know what he was doing until his body was rolled over and into the shallow hole that Krish had scooped out from the mud.

'I don't think I really need it,' Krish said, 'but better a stitch today than a mend tomorrow.' He placed something against Marvan's chest. Marvan's eyes couldn't focus on it, but it was cold, like metal. When Krish struck it, and a chord rang out, he realised that it was a bell-tree. Krish had somehow worked out how to use the magic that was meant to be *his*. But by then he was already sinking deeper and deeper into the ground, as the mud oozed over and into him, entombing him alive beneath the earth.

32

Poor Pelii was only a sprog. She'd already flown from the Islands at a pell-mell pace, and now Eric was making her fly back again. She was labouring in the air, losing height as she went, and he'd half a mind to tell her to stop and rest. But Arwel was on the Hundred Islands. Eric didn't know what he meant to do to stop a whole bloody invasion fleet, but whatever it took, he'd do it, if it meant keeping his son safe.

At least he could finally see the jagged outline of the coast ahead of them and the deep, troubled blue of the sea beyond it. Except now he saw that one of the bays below him, the widest and rockiest, wasn't empty. There was a ship there. It was big: three masted and many sailed, every one of them a bright crimson. At the top of the foremost mast hung a banner with a red wolf's head on it. It was no design Eric had ever seen. Were these the invaders?

'Can you go a bit lower?' he asked Pelii.

She obliged, and the lower they got, the bigger the ship seemed. But it also became clear that it was wrecked. It hadn't moored in this bay, it had shattered on its rocks. There was debris in the water all around it: fragments of wood and crimson cloth from its sails. It looked like blood, floating on the water. There were bodies too, but no sign of anyone living.

'Maybe it's all right,' Eric said, feeling a stirring of hope. 'Looks like they went right past the Islands. Must have got blown off course, then wrecked on the reefs before they stepped foot on land.'

He felt Pelii's chest draw in beneath his thighs as she gathered the breath to speak.

'No, it's all right,' Eric said. 'Save your breath. We can chat when we get there.'

'The water ship sank,' Pelii piped, ignoring him. *'The sky ship is still flying. Look up, Father.'*

He was so startled to be called that, it took him a moment to do as she said. But then he saw it, higher than them, and moving slower: one of the Three's sil-nafön, heading away from the coast and straight for the Hundred Islands. The vanguard of an attack, maybe, or just a spy, but either way, trouble.

'After them,' he said to Pelii.

★

Sang Ki's eyes were fixed forwards, yearning towards the destination that they were finally, after such a very long journey, approaching. The islands were like pebbles from this height, scattered over the water ahead. They were mottled green and grey and also, yes, purple from the sorghum that grew in profusion only there. The closer they got, the more certain he became that this was where the answer lay: the root of godhood itself. But the Hundred Islands hadn't got their name for being few in number. He didn't know where to even begin his search.

'Plant-speaker!' Jalena said.

He shivered. Now that his concentration was broken, he felt the icy wind that blew at this height. The constant sound of the bells was an irritant too, one he'd never quite managed to learn how to ignore.

Jalena pointed to a speck in the sky, approaching from the west.

'A bird? A vulture, perhaps,' he suggested.

'Not a bird. It's too big.'

He squinted at it, but it definitely looked as if it had wings.

'Look closer,' Jalena said. 'There's someone riding it, just like they'd ride a house-beast, only it's not as big as a house-beast. But bigger than a bird.'

Unfortunately, she was right. It could surely only be some magic of the new gods. And it was gaining on them. 'Can we make this thing go faster?' he asked, but he didn't need to see Jalena shake her head. He already knew the answer.

'We'll land then,' he said. 'There'll be places to shelter on the ground, hidden from the air.'

'Yes, but where?' Her hands were on the bells.

He looked down. They were almost at the centre of the archipelago now, or at least above it. But there was, he could see from this great height, something curious about these islands. It was as if someone had drawn a vast square on the outermost of them, interrupted every time land gave way to sea. Were they ruins? He thought they must be, fragments of wall still standing when the roof was gone. But what monumental building could have stretched so wide that it traversed the sea?

He reached a finger to point out the nearest ruin to Jalena and found himself pointing at something else, instead. Because they weren't the only ones approaching this place. Ahead of them, darkening the water, was a fleet of ships. There must have been at least a dozen of them – or a dozen remaining afloat. From this distance, he couldn't be sure what had happened to them. Perhaps there was some shoal, hidden beneath the waters, that had torn chunks from their hulls. Whatever it was, the ships were foundering. He doubted even one of them would make it to the Islands.

As he and Jalena drew nearer, drifting in the air, the screams of the dying travelled thinly up to them.

'We need to help them!' Jalena said.

He opened his mouth to argue that this was a far from wise course of action, but her hands were already ringing the bells that moved their craft. They descended towards the waves and the ships dying on them.

*

If Olufemi hadn't been half-dead from hunger, she might have been more afraid. She might have died, too, when the first great wave hit, if she hadn't grabbed hold of the railing moments before she could be washed overboard. Bruyar would certainly have been lost if Olufemi hadn't grasped *omas* robes to anchor *omas* to the deck.

The journey had taken far longer than they'd bargained for, and the ships would have been unsailable if they'd fed on any more of the crew. But Bruyar, being fuller fleshed than Olufemi, had coped with starvation better. Now that flesh hung in empty folds around *omas* belly, and *oms* was light enough for Olufemi to keep hold of, despite the wild tossing of the ship. All around them, sailors worked desperately in the rigging to right a course that had already doomed them.

The ship tipped, horribly, in the trench of a wave, and for a moment Olufemi was at its highest point and could see the horizon and the sea and the jagged rocks, a little below the waves, that had ripped a hole in their hull. She looked around desperately for other ships, for some hope of rescue, but only two were in sight and they were also on their way to the ocean floor. The fleet had been hopelessly scattered by a storm three days ago and now would never be reunited.

'We should jump,' she said to Bruyar, shouting to be heard above the noise of wind and rain.

'Have you lost your wits?' Bruyar yelled back. 'We'll be smashed on the rocks.'

'If we stay, we'll go down with the ship.' Olufemi began to strip off her robe. Waterlogged, it would make swimming impossible.

Bruyar made no move to follow her example. 'Can you even swim?'

'Yes,' Olufemi said, although in truth she wasn't sure she had the strength. Even the weight of her robe as she undressed felt like too much to bear. But she'd rather die doing something than nothing. If her life could be said to have any principle, she thought that was probably it.

The ship listed to port, flinging Olufemi to her knees on the cracked deck. Splinters sliced beneath her skin and she cried out in pain. She tried to stand, failed and fell back, her strength now utterly spent. So this was how it would end, sat on her buttocks on a sinking ship. No doubt there were some who would think it fitting.

She looked up at the sky, cloud-filled and dour. There were birds circling, waiting to feast on the corpses. They'd find lean pickings after these weeks at sea. Two of them were swooping now, more eager than the rest. Lower still, and Olufemi began to see their size. But . . . weren't they too large for birds? And then she smelt it: a waft of mouldy cinnamon on the wind.

'Rii!' she shouted, somehow finding the strength to stagger to her feet.

Then the creature swooped lower, and Olufemi saw that it wasn't Rii at all – far too small, but still large enough to grab Olufemi between its back-to-front legs and lift her from the deck.

She heard the leathery flap of the wings above her and the beast's gasps with every beat of them. It was struggling for breath, and struggling to rise. She was ten paces above the deck, fifteen. Then they were hovering, not gaining any more height. And then, very slowly, sinking again.

Below her, Bruyar watched the spectacle, speechless for once. Olufemi thought, briefly and absurdly, that Bruyar must have an excellent view of her underclothes. And then *omas* gaze shifted, leftwards and up, and Olufemi saw rushing towards her yet *another* object that had no business being in the sky, while a voice shouted, 'Here! Bring her here!'

Hands reached out and grasped her. She fell over the side and onto the floor of what seemed very much like a wagon. She could do nothing but lie there on her front, gasping for breath, as there was more shouting, more scrambling and a body that was probably Bruyar's fell beside her. She felt the lurch as the improbable vessel rose, and closed her eyes, allowing herself one moment to enjoy the fact that she was still alive.

A moment later, hands helped her to her feet. She found herself staring into the face of a man that she knew she recognised, though couldn't place. The man peered back at her, seemingly equally unable to identify her. Then his eyes widened.

'I know you! We met at Mirror Town. Otufeli, was it? The mage who served the prince.'

'Olufemi,' she said. And on hearing his voice – the aristocratic Ashane accent at odds with his half-blood looks – she knew him too. 'You're Sang Ki, Lord Thilak's son.'

'And this is Jalena.' He stood aside so that she could see the flying vessel's other rider. She was young, barely into adulthood, but the sight sent a shock of feeling through Olufemi. This was a face from the savannah. Vordanna had been of that people too, though stolen from them as a child. But Vordanna's face had always been calm, gentled by the bliss. This girl had a fierceness and an energy that Olufemi's lover never had.

'Well, how delightful to find ourselves among friends,' Bruyar said. Bedraggled and half-starved, *oms* had regained *omas* composure with remarkable speed.

They were rising still. Olufemi looked down, where the dying fleet was growing ever more distant. She saw now that they'd foundered very close to shore, and she could see also what shore it was. 'The Hundred Islands,' she said, then laughed. She was aware that there was a slightly manic note to it. 'See, Bruyar – you led us true after all. We've reached Ashanesland.'

The creature which had rescued them swooped into view. It must surely be a child of Rii's. The resemblance was too strong, although all in miniature. Its claws grasped the side of the flying vessel, and then yet another passenger was scrambling aboard whom Olufemi recognised. This time the name came to her at once.

'Oh good,' Eric said. 'You're safe. We saw you on that boat and we knew you for mages. The rest was all pale, like the folk of the savannah.' He seemed to notice Jalena for the first time. 'Like you, I suppose,' he said to her, and then to Olufemi, 'But you ain't just any mage. I met you in Mirror Town, didn't I?'

'This is Olufemi,' Sang Ki said. 'My companion is Jalena. I am Sang Ki, and I too was in Mirror Town, when all three of us were briefly in the service of Prince Krishanjit. How curious that we should be reunited here.'

'I still serve Krish, or at any rate he's a pal of mine,' Eric said. 'I came back to the Islands to stop an invasion, but I reckon the rocks did my work for me already. That and the wind – half the ships flew straight past and crashed on the mainland. We saw a half a dozen on the way here.'

'Our route was far more circuitous,' Bruyar said. 'But it hardly bears mentioning now. I am Bruyar, not a mage but a Mortal of Ofiklanod. And I have so many questions, I hardly know where to begin with them. But since 'tis better to start than to hesitate, I must ask: what is this curious vessel?'

Eric stared at *omas*. 'Where have you been hiding, then? It's a sil-nafön, made with the Three's magic and flown by the bells. You know about the Three, don't you? The new gods what rose when the sun and moon fell.'

'We are aware of them,' Bruyar said blandly.

Olufemi forbore to explain their own role in those gods' rise.

'Are you working for them?' Eric asked Sang Ki. 'Only you're flying one of their sil-nafön.'

Sang Ki shrugged. 'I'm afraid to admit that we stole it.'

Eric frowned. 'Then if you ain't serving Krish, and you ain't serving the Three, what *are* you doing here?'

Sang Ki hesitated. He had a clever face beneath his pale hair, but not a guarded one. Olufemi saw him considering a lie, and then the moment when he discarded it. 'I've come to put an end to gods entirely,' he said. 'I believe all of us here can vouch that their presence in the world has hardly been a boon.'

'A lofty aim,' Bruyar said. 'But not an easy one. The making of gods has been the study of many lifetimes. Surely the unmaking of them will be harder yet.'

'Maybe for the Ostatni Ludia,' Jalena said. 'But a plant-speaker knows more than you. He knows more than anyone, especially if he's a good plant-speaker, and there's no one better than him.'

Sang Ki smiled fondly at her. 'I'm afraid I'm unable to live up to such praise. But I have . . . seen things that others perhaps have not. I've seen the place where the power of the gods lives. And I've felt its creator, buried at the heart of it – the very first god, who began all this. I believe that Jalena's people were once his worshippers—'

Jalena covered her ears, looking horrified. 'No, you mustn't say it, plant-speaker. It's been forgotten – we swore to forget it.'

'Why would you go and do that?' Eric asked. 'Madam

Aeronwen always used to say, if you don't remember your mistakes, you'll make 'em again, and worse the second time.'

'The folk of the savannah chose to forget,' Sang Ki said, 'precisely to stop themselves repeating a very grave error. They deliberately suppressed the knowledge that had allowed them to make it.'

'The error of god-making.' Olufemi smiled bleakly. 'So they foreswore it and allowed others to make the error again in their place.'

Sang Ki nodded. 'These Hundred Islands are where they first made landfall, aren't they? I believe your people remember.' This was to Bruyar.

'A very long time ago,' *oms* replied absently. 'Our records are fragmentary. They speak of a great civilisation that flourished and built and fell, all within the span of a lifetime.'

'I don't know,' Sang Ki said, 'quite how they made that first god – or perhaps it would be more accurate to say, how one man transformed *himself* into that god. But I know that he shaped the world-beneath-the-world to be the source of his power. And I know that he used the purple sorghum to do it. The first magic, it seems, was the magic of growing things. It's been forgotten, the god banished, but the purple sorghum and the world-beneath-the-world remain. And with it, the ability to make more gods, on and on without end. The error is endlessly repeated.'

Olufemi tried to exchange a glance with Bruyar, but *omas* attention was elsewhere, gazing somewhere outside the sil-nafön. 'We know something of the first god,' Olufemi said. 'We saw his birthplace, I believe. We saw a map there too, of the world as it was. There was a city here once, before it sank beneath the waves along with nearly all the land. So I believe you may be right. This was where the god came, when he left his own land.'

'He *is* correct,' Bruyar said, still gazing outwards and downwards. Olufemi heard a great, suppressed excitement in *omas* voice. 'The map we saw showed a structure here, a great building in the shape of a pyramid It mirrored one in the Motherlands, and like that one stood at the heart of the city, at the centre of his power. And its remains are there still. Look.'

The vessel lurched sickeningly as all of them moved at once to look over its side, but Olufemi barely cared, because Bruyar was right. There, below them, in fragments on each island, was a line of ruins that could only be the base of that structure. It was the mirror of the one they'd visited in the Motherlands, but on an even more monumental scale. Such a building could only have been made with magic.

'What's that, at the centre of the square?' Sang Ki asked. His finger was shaking as it pointed almost directly below them. Olufemi realised there was another square-based structure, far, far smaller than the one of which it was a part, near the shore of the largest island. It was green with grass, no doubt buried under earth after all these years.

'They call that place the Barrow,' Eric told them. 'But no one here remembers who it was a barrow for.'

'The first god,' Sang Ki said. 'That must surely be where his body lies buried. His spirit in the world-beneath-the-world is untouchable, but his body is its anchor, just as he is the chain that keeps that world in place. It's the root of . . . of everything. And that's where we can pluck it out.'

33

Dae Hyo had lost all sense of direction. In among the streets, the white tower wasn't always visible, and besides, he needed to keep his attention on his enemies. The stink of blood and death was everywhere. He struck aside a spear with the haft of his left-hand axe and on the return stroke took out his attacker's throat. Beside him, Dinesh had pushed his opponent's spear back and then forwards, into his kidney, copying the trick Dae Hyo had used to take him down. No one could say the boy wasn't quick.

There were other people crowding the streets. Not fighters, residents, all intent on fleeing but none of them seeming to know where to. They got underfoot at the worst moments. He noticed two of them, frantically pushing past the fringes of the fight towards a narrow side street. One of them turned to survey the skirmish and Dae Hyo saw a brief flash of a long, smiling face that he was sure he recognised. Then the man turned away, a guard tried to pin Dae Hyo's arm, and he put his attention back on the fight.

There were others of their party left fighting behind them, although not many. He had to hope that those who were carrying the bells had at least survived, but there was no time to worry about it. He pressed onwards, into the thickest opposition. He might not be able to see the white tower, but he knew that wherever their enemies didn't want them to go, that was where they needed to be.

A twin flick of his axes took another man through the chest, crunching his ribs with the power of the blow. Dae Hyo pushed him down and stepped over his corpse, ready for his next opponent – but there was none. The street ahead was empty. Had they reached the end of their enemies, or was it merely one of those lulls that sometimes happened even in the fiercest battles?

It would be easier to know the answer if he could hear anything beyond the sound of his own blood in his ears. He looked around again, for bells this time, but there were none of those either, and he chanced taking the plugs from his ears. The moment he did, the sound roared back in: cries and screams and shouts, none of them very far away. It was a lull, then, and not yet a victory.

He was about to replace the wax plugs, when he saw Dinesh remove his. The boy was looking at him intently, and not with his usual disdain.

'What?' Dae Hyo asked.

'All these people.' Dinesh gestured behind them, where the corpses were piled. 'The, the, the living ones, I mean. They'll all die when we change the bells. There's hundreds of them.'

Dae Hyo shrugged, and now the disdain was back on Dinesh's face.

'It's not their fault,' Dinesh said. 'The bells enslave them. They have to do as they're told. They don't deserve to die.'

That earned a shout of laughter from Dae Hyo. 'Svarog's cock, boy, when did *deserving* ever come into it? Men who do evil to women live to see their grandchildren while babies die of the pox. Nobody gets what they deserve.'

'But they should. I won't accept things as they are. I won't give up like you.'

His feet looked rooted to the roadway. Dae Hyo thought he really did mean to stand and wait and let this whole thing fall apart. What would Krish say to him? Dae Hyo wasn't sure, but he tried, 'You said it yourself, they're all belled. They're all slaves. I tell you what, I think you already know the answer. Would you rather live a slave or die free?'

For once, Dae Hyo seemed to have said the right thing. Dinesh's posture loosened and his hand tightened on his sword.

'I'd rather live free. But I, I, I was never given the choice. It should be a choice.'

'If we had the time, I'd ask each one of them. But we don't, so I'm choosing to free them. Are you with me?'

Dinesh hesitated only a moment before nodding. A moment later, Dae Hyo heard the thunder of booted feet approaching, and shouts in the language of the Ofiklanders. He pressed the wax back into his ears, raised his axe and charged forwards.

★

This was the third battle Renar had been caught in, and she wasn't enjoying it any more than the other two. It was impossible to tell who was with the prince and who against him, so she did her best to avoid all of them. She didn't know if Krish's side was winning. She didn't intend to stay long enough to see the conclusion of the fight.

'Is this Fourth Street or Seventh Boulevard?' Lanalan asked. 'I've lost all sense of things.' His hand was slippery with sweat in hers, but she kept a firm hold of it.

'It's Fifth Street,' she said, 'and the docks are at its end. We're nearly there.'

'We're not the only ones with the thought.'

He wasn't wrong. The street ahead was clogged with people. 'There are sil-nafön enough for everyone,' she reassured him. 'Every vessel in Ashanesland was recalled at my suggestion.'

Lanalan nodded, and they saved their breath for the last, desperate shove through the crowd towards the docks. They squeezed between a fat Ashanewoman and an elderly Ofiklander and knocked aside a teenaged girl, until finally there was no one left between them and their destination. Lanalan grinned his boyish grin at her.

Renar didn't smile back. Unlike him, she'd already looked at the docks. He followed her gaze, and his smile dropped.

'Where have they gone?' he asked. 'Did Nabofik send the sil-nafön out again? La, but that will be a disaster for the prince's plans.'

Renar didn't care about Krish's plans. She cared about their ability to escape the consequences of them. They'd parted from Nabofik with the excuse that they needed food, but *oms* would realise they were gone soon enough. *Oms* had probably already realised it.

'No, look!' Lanalan said. 'There are two at the far end.'

He wasn't the only one who'd noticed them. They raced all the other frantic people to the far end of the dock. But when they got there, it was to find one of the sil-nafön cast off and the men inside it leaning over into the second, doing something she couldn't make out. The people in the first sil-nafön were Ashane. Could they be Krish's people? If so, perhaps they *would* make it out of here after all.

'Let us aboard!' she shouted to the men. 'We're allies of the Wheelheir.'

The men didn't react. They didn't even seem to hear her. They were too busily at work on the second sil-nafön. Renar couldn't fathom what they were doing until one of them let out a triumphant cry and jumped away, just as the sil-nafön he'd been working on stopped floating and started falling. Something smaller fell through the air beside it.

'They cut away the bells!' Lanalan said.

That must have been the fate of all the other sil-nafön, sent to destruction hundreds of paces below them on the ground. Krish was nothing if not clever. Renar cursed him in her mind.

'You!' Lanalan shouted. 'Ashanemen – we're King Nayan's people. Won't you help us?'

There was, again, no reaction. The men were looking at each other. Gesturing in some complicated way with their hands. *Talking* with their hands, Renar realised. Of course. The prince wouldn't have wanted them vulnerable to the suggestive power of the bells. They would have stopped their ears. They couldn't hear Renar and Lanalan, they clearly didn't recognise them, and they were already moving away from the dock in the one remaining sil-nafön.

'They'll be heading for the Mortals' dock next,' Renar said, grabbing Lanalan's hand again. 'We'll have to get there before them. I have a key to the gate. Come on!'

★

Dae Hyo and Dinesh had reached the tower and none of their enemies had. It should have been a moment of triumph, but they'd reached the tower alone. There was no sign of their companions or the crucial bells they carried.

The white ceramic tower was broad at the base, narrow in its waist and flared at its top to hold the platform that gave access to the bells above it. The bells which in their turn held the whole enormous city aloft. It was a very long way up, and it was impossible to know what waited for them inside.

Dinesh took out the wax plugs from his ears. 'We should wait for the others,' he said, his eyes scanning the streets that led to the tower for any sign of them.

'We'll clear the way for them,' Dae Hyo countered. 'They can follow.'

Dinesh took one last look behind him, then nodded to Dae Hyo and faced the door. Dae Hyo's first kick rattled it on its hinges but didn't move it. He grimaced, because now he'd warned whoever was inside that they were coming. But he kicked again, and this time the door flew inwards and he and Dinesh leapt through.

There was no one to greet them. The chamber they found themselves in looked to be a library, the walls lined with shelves and the shelves stacked with scrolls and books, but not a single person to read them. Dae Hyo and Dinesh exchanged a look, tightened their hands on their weapons and moved on.

The next room was a dining hall, large enough to seat a war band, but equally empty. Beyond it were the stairs, and on the next floor they found people at last, but not living ones.

'Maybe the others got here before us,' Dinesh said.

Dae Hyo looked at the old mage lying sprawled across a woollen rug. There were dried streaks of blood coming from her mouth and ears. Her eyes were gone entirely, but they didn't look as if they'd been put out. They seemed to have burst all of their own accord.

'This wasn't our people's work,' he said.

There were more corpses as they climbed the stairs, but no sound of conversation. There was nothing but the endless ringing of the bells above, growing louder and louder as they climbed. Until at last they reached the platform, and there they were: twelve of them, stepping up from the size of a man's head to the size of a mammoth's. They were suspended on great thick chains, from a bar that Dae Hyo would have had to climb onto his own shoulders to reach. And above them hung the vast canopy that held the city stable in the air.

He could see how the bells were rung. It was cunning. Ropes hung from wheels at the tops of each of them. Pull on them and the bell would swing and ring. But the ropes were hanging slack and the bells were ringing anyway, a complicated, layered tune, note piled on top of note.

Dinesh looked over the edge of the platform, dizzyingly high, to the streets below. They were still empty. 'They're not coming,' he said hopelessly. 'We can't do it without the bells. And how do we stop these ones?'

Dae Hyo studied the bells, the ropes, the whole contraption. His brother was the thinker, not him, but his brother wasn't there. He tried to recall how he'd felt before, when the rune had kept his mind clear. He'd been able to hold very big ideas inside it then. He needed to find that place again, where there was only thought and no feeling.

'We need to, to, to leave.' Dinesh took Dae Hyo's arm and tried to draw him back towards the stairs.

Dae Hyo shook him off. 'Krish said the tune sustains itself, like a snake eating its own tail. But they must be able to change the tune. The city rises and falls.' He grasped one of the ropes, and the moment his fingers touched it, the bell stilled and the whole city beneath them juddered. Dae Hyo smiled and reached for the next rope to silence its bell.

The city lurched more violently this time. It knocked Dinesh from his feet, and Dae Hyo only kept his by grasping another rope.

'If the city falls, we'll all die!' Dinesh said.

Dae Hyo shook his head. 'It won't fall, if we give the bells a new song to sing. We don't need the ones we brought, we can use these. I've heard you sing, boy. You've a voice as pretty as a knife woman's. What was the tune Krish made?'

Dinesh stared at him as if he'd lost his mind.

'The song!' Dae Hyo snapped.

Hesitantly at first, and then more strongly, Dinesh sang it. There had been a harmony to it that Dinesh couldn't sing while he held the tune, but Dae Hyo thought he could remember it. Sometimes the tribe had sung it, to greet the turning of the season or the arrival of the foals. It had been a beautiful sound, rough voices and young voices and those who sang too high or too low, but all of them together. Dae Hyo could picture every face: his sisters, his cousins, his comrades. He hadn't forgotten a one of them, not in all these long years.

The bells were arranged small to large, high note to low note. Dae Hyo pulled on the first rope, the third, the fifth together, then another chord and another, a whole sequence. But the tune he made wasn't quite right. The city started, ponderously, to turn in the air. The sound of the bells was deafening. That vast discord was almost unbearable, the wrongness of it. Dae Hyo felt blood beginning to seep from his ears.

'Start again,' he shouted to Dinesh.

He could barely make out the sound of the boy's voice over the clamour of the bells, but it was enough. It was the sixth note he'd got wrong, and the ninth – he'd made it fall when it should have risen. He grabbed frantically for the ropes to still them, then began again, pulling three at once to make the harmony that the magic required.

There was a profound stillness after he'd completed the tune. He took his hands away from the ropes, knowing he'd done all he could.

The wait felt as if it lasted an eternity – until, without his guidance, the bells swung of their own accord, keeping up the tune he'd given them, playing it over and over.

The city stopped its spinning. For a moment it seemed to hang absolutely stationary in the air. And then the floor pressed up against the soles of Dae Hyo's boots, and the whole, huge structure began to rise.

'We did it!' Dinesh said.

Dae Hyo smiled. But from his perch on the edge of the roof, he saw that the streets below were no longer empty. A cohort of guards was sprinting towards the tower.

Dinesh saw them too. He picked up the sword he'd dropped when the city had begun its wild motion. 'We'll have to guard the bells.'

'*I* have to guard the bells,' Dae Hyo said. 'You need to go, boy. Get to the sil-nafön and get away. The men there won't wait long.'

'If you stay, you'll die.' The boy didn't sound too sad about the idea. But he didn't look too happy, either.

'Yes,' Dae Hyo said. 'Belbog's balls, I'm not the idiot you think I am. I always knew it would have to end this way. Go, and I'll bar the doors behind you. I'll keep them away from the bells for long enough. Do you doubt my strength?'

Dinesh shook his head, but still hesitated.

'I've been a drunk and a miner and a mage and a drunk again,' Dae Hyo told him. 'I've travelled the Silent Sands and the ocean. I've done many things and most of them badly. There's nothing left. My work in the world is finished. Yours is just beginning. Didn't you tell me you mean to lead the slaves of Mirror Town? I tell you what, you won't do that by staying here. If they need a home, the Dae lands are free. There's no place on the plains more beautiful and the rabbits are plump and the ponies swift. Let the Dae die with me.'

'No,' Dinesh said. 'No. We, we, we don't have a name. The slaves. The Mages took ours from us. But we can take the Dae one, if you let us.'

Dae Hyo smiled. 'Take it then, and wield it better than I did. Now go!'

Renar turned the last corner towards the Mortals' dock to see one solitary sil-nafön still tethered there and no sign yet of the prince's men. There was only one other figure standing on the wooden platform, its back turned to Renar and Lanalan.

'Come on,' Renar said, 'before they take the last sil-nafön.'

There was something wrong with the city: it seemed to be travelling relentlessly upwards. Was this part of Krish's plan? Or was it his plan going wrong? It wouldn't matter either way if they could get away. Renar took Lanalan's hand and led him stumbling towards the dock. Their footsteps were loud, but the figure didn't move. Until, when they were only twenty paces apart, the ground lurched beneath them like a horse bucking, and they were both flung to the ground.

The figure stumbled too – and as *oms* twisted and fell, Renar recognised Nabofik.

'Hello, Renar,' *oms* said.

Renar wanted to run. She didn't know where, but any place that didn't contain Nabofik would do.

'I've been looking everywhere for you.' Renar heard the tremble in her own voice. She couldn't convince even herself.

Nabofik smiled and stepped towards her. *Omas* face, usually so open, was hard to read. *Oms* was smiling, but it was a smile that moved only *omas* mouth.

'Why would you be looking for me here?' Nabofik asked.

Lies had always come easily to Renar, but they deserted her now. Nabofik knew, she was sure of it. And further dissembling could only make things worse for her, if indeed it was possible for them to get any worse.

'How did you find me?' she asked.

'Marvan told me not to trust you. I thought it was stupid, because why would you betray me? But I put someone to follow you anyway, just to make him happy.'

Renar set her shoulders and gestured at Lanalan. 'He didn't know anything about it. It was all me.'

Nabofik barely spared her sib a glance. 'Of course it was. He's an idiot and you're a plotter. Renar the Fox! You're famous for it. Of course it was all you. How long have you been working against me?' *Oms* asked the question so casually, as if it didn't matter.

The city was rising fast, now. Renar felt the press of it against her feet. Her breath was coming harder into her lungs, but perhaps that was merely terror. They were only a dozen paces away from the edge of the dock and the last sil-nafön. But Nabofik was watching them, eyes narrowed. Renar didn't dare move. If they were to escape, Nabofik needed to be distracted. And the easiest emotion to rouse in *omas* had always been anger.

'I've barely worked against you at all,' Renar said. 'I've barely needed to, when you work so well against yourself. I've never before been in the employ of someone so incompetent, and I was once hired to run his campaign by Liegöf the Wealthy, who is quite widely considered the worst Triumvir of the last century. 'Tis a wonder, I've often thought, that you can even dress yourself in the morning.'

Despite everything, it felt quite remarkably good to say these things she *hadn't* been saying for months now. Not just to Nabofik, but to all those she'd worked for over the years who'd proven so unworthy of her talents. In her mind she was saying them to Bruyar too, who'd used her in *omas* scheme to create these pitiful, terrifying gods, and not even done Renar the courtesy of letting her know what she was helping to birth.

Nabofik's face twisted briefly into a childlike hurt, and then into the petulant rage that Renar had come to know all too well. But the city was still rising, and Nabofik didn't seem to have noticed, even though they were all three now gasping for breath. If Krish's plan worked after all, Renar supposed she could grant that her life was a price worth paying, for the world if not for her.

'You can't speak to me like that!' *oms* said. 'I'm a god!'

Renar shrugged, the gesture jerky. 'You're going to kill me anyway – you may as well hear the truth. You behave as a child, Nabofik, but you're quite old enough to know better. I've met children not yet weaned with more self-control than you. I thought at first it was the power of godhood that had twisted you. I even found it in me to pity you, despite what you'd done. But I think now I was mistaken. It was quite the reverse. You've been made into a worthless god because you were already a worthless person.'

There was a lot more she would have liked to say, but her head was spinning and she needed all her breath to stay conscious.

Nabofik was silent for perhaps the longest moment of Renar's life. Then *oms* said, 'I'm not going to kill you. That isn't any sort of punishment at all. If you're dead you won't be able to feel sorry, and I want you to be really, really sorry. So I'm going to kill him instead.'

Before Renar could react, before she could even fully register what Nabofik had said, *oms* turned to Lanalan, opened *omas* mouth and said, 'Cut your own throat.'

Renar leapt towards him. She reached desperately for his arm as it fumbled towards his belt and managed only to brush it with her fingers as he lifted his own knife free and put it to his throat. There was no time for even a single word. They were given only one brief moment for his eyes to meet hers, and then the knife slashed, the blood gushed, and her sib was gone.

Nabofik's smile of triumph was the most adult expression that Renar had ever seen on *omas* face. But a moment later, the expression switched to confusion. *Oms* staggered a step back and nearly fell. 'Oh, I don't feel very well. Why can I feel the city rising?'

Nabofik's eyes flicked to the sil-nafön, the only remaining one in all of the City On High, the only way left to escape. And if Nabofik took it, all this would have been in vain. Lanalan's death would have been in vain. Renar felt brittle with shock, but she made herself move, staggering the ten paces across the dock and flinging herself into the sil-nafön.

Nabofik opened *omas* mouth. Renar saw *omas* lips move and thought that *oms* meant to say stop. But the breath was gone from *omas* too, and Renar had time to take out her own knife and cut through the rope binding the sil-nafön to the dock. It lurched as it was released and Renar was given one final glimpse of Nabofik, standing above Lanalan's corpse, and then the darkness took her.

34

Krish sat rocking on a boat in the stinking marsh, face tipped skywards to watch a battle that was entirely outside his control. He watched as the sil-nafön crowded round the City On High, like flies around a corpse, and then he watched as they fell away again. Did this mean that his plan had worked, or failed? It was impossible to tell.

A little while later, he saw the great city lurch and then, very slowly, begin to spin. It wasn't what was meant to happen, but at least it meant *something* was happening. Until, when the sun was halfway between zenith and horizon, the City On High at long last began to rise. He watched as it touched the clouds and as it was lost among them. And then he kept watching, fists clenched, to see if the city would emerge again, unscathed, and descend to wreak revenge on the people who had nearly bested it.

For the span of a hundred heartbeats, it didn't. He waited another hundred, unable to believe that Dae Hyo and Dinesh had truly succeeded. He was so unused to things going as he'd intended that he struggled to make himself accept it.

But even if he'd prevailed here, the war wasn't yet won. For so long, he realised, he'd been waiting for things to be over. When he'd killed his da, that had felt like an ending. But it had turned out to be a beginning. Fighting, and then uniting with his real father – that had felt like a conclusion too. Instead it had solved almost nothing. Even giving up his godhood hadn't brought things to an end, not for good, because he'd made the choice to return.

Maybe nothing ever ended. Maybe it was all cycles like the

seasons: warmth would always follow cold, and cold warmth. But even if that was true, he knew he had to live as if it wasn't. Otherwise, what reason could he find for doing anything? And he'd learned that he wasn't a person who could be content to do nothing. He had to think that some tasks, once done, were done for good. And this one was only two-thirds accomplished.

Marvan was gone, lost beneath the earth. Krish didn't feel a moment's guilt about that. He was glad he didn't feel too much satisfaction, either. He'd be too much like Marvan if he took pleasure in condemning a man to that fate. This Nabofik had been removed too. Maybe *oms* would find a way back down, but for now they needn't worry about *omas*.

Only Alfreda remained, the god who Marvan claimed hated Krish. And if Pelii's message was right, she'd already come to the Islands. Krish's plan had left them almost entirely undefended. The allies that his father had such confidence in had failed to appear. And without them, Nayan could muster barely a hundred men. The rest had all come to the mainland with Krish. It should have occurred to him that their enemies would plot a counterstroke, but he'd been too impressed with his own cleverness. And Eric had returned to face whatever was coming. Krish found that this was what worried him most of all.

And yet here, alone in the marsh with the dun-coloured birds and the biting insects, waiting for someone to come for him – if there was anyone left to come – he was powerless. Despite his worry, there was a sort of peace in that. He wondered if that was what Dae Hyo looked for in the drink: the feeling that things were beyond his control, and so he had no responsibility to do anything.

Except there, falling towards him from the sky, was a dark blur that soon resolved into a sil-nafön. Closer still, Krish saw Dinesh's face, peering over the side. He fumbled in his pack for the red cloth they'd decided on for a signal. When he waved it above his head, the sil-nafön veered and came straight for him.

Dinesh didn't have the steering quite right. It splashed too heavily, half on shore and half in the muck. Krish was sprayed with mud that smelled of old eggs. When he wiped his eyes clear of it, he saw Dinesh dismounting from the sil-nafön, staggering a little on the rough ground.

Dinesh, but nobody else.

It was strange. Krish realised that a part of him had expected this. A part of him already knew, even before Dinesh said, 'I, I, I'm sorry. Dae Hyo stayed. He wanted to make sure that nothing went wrong.'

And yet, even knowing, Krish wept helplessly. He turned his back on Dinesh, ashamed of it. They were the only tears he'd shed since he became a man. But Dae Hyo had been his first friend. For a long time, his only one.

'He let me have the Dae name,' Dinesh said. 'He told me to take the tribe's land. Why did he do that, when I hated him?'

Krish wiped his eyes and turned back to him. 'The tribe mattered to him more than his pride. More than anything. He must have thought you were worthy of it.' He'd thought Krish was too, but Krish could never be simply Dae. Maybe Dinesh could. There'd be no grave marker for Dae Hyo, lost among the clouds. He'd left only the name behind.

'Am I worthy of it?' Dinesh asked. He sounded young and uncertain, close to the slave boy that Krish had first met.

'You can try to be,' Krish said.

He looked up at the sky, as if he could somehow see Dae Hyo there, catch a last glimpse of him. But instead his eyes were drawn by a distant, silver fleck that moved past the face of the sun. For a moment he thought it might be the City On High returned and he felt hope rather than fear, that Dae Hyo might have been spared. But as it drew a little closer, he saw that it was something entirely different, although almost of the same scale. It looked like a vast bird made entirely of metal.

Dinesh followed his gaze, shading his eyes against the sun. 'What is that?'

'The next battle. There's always one more battle. We need to get back to the Islands.'

★

Alfreda stood in the prow of her creation, and sang it through the sky. The platform beneath her was the size of a mansion, perfectly smooth and made of metal thinner than a hair but stronger than any anvil. If the thing she'd made had really been the hawk it was fashioned to resemble, Alfreda would have been standing between its eyes. But *she* was its eyes, and its muscles. It existed because she'd made it, and it moved because she willed it. She'd named it the *Edred*, for the horse who'd once served her and Algar so faithfully.

The great beating of its metal wings, the creaks and clanks of them, almost drowned out the sound of her voice, but it was enough. She'd made this thing with the skills she'd learned alongside Algar and in honour and memory of Cwen. It was as true as they'd both been. It kept flying, the song lodged inside it now, moving all the tiny invisible parts of it in the way that Alfreda had ordered them, in the direction she'd set, towards her sibling gods.

Except, her sibling gods were nowhere to be found. This was the place where Nabofik had told her to come, Alfreda was sure of it. The ground was very far below, but those five blue blots, as small as buttons, were the lakes on which the Five Stars floated. And there was a feeling, too, a terrible hollow emptiness inside her where Marvan and Nabofik should have been. They'd been her constant company and comfort since the day they'd all been made gods, and now they were gone.

The sky was empty of everything but birds. Even they winged a wide course around this freakish, giant silver version of themselves. All except one, Alfreda realised. Above her, just where she'd expected the City On High to be, there was something else, heading straight for them. No, *falling* towards them. It was a sil-nafön, the only one she'd seen since she came to the skies of Ashanesland.

The *Edred* answered slowly to her voice. It was too vast to manoeuvre with any speed, and the sil-nafön had fallen below them before Alfreda could turn their nose towards it. Once she had, she sent the *Edred* down, so fast the wind was like a spray of ice against her skin. In moments they were a score of paces beneath the sil-nafön. It fell that last distance and landed on the foredeck in front of her.

The speed had been too great for it to land gently. The base of the thing was wooden and it shattered into splinters at the impact as one solitary person rolled out of it.

It was an Ofiklander, but not Nabofik. This was a woman, a little older than Alfreda. She seemed to be unconscious.

On the platform behind her, two belled soldiers stirred, but she waved them back before they could move. What possible danger could this woman be to her? She knelt on the cold metal deck and inspected her body for wounds. There was no sign of any, only an unhealthy blue tinge to her lips. Alfreda put her fingers in front of them, to feel for breath.

There was a gentle whisper of it, barely warming her fingertips. Then the woman coughed. Spittle sprayed over Alfreda's hand before she snatched it back. The woman twisted onto her side and hacked up more phlegm, her body convulsing with every cough, until she finally stilled.

'You came from the City On High?' Alfreda asked.

The woman rolled to her back to stare up at her with dead eyes.

'Well?' Alfreda said, letting her power into her voice. 'Speak.'

'Yes, I came from the city,' the woman said, her tone flat.

'And where is it?'

'Gone. Gone forever.'

'How?'

The woman sat up. Expression was returning to her face, but it wasn't a happy one. 'It was Krishanjit's plan to send the City On High up.'

'And Nabofik?' But Alfreda already knew the answer.

'Gone with it.'

Despite having known this was coming, it rocked Alfreda back on her heels. 'What about Marvan? Was he in the city too?'

The woman shrugged, and Alfreda wanted to strike her, but she clenched her fists instead. This woman might possess the only knowledge she'd ever find of her sibling-gods' fate.

'Krishanjit did this, aye? Then where is he now?' Alfreda's voice was like a whip and the woman flinched at it.

'I don't know. Back to the Hundred Islands, perhaps, where he has his base. Why should I care? Why should I care about any of you? Nabofik got what *oms* deserved. If Marvan is dead then he did too. The world is well rid of them.'

There was a savagery in her words but not in her tone. It was dead and flat and hopeless. It was the only thing that saved her. If she'd spoken with relish, Alfreda didn't think she could have stopped herself from ripping out her throat. But there was a note in her voice that Alfreda recognised. It was the voice of someone who'd lost everything. Maybe everyone did, in the end.

Whatever had happened to this woman, Prince Krishanjit was responsible. He was the cause of everything, the first cause, the finger that tipped the block that knocked off the log that fell and crushed the innocent beneath it. Now Alfreda knew where to find him to make him pay. And this time, when she killed him, he would stay dead.

35

Sang Ki felt an ending in the air. He'd always thought himself a man of reason, a thinker, not one who was ruled by his emotions. When he and Mahvesh had come to the savannah, he'd taken the position of plant-speaker that was offered him and silently scoffed at it even as he played the part. Now here he was, acting purely on instinct. And yet, he knew that he was right.

Jalena had brought the sil-nafön lower as they neared the coast. Their destination was close to it: a hill that, from the air, revealed the unnatural squareness of its shape. There was a structure made by man buried beneath it, he was quite sure. And inside that structure, the root of everything.

Nearer, hugging the coast, he saw what he at first took to be a town, as ramshackle as Smiler's Fair. When they were a mere two hundred paces above it, he understood it to be a collection of ships, all roped together. He'd read about the place once, he recalled. Fleet: the maritime capital of the Islands. He still found it strange, how many of the places he'd once read about, he'd since seen with his own eyes. His life hadn't taken the path he expected, but then whose did?

'I'm gonna leave you here,' Eric said, then whistled for his mount.

The sil-nafön rocked nauseatingly as the beast took up a perch on its side. Eric barely seemed to notice the motion or the drop beneath him as he climbed onto its back.

'Deserting us?' Olufemi asked.

'Getting help. It ain't gonna be easy to dig through all that earth. You go on ahead. I'll catch you up.' And with that, he and the beast were off, winging downwards towards the floating town.

The rest of them flew on, a mile or so further round the coast to where the barrow mound sat. Jalena's concentration was completely on her navigation, ringing and silencing bells as required to keep their course steady against the wind. She'd mastered the management of the sil-nafön far better than Sang Ki. She was a fast learner. When they'd begun their travels, Sang Ki had sometimes mistaken her naivety for stupidity, but he knew better now. And besides, their journey had worn away a little of her innocence. Only her childlike faith in him truly remained of who she'd once been. And, he realised with a sickening swoop of his stomach, he was about to betray that faith.

'Jalena,' he said cautiously. 'There's something you should know. About what I intend to do when we reach our destination.' Sang Ki could already see the square grey stones scattered around the barrow, remnants perhaps of some larger structure that had once contained it.

'You're going to kill these new gods,' Jalena said. 'I don't really understand how, but I'm not a plant-speaker.'

'Not just these gods, all gods.' And then, before he could lose the urge for honesty, 'All the gods and the world-beneath-the-world with them. It's what sustains them. If we succeed here, it will be gone, for good – or perhaps not gone, but inaccessible to those who want to use its power, as it was always meant to be. It will return to being what it was, an idea without form or name. There'll be no more speaking with the plants, for me or anyone.'

Jalena's back was still turned to him. He couldn't see her expression, but he saw her shrug. 'If you think that's best, then that's what we'll do.'

'But Jalena, your whole way of living, the whole reason you followed me—'

She did turn around at that. Her expression was angry. 'You're very stupid for a person who's so clever. I don't follow you because you're a plant-speaker. I follow you because you're you. If we'd still been among the real people, I would have woven a mat for you using red rush, and you would have understood that

I wanted to make new people with you. But we're not and I haven't.'

'Oh,' he said. 'Oh. I . . .' He found that, for once, he was out of words. There was a feeling in his chest he found it hard to name, unfamiliar as it was. He thought it might be joy.

She turned back to the bells before he could answer. They'd arrived at their destination. He kept his eyes away from the scorn on Olufemi's face and the mockery on Bruyar's as they glided towards the ground.

The sil-nafön settled on the earth twenty paces from the unnatural hill. He fumbled at the door catch, suddenly desperate to be out of that small space and all the feelings in it. The latch sprang free, he stepped out . . .

. . . and the instant his feet touched the ground, touched the purple sorghum that sprouted there in such profusion, the physical connection became a spiritual one, his mind reaching out on instinct to touch the world-beneath-the-world. And a pain went through him so searing that it took his legs out from under him.

Jalena was speaking. He thought the others might be too. He heard the sound but couldn't understand the words. The pain was too huge and he was too small inside it. He fought it back, trying to make space for his own thoughts. And in the moment that he succeeded, he realised it wasn't his own pain he felt, but the earth's.

'Poison,' he gasped. He could feel the filthy stain of it all around, in this world and the other. 'There's poison in the soil. A seed of death is growing.'

He had one moment to take in Olufemi's horrified face, staring down at him, and then the pain swallowed him.

★

When Krish had first seen the metal bird, it had been miles behind them, only visible because of its vast size as glints of sunlight struck it from between the slowly dispersing storm clouds. Now it had closed the distance between them to little more than a mile. If it was the hawk, he and Dinesh and their vessel, so tiny beside its bulk, were the mouse it was stooping to kill.

They must be no more than a speck in the sky to whoever was aboard it. There was no reason to think it was pursuing them specifically. The Islands as a whole could have been its target; the forces of the Three must know that their opponents were based here. And yet Krish knew that he was its prey. He sensed it, sensed the presence of a god inside it, just as he'd once sensed that same god in the place that Sang Ki had called the world-beneath-the-world. It was a god who hated him and was bending all her power towards his death.

All hope wasn't lost, though. They were at the shore of the Graveyard, directly above Fleet. Their pursuer could swallow their vessel in the air in one snap of its metal beak, but they'd be harder targets on the ground, where they could find shelter and cover. But it wasn't only that. Krish sensed Sang Ki too, somewhere a little ahead of him, as if their time together in that other world had forged an unseen bond between them, which was now drawing taut.

Drawing taut – and then, with a surge of pain, snapping. Krish cried out, briefly blinded by it, and Dinesh turned to him in concern. When Krish's sight returned, he looked below, at the coast and the crawling sea, but he couldn't see Sang Ki. They were still too high. There was another shape he recognised, though: a hill in the shape of a square-based pyramid. He'd walked past it a dozen times. His last flight, he'd been pressed too close to Eric to pay attention to the ground. But now, from the air, it was as familiar to him as the village of his birth. It was the shape which was multiplied a million times to form the bones of the world-beneath-the-world. And it was the shape of the thing that had lain, unreachable, at the heart of that place for all the time he'd been there.

'Land!' he said to Dinesh. 'Land here.'

When they did, with a painful jolt, he saw that he'd been right. Sang Ki was here, lying on the ground. There was a young woman Krish didn't recognise brushing the hair gently from his eyes, an older Ofiklander, also a stranger – and Olufemi, where he couldn't possibly have expected her.

Sang Ki groaned. Krish knelt beside him, but he couldn't see a wound.

'What happened, Jalena?' Sang Ki asked weakly.

Her face was drawn with worry as she replied, 'Poison. You said the land was poisoned.' Her expression hardened as she pointed at Olufemi. '*She* knows what it means, but she won't say.'

Olufemi exchanged a troubled look with the Ofiklander. It was clear to Krish that this Jalena was right. They *did* know.

'Is it the Three?' he asked. 'Is that what he senses?'

'Not them,' Olufemi said. 'Us.' The Ofiklander opened *omas* mouth, as if *oms* meant to protest, but Olufemi scowled *omas* into silence. 'No, Bruyar. We brought this death here, the least we can do is confess it. Our mistakes have been so many – here's one standing before us, and another winging through the sky towards us. What's one more to add to them?'

'You're Krishanjit?' Bruyar asked.

Krish nodded. He realised that he recognised the name, if not the person. This was who Renar had been serving when she'd come to him as an envoy.

'Krishanjit, but not the moon god, not any longer,' *oms* said. "Tis a pity, as a god might solve the problem we have here. We've come a very long way, from a very distant shore. The Motherlands, I believe your people call them. Mother no longer. They're barren – cursed with magic so powerful that every plant and tree is turned against humanity. To eat any of them is death.'

'You, you, you brought the death here?' Dinesh asked. Behind him, the metal hawk had grown in the sky to the size of a house. Krish almost laughed. It seemed absurd that they had this new death to worry about, when another was so close.

Bruyar shrugged. 'Not deliberately, I assure you. I suppose some seeds might have found a home on our ship, and washed ashore here.'

'It might be confined to this island,' Olufemi said. 'This place is doomed. The death, once planted, can't be torn up. It spreads from plant to plant through some malign magic, the oldest magic, I suppose. Every plant that absorbs it will become poisonous, deadly to those who eat it. But—'

Bruyar smiled thinly. 'When has our luck ever been so good? Our fleet was scattered by a storm. No doubt its ships and wrecks now line the Ashane coast. The seeds will be everywhere by now. And from Ashanesland they'll spread to every corner of this continent. There's no stopping it. It may take a decade, centuries perhaps, but one day this place will be as inhospitable as the Motherlands, where everyone who ever lived has died.'

'No,' Krish said. 'No. I won't accept it. There must be something we can do. If we can find all the seeds before they grow . . .'

'It won't work,' Sang Ki said. His face was pale and clammy, still riven with pain, but he sat up. 'The world-beneath-the-world itself has been poisoned, and all plants draw their strength from it. There's only one way to stop it. We must pull up the root. We must kill the first god – kill his body, so that his spirit can finally die.' His words were lost in a hacking cough.

Jalena rushed to hold him as he gasped for breath, but her eyes were on Krish. 'The god's buried in the earth there.' She nodded at the hill beside them. 'That's what the plant-speaker said. You have to dig it out.'

'But how?' Dinesh asked.

The metal bird was only minutes from the shoreline. It would reach them very soon. 'We'll use our hands,' Krish said grimly. 'Or our swords, whatever we have.' But even as he followed his own instructions, he knew it was futile. The rain had loosened only the topmost layer of soil. When he tore it away, there was packed earth and stone beneath. He took out his knife and dug its point in, prising it out one small lump at a time, not because he thought he had any chance of success, but only so that he'd be doing *something*.

He was so focused on the futile task he barely registered the heavy tread behind him. But as his nose filled with the smell of mouldy cinnamon, a claw took up the work his knife was doing – a claw that was ten times the size of the knife and far more powerful. Clods of earth began to fly past.

'Rii,' Krish said. He stood back, leaving her to work. And not just her. She'd brought her children with her. They used their smaller, sharper claws to tear through the earth beside her, piling a growing, loamy mound of it behind them.

'Thought we might need her,' Eric said, grinning from his perch high up on Rii's back. Her hairy legs were caked in mud all the way up, and Krish realised that she must have walked the mile from Fleet to this place, dragging the enormous bulk of her body step by step now that it could no longer fly.

Krish smiled back, but the smile slipped at what he saw over Eric's shoulder. The metal bird was now above the island's innermost reefs. It would arrive long before they'd completed this task, even with Rii's help.

*

Alfreda knew that Krish lay ahead of her. So close now, she could sense him with a sense she hadn't known she possessed until this moment. She watched as his tiny vessel landed near the coast and she knew that very soon he'd be hers.

She'd been reaching out with that same sense to feel for Nabofik, or Marvan. Of him there was the faintest trace, so muted it was impossible to place. Of Nabofik, nothing. Alfreda was alone again. Everyone she ever loved was taken from her. Maybe she would tell her army to water these Hundred Islands with the blood of their residents, then sow them with salt. Maybe she would make Krishanjit watch before she killed him too. She suspected that when he was in her grasp, she'd be too impatient and kill him first.

'God-Triumvir! God-Triumvir!' It was the voice of one of her generals. She thought he must have been speaking for a while, from the frantic tone.

With difficulty, she took her eyes from her quarry. 'Well, what is it?'

Before he could reply, there was the clang of something very heavy striking *Edred*'s roof. A moment later there was a sound that was a little like a clap. She couldn't guess the source, because the sky around them was suddenly filled with vessels. They must have come from above. It was the only direction from which they could have come undetected.

The clang and then the clap came again and the *Edred* juddered. Hearing the sound a second time, Alfreda recognised it. It was black powder igniting, the sound of her own fire javelin – the weapon Algar had invented and been killed by. Someone had recreated it, and they were using it against her.

The vessels attacking them weren't stolen sil-nafön. They were a far more primitive design. Each seemed to have a fire in its wagon bed and above it there was a canopy made not of metal, like those on her own vessels, but of a material that looked a little like silk.

As she watched, one of her people fired *omas* own black powder weapon. Alfreda had perfected the design since she'd become a god. It must have struck one of the attacker's canopies. The material tore and emptied of air and the vessel went spiralling towards the ground. The *Edred* shook at two more detonations in quick succession, towards its tail. But the number of attackers had already been thinned. They could do little more than slow Alfreda down.

Except then she heard another detonation, far louder than the first, and then another, a rolling thunder of them. And this time the blows struck *Edred*'s underside. The metal held at the first impact, held at the second – and then cracked open at another full volley from below.

Now it was the *Edred* heading towards the ground. No, not the ground, the sea. They hadn't yet reached the shore. And all along it, facing them, were the black snub shapes of fire javelins, ready to send more barrages against them.

★

Krish watched the swarm of tiny vessels attacking the metal monster in shock. They should have been no more than a nuisance to it, and yet it was falling – it was *plummeting* – towards the sea.

These must be the allies his father had spoken about. They could only have arrived after Krish left the island, at the last possible hour.

'The Rah,' Sang Ki said faintly. 'So Ensee did listen to me after all.'

There was a sound accompanying the fight. It took Krish a little time to place it. He'd last heard it years ago, in Mirror Town, from the forces allied to his father. The weapon had sent metal to tear great chunks through his people. It did seem very like the Rah to have learned the trick of it.

Behind him there was a harsher sound: Rii's breathing, rasping in and out like a bellows. Beneath her claws and those of her children, the earth of the mound had melted away. There was a shape carved out of it that looked as if a giant jaw had taken a bite. Rii's children were still digging with a frenzy, but she'd slowed. Every movement of her muddy legs seemed to cost her more and more effort.

Eric slid from her back to look into her eye. It was as big as his head, but clouded now. It seemed to take a while to focus on him.

'You ain't as young as you used to be,' Eric said. 'You've done enough. Why don't you rest now?'

'Because the task is not yet complete, morsel.' Her voice, always thin and higher than seemed possible from so huge a creature, was even thinner and higher now. Krish thought that even speech must be exhausting her. But she turned from Eric and back to the hill. Her claws took out one huge gouge of earth, and then another. And the third time she moved, her claws struck something that wasn't earth. It sounded like hollow wood.

Rii lifted her claw again, to clear the earth further, then let it fall. Her head drooped towards her chest. *'Yron, I have done as thou wished,'* she said. Her voice was so quiet now, it was almost human. *'I am finished. I was not made for a world without thy power.'*

'No! You ain't allowed to die!' Eric said fiercely. There were tears streaming down his cheeks and he swiped them impatiently away.

Rii moved her head a fraction, until her snout could briefly nuzzle Eric's cheek. *'Grieve not, morsel. I have abided a long while in this world, and lived to see the defeat of mine enemies. What more could any creature ask? Our children are thine now, to guard. Care for them as well as I have cared for thee.'* With that last word, her head dropped to rest between her claws. She released one long, sighing breath, and then was silent.

Eric let out a choked cry and fell to his knees beside her. He rested his face in her grubby fur and wept. All around him Rii's children keened for their mother, a high, eerie sound that raised all the hairs on Krish's neck.

But she had succeeded. Resting beneath her outstretched claw was a box not much larger than a man. It seemed to be made of oak. Could this truly be the root of all godhood? It seemed impossible that something so small could have caused problems so large.

Behind them, an enormous splash briefly drew Krish's attention. The metal bird had struck the water. Struck, and begun to sink. A ten-foot-tall wave swept the beach in the wake of that landing, flattening the sand dunes at its rear and only coming to a frothing stop at the feet of a herd of startled cattle in the field beyond.

Krish turned back to the hill and what had been uncovered within it.

'Open it, then,' Olufemi said.

Her voice had been dead before, hopeless. Now she sounded more like herself. Of course she'd be interested in the source of all godhood. It had been her life's study. But Krish wouldn't let her use this to create any more. The world had seen enough gods.

He walked towards the wooden box, flanked by Olufemi. Sang Ki came forwards too, supported with his arm across Jalena's shoulders. The lid was heavy and fixed with a metal clasp. In the end, it took all four of them to lever it open.

There was a corpse inside that was no more than a skeleton dressed in skin. It was so withered and small that it took Krish a moment to realise that it was a man. He wondered what he was meant to do with it – and then its eyes opened.

The corpse's – the man's – mouth moved, but no sound came out of it, only a dry croak. His limbs twitched feebly. It was both the most pitiful and the most horrifying thing Krish had ever seen.

'A burial chamber lay on these islands. That's what it said on the map we saw in the abandoned city, Olufemi,' Bruyar said. 'Now we know who was buried here.'

Olufemi scowled at *omas*. 'You let me believe you couldn't read it.'

'I've never been renowned for my honesty.'

Sang Ki rested his hand against the rim of the oak box. He looked down at the feeble, twitching figure, then at Krish. 'I recognise it, don't you?'

Krish nodded. 'This was what I felt in the world-beneath-the-world. This was what rested at the base of it.'

'The first god,' Sang Ki said. 'The one who began it all, millennia ago. And still holds it together.'

Olufemi looked behind them, and shuddered. The sea, which had been so wild moments ago, was now ice. The waves had frozen in perfect peaks and curls, and a woman was walking on them, striding inexorably across the few hundred yards that separated them. 'Kill him,' she said to Krish. 'End this forever. The poison plague was made with magic. Maybe if it's taken from this world, the plague will end.'

Sang Ki nodded. 'Yes. I believe you're right. If the world-beneath-the-world is freed of the god's influence, his corruption, the poison will have no way to spread from plant to plant.' But he still hesitated, looking down at this ancient, undying figure.

'What are you waiting for?' Jalena asked. She drew her knife and plunged it towards the god's chest.

Towards, but not into it. When the tip of the metal met that desiccated flesh, it skidded aside to score a gouge in the wall of the box. She frowned and tried again, with more force, and this time the knife blade snapped, the tip flying one way and the jagged end left in her hand.

'I'll, I'll, I'll do it,' Dinesh said. He drew his sword and slashed it down – with exactly the same effect.

Olufemi put a hand against his arm to stop him swinging again. 'I think I understand. I should have guessed – I knew the rule already. Only a god can kill a god.' She turned to Krish. 'You do it.'

Even now it seemed wrong, to attack something so weak and defenceless. But the god's eyes were rolling in his head. They looked insane, and who wouldn't be, after thousands of years underground? His expression was despairing, as if he didn't believe his suffering could ever end. So Krish drew his knife and pressed it against the flesh of his throat.

But his blade skidded aside too.

'A god no longer,' Bruyar laughed. It sounded, improbably, like genuine amusement. 'I should have known. What's done can't be undone. 'Tis one of the very foundational rules of politics. The Fox was fond of quoting it to me when I made unreasonable demands of her.'

Krish turned to look at the frozen sea, but Alfreda was no longer on it. She'd crossed the beach and was heading over the field towards them. She'd reach them in minutes.

'I need to take the children away,' Eric said. His eyes were red and swollen but there was a steely resolve on his face. 'That's the last thing Rii asked of me and I ain't gonna let her down. We need to hide. Or find a boat. Sail away from here.'

'Yes,' Krish said. 'You should go.' He stepped forwards. 'It's me she wants. It's me she hates. If I distract her, you'll have time to get away.'

Eric looked between Krish and the pups, his expression torn. But when he called to them, the pups didn't come. They fluttered in the sky above their mother's cooling body, as if they couldn't bear to leave it.

Dinesh swayed from foot to foot. His gaze flicked between the approaching woman and Krish.

'Run,' Krish said. 'Do what Dae Hyo asked of you. Let the Dae live again. You heard what Olufemi said. The poison could take decades to spread. You'd have time to live out your life.'

Dinesh hesitated a moment longer, then planted his feet squarely beside Krish. He raised the tip of his sword until it was pointing futilely at the approaching god. 'No. I'm a free man, not your slave. You don't make my choices any more, and I choose to fight.'

By then it was too late, anyway. Alfreda had reached them. She looked, Krish thought, more like a god than he ever had. She was tall and broad-shouldered with a tangle of curly honey-coloured hair and the washed-out skin of the Moon Forest folk. There was a strength in her that he didn't think came from her magic. He stepped forwards to face her. He'd travelled so very far. It seemed right that he'd reached the end of his journey in his own homeland, in a place as bleak and beautiful as the one in which he'd spent his childhood.

'I'm the one you want,' he said. 'These others have never hurt you.'

Alfreda stepped closer. She didn't seem to know what to do with her hands. 'It's your fault. Cwen and Jinn died fighting you. Marvan and Nabofik. Algar. You're the reason for all of it.' But she didn't sound certain.

Krish shook his head and stepped aside, so that she could see the oak box and the pitiful, undying figure in it. '*That's* the reason for all of it. The first god. He made me possible, and you. He took something that was in everyone and trapped it in another place, in a cage, where only gods could use its power.'

'What thing?' she asked, her eyes fixed on the figure in the coffin.

Krish shrugged. 'No one will know, until they have it back.'

She reached out a hand, but hesitated short of touching that ancient flesh. 'But how? How was it possible?'

'Because people let him,' Sang Ki said. 'They wanted a god, and they let him become one. Just like Olufemi did. Just like your creators did. People always think they want the things gods offer them – the chance to break the rules of nature, to do things the easy way. By the time they realise they've lost more than they've gained, it's too late.'

'People are fools,' Alfreda said. 'Every one of them. They deserve what they get.'

'Even the children?' Sang Ki asked. 'Even the babies not yet a day old? There's a plague, a poison spreading in this land that was caused, long ago, by him. It will kill every person on this continent, eventually. The only way to end it is to end him and thereby end his magic. End *all* magic. But you're the only one left in the world who can do it.'

She took one last look down, then turned back to Krish. 'Why should I care about the world? It's never cared for me. And why should I mind if everyone dies? There's not a single person left that I'd weep for. I amn't a fool. Maybe that . . . thing made the power, but you *used* it. You chose to use it.'

'Yes,' Krish said, 'I did.'

'And so did Nabofik,' another voice said. It was Renar, limping across the grass. She must have come from the fallen hawk-ship too. 'You lost your brother? So did I. Your sibling-god murdered him. Lanalan had never hurt a living thing. He was as pure-hearted as it's possible for a man to be. And Nabofik killed him just to hurt me.'

'No,' Alfreda said. 'No.'

'If you remain a god,' Krish told her, 'you'll become what you hate. We all do.'

Renar's expression was relentless. 'Nabofik was a monster. Marvan was a murderer. The Three were worse than any gods who came before.'

'But I loved them,' Alfreda said, still to Krish. Her eyes were bright with tears. 'They were all I had left and you took them away.'

'And you'll be grieving them forever, if you stay a god. Look at the first of us – look at him! Is that what you want? It's your future, unless you change it.' He stepped up to her, took her hand in his and lifted it until it rested against his throat. It looked more than strong enough to do the job. 'Kill me first if you need to. But kill him second. Let the power go. The people it hurts most of all are the people who have it.'

The moment seemed to stretch into eternity. As last moments went, it didn't seem the worst. He was glad to have Eric there, someone who cared for him only as a person. And he was glad it would happen under the open sky, with a fresh salt wind in his face.

Alfreda's hand squeezed against his throat. His vision began to grey as her fingers pressed harder and harder. Then she let out a desperate, wrenching cry, turned to reach inside the coffin, and snapped *that* neck instead, with a crack so quiet it could only just be heard, over the calling of the birds.

There was a long, hissing sigh, a last twitch. Until, finally, the man inside the coffin stilled his restless motion. He lay, unmoving, as dead as he long ago should have been.

Alfreda stayed there, frozen. Krish stared at her, at the beach and the grass and the fresh earth around the hill. He'd expected the world to feel fundamentally different after the death of all gods, but it felt fundamentally the same.

'It's gone,' Sang Ki said. 'The world-beneath-the-world. I can't feel it any more. I think it's done.'

'But I'm still here!' Alfreda cried. The tears were openly streaming down her face now. 'Why am I still here? You said it would be over. What am I meant to do now?'

'I don't know,' Krish said. He looked at Eric, who'd gone back to kneel beside Rii's vast corpse, gently smoothing out the rictus grin of death from her lips. 'I don't know what happens next. Maybe people will be better, now they have back what the first god stole. Or maybe they won't. We'll always have the choice to do wrong. But you did right today. I think that's the best we can ever say.'

Epilogue

They returned to the savannah in style, carried on the backs of two of Rii's children. Sang Ki had told Krish he'd be happy to make the journey the slow way, now that the sil-nafön no longer flew, but when he crossed the border between the Silent Sands and the grasslands, he realised how very happy he was to be back.

They'd left Dinesh at Mirror Town, or what remained of it, to lead the former slaves from the dying city to the Dae lands. It would be no easy task, but Sang Ki thought he'd succeed at it. There'd turned out to be an iron will hidden beneath the bliss which had enslaved him. People were, Sang Ki had found, very frequently surprising.

He looked across at Jalena and she grinned back at him from her own mount. She'd taken to riding the pup, as she'd taken to most things, like a bee to a flower.

They hadn't yet spoken about what she'd told him, before that final confrontation at the first god's tomb. But when they made camp for the night, he sometimes caught her looking at him. She was young, but not so young as she had been when they set out together. He still couldn't quite fathom the idea that someone might look at him, and see a husband. But he thought that with time he might become used to it.

They stopped just short of the obec's land to make camp for the night beneath the shade of a lone, crooked tree. It might even be the one they'd stopped at when they first fled their home.

'What place do you think I'll have in the obec, now that I no longer speak to the plants?' he asked.

'You don't need to tell them,' Jalena said stubbornly, as she'd said before. It was an argument they'd had more than once. '*They* never saw the world-beneath-the-world. They won't know it's gone. And you're cleverer than any of them. They should listen to you.'

'Perhaps,' he said noncommittally, but he was beginning to form a plan.

And then, a little after dawn the next morning, they came to Juh Obec. It looked utterly unchanged. It was strange, after so many years seeking out novelty, to find himself so pleased by this. Although when Sang Ki counted the house-beasts, he saw that there were three more, far smaller than the rest. Ladislao's house must have birthed her litter at last. That seemed like a degree of change he could be comfortable with.

They landed in the dusty square at the centre of the obec. Jalena, he saw, had her head held high and a stern expression on her face. She was enjoying this performance. It would certainly do a great deal to increase her standing in the obec. In a place where so little happened, an event such as this would be remembered. At least until their deaths, when it must of course be forgotten. There was a comfort in that too: the knowledge that nothing he did could change the world too much or too permanently.

The three members of the conclave stepped forwards hesitantly to greet them: the chief gatherer and the harvester and the crafter. They'd aged a little, of course, but they were the same people who'd tried to hobble him, more than three years ago. The last time he'd seen them, they'd been smug and confident. Now they were unsure.

'I have come back to you,' Sang Ki said grandly. He often found it best to begin by stating the obvious. 'Borne on the back of those who serve the world-beneath-the-world.'

Sii's dark eyes glanced at Sang Ki askance, but he didn't speak. The pups were wiser than their years suggested.

'We thought you dead,' the chief gatherer said.

'Merely voyaging as the plants led me,' Sang Ki told him, which was in fact the truth.

'We've got rid of the danger the plant-speaker saw,' Jalena said, then more belligerently, 'The one you didn't believe in. He did a very big, very good thing, and Juh Obec should be thanking its luck that he's chosen to return to us.'

Sang Ki smiled round at them, warm and magnanimous. 'But I'm delighted to be here. To be home.'

After that, they crowded round him, shouting and laughing and talking. Very soon, he knew, it would be as if he'd never left. The folk of the savannah were very like the grass on which they lived. The obecs passed over it, and within weeks there was no sign of their passage.

His picked out Mahvesh among the crowd. She was, he was delighted to see, wearing the oyster-shell pendant of a woman who'd made a pairing bond. Perhaps he'd be wearing such a necklace himself soon. She came up to him as he was ruffling the hair of some new cousin of Jalena's and handed him a cup of sugar-grass tea.

'What happened out there?' she asked quietly.

He smiled and shook his head. 'Nothing that need concern us. This is our world now. The rest can be forgotten.'

★

Olufemi went back with Bruyar to Ofiklanod. What else could she do? There was nothing but dusty ruins left of Mirror Town, and she didn't have a place in the new Ashane court.

Of course, Ofiklanod wasn't in too fit a state itself: fully three quarters of its people were dead, its vineyards withering and its windmills still. But she wanted, if nothing else, to learn Yemisi's fate. And she found that she wasn't yet ready to give up Bruyar's company. The inter could hardly be called a friend, but over the last months, Olufemi had become accustomed to *omas* company.

Yemisi, it transpired, was dead. Murdered by the god she'd chosen to serve. Olufemi looked for some sorrow inside herself and ruthlessly tamped down any satisfaction that she'd been proven right. In the end, the best she could muster was a sort of muted melancholy. The teacher she'd once respected had died in every way that mattered in Mirror Town. Now her body had gone to the grave, travelling its backward route through time.

There were few Mortals remaining in what was left of Täm. Those who'd served Nabofik in Ofiklanod wouldn't be returning. They'd disappeared forever in their impossible city. Olufemi had wondered if it would return to earth once the magic was gone, but it hadn't. Perhaps it would join the moon and stars in their endless, cold circles through the darkness.

Bruyar was welcomed back. No one cared to comment on *omas* disappearance during the reign of the Three. They were just glad of someone to tell them what to do. There was a very great deal of it required, if life in Ofiklanod was to return to anything approaching normality.

Except, on the afternoon of their second day back, Olufemi realised that Bruyar was nowhere to be found. She wasn't sure what instinct made her search in the City Below, the city of the sun that had been buried, unburied and then brought to ruin by the sun's death. Perhaps it was merely that this was a place no one else would think to look.

She found Bruyar at last in what must once have been the courtyard of a fine house. The fountain in its centre was ringed by marble fish, their open mouths now dry, as if they'd been caught in the moment of their death, gasping at air.

The marble table was better preserved. Bruyar sat at it alone, with a bottle of wine and one half-empty glass in front of *omas*. *Oms* looked up at Olufemi's approach.

'Did you know,' Bruyar said, as if they were already mid-conversation, 'that my family were imprisoned for the entirety of my absence?'

Olufemi sat cautiously on the marble bench opposite *omas*. She didn't like the look in Bruyar's eyes. They were a little glassy, as if *oms* had drunk a full bottle of that wine already.

'I'm sorry,' she said. 'I suppose it was to be expected.'

There was a flash of anger in Bruyar's expression. 'They tortured my husband and my wife for information on my whereabouts. Was that to be expected too?'

Olufemi bowed her head and didn't answer.

'Maybe we should have let the poison run its course — have you considered that?' Bruyar asked. 'I struggle to see what there could be in this world worth saving.'

'Oh, please, spare me the self-pity. You made a choice. It had consequences. Now you must live with them.'

'Or not,' Bruyar said, raising *omas* glass in an ironic toast.

For the first time, Olufemi recognised the smell of it, a bitterness that wasn't wine. It was poison. A normal one, not the magical kind that she and Bruyar had so nearly unleashed. Olufemi dashed the glass out of *omas* hand before it could reach *omas* lips again. It splashed red like blood across the white marble table and the white marble bench.

Bruyar looked down at it, then back up at Olufemi. 'Well, that was a waste, but I've a whole storehouse full of it. It was a most useful way to dispose of my enemies without causing an inconvenient fuss.'

'You coward,' Olufemi said viciously. 'You utter craven. Your family is still alive. Your country still lives. They need you. So you've made mistakes — you're far from the only one. They're no more grave than mine. But I at least lived with them. I looked them in the eye.'

'To what purpose?' Bruyar asked. *Omas* eyes were pinned on Olufemi, less unfocused now. The question was perhaps genuine.

'To mend them,' Olufemi said. 'There's no one else to do it but us, and I have few years left. Soon the task will be yours alone. Will you really shirk it?'

Bruyar didn't reply, but *oms* didn't reach for the wine either. That, Olufemi thought, was the best she could hope for.

*

Rii was buried at sea. It was the way of the Islands. They put a sail on her raft, surrounded her corpse with logs, and set it free to drift across the ocean, aflame. Nayan's corpse had been laid beside her. He'd died in the final defence of the Islands, drowned in the wave that Alfreda's falling vessel had caused.

I did kill him in the end, Krish thought, *or at least my plan did.*

But he thought his father might have been content with this conclusion to his reign. Krish was surprised at the depth of his feeling as he watched the flaming raft sail towards the horizon. He hadn't known he cared for his father that much. But maybe his grief was more for Dae Hyo, who'd left no body for Krish to mourn or bury. And for everyone else who'd died in wars they hadn't chosen.

The waters were crowded with boats, mostly small fishing vessels and some of the huge ships that were more normally at the heart of Fleet. The islanders had all come to say farewell to their Queen. They had a new leader now. Krish hoped they'd learn to love him as well as they'd loved her.

There were fewer people on the beach, and one by one they drifted away, as the glow of the funeral pyre faded across the water. Soon only Krish and Renar remained. She stood grim and silent at his shoulder. She too, he suspected, had come to Rii's funeral to mourn another. Lanalan, like Dae Hyo, had left no corpse behind.

He turned to her. 'Will you walk with me? There's something I'd like to talk about.'

She nodded silently. She'd barely spoken since her brother's death. It was as if he'd taken all her words away with him.

'I'm the King of Ashanesland now,' he said. It felt absurd, even saying it. 'Except that I'm not. I'm a goatherd. I know something about fighting. I know a lot about surviving. But I don't know anything about ruling.'

'You wish to ask me to serve you as I served your father?' Her mouth turned down further. 'And Nabofik after him.'

'And Bruyar before.'

'My counselling days are over,' she said firmly. 'I've done enough harm.'

He stopped at the top of the first low hill, with its view out over the waves and across the island. The half-torn-away hill that had been the first god's grave was hidden from view here. Krish had ordered that the whole thing be razed. 'Then do some good,' he said. 'I can't do this alone. I'm not sure I can do it at all. You know much more about ruling than I do.'

'You mean to share the throne of Ashanesland with me? La, I fear your shiplords might have a thing or two to say about that.'

'There *are* no shiplords, or hardly any. Nabofik killed a quarter of them, and another quarter fled. There are so few left I've had to leave Imesha in charge of Fell's End, just so there's someone to keep order there. I don't want to give you the Oak Wheel. I want you to be Lord of Delta's Strength. It's the most important fort, except Ashfall. The strongest. It needs to be led by someone who knows what they're doing.'

'And who you believe to be loyal to you.'

'Yes, that too. It will only be for a time.'

The listlessness was back on her face. She turned away from him. 'I have no appetite for it.'

'Then what do you have an appetite for? Are you going to become Alfreda, mourning her brother forever?'

'Would you rather I forgot him?' she snapped.

'I didn't know Lanalan very well, but I think I know what he'd say. He'd tell you that you've got more cunning in your little finger than most people will have in a lifetime. He'd say that you mustn't let it go to waste. He might say that if you were Lord, you could make sure he's never forgotten. There'll be histories written about this time, and it will be those with power who write them. Why not make sure he has his place in them?'

'A low blow,' she said. 'A jab to the kidneys.' But then she smiled a little. 'I could write him down as the greatest actor of his age. He could be remembered as the most dazzling walker on the stages of Täm.'

'He could.'

'I hear you permitted Alfreda to depart with Ensee. If you'd sought my counsel then, I'd have spoken against it.'

Krish shrugged. 'They both like to make new things. Alfreda might find meaning in working with her.'

'Too much meaning. The Rah are an ambitious people. They won't stay in their swamp for long, and you've given them the world's pre-eminent weapon maker. Did you hear? Ensee's people have been spreading sedition among your landborn. Speaking of the death of kings.'

'Perhaps kings *should* die,' Krish said. 'The world is rid of gods. I think it should be rid of kings and lords as well. Your people learned to live without them all. I want you to help me teach mine to do the same. In Ofiklanod they told me you used to take on the most hopeless candidates and somehow lead them to victory. You enjoyed the challenge. I want to change a whole country, a whole people. I want them to follow me just long enough to learn that they don't need to follow anyone. Is that challenge enough for you?'

*

Krish ate dinner with Eric. The children were there too, both Arwel's and Rii's, hanging from the boat's beams by their feet as they drained the blood from the trout that had been brought for them. But when the meal was over, Eric sent them out to play.

'Drut – I meant to say, Thilini, will keep her eye on them. Far as anyone can, that is. They're right terrors.'

'They'll have the entire island watching them,' Krish said. 'Their Queen's children. The last things they have left of her.'

Eric looked down at his plate, using his fork to arrange the fishbones into the shape of a tree. 'It ain't gonna be easy to rule them, not after Rii. She was always so certain of things. And I ain't certain of anything, not these days.'

'I think these are the days for doubt. We've had too much certainty. I made you lord here because of your ties to Rii. It should only be for a while, and you're the only one they'd accept. But I think you'll be good at it.'

'Do you?' Eric's eyes were intent on Krish's. 'A whore of Smiler's Fair turned into a lord?'

'It's no worse than a goatherd becoming a king.'

Eric laughed. 'Yeah, I suppose. I was thinking I might invite the fair here. They ain't never come to the Islands before. Might help show these folk a more distant horizon.'

'And show the people of the fair how far you've risen.'

'Yeah,' Eric said. 'I can't say that ain't crossed my mind. I heard you made Babi the lord of Smallwood *and* Whitewood. I reckon she's well suited to it too.'

Krish studied him in silence, trying to see in this man the shape of the boy who'd flown to his rescue in Mirror Town, not that many years ago. His outline was there, but it was faint. The deaths that they'd suffered hadn't all been of friends. The people they'd once been had died too. But he liked who Eric was now. There was strength in his face as well as humour. Strength and beauty.

'I'm sorry about Dae Hyo,' Eric said, after he'd allowed Krish to look him over a while. 'Even though he was a pain in my arse the whole time we was with the Drifters.'

'He was my only friend, for a long time.'

Eric nodded. 'Rii was mine. I never thought of her that way. Can't imagine what she'd have said if I called her that – nothing flattering most likely. But she was.'

'*We* could be friends,' Krish said. 'We are friends. Aren't we?'

Eric studied him, his head tipped to the side. Then he grinned, full of mischief, looking briefly exactly like the boy he'd once been. 'Is that what we are?'

Krish found he didn't have a reply.

'You said "rule for a while", not forever,' Eric said.

'I don't want any of us to rule forever. I want the Ashane to rule themselves, the way the Ofiklanders did, before the Mortals decided they needed gods again.'

'And then you'll just walk away? What does a king do when he stops being a king?'

'The other lands. The Motherlands. The poison will be gone from them now. I was thinking I might travel there. See the place that we all came from.' Without having quite intended to add it, he asked, 'Do you think you'd want to come too? If you brought Rii's pups they could make a home there. A land of their own.'

'Somewhere they wouldn't draw eyes everywhere they go,' Eric said. 'Them or Arwel. Yeah, that ain't the worst idea. In the meantime, you come and visit me, King Krishanjit, you hear?

Don't wait too long. I can send one of the pups for you any time you want. I'd like to get to know you better, if you're willing.'

Krish smiled. 'I think I'd like that.'

Acknowledgements

Firstly, I'd like to thank those readers who've stuck it out until the not-so-bitter end. I hope you've enjoyed your stay in this world – I'm incredibly grateful that you let me be your tour guide in it.

Many thanks also to Andy Ryan for the brilliant structural edit and to Gabrielle Chant for the fantastic copy edit – the book is much better for your input.

I'm grateful as ever for my agent James Wills' unwavering support. And to all my friends, who've been there when I needed them. I would never have been able to write these books without you.

HODDERSCAPE

WANT MORE HODDERSCAPE? JOIN US!

Sign up to our mailing list to get exclusive early sneak peeks and offers:

Follow us on our social channels:
 @hodderscape

Buy our books, find out more, and discover exclusive content:
www.hodderscape.co.uk